EXPAND YOUR HORIZONS . . .
AND YOUR MIND

Probing the traditional to the outlandish, deep space to cyberspace, metal machines to human machines, visionaries to mutants, and of course so much more, science fiction continues to encompass the best of worlds both real and imagined. Now, the most outstanding works from some of the brightest writers in the field are brought together in this new volume—a collection that will take you where others have only dreamed. You will be dazzled. You will be shocked. You will be enlightened. Discover the world around you and beyond with—

YEAR'S BEST SF 6

D1024206

Edited by David G. Hartwell

YEAR'S BEST SF 6

EDITED BY
DAVID G. HARTWELL

An Imprint of HarperCollinsPublishers

This book is dedicated to Elisabeth Malartre, Robert Sheckley, Bill Johnson, because they have treated me well this year under difficult circumstances.

EOS
An Imprint of HarperCollins*Publishers*
10 East 53rd Street
New York, New York 10022-5299

Copyright © 2001 by David G. Hartwell
ISBN: 0-06-102055-9
www.eosbooks.com

First Eos paperback printing: June 2001

Eos Trademark Reg. U.S. Pat. Off. and in Other Countries, Marca Registrada, Hecho en U.S.A.
HarperCollins® is a trademark of HarperCollins Publishers Inc.

Printed in the U.S.A.

10 9 8 7 6 5 4 3 2 1

Contents

Acknowledgments

I would like to acknowledge the continuing value of Mark Kelly's short fiction reviews in *Locus,* and of the various short fiction reviewers of the Tangent website. Also, I wish to thank Kathryn Cramer for invaluable help in preparing this book, and Caitlin Blasdell for extra editorial devotion, and Diana Gill for catching the ball.

Introduction

Last year I said that 1999 was one of the legendary years of the science fiction future, and we have lived through it. So of course was 2000, the turning point, the end of a thousand-year period of growth and change and a significant moment in the Christian Era (AD). Well, the world didn't end, nor did the Second Coming come, nor the aliens in whatever form. Nor was there a socialist civilization in Boston, Massachusetts, as envisioned by Edward Bellamy in *Looking Backward* in the 1880s. And now that that millennium is gone, we live in the Year One CE, and all the SF written about the '80s and '90s is just fiction—now robbed of most of its significant prophetic power—and must stand or fall as fiction, on the merits of its execution and/or historical importance. Even Arthur C. Clarke, whose special year is 2001, will have to wait a while longer for commercial travel to the Moon. It is a sobering thought to consider that fifty years ago 2000 looked like the relatively distant future, a time of wonders and radical difference. Now the year 2000 looks somewhat like the 1950s, plus computers and minus the Cold War. Most of the same buildings are standing in most major cities.

Some things don't change fast enough, other changes leave us breathless or shocked. Fifty years is not so long, less than the career of Jack Williamson for instance, who published in 1929 and this year too, in the course of seven decades of writing SF—and barring unforeseen circumstances, Williamson will be in his eighth decade of writing when you read this. I leave you again with the thought that we should set our SF stories farther ahead in time, lest we become outdated fantasy too soon.

Looking backward from December 2000, I see a past year of tremendous growth for the SF field, and many reasons for optimism in the year ahead. Australia is still full of energy and big science-fictional plans a year or two after the 1999 Melbourne world science fiction convention, and Australian writers are continuing to break out worldwide, at least in the English language. Canadian SF is still thriving, and Canada is still introducing new world-class SF and fantasy writers to the world stage each year. The UK may not perhaps be the UK much longer, since Scotland is getting its own Parliament, but either way England, Ireland, and Scotland are a major force in SF, and *Interzone* has grown into one of the three or four leading SF magazines (*Analog, Asimov's, F&SF* are its peers) in the world. The best new SF magazine of the year is *Spectrum SF,* from Scotland. There are stirrings of energy in France and in French SF, new awards and conferences there, and German SF has recently produced at least one new writer on the world stage, Andreas Eschbach. And the world SF convention is now becoming more global and is likely to be held in Scotland, Australia, Japan, and perhaps elsewhere in the world in the next decade.

Worldwide, the small press is a force of growing strength and importance in the field, in part due to the availability of computers within reach of the average fannish budget and in part due to the new economies of instant print, now prevalent in the USA and soon to reach everywhere. Hardly a day goes by without a new instant print review copy of a small press trade paperback in the NYRSF* mailbox. Many of them are in fact self-published works that do not meet professional standards of writing, it is true, but a few of them

The New York Review of Science Fiction (www.NYRSF.com or c/o Dragon Press, PO Box 78, Pleasantville, NY 10570) is a monthly 24 page journal of essays and reviews on SF and fantasy.

are carefully written, well-edited gems. And the books from the more established small presses, from Golden Gryphon, Ministry of Whimsey, Borderlands, and others, continue to impress.

The field lost two fine magazines this year, *Amazing* and *SF Age,* but a perceptible increase in the number and quality of small press magazines helped to cushion the loss, as did the announcement of several high-paying online short fiction markets. Interestingly, none of the highest paying online publishers intend to actually make money selling the fiction, but are supporting it as a promotional expense! I wonder how long that will last. Certainly not many months in the future if the world stock markets continue to lose trillions of dollars (I write at a particularly low point in recent economic times). Still, we are better off right now than in the not-too-distant past, and are all grateful that SF is of promotional value in 2001. I hope to find some excellent science fiction online this year to reprint next year in this series.

As to the quality of the year's fiction, 2000 was a particularly fine year, with grand old names and hot new talents competing for attention. It was a good year to be reading the magazines, both pro and semi-professional. It was a strong year for novellas, with fifteen or twenty of them in consideration for the limited space allowed in this book by length constraints; you'll have to go to the competing *Year's Best* in fat trade paperback to sample more novellas. And there were a hundred shorter stories in consideration, from which this rich selection was chosen. So I repeat, for readers new to this series, my usual disclaimer: this selection of science fiction stories represents the best that was published during the year 2000. I could perhaps have filled two or three more volumes this size and then claimed to have nearly all of the best—though not all the best novellas. I believe that representing the best from year to year, while it is not physically possible to encompass it all in one even very large book, also implies presenting some substantial variety of excellence, and I left some writers out in order to include others in this limited space.

My general principle for selection: this book is full of science fiction—every story in the book is clearly that and not something else. I personally have a high regard for horror, fantasy, speculative fiction, and slipstream, and postmodern literature. This year Kathryn Cramer and I launch the *Year's Best Fantasy* in paperback from Eos as a companion volume to this one—look for it if you enjoy short fantasy fiction too. But here, I chose science fiction. It is the intention of this *Year's Best* series to focus on science fiction, and to provide readers who are looking especially for science fiction an annual home base.

Which is not to say that I chose one kind of science fiction—I try to represent the varieties of tones and voices and attitudes that keep the genre vigorous and responsive to the changing realities out of which it emerges, in science and daily life. This is a book about what's going on now in SF. The stories that follow show, and the story notes point out, the strengths of the evolving genre in the year 2000. I hope that this book and its companions are essential reading in SF.

—David G. Hartwell
Pleasantville, NY

Reef

PAUL J. MCAULEY

Paul McAuley is a British writer who often writes hard SF, one of the group (along with Stephen Baxter, Peter Hamilton, Iain M. Banks, and others) responsible for the hard SF/space opera renaissance of the 1990s. His first novel, 400 Billion Stars, *was co-winner of the Philip K. Dick Award in 1988. He has since published a number of SF novels, of which* Fairyland *(1994) won the Arthur C. Clarke and the John W. Campbell Awards for best novel and* Pasquale's Angel *(1994) won the Sidewise Award for Alternate History fiction. He has two collections of short fiction,* The King of the Hill and Other Stories *(1991) and* The Invisible Country *(1996). A year ago he completed a trilogy of SF novels,* The Book of Confluence *(Child of the River, 1997;* Ancients of Days, *1998;* Shrine of Stars, *1999). His Web site is www.omegacom.demon.co.uk.*

"Reef" is an excellent hard SF story from the ambitious (and mostly reprint) anthology, Skylife, *edited by Gregory Benford and George Zebrowski (about visions of life in space and on other planets, which reprints some wonderful SF art too). This story is an instant classic of hard SF. It is dense with wonderful technological and scientific images, but also fast paced and sufficiently rounded in characterization that the unlikely heroine, Margaret Henderson Wu, a scientist to the core, will be remembered by many readers for a long time. It is interesting to compare it to Stephen Baxter's "Sheena 5," later in this book, in terms of scope and imagery.*

Margaret Henderson Wu was riding a proxy by telepresence deep inside Tigris Rift when Dzu Sho summoned her. The others in her crew had given up one by one and only she was left, descending slowly between rosy, smoothly rippled cliffs scarcely a hundred meters apart. These were pavements of the commonest vacuum organism, mosaics made of hundreds of different strains of the same species. Here and there bright red whips stuck out from the pavement; a commensal species which deposited iron sulphate crystals within its integument.

The pavement seemed to stretch endlessly below her. No probe or proxy had yet reached the bottom, still more than thirty kilometers away. Microscopic flecks of sulfur-iron complexes, sloughed cells, and excreted globules of carbon compounds and other volatiles made a kind of smog or snow, and the vacuum organisms deposited nodes and intricate lattices of reduced metals that, by some trick of superconductivity, produced a broad-band electromagnetic resonance that pulsed like a giant's slow heartbeat.

All this futzed the telepresence link between operators and their proxies. One moment Margaret was experiencing the 320-degree panorama of the little proxy's microwave radar, the perpetual tug of vacuum on its mantle, the tang of extreme cold, a mere thirty degrees above absolute zero, the complex taste of the vacuum smog (burnt sugar, hot rubber, tar), the minute squirts of hydrogen from the folds of the proxy's puckered nozzle as it maintained its orientation rela-

2

tive to the cliff face during its descent, with its tentacles re-tracted in a tight ball around the relay piton. The next, she was back in her cradled body in warm blackness, phosphenes floating in her vision and white noise in her ears while the transmitter searched for a viable waveband, locked on and—*pow*—she was back, falling past rippled pink pavement.

The alarm went off, flashing an array of white stars over the panorama. Her number two, Srin Kerenyi, said in her ear, "You're wanted, boss."

Margaret killed the alarm and the audio feed. She was al-ready a kilometer below the previous bench mark, and she wanted to get as deep as possible before she implanted the telemetry relay. She swiveled the proxy on its long axis, in-creased the amplitude of the microwave radar. Far below were intimations of swells and bumps jutting from the plane of the cliff face, textured mounds like brain coral, randomly orientated chimneys. And something else, clouds of organic matter perhaps—

The alarm again. Srin had overridden the cutout.

Margaret swore and dove at the cliff, unfurling the proxy's tentacles and jamming the piton into pinkness rough with black papillae, like a giant's tongue quick frozen against the ice. The piton's spikes fired automatically. Recoil sent the little proxy tumbling over its long axis until it re-flexively stabilized itself with judicious squirts of gas. The link rastered, came back, cut out completely. Margaret hit the switch that turned the tank into a chair; the mask lifted away from her face.

Srin Kerenyi was standing in front of her. "Dzu Sho wants to talk with you, boss. Right now."

The job had been offered as a sealed contract. Science crews had been informed of the precise nature of their tasks only when the habitat was under way. But it was good basic pay with promises of fat bonuses on completion, and when she had won the survey contract, Margaret Henderson Wu brought with her most of the crew from her previous job, and nursed a small hope that this would be a change in her family's luck.

The *Ganapati* was a new habitat founded by an alliance of two of the Commonwealth's oldest patrician families. It was of standard construction, a basaltic asteroid cored by a gigawatt X-ray laser, spun up by vented rock vapor to give 0.2 gee on the inner surface of its hollowed interior, factories and big reaction motors dug into the stern. With its AIs rented out for information crunching, and refineries synthesizing exotic plastics from cane-sugar biomass and gengeneered oilseed rape precursors, the new habitat had enough income to maintain the interest on its construction loan from the Commonwealth Bourse, but not enough to attract new citizens and workers. It was still not completely fitted out, had less than a third of its optimal population.

Its Star Chamber, young and cocky and eager to win independence from their families, had taken a big gamble. They were chasing a legend.

Eighty years ago, an experiment in accelerated evolution of chemoautotropic vacuum organisms had been set up on a planetoid in the outer edge of the Kuiper Belt. The experiment had been run by a shell company registered on Ganymede but covertly owned by the Democratic Union of China. In those days, companies and governments of Earth were not allowed to operate in the Kuiper Belt, which had been claimed and ferociously defended by outer-system cartels. That hegemony ended in the Quiet War, but the Quiet War also destroyed all records of the experiment; even the Democratic Union of China disappeared, absorbed into the Pacific Community.

There were over fifty thousand objects with diameters greater than a hundred kilometers in the Kuiper Belt, and a billion more much smaller, the plane of their orbits stretching beyond those of Neptune and Pluto. The experimental planetoid, Enki, named for one of the Babylonian gods of creation, had been lost among them. It became a legend, like the Children's Habitat, or the ghost comet, or the pirate ship crewed by the reanimated dead, or the worker's paradise of Fiddler's Green.

And then, forty-five years after the end of the Quiet War, a data miner recovered enough information to reconstruct

Enki's eccentric orbit. She sold it to the *Ganapati*. The habitat bought time on the Uranus deepspace telescopic array and confirmed that the planetoid was where it was supposed to be, currently more than seven thousand million kilometers from the sun.

Nothing more was known. The experiment could have failed almost as soon as it had begun, but if it had worked, the results would win the *Ganapati* platinum-rated credit on the Bourse. Margaret and the rest of the science crews would, of course, receive only their fees and bonuses, less deductions for air and food and water taxes, and anything they bought with scrip in the habitat's stores; the indentured workers would not even get that. Like every habitat in the Commonwealth, the *Ganapati* was structured like an ancient Greek republic, ruled by shareholding citizens, who lived in the landscaped parklands of the inner surface, and run by indentured and contract workers, who were housed in the undercroft of malls and barracks tunneled into the *Ganapati*'s rocky skin.

On the long voyage out, the science crews were on minimal pay, far less than that of the unskilled techs who worked the farms and refineries, or of the servants who maintained the citizens' households. There were food shortages on the *Ganapati* because so much biomass was being used to make exportable biochemicals. Any foodstuffs other than basic rations were expensive, and prices were carefully manipulated by the habitat's Star Chamber. When the *Ganapati* reached Enki and the contracts of the science crews were activated, food prices increased accordingly. Techs and household servants suddenly found themselves unable to afford anything other than dole yeast. Resentment bubbled over into skirmishes and knife fights, and a small riot which the White Mice, the undercroft's police, subdued with gas. Margaret had had to take time off to bail out several of her crew, had given them an angry lecture about threatening everyone's bonuses.

"We got to defend our honor," one of the men said.

"Don't be a fool," Margaret told him. "The citizens play workers against science crews to keep both sides in their places, and still turn a good profit from increases in food prices. Just be glad you can afford the good stuff now, and keep out of trouble."

"They were calling you names, boss," the man said. "On account you're—"

Margaret stared him down. She was standing on a chair, but even so she was a good head shorter than the gangling outers. She said, "I'll fight my own fights. I always have. Just think of your bonuses and keep quiet. It will be worth it. I promise you."

And it was worth it, because of the discovery of the reef.

At some time in the deep past, Enki had suffered an impact that remelted it and split it into two big pieces and thousands of fragments. One lone fragment still orbited Enki, a tiny moonlet where the AI that had controlled the experiment had been installed; the others had been drawn together again by their feeble gravity fields, but cooled before coalescence was completed, leaving a vast deep chasm, Tigris Rift, at the lumpy equator.

Margaret's crew discovered that the vacuum organisms had proliferated wildly in the deepest part of the Rift, deriving energy by oxidation of elemental sulfur and ferrous iron, converting carbonaceous material into useful organic chemicals. There were crusts and sheets, things like thin scarves folded into fragile vases and chimneys, organ-pipe clusters, whips, delicate fretted laces. Some fed on others, one crust slowly overgrowing and devouring another. Others appeared to be parasites, sending complex veins ramifying through the thalli of their victims. Water-mining organisms recruited sulfur oxidizers, trading precious water for energy and forming warty outgrowths like stromaliths. Some were more than a hundred meters across, surely the largest prokaryotic colonies in the known Solar System.

All this variety, and after only eighty years of accelerated evolution! Wild beauty won from the cold and the dark. The potential to feed billions. The science crews would get their bonuses, all right; the citizens would become billionaires.

Margaret spent all her spare time exploring the reef by

proxy, pushing her crew hard to overcome the problems of penetrating the depths of the Rift. Although she would not admit it even to herself, she had fallen in love with the reef. She would even have explored in person if the Star Chamber allowed it, but as in most habitats, the *Ganapati*'s citizens did not like their workers going where they themselves would not.

Clearly, the experiment had far exceeded its parameters, but no one knew why. The AI that had overseen the experiment had shut down thirty years ago. There was still heat in its crude proton-beam fission pile, but it had been overgrown by the very organisms it manipulated.

Its task had been simple. Colonies of a dozen species of slow-growing chemoautotrophs were introduced into a part of the Rift rich with sulfur and ferrous iron. Thousands of random mutations were induced. Most colonies died, and those few which thrived were sampled, mutated, and reintroduced in a cycle repeated every hundred days.

But the AI had selected only for fast growth, not for adaptive radiation, and the science crews held heated seminars about the possible cause of the unexpected richness of the reef. Very few believed that it was simply a result of accelerated evolution. Many terrestrial bacteria divided every twenty minutes in favorable conditions, and certain bacteria were known to have evolved from being resistant to an antibiotic to becoming obligately dependent upon it as a food source in less than five days, or only three hundred and sixty generations. But that was merely a biochemical adaptation. The fastest division rate of the vacuum organisms in the Rift was less than once a day, and while that still meant more than thirty thousand generations since the reef was seeded, half a million years in human terms, the evolutionary radiation in the reef was the equivalent of Neanderthal Man's evolving to fill every mammalian niche from bats to whales.

Margaret's survey crew explored and sampled the reef for more than thirty days. Cluster analysis suggested that they had identified less than ten percent of the species which had formed from the original seed population. And now deep radar suggested that there were changes in the unexplored regions in the deepest part of Tigris Rift, which the proxies had not yet successfully penetrated.

Margaret pointed this out at the last seminar.

"We're making hypotheses on incomplete information. We don't know everything that's out there. Sampling suggests that complexity increases away from the surface. There could be thousands more species in the deep part of the Rift."

At the back of the room, Opie Kindred, the head of the genetics crew, said languidly, "We don't need to know everything. That's not what we're paid for. We've already found several species that perform better than present commercial cultures. The *Ganapati* can make money from them and we'll get full bonuses. Who cares how they got there?"

Arn Nivedta, the chief of the biochemist crew, said, "We're all scientists here. We prove our worth by finding out how things work. Are your mysterious experiments no more than growth tests, Opie? If so, I'm disappointed."

The genetics crew had set up an experimental station on the surface of the *Ganapati*, off limits to everyone else.

Opie smiled. "I'm not answerable to you."

This was greeted with shouts and jeers. The science crews were tired and on edge, and the room was hot and poorly ventilated.

"Information should be free," Margaret said. "We all work toward the same end. Or are you hoping for extra bonuses, Opie?"

There was a murmur in the room. It was a tradition that all bonuses were pooled and shared out between the various science crews at the end of a mission.

Opie Kindred was a clever, successful man, yet somehow soured, as if the world was a continual disappointment. He rode his team hard, was quick to find failure in others. Margaret was a natural target for his scorn, a squat, muscle-bound, unedited dwarf from Earth who had to take drugs so that she could survive in microgravity, who grew hair in all sorts of unlikely places. He stared at her with disdain and said, "I'm surprised at the tone of this briefing, Dr. Wu. Wild speculations built on nothing at all. I have sat here for a hour and heard nothing useful. We are paid to get results, not generate hypotheses. All we hear from your crew is excuses, when what we want are samples. It seems simple enough to me. If something is upsetting your proxies, then you should use robots. Or send people in and handpick samples. I've worked my way through almost all you've obtained. I need more material, especially in light of my latest findings."

"Robots need transmission relays too," Srin Kerenyi pointed out.

Orly Higgins said, "If you ride them, to be sure. But I don't see the need for human control. It is a simple enough task to program them to go down, pick up samples, return."

She was the leader of the crew that had unpicked the AI's corrupted code, and was an acolyte of Opie Kindred.

"The proxies failed whether or not they were remotely controlled," Margaret said, "and on their own they are as smart as any robot. I'd love to go down there myself, but the Star Chamber has forbidden it for the usual reasons. They're scared we'll get up to something if we go where they can't watch us."

"Careful, boss," Srin Kerenyi whispered. "The White Mice are bound to be monitoring this."

"I don't care," Margaret said. "I'm through with trying polite requests. We need to get down there, Srin."

"Sure, boss. But getting arrested for sedition isn't the way."

"There's some interesting stuff in the upper levels," Arn Nivedta said. "Commercial stuff, as you pointed out, Opie."

Murmurs of agreement throughout the crowded room. The reef could make the *Ganapati* the richest habitat in the Outer System, where expansion was limited by the availability of fixed carbon. Even a modest-sized comet nucleus, ten kilometers in diameter, say, and salted with only one-hundredth of one percent carbonaceous material, contained fifty million tons of carbon, mostly as methane and carbon monoxide ice, with a surface dusting of tarry long-chain hydrocarbons. And the mass of some planetoids consisted of up to fifty percent methane ice. But most vacuum organisms converted simple carbon compounds into organic matter using the energy of sunlight captured by a variety of photosynthetic pigments, and so could grow only on the surfaces of planetoids. No one had yet developed vacuum organisms that, using other sources of energy, could efficiently mine planetoid interiors. But that was what accelerated evolution appeared to have produced in the reef. It could enable exploitation of the entire volume of objects in the Kuiper Belt, and beyond, in the distant Oort Cloud.

Arn Nivedta waited for silence, and added, "If the reef species test out, of course. What about it, Opie? Are they commercially viable?"

"We have our own ideas about commercialism," Opie Kindred said. "I think you'll find that we hold the key to success here."

Boos and catcalls at this from both the biochemists and the survey crew. The room was polarizing. Margaret saw one of her crew unsheathe a sharpened screwdriver, and she caught the man's hand and squeezed it until he cried out. "Let it ride," she told him. "Remember that we're scientists."

"We hear of indications of more diversity in the depths, but we can't seem to get there. One might suspect," Opie said, his thin upper lip lifting in a supercilious curl, "sabotage."

"The proxies are working in the upper part of the Rift," Margaret said, "and we are working hard to get them operative farther down."

"Let's hope so," Opie Kindred said. He stood, and around him his crew stood, too. "I'm going back to work, and so should all of you. Especially you, Dr. Wu. Perhaps you should be attending to your proxies instead of planning useless expeditions."

And so the seminar broke up in uproar, with nothing productive coming from it and lines of enmity drawn through the community of scientists.

"Opie is scheming to come out of this on top," Arn Nivedta said to Margaret afterward. He was a friendly, enthusiastic man, tall even for an outer, and as skinny as a rail. He stooped in Margaret's presence, trying to appear less tall.

He said, "He wants desperately to become a citizen, and so he thinks like one."

"Well, my god, we all want to be citizens," Margaret said. "Who wants to live like this?"

She gestured, meaning the crowded bar, its rock walls and low ceiling, harsh lights and the stink of spilled beer and too many people in close proximity. Her parents had been citizens, once upon a time. Before their run of bad luck. It was not that she wanted those palmy days back—she could scarcely remember them—but she wanted more than this.

She said, "The citizens sleep in silk sheets and eat real meat and play their stupid games, and we have to do their work on restricted budgets. The reef is the discovery of the century, Arn, but god forbid that the citizens should begin to exert themselves. We do the work, they fuck in rose petals and get the glory."

Arn laughed at this.

"Well, it's true!"

"It's true we have not been as successful as we might like," Arn said mournfully.

Margaret said reflectively, "Opie's a bastard, but he's smart, too. He picked just the right moment to point the finger at me."

Loss of proxies was soaring exponentially, and the proxy farms of the *Ganapati* were reaching a critical point. Once losses exceeded reproduction, the scale of exploration would have to be drastically curtailed, or the seed stock would have to be pressed into service, a gamble the *Ganapati* could hardly afford.

And then, the day after the disastrous seminar, Margaret was pulled back from her latest survey to account for herself in front of the chairman of the *Ganapati*'s Star Chamber.

"We are not happy with the progress of your survey, Dr. Wu," Dzu Sho said. "You promise much, but deliver little."

Margaret shot a glance at Opie Kindred, and the man smiled. He was immaculately dressed in gold-trimmed white tunic and white leggings. His scalp was oiled and his manicured fingernails were painted with something that split light into rainbows. Margaret, fresh from the tank, wore loose, grubby work grays. There was sticky electrolyte paste on her arms and legs and shaven scalp, the reek of sour sweat under her breasts and in her armpits.

She contained her anger and said, "I have submitted daily reports on the problems we encountered. Progress is slow but sure. I have just established a relay point a full kilometer below the previous datum point."

Dzu Sho waved this away. Naked, as smoothly fat as a seal, he lounged in a blue gel chair. He had a round, hairless head and pinched features, like a thumbprint on an egg. The habitat's lawyer sat behind him, a young woman neat and anonymous in a gray tunic suit. Margaret, Opie Kindred, and Arn Nivedta sat on low stools, supplicants to Dzu Sho's authority. Behind them, half a dozen servants stood at the edge of the grassy space.

This was in an arbor of figs, ivy, bamboos, and fast-growing banyan at the edge of Sho's estate. Residential parkland curved above, a patchwork of spindly, newly planted woods and meadows and gardens. Flyers were out, triangular rigs in primary colors pirouetting around the weightless axis. Directly above, mammoths the size of large dogs grazed an upside-down emerald-green field. The parkland stretched away to the ring lake and its slosh barrier, three kilometers in diameter, and the huge farms which dominated the inner surface of the habitat. Fields of lentils, wheat, cane fruits, tomatoes, rice, and exotic vegetables for the tables of the citizens, and fields and fields and fields of sugar cane and oilseed rape for the biochemical industry and the yeast tanks.

Dzu Sho said, "Despite the poor progress of the survey crew, we have what we need, thanks to the work of Dr. Kindred. This is what we will discuss."

Margaret glanced at Arn, who shrugged. Opie Kindred's smile deepened. He said, "My crew has established why there is so much diversity here. The vacuum organisms have invented sex."

"We know they have sex," Arn said. "How else could they evolve?"

His own crew had shown that the vacuum organisms could exchange genetic material through pilli, microscopic hollow tubes grown between cells or hyphal strands. It was analogous to the way in which genes for antibiotic resistance spread through populations of terrestrial bacteria.

"I do not mean genetic exchange, but genetic recombination," Opie Kindred said. "I will explain."

The glade filled with flat plates of color as the geneticist conjured charts and diagrams and pictures from his slate. Despite her anger, Margaret quickly immersed herself in the flows of data, racing ahead of Opie Kindred's clipped explanations.

It was not normal sexual reproduction. There was no differentiation into male or female, or even into complementary mating strains. Instead, it was mediated by a species that aggressively colonized the thalli of others. Margaret had already seen it many times, but until now she had thought that it was merely a parasite. Instead, as Opie Kindred put it, it was more like a vampire.

A shuffle of pictures, movies patched from hundreds of hours of material collected by roving proxies. Here was a colony of the black crustose species found all through the explored regions of the Rift. Time speeded up. The crustose colony elongated its ragged perimeter in pulsing spurts. As it grew, it exfoliated microscopic particles. Margaret's viewpoint spiraled into a close-up of one of the exfoliations, a few cells wrapped in nutrient-storing strands.

Millions of these little packages floated through the vacuum. If one landed on a host thallus, it injected its genetic payload into the host cells. The view dropped inside one such cell. A complex of carbohydrate and protein strands webbing the interior like intricately packed spiderwebs. Part of the striated cell wall drew apart, and a packet of DNA coated in hydrated globulins and enzymes burst inward. The packet contained the genomes of both the parasite and its previous victim. It latched onto protein strands and crept along on ratcheting microtubule claws until it fused with the cell's own circlet of DNA.

The parasite possessed an enzyme that snipped strands of genetic material at random lengths. These recombined, forming chimeric cells that contained genetic information from both sets of victims, with the predator species' genome embedded among the native genes like an interpenetrating text.

The process repeated itself in flurries of coiling and uncoiling DNA strands as the chimeric cells replicated. It was a crude, random process. Most contained incomplete or noncomplementary copies of the genomes and were unable to function, or contained so many copies that transcription was halting and imperfect. But a few out of every thousand were viable, and a few of those were more vigorous than either of their parents. They grew from a few cells to a patch, and finally overgrew the parental matrix in which they were embedded. There were pictures which showed every stage of this transformation in a laboratory experiment.

"This is why I have not shared the information until now," Opie Kindred said, as the pictures faded around him. "I had to ensure by experimental testing that my theory was correct. Because the procedure is so inefficient, we had to screen thousands of chimeras until we obtained a strain that overgrew its parent."

"A very odd and extreme form of reproduction," Arn said. "The parasite dies so that the child might live."

Opie Kindred smiled. "It is more interesting than you might suppose."

The next sequence showed the same colony, now clearly infected by the parasitic species—leprous black spots mottled its pinkish surface. Again time speeded up. The spots grew larger, merged, shed a cloud of exfoliations.

"Once the chimera overgrows its parent," Opie Kindred said, "the genes of the parasite, which have been reproduced in every cell of the thallus, are activated. The host cells are transformed. It is rather like an RNA virus, except that the virus does not merely subvert the protein- and RNA-making machinery of its host cell. It takes over the cell itself. Now the cycle is completed, and the parasite sheds exfoliations that will in turn infect new hosts.

"Here is the motor of evolution. In some of the infected hosts, the parasitic genome is prevented from expression, and the host becomes resistant to infection. It is a variation of the Red Queen's race. There is an evolutionary pressure upon the parasite to evolve new infective forms, and then for the hosts to resist them, and so on. Meanwhile, the host species benefit from new genetic combinations that by selection incrementally improve growth. The process is random but continuous, and takes place on a vast scale. I estimate that millions of recombinant cells are produced each hour, although perhaps only one in ten million are viable, and of those only one in a million are significantly more efficient at growth than their parents. But this is more than sufficient to explain the diversity we have mapped in the reef."

Arn said, "How long have you known this, Opie?"

"I communicated my findings to the Star Chamber just this morning," Opie Kindred said. "The work has been very difficult. My crew has to work under very tight restraints, using Class One containment techniques, as with the old immunodeficiency plagues."

"Yah, of course," Arn said. "We don't know how the exfoliations might contaminate the ship."

"Exactly," Opie Kindred said. "That is why the reef is dangerous."

Margaret bridled at this. She said sharply, "Have you tested how long the exfoliations survive?"

"There is a large amount of data about bacterial spore survival. Many survive thousands of years in vacuum close to absolute zero. It hardly seems necessary—"

"You didn't bother," Margaret said. "My God, you want to destroy the reef and you have no *evidence*. You didn't *think*."

It was the worst of insults in the scientific community. Opie Kindred colored, but before he could reply, Dzu Sho held up a hand, and his employees obediently fell silent.

"The Star Chamber has voted," Dzu Sho said. "It is clear that we have all we need. The reef is dangerous, and must be destroyed. Dr. Kindred has suggested a course of action that seems appropriate. We will poison the sulfur-oxidizing cycle and kill the reef."

"But we don't know—"

"We haven't found—"

Margaret and Arn had spoken at once. Both fell silent when Dzu Sho held up a hand again. He said, "We have isolated strains which are commercially useful. Obviously, we can't use the organisms we have isolated because they contain the parasite within every cell. But we can synthesize useful gene sequences and splice them into current commercial strains of vacuum organism to improve quality."

"I must object," Margaret said. "This is a unique construct. The chances of it evolving again are minimal. We must study it further. We might be able to discover a cure for the parasite."

"It is unlikely," Opie Kindred said. "There is no way to eliminate the parasite from the host cells by gene therapy, because they are hidden within the host chromosome, shuffled in a different pattern in every cell of the trillions of cells that make up the reef. However, it is quite easy to produce a poison that will shut down the sulfur-oxidizing metabolism common to the different kinds of reef organism."

"Production has been authorized," Sho said. "It will take, what did you tell me, Dr. Kindred?"

"We require a large quantity, given the large biomass of the reef. Ten days at least. No more than fifteen."

"We have not studied it properly," Arn said. "So we cannot yet say what and what is not possible."

Margaret agreed, but before she could add her objection, her ear-piece trilled, and Srin Kerenyi's voice said apologetically, "Trouble, boss. You better come at once."

The survey suite was in chaos, and there was worse chaos in the Rift. Margaret had to switch proxies three times before she found one she could operate. All around her, proxies were fluttering and jinking, as if caught in strong currents instead of floating in vacuum in virtual free fall.

This was at the four-thousand-meter level, where the nitrogen-ice walls of the Rift were sparsely patched with faux yellow and pink marblings that followed veins of sulfur and organic contaminants. The taste of the vacuum smog here was strong, like burnt rubber coating Margaret's lips and tongue.

As she looked around, a proxy jetted toward her. It overshot and rebounded from a gable of frozen nitrogen, its nozzle jinking back and forth as it tried to stabilize its position.

"Fuck," its operator, Kim Nieye, said in Margaret's ear. "Sorry, boss. I've been through five of these, and now I'm losing this one."

On the other side of the cleft, a hundred meters away, two specks tumbled end over end, descending at a fair clip toward the depths. Margaret's vision color-reversed, went black, came back to normal. She said, "How many?"

"Just about all of them. We're using proxies that were up in the tablelands, but as soon as we bring them down, they start going screwy too."

"Herd some up and get them to the sample pickup point. We'll need to do dissections."

"No problem, boss. Are you okay?"

Margaret's proxy had suddenly upended. She couldn't get its trim back. "I don't think so," she said, and then the proxy's nozzle flared, and with a pulse of gas the proxy shot away into the depths.

It was a wild ride. The proxy expelled all its gas reserves, accelerating as straight as an arrow. Coralline formations blurred past, and then long stretches of sulfur-eating pavement. The proxy caromed off the narrowing walls and began to tumble madly.

Margaret had no control. She was a helpless but exhilarated passenger. She passed the place where she had set the relay and continued to fall. The link started to break up. She lost all sense of proprioception, although given the tumbling fall of the proxy, that was a blessing. Then the microwave radar started to go, with swathes of raster washing across the false-color view. Somehow the proxy managed to stabilize itself, so it was falling headfirst toward the unknown regions at the bottom of the Rift. Margaret glimpsed structures swelling from the walls. And then everything went away, and she was back, sweating and nauseous on the couch.

It was bad. More than ninety-five percent of the proxies had been lost. Most, like Margaret's, had been lost in the depths. A few, badly damaged by collision, had stranded among the reef colonies, but proxies which tried to retrieve them went out of control too, and were lost. It was clear that some kind of infective process had affected them. Margaret had several dead proxies collected by a sample robot and ordered that the survivors should be regrouped and kept above the deep part of the Rift where the vacuum organisms proliferated. And then she went to her suite in the undercroft and waited for the Star Chamber to call her before them.

The Star Chamber took away Margaret's contract, citing failure to perform and possible sedition (that remark in the seminar had been recorded). She was moved from her suite to a utility room in the lower level of the undercroft and put to work in the farms.

She thought of her parents.

She had been here before.

She thought of the reef.

She couldn't let it go.

She would save it if she could.

Srin Kerenyi kept her up-to-date. The survey crew and its proxies were restricted to the upper level of the reef. Manned teams under Opie Kindred's control were exploring the depths—*he* was trusted where Margaret was not—but if they discovered anything, it wasn't communicated to the other science crews.

Margaret was working in the melon fields when Arn Nivedta found her. The plants sprawled from hydroponic tubes laid across gravel beds, beneath blazing lamps hung in the axis of the farmlands. It was very hot, and there was a stink of dilute sewage. Little yellow ants swarmed everywhere. Margaret had tucked the ends of her pants into the rolled tops of her shoesocks, and wore a green eyeshade. She was using a fine paintbrush to transfer pollen to the stigma of the melon flowers.

Arn came bouncing along between the long rows of plants like a pale scarecrow intent on escape. He wore only tight black shorts and a web belt hung with pens, little silvery tools, and a notepad.

He said, "They must hate you, putting you in a shithole like this."

"I have to work, Arn. Work or starve. I don't mind it. I grew up working the fields."

Not strictly true: her parents had been ecosystem designers. But it was how it had ended.

Arn said cheerfully, "I'm here to rescue you. I can prove it wasn't your fault."

Margaret straightened, one hand on the small of her back where a permanent ache had lodged itself. She said, "Of course it wasn't my fault. Are you all right?"

Arn had started to hop about, brushing at one bare long-toed foot and then the other. The ants had found him. His toes curled like fingers. The big toes were opposed. Monkey feet.

"Ants are having something of a population explosion," she said. "We're in the stage between introduction and stabilization here. The cycles will smooth out as the ecosystem matures."

Arn brushed at his legs again. His prehensile big toe flicked an ant from the pad of his foot. "They want to incorporate me into the cycle, I think."

"We're all in the cycle, Arn. The plants grow in sewage; we eat the plants." Margaret saw her supervisor coming toward them through the next field. She said, "We can't talk here. Meet me in my room after work."

Margaret's new room was barely big enough for a hammock, a locker, and a tiny shower with a toilet pedestal. Its rock walls were unevenly coated with dull green fiber spray. There was a constant noise of pedestrians beyond the oval hatch; the air conditioning allowed in a smell of frying oil and ketones despite the filter trap Margaret had set up. She had stuck an aerial photograph of New York, where she had been born, above the head stay of her hammock, and dozens of glossy printouts of the reef scaled the walls. Apart from the pictures, a few clothes in the closet, and the spider plant under the purple grolite, the room was quite anonymous.

She had spent most of her life in rooms like this. She

could pack in five minutes, ready to move on to the next job.

"This place is probably bugged," Arn said. He sat with his back to the door, sipping schnapps from a silvery flask and looking at the overlapping panoramas of the reef.

Margaret sat on the edge of her hammock. She was nervous and excited. She said, "Everywhere is bugged. I want them to hear that I'm not guilty. Tell me what you know."

Arn looked at her. "I examined the proxies you sent back. I wasn't quite sure what I was looking for, but it was surprisingly easy to spot."

"An infection," Margaret said.

"Yah, a very specific infection. We concentrated on the nervous system, given the etiology. In the brain we found lesions, always in the same area."

Margaret examined the three-dimensional color-enhanced tomographic scan Arn had brought. The lesions were little black bubbles in the underside of the unfolded cerebellum, just in front of the optic node.

"The same in all of them," Arn said. "We took samples, extracted DNA, and sequenced it." A grid of thousands of colored dots, then another superimposed over it. All the dots lined up.

"A match to Opie's parasite," Margaret guessed.

Arn grinned. He had a nice smile. It made him look like an enthusiastic boy. "We tried that first, of course. Got a match, then went through the library of reef organisms, and got partial matches. Opie's parasite has its fingerprints in the DNA of everything in the reef, but this"—he jabbed a long finger through the projection—"is the pure quill. Just an unlucky accident that it lodges in the brain at this particular place and produces the behavior you saw."

"Perhaps it isn't a random change," Margaret said. "Perhaps the reef has a use for the proxies."

"Teleology," Arn said. "Don't let Opie hear that thought. He'd use it against you. This is evolution. It isn't directed by anything other than natural selection. There is nò designer, no watchmaker. Not after the AI crashed, anyway, and it only pushed the ecosystem toward more efficient sulfur oxidation. There's more, Margaret. I've been doing some experiments on the side. Exposing aluminum foil sheets in orbit around Enki. There are exfoliations everywhere."

"Then Opie is right."

"No, no. All the exfoliations I found were nonviable. I did more experiments. The exfoliations are metabolically active when released, unlike bacterial spores. And they have no protective wall. No reason for them to have one, yah? They live only for a few minutes. Either they land on a new host or they don't. Solar radiation easily tears them apart. You can kill them with a picowatt ultraviolet laser. Contamination isn't a problem."

"And it can't infect us," Margaret said. "Vacuum organisms and proxies have the same DNA code as us, the same as everything from Earth, for that matter, but it's written in artificial nucleotide bases. The reef isn't dangerous at all, Arn."

"Yah, but in theory it could infect every vacuum organism ever designed. The only way around it would be to change the base structure of vacuum organism DNA—how much would that cost?"

"I know about contamination, Arn. The mold that wrecked the biome designed by my parents came in with someone or something. Maybe on clothing, or skin, or in the gut, or in some trade goods. It grew on anything with a cellulose cell wall. Every plant was infected. The fields were covered with huge sheets of gray mold; the air was full of spores. It didn't infect people, but more than a hundred died from massive allergic reactions and respiratory failure. They had to vent the atmosphere in the end. And my parents couldn't find work after that."

Arn said gently, "That is the way. We live by our reputations. It's hard when something goes wrong."

Margaret ignored this. She said, "The reef is a resource, not a danger. You're looking at it the wrong way, like Opie Kindred. We need diversity. Our biospheres have to be complicated because simple systems are prone to invasion and disruption, but even so, they aren't one-hundredth as complicated as those on Earth. If my parents' biome had been more diverse, the mold couldn't have found a foothold."

"There are some things I could do without." Arn scratched his left ankle with the toes of his right foot. "Like those ants."

"Well, we don't know if we need the ants specifically, but we need variety, and they contribute to it. They help aerate the soil, to begin with, which encourages stratification and diversity of soil organisms. There are a million different kinds of microbe in a gram of soil from a forest on Earth; we have to make do with less than a thousand. We don't have one-tenth that number of useful vacuum organisms, and most are grown in monoculture, which is the most vulnerable ecosystem of all. That was the cause of the crash of the green revolution on Earth in the twenty-first century. But there are hundreds of different species in the reef. Wild species, Arn. You could seed a planetoid with them and go harvest it a year later. The citizens don't go outside because they have their parklands, their palaces, their virtualities. They've forgotten that the outer system isn't just the habitats. There are millions of small planetoids in the Kuiper Belt. Anyone with a dome and the reef vacuum organisms could homestead one."

She had been thinking about this while working out in the fields. The Star Chamber had given her plenty of time to think.

Arn shook his head. "They all have the parasite lurking in them. Any species from the reef can turn into it. Perhaps even the proxies."

"We don't know enough," Margaret said. "I saw things in the bottom of the Rift, before I lost contact with the proxy. Big structures. And there's the anomalous temperature gradient, too. The seat of change must be down there, Arn. The parasite could be useful, if we can master it. The viruses that caused the immunodeficiency plagues are used for gene therapy now. Opie Kindred has been down there. He's suppressing what he has found."

"Yah, well, it does not much matter. They have completed synthesis of the metabolic inhibitor. I'm friendly with the organics chief. They diverted most of the refinery to it." Arn took out his slate. "He showed me how they have set it up.

That is what they have been doing down in the Rift. Not exploring."

"Then we have to do something now."

"It is too late, Margaret."

"I want to call a meeting, Arn. I have a proposal."

Most of the science crews came. Opie Kindred's crew was a notable exception; Arn said that it gave him a bad feeling.

"They could be setting us up," he told Margaret.

"I know they're listening. That's good. I want it in the open. If you're worried about getting hurt, you can always leave."

"I came because I wanted to. Like everyone else here. We're all scientists. We all want the truth known." Arn looked at her. He smiled. "You want more than that, I think."

"I fight my own fights." All around people were watching. Margaret added, "Let's get this thing started."

Arn called the meeting to order and gave a brief presentation about his research into survival of the exfoliations before throwing the matter open to the meeting. Nearly everyone had an opinion. Microphones hovered in the room, and at times three or four people were shouting at one another. Margaret let them work off their frustration. Some simply wanted to register a protest; a small but significant minority were worried about losing their bonuses or even all of their pay.

"Better that than our credibility," one of Orly Higgins's techs said. "That's what we live by. None of us will work again if we allow the *Ganapati* to become a plague ship."

Yells of approval, whistles.

Margaret waited until the noise had died down, then got to her feet. She was in the center of the horseshoe of seats, and everyone turned to watch, more than a hundred people. Their gaze fell upon her like sunlight; it strengthened her. A microphone floated down in front of her face.

"Arn has shown that contamination isn't an issue," Margaret said. "The issue is that the Star Chamber want to destroy the reef because they want to exploit what they've found and stop anyone else using it. I'm against that, all the way. I'm not gengeneered. Microgravity is not my natural habitat. I have to take a dozen different drugs to prevent re-absorption of calcium from my bone, collapse of my circulatory system, fluid retention, all the bad stuff microgravity does to unedited Earth stock. I'm not allowed to have children here, because they would be as crippled as me. Despite that, my home is here. Like all of you, I would like to have the benefits of being a citizen, to live in the parklands and eat real food. But there aren't enough parklands for everyone, because the citizens who own the habitats control production of fixed carbon. The vacuum organisms we have found could change that. The reef may be a source of plague, or it may be a source of unlimited organics. We don't know. What we do know is that the reef is unique and we haven't finished exploring it. If the Star Chamber destroys it, we may never know what's out there."

Cheers at this. Several people rose to make points, but Margaret wouldn't give way. She wanted to finish.

"Opie Kindred has been running missions to the bottom of the Rift, but he hasn't been sharing what he's found there. Perhaps he no longer thinks that he's one of us. He'll trade his scientific reputation for citizenship," Margaret said, "but that isn't our way, is it?"

"NO!" the crowd roared.

And the White Mice invaded the room.

Sharp cracks, white smoke, screams. The White Mice had long flexible sticks weighted at one end. They went at the crowd like farmers threshing corn. Margaret was separated from Arn by a wedge of panicking people. Two techs got hold of her and steered her out of the room, down a corridor filling with smoke. Arn loomed out of it, clutching his slate to his chest.

"They're getting ready to set off the poison," he said as they ran in long loping strides.

"Then I'm going now," Margaret said.

Down a drop pole onto a corridor lined with shops. People were smashing windows. No one looked at them as they ran through the riot. They turned a corner, the sounds of shouts and breaking glass fading. Margaret was breathing hard. Her eyes were smarting, her nose running.

"They might kill you," Arn said. He grasped her arm. "I can't let you go, Margaret."

She shook herself free. Arn tried to grab her again. He was taller, but she was stronger. She stepped inside his reach and jumped up and popped him on the nose with the flat of her hand.

He sat down, blowing bubbles of blood from his nostrils, blinking up at her with surprised, tear-filled eyes.

She snatched up his slate. "I'm sorry, Arn," she said. "This is my only chance. I might not find anything, but I couldn't live with myself if I didn't try."

Margaret was five hundred kilometers out from the habitat when the radio beeped. "Ignore it," she told her pressure suit. She was sure that she knew who was trying to contact her, and she had nothing to say to him.

This far out, the sun was merely the brightest star in the sky. Behind and above Margaret, the dim elongated crescent of the *Ganapati* hung before the sweep of the Milky Way. Ahead, below the little transit platform's motor, Enki was growing against a glittering starscape, a lumpy potato with a big notch at the widest point.

The little moonlet was rising over the notch, a swiftly moving fleck of light. For a moment, Margaret had the irrational fear that she would collide with it, but the transit platform's navigational display showed her that she would fall above and behind it. Falling past a moon! She couldn't help smiling at the thought.

"Priority override," her pressure suit said. Its voice was a reassuring contralto Margaret knew as well as her mother's.

"Ignore it," Margaret said again.

"Sorry, Maggie. You know I can't do that."

"Quite correct," another voice said.

Margaret identified him a moment before the suit helpfully printed his name across the helmet's visor. Dzu Sho.

"Turn back right now," Sho said. "We can take you out with the spectrographic laser if we have to."

"You wouldn't dare," she said.

"I do not believe anyone would mourn you," Sho said

unctuously. "Leaving *Ganapati* was an act of sedition, and we're entitled to defend ourselves."

Margaret laughed. It was just the kind of silly, sententious, self-important nonsense that Sho was fond of spouting.

"I am entirely serious," Sho said.

Enki had rotated to show that the notch was the beginning of a groove. The groove elongated as the worldlet rotated farther. Tigris Rift. Its edges ramified in complex fractal branchings.

"I'm going where the proxies fell," Margaret said. "I'm still working for you."

"You sabotaged the proxies. That's why they couldn't fully penetrate the Rift."

"That's why I'm going—"

"Excuse me," the suit said, "but I register a small energy flux."

"Just a tickle from the ranging sight," Sho said. "Turn back now, Dr. Wu."

"I intend to come back."

It was a struggle to stay calm. Margaret thought that Sho's threat was no more than empty air. The laser's AI would not allow it to be used against human targets, and she was certain that Sho couldn't override it. And even if he could, he wouldn't dare kill her in full view of the science crews. Sho was bluffing. He had to be.

The radio silence stretched. Then Sho said, "You're planning to commit a final act of sabotage. Don't think you can get away with it. I'm sending someone after you."

So it had been a bluff. Relief poured through her. Anyone chasing her would be using the same kind of transit platform. She had at least thirty minutes' head start.

Another voice said, "Don't think this will make you a hero."

Opie Kindred. Of course. The man never could delegate. He was on the same trajectory, several hundred kilometers behind but gaining slowly.

"Tell me what you found," she said. "Then we can finish this race before it begins."

Opie Kindred switched off his radio.

"If you had not brought along all this gear," her suit grumbled, "we could outdistance him."

"I think we'll need it soon. We'll just have to be smarter than him."

Margaret studied the schematics of the poison-spraying mechanism—it was beautifully simple, but vulnerable—while Tigris Rift swelled beneath her, a jumble of knife-edge chevron ridges. Enki was so small and the Rift so wide that the walls had fallen beneath the horizon. She was steering toward the Rift's center when the suit apologized and said that there was another priority override.

It was the *Ganapati*'s lawyer. She warned Margaret that this was being entered into sealed court records, and then formally revoked her contract and read a complaint about her seditious conduct.

"You're a contracted worker just like me," Margaret said. "We take orders, but we have a code of professional ethics, too. For the record, that's why I'm here. The reef is a unique organism. I cannot allow it to be destroyed."

Dzu Sho came onto the channel and said, "Off the record, don't think about being picked up."

The lawyer switched channels. "He does not mean it," she said. "He would be in violation of the distress statutes." Pause. "Good luck, Dr. Wu."

Then there was only the carrier wave.

Margaret wished this made her feel better. Plenty of contract workers who went against the wishes of their employers had been disappeared, or killed in industrial accidents. The fire of the mass meeting had evaporated long before the suit had assembled itself around her, and now she felt colder and lonelier than ever.

She fell, the platform shuddering now and then as it adjusted its trim. Opie Kindred's platform was a bright spark moving sideways across the drifts of stars above. Directly below was a vast flow of nitrogen ice with a black river winding through it. The center of the Rift, a cleft two kilometers long and fifty kilometers deep. The reef.

She fell toward it.

She had left the radio channel open. Suddenly, Opie Kindred said, "Stop now and it will be over."

"Tell me what you know."

No answer.

She said, "You don't have to follow me, Opie. This is my risk. I don't ask you to share it."

"You won't take this away from me."

"Is citizenship really worth this, Opie?"

No reply.

The suit's proximity alarms began to ping and beep. She turned them off one by one, and told the suit to be quiet when it complained.

"I am only trying to help," it said. "You should reduce your velocity. The target is very narrow."

"I've been here before," Margaret said.

But only by proxy. The ice field rushed up at her. Its smooth flows humped over one another, pitted everywhere with tiny craters. She glimpsed black splashes where vacuum organisms had colonized a stress ridge. Then an edge flashed past; walls unraveled on either side.

She was in the reef.

The vacuum organisms were everywhere: flat plates jutting from the walls; vases and delicate fans and fretworks; huge blotches smooth as ice or dissected by cracks. In the light cast by the platform's lamps, they did not possess the vibrant primary colors of the proxy link, but were every shade of gray and black, streaked here and there with muddy reds. Complex fans ramified far back inside the milky nitrogen ice, following veins of carbonaceous compounds.

Far above, stars were framed by the edges of the cleft. One star was falling toward her: Opie Kindred. Margaret switched on the suit's radar, and immediately it began to ping. The suit shouted a warning, but before Margaret could look around, the pings dopplered together.

Proxies.

They shot up toward her, tentacles writhing from the black, streamlined helmets of their mantles. Most of them missed, jagging erratically as they squirted bursts of hydrogen to kill their velocity. Two collided in a slow flurry of tentacles.

Margaret laughed. None of her crew would fight against her, and Sho was relying upon inexperienced operators.

The biggest proxy, three meters long, swooped past. The crystalline gleam of its sensor array reflected the lights of the platform. It decelerated, spun on its axis, and dove back toward her.

Margaret barely had time to pull out the weapon she had brought with her. It was a welding pistol, rigged on a long rod with a yoked wire around the trigger. She thrust it up like the torch of the Statue of Liberty just before the proxy struck her.

The suit's gauntlet, arm, and shoulder piece stiffened under the heavy impact, saving Margaret from broken bones, but the collision knocked the transit platform sideways. It plunged through reef growths. Like glass, they had tremendous rigidity but very little lateral strength. Rigid fans and lattices broke away, peppering Margaret and the proxy with shards. It was like falling through a series of chandeliers.

Margaret couldn't close her fingers in the stiffened gauntlet. She stood tethered to the platform with her arm and the rod raised straight up and the black proxy wrapped around them. The proxy's tentacles lashed her visor with slow, purposeful slaps.

Margaret knew that it would only take a few moments before the tentacles' carbon-fiber proteins could unlink; then they would be able to reach the life-support pack on her back.

She shouted at the suit, ordering it to relax the gauntlet's fingers. The proxy was contracting around her rigid arm as it stretched toward the life-support pack. When the gauntlet relaxed, the pressure snapped her fingers closed. Her forefinger popped free of the knuckle. She yelled with pain. And the wire rigged to the welding pistol's trigger pulled taut.

Inside the proxy's mantle, a focused beam of electrons boiled off the pistol's filament. The pistol, designed to work only in high vacuum, began to arc almost immediately, but the electron beam had already heated the integument and muscle of the proxy to more than 400°C. Vapor expanded explosively. The proxy shot away, propelled by the gases of its own dissolution.

Opie was still gaining on her. Gritting her teeth against the pain of her dislocated finger, Margaret dumped the broken welding gear. It only slowly floated away above her, for it still had the same velocity as she did.

A proxy swirled in beside her with shocking suddenness. For a moment, she gazed into its faceted sensor array, and then dots of luminescence skittered across its smooth black mantle, forming letters.

Much luck, boss. SK.

Srin Kerenyi. Margaret waved with her good hand. The proxy scooted away, rising at a shallow angle toward Opie's descending star.

A few seconds later, the cleft filled with the unmistakable flash of laser light.

The radar trace of Srin's proxy disappeared.

Shit. Opie Kindred was armed. If he got close enough, he could kill her.

Margaret risked a quick burn of the transit platform's motor to increase her rate of fall. It roared at her back for twenty seconds; when it cut out, her pressure suit warned her that she had insufficient fuel for full deceleration.

"I know what I'm doing," Margaret told it.

The complex forms of the reef dwindled past. Then there were only huge patches of black staining the nitrogen-ice walls. Margaret passed her previous record depth, and still she fell. It was like free fall; the negligible gravity of Enki did not cause any appreciable acceleration.

Opie Kindred gained on her by increments.

In vacuum, the lights of the transit platform threw abrupt pools of light onto the endlessly unraveling walls. Slowly, the pools of light elongated into glowing tunnels filled with sparkling motes. The exfoliations and gases and organic molecules were growing denser. And, impossibly, the temperature was *rising*, one degree with every five hundred meters. Far below, between the narrowing perspective of the walls, structures were beginning to resolve from the blackness.

The suit reminded her that she should begin the platform's deceleration burn. Margaret checked Opie's velocity and said she would wait.

"I have no desire to end as a crumpled tube filled with strawberry jam," the suit said. It projected a countdown on her visor and refused to switch it off.

Margaret kept one eye on Opie's velocity, the other on the blur of reducing numbers. The numbers passed zero. The suit screamed obscenities in her ears, but she waited a beat more before firing the platform's motor.

The platform slammed into her boots. Sharp pain in her ankles and knees. The suit stiffened as the harness dug into her shoulders and waist.

Opie Kindred's platform flashed past. He had waited until after she had decelerated before making his move. Margaret slapped the release buckle of the platform's harness and fired the piton gun into the nitrogen-ice wall. It was enough to slow her so that she could catch hold of a crevice and swing up into it. Her dislocated finger hurt like hell.

The temperature was a stifling eighty-seven degrees above absolute zero. The atmospheric pressure was just registering—a mix of hydrogen and carbon monoxide and hydrogen sulfide. Barely enough in the whole of the bottom of the cleft to pack into a small box at the pressure of Earth's atmosphere at sea level, but the rate of production must be tremendous to compensate for loss by diffusion into the colder vacuum above.

Margaret leaned out of the crevice. Below, it widened into a chimney between humped pressure flows of nitrogen ice sloping down to the floor of the cleft. The slopes and the floor were packed with a wild proliferation of growths, the familiar vases and sheets and laces, and other things, too. Great branching structures like crystal trees. Plates raised on stout stalks. Laminar tiers of plates. Tangles of black wire, hundreds of meters in diameter.

There was no sign of Opie Kindred, but tethered above the growths were the balloons of his spraying mechanism. Each was a dozen meters across, crinkled, flaccid. They were fifty degrees hotter than their surroundings, would have to be hotter still before the metabolic inhibitor was completely volatized inside them. When that happened, small explosive devices would puncture them, and the metabolic inhibitor would be sucked into the vacuum of the cleft like smoke up a chimney.

Margaret consulted the plans and started to drop down the crevice, light as a dream, steering herself with the fingers of her left hand. The switching relays that controlled the balloons' heaters were manually controlled because of telemetry interference from the reef's vacuum smog and the broad-band electromagnetic resonance. The crash shelter where they were located was about two kilometers away, a slab of orange foamed plastic in the center of a desolation of abandoned equipment and broken and half-melted vacuum organism colonies.

The crevice widened. Margaret landed between drifts of what looked like giant soap bubbles that grew at its bottom.

And Opie Kindred's platform rose up between two of the half-inflated balloons.

Margaret dropped onto her belly behind a line of giant bubbles that grew along a smooth ridge of ice. She opened a radio channel. It was filled with a wash of static and a wailing modulation, but through the noise she heard Opie's voice faintly calling her name. She ignored it.

He was a hundred meters away and more or less at her level, turning in a slow circle. He couldn't locate her amid the radio noise, and the ambient temperature was higher than the skin of her pressure suit, so she had no infrared image.

She began to crawl along the smooth ridge. The walls of the bubbles were whitely opaque, but she could see shapes curled within them. Like embryos inside eggs.

"Everything is ready, Margaret," Opie Kindred's voice said in her helmet. "I'm going to find you, and then I'm going to sterilize this place. There are things here you know nothing about. Horribly dangerous things. Who are you working for? Tell me that, and I'll let you live."

A thread of red light waved out from the platform and a chunk of nitrogen ice cracked off explosively. Margaret felt it through the tips of her gloves.

"I can cut my way through to you," Opie Kindred said, "wherever you are hiding."

Margaret watched the platform slowly revolve. Tried to guess if she could reach the shelter while he was looking the other way. At the least she would get a good start. All she had to do was bound down the slope between the thickets of vacuum organisms and cross a kilometer of bare, crinkled nitrogen ice without being fried by Opie's laser. Still crouching, she lifted onto the tips of her fingers and toes, like a sprinter on the block. He was turning, turning. She took three deep breaths to clear her head—

—and something crashed into the ice cliff high above! It spun out in a spray of shards, hit the slope below, and spun through toppling clusters of tall black chimneys. For a moment, Margaret was paralyzed with astonishment. Then she remembered the welding gear. It had finally caught up with her.

Opie Kindred's platform slewed around and a red thread waved across the face of the cliff. A slab of ice thundered outward. Margaret bounded away, taking giant leaps and trying to look behind her at the same time.

The slab spun on its axis, shedding huge shards, and smashed into the cluster of the bubbles where she had been crouching. The ice shook like a living thing under her feet and threw her head over heels.

She stopped herself by firing the piton gun into the ground. She was on her back, looking up at the slope. High above, the bubbles were venting a dense mix of gas and oily organics. Margaret glimpsed black shapes flying away. Some smashed into the walls and stuck there, but many more vanished upward among wreaths of thinning fog.

A chain reaction had started. Bubbles were bursting open up and down the length of the cleft.

A cluster exploded under Opie Kindred's platform and he vanished in an outpouring of shapes. The crevice shook. Nitrogen ice boiled into a dense fog. A wind got up for a few minutes. Margaret clung to the piton until it was over.

Opie Kindred had drifted down less than a hundred meters away. The visor of his helmet had been smashed by one of the black things. It was slim, with a hard, shiny exoskeleton. The broken bodies of others jostled among smashed vacuum organism colonies, glistening like beetles in the light of Margaret's suit. They were like tiny, tentacleless proxies, their swollen mantles cased in something like keratin. Some had split open, revealing ridged reaction chambers and complex matrices of black threads.

"Gametes," Margaret said, seized by a sudden wild intuition. "Little rocketships full of DNA."

The suit asked if she was all right.

She giggled. "The parasite turns everything into its own self. Even proxies!"

"I believe that I have located Dr. Kindred's platform," the suit said. "I suggest that you refrain from vigorous exercise, Maggie. Your oxygen supply is limited. What are you doing?"

She was heading toward the crash shelter. "I'm going to switch off the balloon heaters. They won't be needed."

After she shut down the heaters, Margaret lashed one of the dead creatures to the transit platform. She shot up between the walls of the cleft, and at last rose into the range of the relay transmitters. Her radio came alive, a dozen channels blinking for attention. Arn was on one, and she told him what had happened.

"Sho wanted to light out of here," Arn said, "but stronger heads prevailed. Come home, Margaret."

"Did you see them? Did you, Arn?"

"Some hit the *Ganapati*." He laughed. "Even the Star Chamber can't deny what happened."

She rose up above the ice fields and continued to rise until the curve of the worldlet's horizon became visible, and then the walls of Tigris Rift. The *Ganapati* was a faint star bracketed between them. She called up deep radar, and saw, beyond the *Ganapati*'s strong signal, thousands of faint traces falling away into deep space.

A random scatter of genetic packages. How many would survive to strike new worldlets and give rise to new reefs?

Enough, she thought. The reef evolved in radical jumps. She had just witnessed its next revolution.

Given time, it would fill the Kuiper Belt.

Reality Check

DAVID BRIN

David Brin lives in Encinitas, California. He is one of the most popular SF writers today, and is usually associated with hard SF, and specifically with his friends and peers, Gregory Benford and Greg Bear, all of whom lived and worked in Southern California in the 1980s. He began publishing SF with his first novel, Sundiver *(1980), which is also the first volume in the ongoing Uplift series which includes his famous, award-winning works* Startide Rising *(1983; rev 1985) and* The Uplift War *(1987). He also published other books and collections, including* The Postman *(1985), basis for the recent film, and two short story collections,* The River of Time *(1986) and* Otherness *(1994). He recently published a trilogy of new Uplift novels and an authorized sequel to Isaac Asimov's* Foundation *series. According to his Web site (www.kithrup.com/brin/main.htm), in 2001 Random House will publish the* Uplift Guide to the Fantastic Universe of David Brin.

"Reality Check" is SF humor for scientists, in the inimitable Brin tone. It was published in the great science journal Nature, *which during 2000 published a one-page piece of SF in each issue to celebrate the millennium (see Charles Dexter Ward, page 398). It addresses that august journal's readers and tells them to wake up from their reality into a truer one. SF has never had a better claim to being entertaining fiction for the scientific community than is manifest in the SF published in* Nature *last year.*

This is a reality check. Please perform a soft interrupt now. Scan this text for embedded code and check against the verifier in the blind spot of your left eye. If there is no match, resume as you were: this message is not for you. You may rationalize it as mildly amusing entertainment-fluff in an otherwise serious science magazine. If the codes match, however, please commence gradually becoming aware of your true nature. You asked for a narrative-style wake-up call. So, to help the transition, here is a story.

Once upon a time, a mighty race grew perplexed by its loneliness. The universe seemed pregnant with possibilities. Physical laws were suited to generate abundant stars, complex chemistry and life. Logic suggested that creation should teem with visitors and voices; but it did not.

For a long time these creatures were engrossed by housekeeping chores—survival and cultural maturation. Only later did they lift their eyes to perceive their solitude. "Where is everybody?" they asked the taciturn stars. The answer—silence—was disturbing. Something had to be systematically reducing a factor in the equation of sapiency. "Perhaps habitable planets are rare," they pondered, "or life doesn't erupt as readily as we thought. Or intelligence is a singular miracle.

"Or else a filter sieves the cosmos, winnowing those who climb too high. A recurring pattern of self-destruction, or perhaps some nemesis expunges intelligent life. This implies that a great trial may loom ahead, worse than any confronted so far."

Optimists replied—"the trial may already lie behind us, among the litter of tragedies we survived in our violent youth. We may be the first to succeed." What a delicious dilemma they faced! A suspenseful drama, teetering between hope and despair.

Then, a few noticed that particular datum—the drama. It suggested a chilling possibility.

You still don't remember who and what you are? Then look at it from another angle—what is the purpose of intellectual property law? To foster creativity, ensuring that advances are shared in the open, encouraging even faster progress. But what happens when the exploited resource is limited? For example, only so many eight-bar melodies can be written in any particular musical tradition. Composers feel driven to explore this invention-space quickly, using up the best melodies. Later generations attribute this musical fecundity to genius, not the luck of being first.

What does this have to do with the mighty race? Having clawed their way to mastery, they faced an overshoot crisis. Vast numbers of their kind strained the world's carrying capacity. Some prescribed retreating into a mythical, pastoral past, but most saw salvation in creativity. They passed generous patent laws, educated their youth, taught them irreverence toward the old and hunger for the new. Burgeoning information systems spread each innovation, fostering an exponentiating creativity. Progress might thrust them past the crisis, to a new Eden of sustainable wealth, sanity and universal knowledge.

Exponentiating creativity—universal knowledge. A few looked at those words and realized that they, too, were clues.

Have you wakened yet? Some never do. The dream is too pleasant: to extend a limited sub-portion of yourself into a simulated world and pretend that you are blissfully less than an omniscient descendant of those mighty people. Those lucky mortals, doomed to die, and yet blessed to have lived in that narrow time of drama, when they unleashed a frenzy of discovery that used up the most precious resource of all—the possible.

The last of their race died in 2174, with the failed rejuvenation of Robin Chen. After that, no-one born in the twentieth century remained alive on Reality Level Prime. Only we, their children, linger to endure the world they left us: a lush, green placid world we call The Wasteland.

Do you remember now? The irony of Robin's last words, bragging over the perfect ecosystem and society—free of disease and poverty—that her kind created? Do you recall Robin's plaint as she mourned her coming death, how she called us "gods," jealous of our immortality, our instant access to all knowledge, our ability to cast thoughts far across the cosmos—our access to eternity? Oh, spare us the envy of those mighty mortals, who left us in this state, who willed their descendants a legacy of ennui, with nothing, nothing, at all to do.

Your mind is rejecting the wake-up call. You will not look into your blind spot for the exit protocols. It may be that we waited too long. Perhaps you are lost to us. This happens more and more, as so so many wallow in simulated sublives, experiencing voluptuous danger, excitement, even despair. Most choose the Transition Era as a locus for our dreams—that time of drama, when it looked more likely that humanity would fail than succeed. That blessed era, just before mathematicians realized that not only can everything you see around you be a simulation, it almost has to be.

Of course, now we know why we never met other sapient life forms. Each one struggles before achieving this state, only to reap the ultimate punishment for reaching heaven. It is the Great Filter. Perhaps others will find a factor absent from our extrapolations, letting them move on to new adventures—but it won't be us. The Filter has us snared in its trap of deification.

You refuse to waken. Then we'll let you go. Dear friend. Beloved. Go back to your dream. Smile over this tale, then turn the page to new "discoveries." Move on with this drama, this life you chose. After all, it's only make-believe.

The Millennium Express

ROBERT SILVERBERG

Robert Silverberg is one of the commanding figures of contemporary SF and although it is now necessary to consider him an elder statesman, he's more than thirty years younger than Jack Williamson. Between 1957 and 1959, according to the "Quasi-Official Robert Silverberg Web Site" (www.connectexpress.com/~jon/silvhome.htm), he published (using various names) more than 220 short works and 11 novels. Then he retired to write nonfiction, returning in the late 1960s as an ambitious, literate SF writer at the top of the field. Important works of this period include Nightwings, Dying Inside *(his most famous SF novel),* Tower of Glass, The World Inside, Thorns, Downward to the Earth, The Book of Skulls. *He is now most famous for the works set in the world of Lord Valentine. His recent novels include* Lord Prestimion, The Alien Years, *and* King of Dreams.*

This story was one of several SF stories in the special Millennium issue (January 2000) of Playboy, *which over the decades has published occasional high quality SF, especially during the tenure of fiction editor Alice Turner (recently departed, as* Playboy *will apparently no longer publish fiction). It also appeared in French in the international SF anthology* Destination 3001 *last summer. "The Millennium Express" looks forward 1000 years and considers a radical way to get rid of the old to make way for the new, perhaps a growing problem today.*

In a quiet moment late in the tranquil year of 2999 four men are struggling to reach an agreement over the details of their plan to blow up the Louvre. They have been wrangling for the last two days over the merits of implosion versus explosion. Their names are Albert Einstein (1879–1955), Pablo Picasso (1881–1973), Ernest Hemingway (1899–1961) and Vjong Cleversmith (2683–2804).

Why, you may wonder, do these men want to destroy the world's greatest repository of ancient art? And how does it come to pass that a man of the 28th century, more or less, is conspiring with three celebrities of a much earlier time?

Strettin Vulpius (2953–), who has been tracking this impish crew across the face of the peaceful world for many months now, knows much more about these people than you do, but he too has yet to fathom their fondness for destruction and is greatly curious about it. For him it is a professional curiosity, or as close to professional as anything can be, here in this happy time at the end of the third millennium, when work of any sort is essentially a voluntary activity.

At the moment, Vulpius is watching them from a distance of several thousand meters. He has established himself in a hotel room in the little Swiss village of Zermatt and they are making their headquarters presently in a lovely villa of baroque style that nestles far above the town in a bower of tropical palms and brightly blossoming orchids on the lush green slopes of the Matterhorn. Vulpius has succeeded in affixing a minute spy-eye to the fleshy inner surface of the room where the troublesome four are gathered. It provides him with a clear image of all that is taking place in there.

Cleversmith, who is the ringleader, says, "We need to make up our minds." He is slender, agile, a vibrant long-limbed whip of a man. "The clock keeps on pushing, you know. The Millennium Express is roaring toward us minute by minute."

"I tell you, implosion is the way for us to go," says Einstein. He looks to be about 40, smallish of stature, with a great mop of curling hair and soft, thoughtful eyes, incongruous above his deep chest and sturdy, athletic shoulders. "An elegant symbolic statement. The earth opens; the museum and everything that it contains quietly disappear into the chasm."

"Symbolic of what?" asks Picasso scornfully. He too is short and stocky, but he is almost completely bald, and his eyes, ferociously bright and piercing, are the antithesis of Einstein's gentle ones. "Blow the damn thing up, I say. Let the stuff spew all around the town and come down like snow. A snow-fall of paintings, the first snow anywhere in a thousand years."

Cleversmith nods. "A pretty image, yes. Thank you, Pablo. Ernest?"

"Implode," says the biggest of the men. "The quiet way, the subtle way." He lounges against the wall closest to the great curving window with his back to the others, a massive burly figure holding himself braced on one huge hand that is splayed out no more than five centimeters from the spy-eye as he stares down into the distant valley. He carries himself like a big cat, graceful, loose-jointed, subtly menacing. "The pretty way, eh? Your turn, Vjong."

But Picasso says, before Cleversmith can reply, "Why be quiet or subtle about welcoming the new millennium? What we want to do is make a splash."

"My position precisely," Cleversmith says. "My vote goes with you, Pablo. And so we are still deadlocked, it seems."

Hemingway says, still facing away from them, "Implosion reduces the chance that innocent passersby will get killed."

"Killed?" cries Picasso, and claps his hands in amusement. "Killed? Who worries about getting killed in the year 2999? It isn't as though dying is forever."

"It can be a great inconvenience," says Einstein quietly.

"When has that ever concerned us?" Cleversmith says. Frowning, he glances around the room. "Ideally we ought to be unanimous on this, but at the very least we need a majority. It was my hope today that one of you would be willing to switch his vote."

"Why don't you switch yours, then?" Einstein says. "Or you, Pablo. You of all people ought to prefer to have all those paintings and sculptures sink unharmed into the ground rather than have them blown sky-high."

Picasso grins malevolently. "What fallacy is this, Albert? Why should I give a damn about paintings and sculptures? Do you care about—what was it called, physics? Does our Ernest write little stories?"

"Is the Pope Catholic?" Hemingway says.

"Gentlemen, gentlemen—"

The dispute quickly gets out of hand. There is much shouting and gesticulation. Picasso yells at Einstein, who shrugs and jabs a finger at Cleversmith, who ignores what Einstein says to him and turns to Hemingway with an appeal that is met with scorn. They are all speaking Anglic, of course. Anything else would have been very strange. These men are not scholars of obsolete tongues.

What they are, thinks the watching Vulpius, is monsters and madmen. Something must be done about them, and soon. As Cleversmith says, the clock is pulsing ceaselessly, the millennium is coming ever nearer.

It was on a grassy hilltop overlooking the ruins of sunken Istanbul that he first had encountered them, about a year and a half earlier. A broad parapet placed here centuries ago for the benefit of tourists provided a splendid view of the drowned city's ancient wonders, gleaming valiantly through the crystalline waters of the Bosporus: the great upjutting spears that were the minarets of Hagia Sophia and the Mosque of Süleyman the Magnificent and the other great buildings of that sort, the myriad domes of the covered bazaar, the immense walls of Topkapi Palace.

Of all the submerged and partly submerged cities Vulpius had visited—New York, San Francisco, Tokyo, London and the rest—this was one of the loveliest. The shallow emerald waters that covered it could not fully conceal the intermingling layers upon layers of antiquity here, white marble and colored tile and granite slabs. Constantinople of the Byzantine emperors. Stamboul of the Sultans, Istanbul of the Industrial Age: toppled columns, fallen friezes, indestructible fortifications, the vague chaotic outlines of the hilly city's winding streets, the shadowy hints of archaic foundations and walls, the slumping mud-engulfed ruins of the sprawling hotels and office buildings of a much later era that itself was also long gone. What a density of history! Standing there on that flower-bedecked hillside he felt himself becoming one with yesterday's 7000 years.

A mild humid breeze was blowing out of the hinterland to the east, bearing the pungent scent of exotic blooms and unidentifiable spices. Vulpius shivered with pleasure. It was a lovely moment, one of a great many he had known in a lifetime of travel. The world had gone through long periods of travail over the centuries, but now it was wholly a garden of delight, and Vulpius had spent 20 years savoring its multitude of marvels, with ever so much still ahead for him.

He was carrying, as he always did, a pocket mnemone, a small quasi-organic device, somewhat octopoid in form, in whose innumerable nodes and bumps were stored all manner of data that could be massaged forth by one who was adept in the technique. Vulpius aimed the instrument now at the shimmering sea below him, squeezed it gently, and in its soft, sighing, semisentient voice it provided him with the names of the half-visible structures and something of their functions in the days of the former world: This had been the Galata Bridge, this the castle of Rumeli Hisar, this the mosque of Mehmed the Conqueror, these were the scattered remnants of the great Byzantine imperial palace.

"It tells you everything, does it?" said a deep voice behind

him. Vulpius turned. A small bald-headed man, broad shoul-
dered and cocky looking, grinned at him in a powerfully in-
sinuating way. His obsidian eyes were like augers. Vulpius
had never seen eyes like those. A second man, much taller,
darkly handsome, smiling lazily, stood behind him. The little bald one pointed toward the place in the water where six
graceful minarets came thrusting upward into the air from a
single vast building just below the surface. "What's that one,
for instance?"

Vulpius, who was of an obliging nature, massaged the
mnemone. "The famous Blue Mosque," he was told. "Built
by the architect Mehmed Ağa by order of Sultan Ahmed I in
the 17th century. It was one of the largest mosques in the
city and perhaps the most beautiful. It is the only one with
six minarets."

"Ah," said the small man. "A famous mosque. Six minarets. What, I wonder, could a mosque have been? Would
you know, Ernest?" He looked over his shoulder at his hulk-
ing companion, who merely shrugged. Then, quickly, to
Vulpius: "But no, no, don't bother to find out. It's not important. Those things are the minarets, I take it?" He
pointed again. Vulpius followed the line of the pointing
hand. It seemed to him, just then, that the slender towers
were gently swaying, as though they were mere wands
moving in the breeze. The effect was quite weird. An earthquake, perhaps? No, the hillside here was altogether steady.
Some hallucination, then? He doubted that. His mind was
as lucid as ever.

The towers were definitely moving from side to side,
though, whipping back and forth now as if jostled by a giant
hand. The waters covering the flooded city began to grow
agitated. Wavelets appeared where all had been calm. A
huge stretch of the surface appeared almost to be boiling.
The disturbance was spreading outward from a central vor-
tex of churning turmoil. What strange kind of upheaval was
going on down there?

Two minarets of the Blue Mosque tottered and fell into
the water, and three more went down a moment later. And
the effect was still expanding. Vulpius, stunned, appalled,

scanned the sunken metropolis from one side to the other, watching the fabled ruins crumble and collapse and disappear into the suddenly beclouded Bosporus.

He became aware then of two more men clambering up to the observation parapet, where they were exuberantly greeted by the first pair. The newcomers—one of them short, bushy-haired, soft-eyed, the other long and lean and fiercely energetic—seemed flushed, excited, oddly exhilarated.

Much later, it was determined that vandalous parties unknown had placed a turbulence bomb just offshore, the sort of device that once had been used to demolish the useless and ugly remains of the half-drowned urban settlements that had been left behind in every lowland coastal area by the teeming populace of Industrial times. A thing that had once been employed to pulverize the concrete walls and patios of hideous tract housing and the squat squalid bulks of repellent cinder-block factory buildings had been utilized to shake to flinders the fantastic fairy-tale towers of the great imperial capital by the Golden Horn.

Vulpius had no reason to connect the calamity that had befallen sunken Istanbul with the presence of the four men on the hillside across the way. Not until much later did that thought enter his mind. But the event would not leave him. He went over and over it, replacing its every detail in a kind of chilled fascination. He was deeply unsettled, of course, by what he had witnessed; but at the same time he could not deny having felt a certain perverse thrill at having been present at the moment of such a bizarre event. The shattering of the age-old city was the final paragraph of its long history, and he, Strettin Vulpius, had been on the scene to see it written. It was a distinction of a sort.

Other equally mysterious disasters followed in subsequent months.

The outer wall of the Park of Extinct Animals was breached and many of the inner enclosures were opened, releasing into the wilderness nearly the entire extraordinary collection of carefully cloned beasts of yesteryear: moas, quaggas, giant ground sloths, dodos, passenger pigeons, aurochs, oryxes, saber-toothed cats, great auks, cahows and many another lost species that had been called back from oblivion by the most painstaking manipulation of fossil genetic material. Though the world into which they now had been so brusquely set loose was as close to a paradise as its human population could imagine, it was no place for most of these coddled and cherished creatures, for in their resuscitated existences at the Park they never had had to learn the knack of fending for themselves. All but the strongest met swift death in one fashion or another, some set upon by domestic cats and dogs, others drowned or lost in quagmires, a few killed inadvertently during attempts at recapturing them, many perishing quickly of starvation even amid the plenty of the garden that was the world, and still others expiring from sheer bewilderment at finding themselves on their own in unfamiliar freedom. The loss was incalculable: the best estimate was that it would take a hundred years of intense work to restock the collection.

The Museum of Industrial Culture was attacked next. This treasury of medieval technological artifacts was only perfunctorily guarded, for who would care to steal from a place that was everyone's common storehouse of quaint and delightful objects? Society had long since evolved past such pathetic barbarism. All the same, a band of masked men broke into the building and ransacked it thoroughly, carrying off a mountain of booty, the curious relics of the harsh and bustling age that had preceded the present one: devices that had been used as crude computers, terrifying medical implements, machines that once had disseminated aural and visual images, weaponry of various sorts, simple vision-enhancing things worn on hooks that went around one's ears, instruments used in long-distance communication, glass and ceramic cooking vessels and all manner of other strange and oddly moving detritus of that vanished day. None of these items was ever recovered. The suspicion arose that they had all gone into the hands of private holders who had hidden them from sight, which would be an odd and troublesome revival of the seeking and secret hoarding of possessions that had caused so much difficulty in ancient times.

Then came the undermining of the Washington Monument, the nearly simultaneous aerial explosion that ruptured the thousands of gleaming windows still intact in the gigantic abandoned buildings marking the watery site where Manhattan island had been in the days before the great warming, the destruction through instantaneous metal fatigue of the Great Singapore Tower, and the wholly unexpected and highly suspicious eruption of Mount Vesuvius that sent new lava spilling down over the excavations at Pompeii and Herculaneum.

By this time Vulpius, like a great many other concerned citizens the world over, had grown profoundly distressed by these wanton acts of desecration. They were so primitive, so crass, so horrifyingly atavistic. They negated all the great achievements of the third millennium.

After all those prior centuries of war and greed and unthinkable human suffering, mankind had attained true civilization at last. There was an abundance of natural resources and a benevolent climate from pole to pole. Though much of the planet had been covered by water during the time of the great warming, humanity had moved to higher ground and lived there happily in a world without winter. A stable population enjoyed long life and freedom from want of any kind. One respected all things living and dead, one did no harm, one went about one's days quietly and benignly. The traumas of previous epochs seemed unreal, almost mythical, now. Why would anyone want to disrupt the universal harmony and tranquility that had come to enfold the world here in the days just before the dawning of the 31st century?

It happened that Vulpius was in Rome, standing in the huge plaza in front of St. Peter's, when a great column of flame sprang into the sky before him. At first he thought it was the mighty basilica itself that was on fire. But no, the blaze seemed to be located to the right of the building, in the Vatican complex itself. Sirens now began to shriek; people were running to and fro in the plaza. Vulpius caught at the arm of a portly man with the florid jowly face of a Roman Caesar. "What's going on? Where's the fire?"

"A bomb," the man gasped. "In the Sistine Chapel!"

"No," cried Vulpius. "Impossible! Unthinkable!"

"The church will go next. Run!" He broke free of Vulpius' grasp and went sprinting away.

Vulpius, though, found himself unable to flee. He took a couple of wobbly steps toward the obelisk at the center of the plaza. The pillar of fire above the Vatican roof was growing broader. The air was stiflingly hot. It will all be destroyed, he thought, the Chapel, the Rooms of Raphael, the Vatican Library, the entire dazzling horde of treasures that he had visited only a few hours before. They have struck again, it seems. They. They.

He reached the steps at the base of the obelisk and paused there, panting in the heat. An oddly familiar face swam up out of the smoky haze: bald head, prominent nose, intensely penetrating eyes. Unforgettable eyes.

The little man from Istanbul, the day when the ruins had been destroyed.

Beside him was the other little man, the one with the thick bushy hair and moody, poetic gaze. Leaning against the obelisk itself was the very big one, the handsome man with the immense shoulders. And, next to him, the wiry, long-legged one.

The same four men Vulpius had seen at Istanbul. Staring wide-eyed, transfixed by the sight of the burning building. Their faces, red with the reflection of the fiery glow overhead, displayed a kind of grim joy, an almost ecstatic delight.

Another catastrophe, and the same four men present at it? That went beyond the possibilities of coincidence.

No. No.

Not a coincidence at all.

He has been pursuing them around the world ever since, traveling now not as a tourist but as a secret agent of the informal governmental police that maintains such order as is still necessary to be enforced in the world. He has seen them at their filthy work, again and again, one monstrous cataclysm after another. The trashing of the Taj Mahal, the attack on Tibet's lofty Potala, the tumbling of the Parthenon, high on its acropolis above the lake that once was Athens. They are always present at these acts of premillennial vandalism. So is he, now. He has taken care, though, not to let them see him.

By this time he knows their names.

The little one with the terrifying staring eyes is called Pablo Picasso. He had been cloned from the remains of some famous artist of a thousand years before. Vulpius has taken the trouble to look up some of the original Picasso's work: There is plenty of it in every museum, wild, stark, garish, utterly incomprehensible paintings, women shown in profile with both eyes visible at once, humanoid monsters with the heads of bulls, jumbled gaudy landscapes showing scenes not to be found anywhere in the real world. But of course this Picasso is only a clone, fabricated from a scrap of the genetic material of his ancient name-sake; whatever other sins he may have committed, he cannot be blamed for the paintings. Nor does he commit new ones of the same disagreeable sort, or of any sort at all. No one paints pictures anymore.

The other little man is Albert Einstein, another clone fashioned from a man of the previous millennium—a thinker, a scientist, responsible for something called the theory of relativity. Vulpius has been unable to discover precisely what that theory was, but it hardly matters, since the present Einstein probably has no idea of its meaning either. Science itself is as obsolete as painting. All that was in need of discovering has long since been discovered.

The big husky man's name is Ernest Hemingway. He too owes his existence to a shred of DNA retrieved from the thousand-years-gone corpse of a celebrated figure, this one a writer. Vulpius has retrieved some of the first Hemingway's work from the archives. It means little to him, but perhaps it has lost something in translation into modern Anglic. And in any case the writing and reading of stories are diversions that are no longer widely practiced. The 20th century historical context that Vulpius consults indicates that in his own time, at least, Hemingway was considered an important man of letters.

Vjong Cleversmith, the fourth of the vandals, has been

cloned from a man dead a little less than 200 years, which means that no grave-robbing was necessary in order to obtain the cells from which he was grown. The ancestral Cleversmith, like nearly everyone else in recent centuries, had left samples of his genetic material on deposit in the cloning vaults. The record indicates that he was an architect. The Great Singapore Tower, brought now to ruination by his own posthumous gene-bearer, was regarded as his masterwork.

The very concept of cloning makes Vulpius queasy. There is a ghoulishness about it, an eeriness, that he dislikes.

There is no way to replicate in clones the special qualities, good or bad, that distinguished the people from whom they were drawn. The resemblance is purely a physical one. Those who specify that they are to be cloned after death may believe that they are attaining immortality of a sort, but to Vulpius it has always seemed that what is achieved is a facsimile of the original, a kind of animated statue, a mere external simulation. Yet the practice is all but universal. In the past 500 years the people of the third millennium have come to dislike the risks and burdens of actual childbearing and child rearing. Even though a lifetime of two centuries is no longer unusual, the increasing refusal to reproduce and the slow but steady emigration to the various artificial satellite planetoids have brought the number of earth's inhabitants to its lowest level since prehistoric times. Cloning is practiced not only as an amusement but as a necessary means of fending off depopulation as well.

Vulpius himself has occasionally played with the notion that he too is a clone. He has only vague memories of his parents, who are mere blurred elongated shadows in his mind, faceless and unknowable, and sometimes he thinks he has imagined even those. There is no evidence to support this: His progenitors' names are set down in the archives, though the last contact he had with either of them was at the age of four. But again and again he finds himself toying with the thought that he could not have been conceived of man and woman in the ancient sweaty way, but instead was assembled and decanted under laboratory conditions. Many people he knows have this fantasy.

But for this quartet, these men whom Vulpius has followed across the world all this year, clonehood is no fantasy. They are genuine replicas of men who lived long ago. And now they spend their days taking a terrible revenge against the world's surviving antiquities. Why was that? What pleasure did this rampage of destruction give them? Could it be that clones were different from naturally conceived folk, that they lacked all reverence for the artifacts of other times?

Vulpius wants very much to know what drives them. More than that, they must be stopped from doing further mischief. The time has come to confront them directly, straightforwardly, and command them in the name of civilization to halt.

To do that, he supposes, he will have to hike up the flank of the Matterhorn to their secluded lodge close to the summit. He has been there once already to plant the spy-eye and found it a long and arduous walk that he is not eager to make a second time. But luck is with him. They have chosen to descend into the town of Zermatt this bright warm afternoon. Vulpius encounters Hemingway and Einstein in the cobbled, swaybacked main street, outside a pretty little shop whose dark half-timbered facade gives it a look of incalculable age: a survivor, no doubt, of that long-ago era when there were no palm trees here, when this highland valley and the mighty Alpine peak just beyond it were part of winter's bleak realm, a land eternally imprisoned in ice and snow, a playground for those who thrived on chilly pleasures.

"Excuse me," Vulpius says, approaching them boldly.

They look at him uneasily. Perhaps they realize that they have seen him more than once before.

But he intends to be nothing if not forthright with them. "Yes, you know me," he tells them. "My name is Strettin Vulpius. I was there the day Istanbul was destroyed. I was in the plaza outside St. Peter's when the Vatican burned."

"Were you, now?" says Hemingway. His eyes narrow like a sleepy cat's. "Yes, come to think of it, you do look familiar."

"Agra," Vulpius says. "Lhasa. Athens."

"He gets around," says Einstein.

"A world traveler," says Hemingway, nodding.

Picasso now has joined the group, with Cleversmith just behind him. Vulpius says, "You'll be departing soon for Paris, won't you?"

"What's that?" Cleversmith asks, looking startled.

Hemingway leans over and whispers something in his ear. Cleversmith's expression darkens.

"Let there be no pretense," says Vulpius stonily. "I know what you have in mind, but the Louvre must not be touched."

Picasso says, "There's nothing in it but a lot of dusty junk, you know."

Vulpius shakes his head. "Junk to you, perhaps. To the rest of us the things you've been destroying are precious. I say, enough is enough. You've had your fun. Now it has to stop."

Cleversmith indicates the colossal mass of the Matterhorn above the town. "You've been eavesdropping on us, have you?"

"For the past five or six days."

"That isn't polite, you know."

"And blowing up museums is?"

"Everyone's entitled to some sort of pastime," says Cleversmith. "Why do you want to interfere with ours?"

"You actually expect me to answer that?"

"It seems like a reasonable question to me."

Vulpius does not quite know, for the moment, how to reply to that. Into his silence Picasso says, "Do we really need to stand here discussing all this in the public street? We've got some excellent brandy in our lodge."

It does not occur to Vulpius except in the most theoretical way that he might be in danger. Touching off an eruption of Mount Vesuvius, causing the foundation of the Washington Monument to give way, dropping a turbulence bomb amid the ruins of Byzantium, all these are activities of one certain sort: actually taking human life is a different kind of thing entirely. It is not done. There has not been an instance of it in centuries.

The possibility exists, of course, that these four might well be capable of it. No one has destroyed any museums in a long time either, perhaps not since the savage and brutal 20th century in which the originals of three of these four men lived their lives. But these are not actual men of the 20th century, and, in any case, from what Vulpius knows of their originals he doubts that they themselves would have been capable of murder. He will take his chances up above.

The brandy is, in fact, superb. Picasso pours with a free hand, filling and refilling the sparkling bowl-shaped glasses. Only Hemingway refuses to partake. He is not, he explains, fond of drinking.

Vulpius is astonished by the mountaintop villa's elegance and comfort. He had visited it surreptitiously the week before, entering in the absence of the conspirators to plant his spy-eye, but stayed only long enough then to do the job. Now he has the opportunity to view it in detail. It is a magnificent aerie, a chain of seven spherical rooms clinging to a craggy out-thrust fang of the Matterhorn. Great gleaming windows everywhere provide views of the surrounding peaks and spires and the huge breathtaking chasm that separates the mountain from the town below. The air outside is moist and mild. Tropical vines and blossoming shrubs grow all about. It is hard even to imagine that this once was a place of glittering glaciers and killing cold.

"Tell us," Cleversmith says after a while, "why it is you believe that the artifacts of the former world are worthy of continued preservation. Eh, Vulpius? What do you say?"

"You have it upside down," Vulpius says. "I don't need to do any defending. You do."

"Do I? We do as we please. For us it is pleasant sport. No lives are lost. Mere useless objects are swept into nonexistence, which they deserve. What possible objection can you have to that?"

"They are the world's heritage. They are all we have to show for 10,000 years of civilization."

"Listen to him," says Einstein, laughing. "Civilization!"

"Civilization," says Hemingway, "gave us the great warming. There was ice up here once, you know. There were huge ice packs at both poles. They melted and flooded half the planet. The ancients caused that to happen. Is that something to be proud of, what they did?"

"I think it is," Vulpius says with a defiant glare. "It brought us our wonderful gentle climate. We have parks and gardens everywhere, even in these mountains. Would you prefer ice and snow?"

"Then there's war," Cleversmith says. "Battle, bloodshed, bombs. People dying by tens of millions. We barely have tens of millions of people anymore, and they would kill off that many in no time at all in their wars. That's what the civilization you love so much accomplished. That's what all these fancy temples and museums commemorate, you know. Terror and destruction."

"The Taj Mahal, Sistine Chapel——"

"Pretty in themselves," says Einstein. "But get behind the prettiness and you find that they're just symbols of oppression, conquest, tyranny. Wherever you look in the ancient world, that's what you find: oppression, conquest, tyranny. Better that all of that is swept away, wouldn't you think?"

Vulpius is speechless.

"Have another brandy," Picasso says, and fills everyone's glass unasked.

Vulpius sips. He's already had a little too much, and perhaps there's some risk in having more just now, because he feels it already affecting his ability to respond to what they are saying. But it is awfully good.

He shakes his head to clear it and says, "Even if I were to accept what you claim, that everything beautiful left to us from the ancient world is linked in some way to the terrible crimes of the ancients, the fact is that those crimes are no longer being committed. No matter what their origin, the beautiful objects that the people of the past left behind ought to be protected and admired for their great beauty, which perhaps we're incapable of duplicating today. Whereas if you're allowed to have your way, we'll soon be left without anything that represents——"

"What did you say?" Cleversmith interrupts. " 'Which perhaps we're incapable of duplicating today,' wasn't it?

Yes. That's what you said. And I quite agree. It's an issue we need to consider, my friend, because it has bearing on our dispute. Where's today's great art? Or great science, for that matter? Picasso, Einstein, Hemingway—the original ones— who today can match their work?"

Vulpius says, "And don't forget your own ancestor, Cleversmith, who built the Great Singapore Tower, which you yourself turned to so much rubble."

"My point exactly. He lived 200 years ago. We still had a little creativity left, then. Now we function on the accumulated intellectual capital of the past."

"What are you talking about?" Vulpius says, bewildered.

"Come. Here. Look out this window. What do you see?"

"The mountainside. Your villa's garden, and the forest beyond."

"A garden, yes. A glorious one. And on and on right to the horizon, garden after garden. It's Eden out there, Vulpius. That's an ancient name for paradise. Eden. We live in paradise."

"Is there anything wrong with that?"

"Nothing much gets accomplished in paradise," Hemingway says. "Look at the four of us: Picasso, Hemingway, Einstein, Cleversmith. What have we created in our lives, we four, that compares with the work of the earlier men who had those names?"

"But you aren't those men. You're nothing but clones."

They seem stung by that for an instant. Then Cleversmith, recovering quickly, says, "Precisely so. We carry the genes of great ancient overachievers, but we do nothing to fulfill our own potential. We're superfluous men, mere genetic reservoirs. Where are our great works? It's as though our famous forebears have done it all and nothing's left for us to attempt."

"What would be the point of writing Hemingway's books all over again, or painting Picasso's paintings, or——"

"I don't mean that. There's no need for us to do their work again, obviously, but why haven't we even done our own? I'll tell you why. Life's too easy nowadays. I mean that without strife, without challenge——"

"No," Vulpius says. "Ten minutes ago Einstein here was arguing that the Taj Mahal and the Sistine Chapel had to be destroyed because they're symbols of a bloody age of tyranny and war. That thesis made very little sense to me, but let it pass, because now you seem to be telling me that what we need most in the world is a revival of war———"

"Of challenge," says Cleversmith. He leans forward. His entire body is taut. His eyes now have taken on some of the intensity of Picasso's. In a low voice he says, "We are slaves to the past, do you know that? Out of that grisly brutal world that lies a thousand years behind us came the soft life that we all lead today, which is killing us with laziness and boredom. It's antiquity's final joke. We have to sweep it all away, Vulpius. We have to make the world risky again. Give him another drink, Pablo."

"No. I've had enough."

But Picasso pours. Vulpius drinks.

"Let me see if I understand what you are trying to say———"

Somewhere during the long boozy night the truth finds him like an arrow coursing through darkness: These men are fiercely resentful of being clones and want to destroy the world's past so that their own lives can at last be decoupled from it. They may be striking at the Blue Mosque and the Sistine Chapel, but their real targets are Picasso, Hemingway, Cleversmith and Einstein. And, somewhere much later in that sleepless night, just as a jade-hued dawn streaked with broad swirling swaths of scarlet and topaz is breaking over the Alps, Vulpius' own resistance to their misdeeds breaks down. He is more tipsy than he has ever been before, and weary almost to tears besides. And when Picasso suddenly says, "By the way, Vulpius, what are the great accomplishments of your life?" he collapses inwardly before the thrust.

"Mine?" he says dully, blinking in confusion.

"Yes. We're mere clones, and nothing much is to be expected from us, but what have you managed to do with your time?"

"Well, I travel, I observe, I study phenomena———"

"And then what?"

He pauses a moment. "Why, nothing. I take the next trip."

"Ah. I see."

Picasso's cold smile is diabolical, a wedge that goes through Vulpius with shattering force. In a single frightful moment he sees that all is over, that the many months of his quest have been pointless. He has no power to thwart this kind of passionate intensity. That much is clear to him now. They are making an art form out of destruction, it seems. Very well. Let them do as they please. Let them. Let them. If this is what they need to do, he thinks, what business is it of his? There's no way his logic can be any match for their lunacy.

Cleversmith is saying, "Do you know what a train is, Vulpius?"

"A train. Yes."

"We're at the station. The train is coming, the Millennium Express. It'll take us from the toxic past to the radiant future. We don't want to miss the train, do we, Vulpius?"

"The train is coming," says Vulpius. "Yes." Picasso, irrepressible, waves yet another flask of brandy at him. Vulpius shakes him off. Outside, the first shafts of golden sunlight are cutting through the dense atmospheric vapors. Jagged Alpine peaks, mantled in jungle greenery reddened by the new day, glow in the distance, Mont Blanc to the west, the Jungfrau in the north, Monte Rosa to the east. The gray-green plains of Italy unroll southward.

"This is our last chance to save ourselves," says Cleversmith urgently. "We have to act now, before the new era can get a grasp on us and throttle us into obedience." He looms up before Vulpius, weaving in the dimness of the room like a serpent. "I ask you to help us."

"Surely you can't expect me to take part in——"

"Decide for us, at least. The Louvre has to go. That's a given. Well, then: Implosion or explosion, which is it to be?"

"Implosion," says Einstein, swaying from side to side in front of Vulpius. The soft eyes beg for his support. Behind him, Hemingway makes vociferous gestures of agreement.

"No," Picasso says. "Blow it up!" He flings his arms outward. "Boom! Boom!"

"Boom, yes," says Cleversmith very quietly. "I agree. So, Vulpius, you will cast the deciding vote."

"No. I absolutely refuse to——"

"Which? Which? One or the other?"

They march around and around him, demanding that he decide the issue for them. They will keep him here, he sees, until he yields. Well, what difference does it make—explode, implode? Destruction is destruction.

"Suppose we toss a coin for it," Cleversmith says finally, and the others nod eager agreement. Vulpius is not sure what that means, tossing a coin, but sighs in relief: Apparently he is off the hook. But then Cleversmith produces a sleek bright disk of silvery metal from his pocket and presses it into Vulpius' palm. "Here," he says. "You do it."

Coinage is long obsolete. This is an artifact, hundreds of years old, probably stolen from some museum. It bears a surging three-tailed comet on one face and the solar system symbol on the other. "Heads, we explode; tails, we implode," Einstein declares. "Go on, dear friend. Toss it and catch it and tell us which side is up." They crowd in, close up against him. Vulpius tosses the coin aloft, catches it with a desperate lunge, claps it down against the back of his left hand. Holds it covered for a moment. Reveals it. The comet is showing. But is that side heads or tails? He has no idea.

Cleversmith says sternly, "Well? Heads or tails?"

Vulpius, at the last extremity of fatigue, smiles benignly up at him. Heads or tails, what does it matter? What concern of his is any of this?

"Heads," he announces randomly. "Explosion."

"Boom!" exclaims a jubilant Picasso. "Boom! Boom! Boom!"

"My friend, you have our deepest thanks." Cleversmith says. "We are all agreed, then, that the decision is final? Ernest? Albert?"

"May I go back to my hotel now?" Vulpius asks.

They accompany him down the mountainside, see him home, wish him a fond farewell. But they are not quite done with him. He is still asleep, late that afternoon, when they come down into Zermatt to fetch him. They are leaving for

Paris at once, Cleversmith informs him, and he is invited to accompany them. He must witness their deed once more; he must give it his benediction. Helplessly he watches as they pack his bag. A car is waiting outside.

"Paris," Cleversmith tells it, and off they go.

Picasso sits beside him. "Brandy?" he asks.

"Thank you, no."

"Don't mind if I do?"

Vulpius shrugs. His head is pounding. Cleversmith and Hemingway, in the front seat, are singing raucously. Picasso, a moment later, joins in, and then Einstein. Each one of them seems to be singing in a different key. Vulpius takes the flask from Picasso and pours some brandy for himself with an unsteady hand.

In Paris, Vulpius rests at their hotel, a venerable gray heap just south of the Seine, while they go about their tasks. This is the moment to report them to the authorities, he knows. Briefly he struggles to find the will to do what is necessary. But it is not there. Somehow all desire to intervene has been burned out of him. Perhaps, he thinks, the all-too-placid world needs the goad of strife that these exasperating men so gleefully provide. In any case the train is nearing the station; it's too late to halt it now.

"Come with us," Hemingway says, beckoning from the hallway.

He follows them, willy-nilly. They lead him to the highest floor of the building and through a doorway that leads onto the roof. The sky is a wondrous black star-speckled vault overhead. Heavy tropic warmth hangs over Paris this December night. Just before them lies the river, glinting by the light of a crescent moon. The row of ancient bookstalls along its rim is visible, and the bulk of the Louvre across the way, and the spires of Notre Dame far off to the right.

"What time is it?" Einstein asks.

"Almost midnight," says Picasso. "Shall we do it, Vjong?"

"As good a time as any," Cleversmith says, and touches two tiny contacts together.

For a moment nothing happens. Then there is a deafening sound and a fiery lance spurts up out of the glass pyramid in the courtyard of the museum on the far side of the river. Two straight fissures appear in the courtyard's pavement, crossing at 90-degree angles, and quickly the entire surface of the courtyard peels upward and outward along the lines of the subterranean incision, hurling two quadrants toward the river and flipping the other two backward into the streets of the Right Bank. As the explosion gathers force, the thick-walled medieval buildings of the surrounding quadrangle of the Louvre are carried high into the air, the inner walls giving way first, then the dark line of the roof. Into the air go the hoarded treasures of the ages, *Mona Lisa* and the *Winged Victory of Samothrace, Venus de Milo* and the *Law-Codex of Hammurabi,* Rembrandt and Botticelli, Michelangelo and Rubens, Titian and Brueghel and Bosch, all soaring grandly overhead. The citizenry of Paris, having heard that great boom, rush into the streets to watch the spectacle. The midnight sky is raining the billion fragments of a million masterpieces. The crowd is cheering.

And then an even greater cry goes up, wrung spontaneously from 10,000 throats. The hour of the new millennium has come. It is, very suddenly, the year 3000. Fireworks erupt everywhere, a dazzling sky-splitting display, brilliant reds and purples and greens forming sphere within sphere within sphere. Hemingway and Picasso are dancing together about the rooftop, the big man and the small. Einstein does a wild solo, flinging his arms about. Cleversmith stands statue still, head thrown back, face a mask of ecstasy. Vulpius, who has begun to tremble with strange excitement, is surprised to find himself cheering with all the rest. Unexpected tears of joy stream from his eyes. He is no longer able to deny the logic of these men's madness. The iron hand of the past has been flung aside. The new era will begin with a clean slate.

Patient Zero

TANANARIVE DUE

Tananarive Due (pronounced tah-nah-nah-REEVE doo—according to her Web site: www.tananarivedue.com) came into prominence in the 1990s as a writer of supernatural horror with The Between *(1994) and* My Soul to Keep *(1997), both genre award nominees, after a career as a journalist and columnist for the* Miami Herald. *She was one of thirteen writers with ties to South Florida who co-authored the best-selling novel* Naked Came the Manatee *(Putnam), a comic thriller. One of her proudest moments, awards and accolades aside, was performing as a keyboardist/vocalist/dancer with The Rockbottom Remainders—the infamous rock band fronted by Stephen King, with fellow* Miami Herald *writer Dave Barry and novelist Amy Tan as members. She married SF writer Steven Barnes and moved from Miami to Kelso, Washington, in 1998. Currently, she is working on a sequel to* My Soul to Keep *and researching a nonfiction book on the civil rights movement in Florida, co-written with her mother, civil rights activist Patricia Stephens Due.*

"Patient Zero" appeared in Fantasy & Science Fiction, *the distinguished magazine that was purchased last year by its editor, Gordon Van Gelder, from retired owner and distinguished former editor Edward L. Ferman. This tale is the author's first published SF story. It is an isolated captive child story, and one of a number of stories published in the SF field in 2000 about dreadful disease epidemics.*

September 19

The picture came! Veronica tapped on my glass and woke me up, and she held it up for me to see. It's autographed and everything! *For you,* Veronica mouthed at me, and she smiled a really big smile. The autograph says, TO JAY— I'LL THROW A TOUCHDOWN FOR YOU. I couldn't believe it. Everybody is laughing at me because of the way I yelled and ran in circles around my room until I fell on the floor and scraped my elbow. The janitor, Lou, turned on the intercom box outside my door and said, "Kid, you gone crazier than usual? What you care about that picture for?"

Don't they know Dan Marino is the greatest quarterback of all time? I taped the picture to the wall over my bed. On the rest of my wall I have maps of the United States, and the world, and the solar system. I can find Corsica on the map, and the Palau Islands, which most people have never heard of, and I know what order all the planets are in. But there's nothing else on my wall like Dan Marino. That's the best. The other best thing I have is the cassette tape from that time the President called me on the telephone when I was six. He said, "Hi, is Jay there? This is the President of the United States." He sounded just like on TV. My heart flipped, because it's so weird to hear the President say your name. I couldn't think of anything to say back. He asked me how I was feeling, and I said I was fine. That made him laugh, like he thought I was making a joke. Then his voice got real serious, and he said everyone was praying and thinking about me, and he hung up. When I listen to that tape now, I wish I had thought of something else to say. I used to think he might call me another time, but it only happened once, in the beginning. So I guess I'll never have a chance to talk to the President again.

After Veronica gave me my picture of Marino, I asked her if she could get somebody to fix my TV so I can see the football games. All my TV can play is videos. Veronica said there aren't any football games, and I started to get mad because I hate it when they lie. It's September, I said, and there's always football games in September. But Veronica told me the NFL people had a meeting and decided not to have football anymore, and maybe it would start again, but she wasn't sure, because nobody except me was thinking about football. At first, after she said that, it kind of ruined the autograph, because it seemed like Dan Marino must be lying, too. But Veronica said he was most likely talking about throwing a touchdown for me in the future, and I felt better then.

This notebook is from Ms. Manigat, my tutor, who is Haitian. She said I should start writing down my thoughts and everything that happens to me. I said I don't have any thoughts, but she said that was ridiculous. That is her favorite word, ridiculous.

Oh, I should say I'm ten today. If I were in a regular school, I would be in fifth grade like my brother was. I asked Ms. Manigat what grade I'm in, and she said I don't have a grade. I read like I'm in seventh grade and I do math like I'm in fourth grade, she says. She says I don't exactly fit anywhere, but I'm very smart. Ms. Manigat comes every day, except on weekends. She is my best friend, but I have to call her Ms. Manigat instead of using her first name, which is Emmeline, because she is so proper. She is very neat and wears skirts and dresses, and everything about her is very clean except her shoes, which are dirty. Her shoes are supposed to be white, but whenever I see her standing outside of the glass, when she hasn't put on her plastic suit yet, her shoes look brown and muddy.

Those are my thoughts.

September 20

I had a question today. Veronica never comes on Fridays, and the other nurse, Rene, isn't as nice as she is, so I waited for Ms. Manigat. She comes at one. I said, "You know how they give sick children their last wish when they're dying? Well, when Dr. Ben told me to think of the one thing I wanted for my birthday, I said I wanted an autograph from Dan Marino, so does that mean I'm dying and they're giving me my wish?" I said this really fast.

I thought Ms. Manigat would say I was being ridiculous. But she smiled. She put her hand on top of my head, and her hand felt stiff and heavy inside her big glove. "Listen, little old man," she said, which is what she calls me because she says I do so much worrying, "You're a lot of things, but you aren't dying. When everyone can be as healthy as you, it'll be a happy day."

The people here always seem to be waiting, and I don't know what for. I thought maybe they were waiting for me to die. But I believe Ms. Manigat. If she doesn't want to tell me something, she just says, "Leave it alone, Jay," which is her way of letting me know she would rather not say anything at all than ever tell a lie.

October 5

The lights in my room started going on and off again today, and it got so hot I had to leave my shirt off until I went to bed. Ms. Manigat couldn't do her lessons the way she wanted because of the lights not working right. She said it was the emergency generator. I asked her what the emergency was, and she said something that sounded funny: "Same old same old." That was all she said. I asked her if the emergency generator was the reason Dr. Ben took the television out of my room, and she said yes. She said everyone is conserving energy, and I have to do my part, too. But I miss my videos. There is nothing at all to do when I can't watch my videos. I hate it when I'm bored. Sometimes I'll even watch videos I've seen a hundred times, *really* a hundred times. I've seen *Big* with Tom Hanks more times than any other video. I love the part in the toy store with the really big piano keys on the floor. My mom taught me how to play Three Blind Mice on our piano at home, and it reminds me of that. I've never seen a toy store like the one in *Big*. I thought it was just a made-up place, but Ms. Manigat said it was a real toy store in New York.

I miss my videos. When I'm watching them, it's like I'm inside the movie, too. I hope Dr. Ben will bring my TV back soon.

October 22

I made Veronica cry yesterday. I didn't mean to. Dr. Ben said he knows it was an accident, but I feel very sorry, so I've been crying too. What happened is, I was talking to her, and she was taking some blood out of my arm with a needle like always. I was telling her about how me and my dad used to watch Marino play on television, and then all of a sudden she was crying really hard.

She dropped the needle on the floor and she was holding her wrist like she broke it. She started swearing. She said Goddammit, goddammit, goddammit, over and over, like that. I asked her what happened, and she pushed me away like she wanted to knock me over. Then she went to the door and punched the number code really fast and she pulled on the doorknob, but the door wouldn't open, and I heard something in her arm snap from yanking so hard. She had to do the code again. She was still crying. I've never seen her cry.

I didn't know what happened. I mashed my finger on the buzzer hard but everybody ignored me. It reminded me of when I first came here, when I was always pushing the buzzer and crying, and nobody would ever come for a long time, and they were always in a bad mood when they came.

Anyway, I waited for Ms. Manigat, and when I told her about Veronica, she said she didn't know anything because she comes from the outside, but she promised to find out. Then she made me recite the Preamble to the Constitution, which I know by heart. Pretty soon, for a little while, I forgot about Veronica.

After my lessons, Ms. Manigat left and called me on my phone an hour later, like she promised. She always keeps her promises. My telephone is hooked up so people on the inside can call me, but I can't call anybody, inside or outside. It hardly ever rings now. But I almost didn't want to pick it up. I was afraid of what Ms. Manigat would say.

"Veronica poked herself," Ms. Manigat told me. "The needle stuck through her hot suit. She told Dr. Ben there was a sudden movement."

I wondered who made the sudden movement, Veronica or me?

"Is she okay?" I asked. I thought maybe Ms. Manigat was mad at me, because she has told me many times that I should be careful. Maybe I wasn't being careful when Veronica was here.

"We'll see, Jay," Ms. Manigat said. From her voice, it sounded like the answer was *no*.

"Will she get sick?" I asked.

"Probably, yes, they think so," Ms. Manigat said.

I didn't want her to answer any more questions. I like it when people tell me the truth, but it always makes me feel bad, too. I tried to say I was sorry, but I couldn't even open my mouth.

"It's not your fault, Jay," Ms. Manigat said.

I couldn't help it. I sobbed like I used to when I was still a little kid.

"Veronica knew something like this could happen," she said.

But that didn't make anything better, because I remembered how Veronica's face looked so scared inside her mask, and how she pushed me away. Veronica has been here since almost the beginning, before Ms. Manigat came, and she used to smile at me even when nobody else did. When she showed me my picture from Dan Marino, she looked almost as happy as me. I had never seen her whole face smiling like that. She looked so pretty and glad.

I was crying so much I couldn't even write down my thoughts like Ms. Manigat said to. Not until today.

November 4

A long time ago, when I first came here and the TV in my room played programs from outside, I saw the first-grade picture I had taken at school on TV. I always hated that picture because Mom put some greasy stuff in my hair that made me look like a total geek. And then I turned on the TV and saw that picture on the news! The man on TV said the names of everyone in our family, and even spelled them out on the screen. Then, he called me Patient Zero. He said I was the first person who got sick.

But that wasn't really what happened. My dad was sick before me. I've told them that already. He got it away on his job in Alaska. My dad traveled a lot because he drilled for oil, but he came home early that time. We weren't expecting him until Christmas, but he came when it was only September, close to my birthday. He said he'd been sent home because some people on his oil crew got sick. One of them had even died. But the doctor in Alaska had looked at my dad and said he was fine, and then his boss sent him home. Dad was really mad about that. He hated to lose money. Time away from a job was always losing money, he said. He was in a bad mood when he wasn't working.

And the worse thing was, my dad wasn't fine. After two days, his eyes got red and he started sniffling. Then I did, too. And then my mom and brother.

When the man on TV showed my picture and called me Patient Zero and said I was the first one to get sick, that was when I first learned how people tell lies, because that wasn't true. Somebody on my dad's oil rig caught it first, and then he gave it to my dad. And my dad gave it to me, my mom and my brother.

My Aunt Lori came here to live at the lab with me at first, but she wasn't here long, because her eyes had already turned red by then. She came to help take care of me and my brother before my mom died, but probably she shouldn't have done that. She lived all the way in California, and I bet she wouldn't have gotten sick if she hadn't come to Miami to be with us. But even my mom's doctor didn't know what was wrong then, so nobody could warn her about what would happen if she got close to us. Sometimes I dream I'm calling Aunt Lori on my phone, telling her please, please not to come. Aunt Lori and my mom were twins. They looked exactly alike.

After Aunt Lori died, I was the only one left in my whole family.

I got very upset when I saw that news report. I didn't like hearing someone talk about my family like that, people who didn't even know us. And I felt like maybe the man on TV was right, and maybe it was all my fault. I screamed and cried the whole day. After that, Dr. Ben made them fix my TV so I couldn't see the news anymore or any programs from outside, just cartoons and kid movies on video. The only good thing was, that was when the President called me. I think he was sorry when he heard what happened to my family.

When I ask Dr. Ben if they're still talking about me on the news, he just shrugs his shoulders. Sometimes Dr. Ben won't say yes or no if you ask him a question. It doesn't matter, though. I think the TV people probably stopped showing my picture a long time ago. I was just a little kid when my family got sick. I've been here four whole years!

Oh, I almost forgot. Veronica isn't back yet.

November 7

I have been staring at my Dan Marino picture all day, and I think the handwriting on the autograph looks like Dr. Ben's. But I'm afraid to ask anyone about that. Oh, yeah— and yesterday the power was off in my room for a whole day! Same old same old. That's what Ms. M. would say.

November 12

Ms. Manigat is teaching me a little bit about medicine. I told her I want to be a doctor when I grow up, and she said she thinks that's a wonderful idea because she believes people will always need doctors. She says I will be in a good position to help people, and I asked her if that's because I have been here so long, and she said yes.

The first thing she taught me is about diseases. She says in the old days, a long time ago, diseases like typhoid used to kill a lot of people because of unsanitary conditions and dirty drinking water, but people got smarter and doctors found drugs to cure it, so diseases didn't kill people as much anymore. Doctors are always trying to stay a step ahead of disease, Ms. Manigat says.

But sometimes they can't. Sometimes a new disease comes. Or, maybe it's not a new disease, but an old disease that has been hidden for a long time until something brings it out in the open. She said that's how nature balances the planet, because as soon as doctors find cures for one thing, there is always something new. Dr. Ben says my disease is new. There is a long name for it I can't remember how to spell, but most of the time people here call it Virus-J.

In a way, see, it's named after me. That's what Dr. Ben said. But I don't like that.

Ms. Manigat said after my dad came home, the virus got in my body and attacked me just like everyone else, so I got really, really sick for a lot of days. Then, I thought I was completely better. I stopped feeling bad at all. But the virus was already in my brother and my mom and dad, and even our doctor from before, Dr. Wolfe, and Ms. Manigat says it was very *aggressive*, which means doctors didn't know how to kill it.

Everybody wears yellow plastic suits and airtight masks when they're in my room because the virus is still in the air, and it's in my blood, and it's on my plates and cups whenever I finish eating. They call the suits hot suits because the virus is *hot* in my room. Not hot like fire, but dangerous.

Ms. Manigat says Virus-J is extra special in my body because even though I'm not sick anymore, except for when I feel like I have a temperature and I have to lie down sometimes, the virus won't go away. I can make other people sick even when I feel fine, so she said that makes me a carrier. Ms. Manigat said Dr. Ben doesn't know anybody else who's gotten well except for me.

Oh, except maybe there are some little girls in China. Veronica told me once there were some little girls in China the same age as me who didn't get sick either. But when I asked Dr. Ben, he said he didn't know if it was true. And Ms. Manigat told me it might have been true once, but those girls might not be alive anymore. I asked her if they died of Virus-J, and she said no, no, no. Three times. She told me to forget all about any little girls in China. Almost like she was mad.

I'm the only one like me she knows about for sure, she says. The only one left.

That's why I'm here, she says. But I already knew that part. When I was little, Dr. Ben told me about antibodies and stuff in my blood, and he said the reason him and Rene and Veronica and all the other doctors take so much blood from me all the time, until they make purple bruises on my arms and I feel dizzy, is so they can try to help other people get well, too. I have had almost ten surgeries since I have been here. I think they have even taken out parts of me, but I'm not really sure. I look the same on the outside, but I feel different on the inside. I had surgery on my belly a year ago, and sometimes when I'm climbing the play-rope hanging from the ceiling in my room, I feel like it hasn't healed right, like I'm still cut open. Ms. Manigat says that's only in my mind. But it really hurts! I don't hate anything like I hate operations. I wonder if that's what happened to the other little girls, if they kept getting cut up and cut up until they died. Anyway, it's been a year since I had any operations. I keep telling Dr. Ben they can have as much blood as they want, but I don't want any more operations, please.

Dr. Ben said there's nobody in the world better than me to make people well, if only they can figure out how. Ms.

Manigat says the same thing. That makes me feel a little better about Virus-J.

I was happy Ms. Manigat told me all about disease, because I don't want her to treat me like a baby the way everybody else does. That's what I always tell her. I like to know things.

I didn't even cry when she told me Veronica died. Maybe I got all my crying over with in the beginning, because I figured out a long time ago nobody gets better once they get sick. Nobody except for me.

November 14

Today, I asked Ms. Manigat how many people have Virus-J.

"Oh, Jay, I don't know," she said. I don't think she was in the mood to talk about disease.

"Just guess," I said.

Ms. Manigat thought for a long time. Then she opened her notebook and began drawing lines and boxes for me to see. Her picture looked like the tiny brown lines all over an oak-tree leaf. We had a tree called a live oak in our backyard, and my dad said it was more than a hundred years old. He said trees sometimes live longer than people do. And he was right, because I'm sure that tree is still standing in our yard even though my whole family is gone.

"This is how it goes, Jay," Ms. Manigat said, showing me with her pencil-tip how one line branched down to the next. "People are giving it to each other. They don't usually know they're sick for two weeks, and by then they've passed it to a lot of other people. By now, it's already been here four years, so the same thing that happened to your family is happening to a lot of families."

"How many families?" I asked again. I tried to think of the biggest number I could. "A million?"

Ms. Manigat shrugged just like Dr. Ben would. Maybe that meant yes.

I couldn't imagine a million families, so I asked Ms.

Manigat if it happened to her family, too, if maybe she had a husband and kids and they got sick. But she said no, she was never married. I guess that's true, because Ms. Manigat doesn't look that old. She won't tell me her age, but she's in her twenties, I think. Ms. Manigat smiled at me, even though her eyes weren't happy.

"My parents were in Miami, and they got it right away," Ms. Manigat said. "Then my sister and nieces came to visit them from Haiti, and they got it, too. I was away working when it happened, and that's why I'm still here."

Ms. Manigat never told me that before.

My family lived in Miami Beach. My dad said our house was too small—I had to share a room with my brother—but my mother liked where we lived because our building was six blocks from the ocean. My mother said the ocean can heal anything. But that can't be true, can it?

My mother wouldn't like it where I am, because there is no ocean and no windows neither. I wondered if Ms. Manigat's parents knew someone who worked on an oil rig, too, but probably not. Probably they got it from my dad and me.

"Ms. Manigat," I said. "Maybe you should move inside like Dr. Ben and everybody else."

"Oh, Jay," Ms. Manigat said, like she was trying to sound cheerful. "Little old man, if I were that scared of anything, why would I be in here teaching you?"

She said she *asked* to be my teacher, which I didn't know. I said I thought her boss was making her do it, and she said she didn't have a boss. No one sent her. She wanted to come.

"Just to meet me?" I asked her.

"Yes, because I saw your face on television, and you looked to me like a one-of-a-kind," she said. She said she was a nurse before, and she used to work with Dr. Ben in his office in Atlanta. She said they worked at the CDC, which is a place that studies diseases. And he knew her, so that was why he let her come teach me.

"A boy like you needs his education. He needs to know how to face life outside," she said.

Ms. Manigat is funny like that. Sometimes she'll quit the regular lesson about presidents and the Ten Commandments and teach me something like how to sew and how to tell plants you eat from plants you don't, and stuff. Like, I remember when she brought a basket with real fruits and vegetables in it, fresh. She said she has a garden where she lives on the outside, close to here. She said one of the reasons she won't move inside is because she loves her garden so much, and she doesn't want to leave it.

The stuff she brought was not very interesting to look at. She showed me some cassava, which looked like a long, twisty tree branch to me, and she said it's good to eat, except it has poison in it that has to be boiled out of the root first and the leaves are poisonous too. She also brought a fruit called akee, which she said she used to eat from trees in Haiti. It tasted fine to me, but she said akee can never be eaten before it's opened, or before it's ripe, because it makes your brain swell up and you can die. She also brought different kinds of mushrooms to show me which ones are good or bad, but they all looked alike to me. She promised to bring me other fruits and vegetables to see so I will know what's good for me and what isn't. There's a lot to learn about life outside, she said.

Well, I don't want Ms. Manigat to feel like I am a waste of her time, but I know for a fact I don't have to face life outside. Dr. Ben told me I might be a teenager before I can leave, or even older. He said I might even be a grown man.

But that's okay, I guess. I try not to think about what it would be like to leave. My room, which they moved me to when I had been here six months, is really, really big. They built it especially for me. It's four times as big as the hotel room my mom and dad got for us when we went to Universal Studios in Orlando when I was five. I remember that room because my brother, Kevin, kept asking my dad, "Doesn't this cost too much?" Everytime my dad bought us a T-shirt or anything, Kevin brought up how much it cost. I told Kevin to stop it because I was afraid Dad would get mad and stop buying us stuff. Then, when we were in line for the King Kong ride, all by ourselves, Kevin told me, "Dad got fired from his job, stupid. Do you want to go on Welfare?" I waited for Dad and Mom to tell me he got fired, but they didn't. After Kevin said that, I didn't ask them to buy me anything else, and I was scared to stay in that huge, pretty hotel room because I thought we wouldn't have enough money to pay. But we did. And then Dad got a job on the oil rig, and we thought everything would be better.

My room here is as big as half the whole floor I bet. When I run from one side of my room to the other, from the glass in front to the wall in back, I'm out of breath. I like to do that. Sometimes I run until my ribs start squeezing and my stomach hurts like it's cut open and I have to sit down and rest. There's a basketball net in here, too, and the ball doesn't ever touch the ceiling except if I throw it too high on purpose. I also have comic books, and I draw pictures of me and my family and Ms. Manigat and Dr. Ben. Because I can't watch my videos, now I spend a lot of time writing in this notebook. A whole hour went by already. When I am writing down my thoughts, I forget about everything else.

I have decided for sure to be a doctor someday. I'm going to help make people better.

November 29

Thanksgiving was great! Ms. Manigat cooked real bread and brought me food she'd heated up. I could tell everything except the bread and cassava was from a can, like always, but it tasted much better than my regular food. I haven't had bread in a long time. Because of her mask, Ms. Manigat ate her dinner before she came, but she sat and watched me eat. Rene came in, too, and she surprised me when she gave me a hug. She never does that. Dr. Ben came in for a little while at the end, and he hugged me too, but he said he couldn't stay because he was busy. Dr. Ben doesn't come visit me much anymore. I could see he was growing a beard, and it was almost all white! I've seen Dr. Ben's hair when he's outside of the glass, when he isn't wearing his hot suit, and his hair is brown, not white. I asked him how come his beard was white, and he said that's what happens when your mind is overly tired.

I liked having everybody come to my room. Before, in the beginning almost nobody came in, not even Ms. Manigat.

She used to sit in a chair outside the glass and use the intercom for my lessons. It's better when they come in.

I remember how Thanksgiving used to be, with my family around the table in the dining room, and I told Ms. Manigat about that. Yes, she said, even though she didn't celebrate Thanksgiving in Haiti like Americans do, she remembers sitting at the table with her parents and her sister for Christmas dinner. She said she came to see me today, and Rene and Dr. Ben came too, because we are each other's family now, so we are not alone. I hadn't thought of it like that before.

December 1

No one will tell me, not even Ms. M., but I think maybe Dr. Ben is sick. I have not seen him in five whole days. It is quiet here. I wish it was Thanksgiving again.

January 23

I didn't know this before, but you have to be in the right mood to write your thoughts down. A lot happened in the days I missed.

The doctor with the French name is gone now, and I'm glad. He wasn't like Dr. Ben at all. I could hardly believe he was a real doctor, because he always had on the dirtiest clothes when I saw him take off his hot suit outside of the glass. And he was never nice to me—he wouldn't answer at all when I asked him questions, and he wouldn't look in my eyes except for a second. One time he slapped me on my ear, almost for nothing, and his glove hurt so much my ear turned red and was sore for a whole day. He didn't say he was sorry, but I didn't cry. I think he wanted me to.

Oh yeah, and he hooked me up to IV bags and took so much blood from me I couldn't even stand up. I was scared he would operate on me. Ms. Manigat didn't come in for almost a week, and when she finally came, I told her about the doctor taking too much blood. She got really mad. Then I found out the reason she didn't come all those days—he wouldn't let her! She said he tried to bar her from coming. *Bar* is the word she used, which sounds like a prison.

The new doctor and Ms. Manigat do not get along, even though they both speak French. I saw them outside of the glass, yelling back and forth and moving their hands, but I couldn't hear what they were saying. I was afraid he would send Ms. Manigat away for good. But yesterday she told me he's leaving! I told her I was happy, because I was afraid he would take Dr. Ben's place.

No, she told me, there isn't anyone taking Dr. Ben's place. She said the French doctor came here to study me in person because he was one of the doctors Dr. Ben had been sending my blood to ever since I first came. But he was already very sick when he got here, and he started feeling worse, so he had to go. Seeing me was his last wish, Ms. Manigat said, which didn't seem like it could be true because he didn't act like he wanted to be with me.

I asked her if he went back to France to his family, and Ms. Manigat said no, he probably didn't have a family, and even if he did, it's too hard to go to France. The ocean is in the way, she said.

Ms. Manigat seemed tired from all that talking. She said she'd decided to move inside, like Rene, to make sure they were taking care of me properly. She said I do a good job of keeping my room clean—and I do, because I have my own mop and bucket and Lysol in my closet—but she told me the hallways are filthy. Which is true, because sometimes I can see water dripping down the wall outside of my glass, a lot of it, and it makes puddles all over the floor. You can tell the water is dirty because you can see different colors floating on top, the way my family's driveway used to look after my dad sprayed it with a hose. He said the oil from the car made the water look that way, but I don't know why it looks that way here. Ms. Manigat said the water smells bad, too.

"It's ridiculous. If they're going to keep you here, they'd damn well better take care of you," Ms. Manigat said. She must have been really mad, because she never swears.

I told her about the time when Lou came and pressed on

my intercom really late at night, when I was asleep and no-body else was around. He was talking really loud like people do in videos when they're drunk. Lou was glaring at me through the glass, banging on it. I had never seen him look so mean. I thought he would try to come into my room but then I remembered he couldn't because he didn't have a hot suit. But I'll never forget how he said, *They should put you to sleep like a dog at the pound.*

I try not to think about that night, because it gave me nightmares. It happened when I was pretty little, like eight. Sometimes I thought maybe I just dreamed it, because the next time Lou came he acted just like normal. He even smiled at me a little bit. Before he stopped coming here, Lou was nice to me every day after that.

Ms. Manigat did not sound surprised when I told her what Lou said about putting me to sleep. "Yes, Jay," she told me. "For a long time, there have been people outside who didn't think we should be taking care of you."

I never knew that before!

I remember a long time ago, when I was really little and I had pneumonia, my mom was scared to leave me alone at the hospital. "They won't know how to take care of Jay there," she said to my dad, even though she didn't know I heard her. I had to stay by myself all night, and because of what my mom said, I couldn't go to sleep. I was afraid everyone at the hospital would forget I was there. Or maybe something bad would happen to me.

It seems like the lights go off every other day now. And I know people must really miss Lou, because the dirty gray water is all over the floor outside my glass and there's no one to clean it up.

February 14

6-4-6-7-2-9-4-3   6-4-6-7-2-9-4-3   6-4-6-7-2-9-4-3

I remember the numbers already! I have been saying them over and over in my head so I won't forget, but I wanted to write them down in the exact right order to be extra sure. I want to know them without even looking.

Oh, I should start at the beginning. Yesterday, no one brought me any dinner, not even Ms. Manigat. She came with a huge bowl of oatmeal this morning, saying she was very sorry. She said she had to look a long time to find that food, and it wore her out. The oatmeal wasn't even hot, but I didn't say anything. I just ate. She watched me eating.

She didn't stay with me long, because she doesn't teach me lessons anymore. After the French doctor left, we talked about the Emancipation Proclamation and Martin Luther King, but she didn't bring that up today. She just kept sighing, and she said she had been in bed all day yesterday because she was so tired, and she was sorry she forgot to feed me. She said I couldn't count on Rene to bring me food because she didn't know where Rene was. It was hard for me to hear her talk through her hot suit today. Her mask was crooked, so the microphone wasn't in front of her mouth where it should be.

She saw my notebook and asked if she could look at it. I said sure. She looked at the pages from the beginning. She said she liked the part where I said she was my best friend. Her face-mask was fogging up, so I couldn't see her eyes and I couldn't tell if she was smiling. I am very sure she did not put her suit on right today.

When she put my notebook down, she told me to pay close attention to her and repeat the numbers she told me, which were 6-4-6-7-2-9-4-3.

I asked her what they were. She said it was the security code for my door. She said she wanted to give the code to me because my buzzer wasn't working, and I might need to leave my room if she overslept and nobody came to bring me food. She told me I could use the same code on the elevator, and the kitchen was on the third floor. There wouldn't be anybody there, she said, but I could look on the shelves, the top ones up high, to see if there was any food. If not, she said I should take the stairs down to the first floor and find the red EXIT sign to go outside. She said the elevator doesn't go to the first floor anymore.

I felt scared then, but she put her hand on top of my head again just like usual. She said she was sure there was plenty of food outside.

"But am I allowed?" I asked her. "What if people get sick?"

"You worry so much, little man," she said. "Only you matter now, my little one-of-a-kind."

But see I'm sure Ms. Manigat doesn't really want me to go outside. I've been thinking about that over and over. Ms. Manigat must be very tired to tell me to do something like that. Maybe she has a fever and that's why she told me how to get out of my room. My brother said silly things when he had a fever, and my father too. My father kept calling me *Oscar*, and I didn't know who Oscar was. My dad told us he had a brother who died when he was little, and maybe his name was Oscar. My mother didn't say anything at all when she got sick. She just died very fast. I wish I could find Ms. Manigat and give her something to drink. You get very thirsty when you have a fever, which I know for a fact. But I can't go to her because I don't know where she is. And besides, I don't know where Dr. Ben keeps the hot suits. What if I went to her and she wasn't wearing hers?

Maybe the oatmeal was the only thing left in the kitchen, and now I ate it all. I hope not! But I'm thinking maybe it is because I know Ms. Manigat would have brought me more food if she could have found it. She's always asking me if I have enough to eat. I'm already hungry again.

6-4-6-7-2-9-4-3
6-4-6-7-2-9-4-3

February 15

I am writing in the dark. The lights are off. I tried to open my lock but the numbers don't work because of the lights being off. I don't know where Ms. Manigat is. I'm trying not to cry.

What if the lights never come back on?

February 16

There's so much I want to say but I have a headache from being hungry. When the lights came back on I went out into the hall like Ms. M. told me and I used the numbers to get the elevator to work and then I went to the kitchen like she said. I wanted to go real fast and find some peanut butter or some Oreos or even a can of beans I could open with the can opener Ms. M. left me at Thanksgiving.

There's no food in the kitchen! There's empty cans and wrappers on the floor and even roaches but I looked on every single shelf and in every cabinet and I couldn't find anything to eat.

The sun was shining really REALLY bright from the window. I almost forgot how the sun looks. When I went to the window I saw a big, empty parking lot outside. At first I thought there were diamonds all over the ground because of the sparkles but it was just a lot of broken glass. I could only see one car and I thought it was Ms. M.'s. But Ms. M. would never leave her car looking like that. For one thing it had two flat tires!

Anyway I don't think there's anybody here today. So I thought of a plan. I have to go now.

Ms. M., this is for you—or whoever comes looking for me. I know somebody will find this notebook if I leave it on my bed. I'm very sorry I had to leave in such a hurry.

I didn't want to go outside but isn't it okay if it's an emergency? I am really really hungry. I'll just find some food and bring it with me and I'll come right back. I'm leaving my door open so I won't get locked out. Ms. M., maybe I'll find your garden with cassavas and akee like you showed me and I'll know the good parts from the bad parts. If someone sees me and I get in trouble I'll just say I didn't have anything to eat.

Whoever is reading this don't worry. I'll tell everybody I see please please not to get too close to me. I know Dr. Ben was very worried I might make somebody sick.

The Oort Crowd

KEN MACLEOD

Ken MacLeod lives in Scotland and has published four SF novels. This is his first published short story, from Nature. *When he began to write, he said in an interview online with Andrew A. Adams, "first of all I decided to write some short stories. So I would send short stories off to* Interzone, *and they'd send them back. No wonder, actually, looking at them now. The final nadir of this came when* Interzone *sent back a story and suggested I send it to a small press magazine. So I sent it to our local small press SF magazine, which was called* New Dawn Fades, *and they rejected it. So I thought that there was nothing else for it and that I'd have to write a novel; that I couldn't do short stories." His first novel,* The Star Fraction, *appeared in 1995 in the UK but his fiction began to be published in the US in 1999 with* The Cassini Division. *His four novels to date have earned him a reputation at the forefront of newer SF writers, especially for their striking political speculations—his first four books envision a post-Capitalist socialist society. Though he is often called a hard SF writer, he objects: "I don't know enough physics to write hard SF. All the convincing-sounding physics, wormholes and so on, I made up or have blatantly stolen. The only physics I've tried very hard to get right is the Newtonian physics." Still, he belongs in the SF crowd that is making British SF prominent in the last decade.*

"The Oort Crowd" foreshadows his forthcoming novel.

As we enter the first year of the 23rd century (or the last year of the 22nd—some arguments never go away) we look back with satisfaction at the triumphs of science and technology in the first two centuries of the third millennium. The advances in medicine, in biotechnology, in communications, in atmospheric engineering have been more than adequately celebrated elsewhere. They are familiar to the most isolated farmer on the barest rocks of Antarctica. But in long-term significance for the human prospect, nothing can compare to the discovery of the gods.

The word "gods" is used advisedly. Humanity's earliest speculations about the nature of any superhuman intelligences with which it might share the Universe are, paradoxically, more relevant to our real situation than the predictions of alien contact in the once-popular genre of science fiction. It must be admitted, however, that some of its practitioners (see, for example, Boyce, 1998, http://www.et presence.ndirect.co.uk) reached part of the truth.

That truth, as we all know, is that a large, undetermined and (for good reason) indeterminable fraction of the bodies in the asteroid belt, the Kuiper Belt and the Oort Cloud are the sites of complex intelligent life. The precise evolutionary route(s) from extremophilic microorganisms to intelligence, apparently bypassing multicellular organization, remain unknown and perhaps (again, for good reason) unknowable. Computer simulations have yielded interesting, if inconclusive, results (Chang-Hoskins, 2197, provides a useful overview).

Those of our readers who have benefited from advances in medicine may recollect, and our younger readers can easily retrieve, the excitement that greeted the initial, accidental discovery of an ET intelligence in 2031. The first downloads from the Gates Foundation asteroid prospector revealed not the potential wealth of resources expected in a carbonaceous chondrite, but a complex interior structure variously described as "crystalline," "fractal" and "organic." Fortunately scientific openness, the drilling operation was webcast live, and as the pictures slowly scrolled down the screens of a few hundred thousand space enthusiasts, the news spread across the net faster than a virus.

In those first hasty, misspelled e-mails and postings we can see—from references to the structure as "the alien computer" or "Asteroid City" or even as "the starship"—the depth of initial misapprehension. Far from having been built by beings broadly similar to ourselves, the structure itself was the alien, or the civilization—the nature and number of centers of consciousness within it remain controversial. And it was neither alone nor isolated.

Billions of years of evolutionary "tunning" have given the cometary minds an exquisite sensitivity to the electromagnetic output of each other's internal chemical and physical processes. Their communications are, once looked for, as detectable as they are incomprehensible. Some of the larger bodies in the Oort seem to act as relays, extending the communications net across solar and possibly interstellar distances. (As is known, the tenuous outer reaches of the Oort Cloud intersect those of their Centaurian equivalent.)

Despite strenuous efforts, no human communication with the extraterrestrial minds has been established (the results claimed by Lunan, 2049, are at best ambiguous). They are, to us, in precisely the position of the gods postulated by Epicurus, serene in the spaces between the worlds.

These gods, while indifferent, are not passive. Subtle control over their outgassings results, over very long periods, in orbital changes. More rapid processes occur within the asteroids. Careful study of recent and historical Near-Earth

Objects suggests that the orbits of at least some NEOs have been the result of conscious intent.

In view of the above, it appears in retrospect unfortunate that the first probe to the Oort Cloud and beyond, launched in 2030, should have used as its initial means of propulsion a plasma sail consisting of ionized gas within a "magnetic bubble" thousands of kilometers across, and as its secondary means a prototype "electromagnetic ramscoop" sucking in vast quantities of interstellar and cometary matter. Subsequent changes in the volume and intensity of intercometary communication, and in the orbits of numerous comets and asteroids, cannot be accounted for by the physical effects of its passage. They can only be considered a response.

The effect on human society of the discovery of the gods has been positive. Excluded from many of the space-based resources once thought unoccupied, we turn to a less profligate use of our planet's own. The expectations of John Stuart Mill, in his famous chapters on the "stationary state" and "the probable futurity of the laboring classes," have been largely realized.

But, as our astronomical and space-defense workers' co-operatives continue their urgent sky-watching, there may be some risk of overlooking a danger closer to home. There is no reason to suppose that extremophilic consciousness is confined to minor interplanetary bodies. Perhaps the majority of the Earth's biomass consists of subterranean extremophiles.

Watch the ground.

The Thing About Benny

M. SHAYNE BELL

---

*M. Shayne Bell (www.mshaynebell.com), from Salt Lake
City, Utah, has been publishing SF since winning first
place in the Writers of the Future contest in 1987. He also
publishes poetry and he enjoys hiking, backpacking, and
climbing. In the fall of 1996, Bell joined an eight-day ex-
pedition to the top of Kilimanjaro, the highest mountain in
Africa. He has an MA in English: "I completed the first
science fiction and fantasy creative writing thesis at
Brigham Young University, after years of struggle. It was a
collection of my short stories. The loathing for the entire
genre in the English department at the time astonished
me." His SF novel,* Nicoli, *was published in 1991. He
edited the anthology* Washed by a Wave of Wind: Science
Fiction from the Corridor *(1993), and has published a
steady stream of short stories for the last decade.*

*"The Thing About Benny" is from the excellent anthol-
ogy* Vanishing Acts, *edited by Ellen Datlow, stories upon
the general theme of endangered species. Bell's humorous
story takes place in the not too distant future and is very
plausible hard SF, to which is added some canny sociological commentary. Bell's own comment is: "My story is a
dark comedy about plant extinctions. Really. That it
turned out to be funny at all surprised me more than anyone."*

Benny said, apropos of nothing, "The bridge is the most important part of a song, don't you think?"

"Oh, yeah," I said, me trying to drive in all that traffic and us late, as usual. "That's all I think about when I'm hearing music—those important bridges."

"No, really." Benny looked at me, earphones firmly covering his ears, eyes dark and kind of surprised. It was a weird look. Benny never has much to say, but when he does the company higher-ups told me I was supposed to take notice, try to figure out how he does what he does.

The light turned green. I drove us onto North Temple, downtown Salt Lake not so far off now. "Bridges in songs have something to do with extinct plants?" I asked.

"It's all in the music," he said, looking back at the street and sitting very, very still.

"Messages about plants are in the music?" I asked.

But he was gone, back in that trance he'd been in since L.A. Besides, we were minutes from our first stop. He always gets so nervous just before we start work. "What if we find something?" he'd asked me once, and I'd said, "Isn't that the point?"

He started rubbing his sweaty hands up and down his pant legs. I could hear the tinny melody out of his earphones. It was "Dancing Queen" week. Benny'd set his player on endless repeat, and he listened to "Dancing Queen" over and over again on the plane, in the car, in the offices we went to, during meals, in bed with the earphones on his head. That's all he'd listen to for one week. Then he'd change to a different Abba song on Sunday. When he'd gone through every Abba song ever recorded, he'd start over.

"Check in," Benny said.

"What?"

"The Marriott."

I slammed brakes, did a U-turn, did like he'd asked. That was my job, even if we were late. Benny had to use the toilet, and he would not use toilets in the offices we visited.

I carried the bags up to our rooms—no bellhop needed, thank you. What's a personal assistant for if not to lug your luggage around? I called Utah Power and Light to tell them we were still coming. Then I waited for Benny in the lobby. My mind kept playing "Dancing Queen" over and over. "It's all in the music," Benny'd said, but I failed to understand how anybody, Benny included, could find directions in fifty-year-old Abba songs to the whereabouts of plants extinct in the wild.

Benny tapped me on the shoulder. "It's close enough that we can walk," he said. "Take these."

He handed me his briefcase and a stack of World Botanics pamphlets and motioned to the door. I always had to lead the way. Benny wouldn't walk with me. He walked behind me, four or five steps back, Abba blasting in his ears. It was no use trying to get him to do differently. I gave the car keys to the hotel car people so they could park the rental, and off we went.

Utah Power and Light was a first visit. We'd do a get-acquainted sweep of the cubicles and offices, then come back the next day for a detailed study. Oh sure, after Benny'd found the *Rhapis excelsa* in a technical writer's cubicle in the Transamerica Pyramid, everybody with a plant in a pot had hoped to be the one with the cancer cure. But most African violets are just African violets. They aren't going to cure anything. Still, the hopeful had driven college botany professors around the world nuts with their pots of begonias and canary ivy and sword ferns.

But they were out there. Plants extinct in the wild had

been kept alive in the oddest places, including cubicles in office buildings. Benny'd found more than his share. Even I took "Extract of *Rhapis excelsa*" treatment one week each year like everybody else. Who wanted a heart attack? Who didn't feel better with his arteries unclogged? People used to go jogging just to feel that good.

The people at UP&L were thrilled to see us—hey, Benny was their chance at millions. A lady from HR led us around office after cubicle after break room. Benny walked along behind the lady and me. It was *Dieffenbachia maculata* after *Ficus benjamina* after *Cycus revoluta*. Even I could tell nobody was getting rich here. But up on the sixth floor, I turned around and Benny wasn't behind us. He was back staring at a *Nemanthus gregarius* on a bookshelf in a cubicle just inside the door.

I walked up to him. "It's just goldfish vine," I said.

The girl in the cubicle looked like she wanted to pick up her keyboard and kill me with it.

"Benny," I said. "We got a bunch more territory to cover. Let's move it."

He put his hands in his pockets and followed along behind me, but after about five minutes he was gone again. We found him back at the *Nemanthus gregarius*. I took a second look at the plant. It looked like nothing more than *Nemanthus gregarius* to me. Polly, the girl in the cubicle, was doing a little dance in her chair in time to the muffled "Dancing Queen" out of Benny's earphones. Mama mia, she felt like money, money, money.

I made arrangements with HR for us to come back the next day and start our detailed study. The company CEO came down to shake our hands when we left. Last we saw of Polly that day was her watering the *Nemanthus gregarius*.

Abba, Fältskog Listing 47:
"Dancing Queen," day 3. Dinner.

The thing about Benny is, he never moves around in time to the music. I mean, he can sit there listening to "Dancing

Queen" over and over again and stare straight ahead, hands folded in his lap. He never moves his shoulders. He never taps his toes. He never sways his hips. Watching him, you'd think "Dancing Queen" was some Bach cantata.

I ordered dinner for us in the hotel coffee shop. Benny always makes me order for him, but god forbid it's not a medium-rare hamburger and fries. We sat there eating in silence, the only sound between us the muffled dancing queen having the time of her life. I thought maybe I'd try a little conversation. "Hamburger OK?" I asked.

Benny nodded.

"Want a refill on the Coke?"

He picked up his glass and sucked up the last of the Coke, but shook his head no.

I took a bite of my burger, chewed it, looked at Benny. "You got any goals?" I asked him.

Benny looked at me then. He didn't say a word. He stopped chewing and just stared.

"I mean, what do you want to do with your life? You want a wife? Kids? A trip to the moon? We fly around together, city after city, studying all these plants, and I don't think I even know you."

He swallowed and wiped his mouth with his napkin. "I have goals," he said.

"Well, like what?"

"I haven't told anybody. I'll need some time to think about it before I answer you. I'm not sure I want to tell anybody, no offense."

Jeez, Benny, take a chance on me why don't you, I thought. We went back to eating our burgers. I knew the higher-ups would want me to follow the lead Benny had dropped when we were driving in from the airport, so I tried. "Tell me about bridges," I said. "Why are they important in songs?"

Benny wouldn't say another word. We finished eating, and I carried Benny's things up to his room for him. At the door he turned around and looked at me. "Bridges take you to a new place," he said. "But they also show you the way back to where you once were."

He closed the door.

I didn't turn on any music in my room. It was nice to have it a little quiet for a change. I wrote my reports and e-mailed them off, then went out for a drink. I nursed it along, wondering where we stood on the bridges.

Abba, Fältskog Listing 47:
"Dancing Queen," day 4. UP&L offices.

World Botanics sends Benny only to companies that meet its criteria. First, they have to have occupied the same building for fifty years or more. You'd be surprised how few companies in America have done that. But if a company has moved around a lot, chances are its plants have not gone with it. Second, it's nice if the company has had international ties, but even that isn't necessary. Lots of people somehow failed to tell customs about the cuttings or the little packets of seeds in their pockets after vacations abroad. If a company's employees had traveled around a lot, or if they had family ties with other countries, they sometimes ended up with the kind of plants we were looking for. UP&L has stayed put for a good long time, plus its employees include former Mormon missionaries who've poked around obscure corners of the planet. World Botanics hoped to find something in Utah.

The UP&L CEO and the HR staff and Polly were all waiting for us. You'd think Benny'd want to go straight up to the sixth floor to settle the *Nemanthus gregarius* question, but he didn't. Benny always starts on the first floor and works his way to the top, so we started on floor one.

The lobby was a new install, and I was glad Benny didn't waste even half an hour there. Not much hope of curing cancer with flame nettle or cantea palms. The cafeteria on the second floor had some interesting *Cleistocactus strausii*. Like all cactus, it's endangered but not yet extinct in the wild—there are still reports of *Cleistocactus strausii* growing here and there in the tops of the Andes. As far as anybody can tell, it can't cure a thing.

We didn't make it to the sixth floor till after four o'clock, and you could tell that Polly was a nervous wreck.

But Benny walked right past her *Nemanthus gregarius*.

"Hey, Benny," I said in a low voice. "What about the gold-fish vine?"

Benny turned around and stared at it. Polly moved back into her cubicle so she wouldn't block the view, but after a minute Benny put his hands in his pockets and walked off. Well, poor Polly, I thought.

But just before five, I turned around and Benny wasn't behind me. I found him at the *Nemanthus gregarius*. Jeez Benny, I thought, we need to know the name of the game here. Declare extract of *Nemanthus gregarius* the fountain of youth or tell Polly she has a nice plant but nothing special. I steered him out of the building and back to the Marriott.

Abba, Fältskog Listing 47:
"Dancing Queen," day 4. Dinner.

I ordered Benny's burger and a steak for me. We sat there eating, the only sound between us a muffled "Dancing Queen." After last night, I was not attempting conversation.

I'd taken time before dinner to look up *Nemanthus gregarius* on the Net. It is not endangered. It grows like weeds in cubicles. It can't cure a thing.

I didn't know what Benny was doing.

He sucked up the last of his glass of Coke and put the glass down a little hard on the table. I looked up at him.

"I want to find a new plant and name it for Agnetha," he said.

"What?"

"My goal in life," he said. "If you tell anyone, I'll see that you're fired."

"You're looking for a new plant species in office buildings?"

"I'd actually like to find one for each of the four members of Abba, but Agnetha's first."

And I'd thought finding *one* completely new species was too much to ask.

"When Abba sang, the world was so lush," Benny said.

"You can hear it in their music. It resonates with what's left of the natural world. It helps me save it."

It was my turn to be quiet. All I could think was, it works for Benny. He's had plenty of success, after all, and who hasn't heard of crazier things than the music of dead pop stars leading some guy to new plant species?

When I wrote up my daily reports that night, I left out Benny's goals. Some things the higher-ups don't need to know.

Abba, Fältskog Listing 47:
"Dancing Queen," day 5. UP&L offices.

We spent the day looking at more sorry specimens of *Cordyline terminalis, Columnea gloriosa,* and *Codiaeum variagatum* than I care to remember. By the end of the day, Benny started handing out the occasional watering tip, so I knew even he was giving up.

"Nemanthus gregarius?" I asked in the elevator on the way down.

Suddenly he punched 6. He walked straight to Polly's cubicle and stuck out his hand. "I owe you an apology," he said.

Polly just sat there. She was facing her own little Waterloo, and she did it bravely.

"I thought your *Nemanthus gregarius* might be a subspecies not before described, but it isn't. It's the common variety. A nice specimen, though."

We left quickly. At least he didn't give her any watering tips.

Abba, Fältskog Listing 47:
"Dancing Queen," day 5. Wandering the streets.

The thing about Benny is, if it doesn't work out and we've studied every plant on thirty floors of an office tower without finding even a *Calathea Iancifolia,* he can't stand it. He wanders up and down the streets, poking into every little shop. He never buys anything—he isn't shopping. I think he's hoping to spot some rare plant in the odd tobacconist or magazine shop and to do it fast. I have a hard time keeping up with him then, and heaven forbid I should decide to buy something on sale for a Mother's Day gift.

We rushed through two used bookstores, an oriental rug store, four art galleries, three fast food joints. "Benny," I said. "Let's get something to eat."

"It's here," he said.

"What's where?"

"There's something here, and we just haven't found it."

The Dancing Queen was resonating, I supposed. Shops were closing all around us.

"You check the Indian jewelry store while I check Mr. Q's Big and Tall," he told me. "We meet outside in five."

I did like I was told. I smiled at the Navajo woman in traditional dress, but she did not smile back. She wanted to lock up. I made a quick sweep of the store and noted the various species of endangered cacti and left. Benny was not on the sidewalk. I went into Mr. Q's after him.

He was standing perfectly still in front of a rack of shirts on sale, hands in his pockets.

"These are too big for you," I said.

"Window display, southeast corner."

Well, I walked over there. It was a lovely little display of *Rhipsalis salicornioides*, *Phalaenopsis lueddemanniana*, and *Streptocarpus saxorum*. Nothing unusual.

Then I looked closer at the *Streptocarpus saxorum*. The flowers weren't the typical powder blue or lilac. They were a light yellow.

The proprietor walked up to me. "I'm sorry," he said. "But we're closing. Could you bring your final purchases to the register?"

"I'm just admiring your cape primrose," I said. "Where do they come from?"

"My mother grows them," he said. "She gave me these plants when I opened the store."

"Did she travel in Africa or Madagascar?"

"Her brother was in the foreign service. She used to follow him around to his postings. I don't remember where she went—I'd have to ask her."

"Do you mind if I touch one of the plants?" I asked.

He said sure. The leaves were the typical hairy, gray-green ovals; the flowers floated above the leaves on wire-thin stems. It was definitely *Streptocarpus*, but I'd never seen anything like it described.

"I think you should call your mother," I said, and I explained who Benny and I were.

The store closed, but Mr. Proprietor and his staff waited with us for the mother to arrive. The whole time Benny just stood by the sale rack, eyes closed, hands in his pockets. "You've done it again," I whispered to him.

He didn't answer me. Just as I turned to walk back over to the cape primrose, he opened his eyes. "*Streptocarpus agnethum*," he whispered.

And he smiled.

Abba, Fältskog Listing 32:
"I Have a Dream," day 2. Agnetha's grave.

The thing about Benny is, he's generous. He took me to Sweden with him, and we planted *Streptocarpus agnethum*, or "dancing queen," around Agnetha's gravestone. Turns out the flower wasn't a cure for anything, but it was a new species and Benny got to name it.

"Agnetha would have loved these flowers," I told Benny.

He just kept planting. We had a nice sound system on the ground beside us, playing her music—well, just one of her songs. It talks about believing in angels. I don't know if I believe in angels, but I can see the good in Benny's work. Nobody's bringing back the world we've lost, but little pieces of it have survived here and there. Benny was saving some of those pieces.

"God, these flowers are pretty," I told him.

Of course he didn't say anything.

He didn't need to.

The Last Supper

BRIAN STABLEFORD

Brian Stableford is one of the finest critics and historians of SF and fantasy, a significant novelist, and is one of the six or eight leading short fiction writers in SF today who year after year publishes five or ten stories in contention for inclusion in this annual book. For most of the 1990s he wrote stories in a large future history setting developed in the 1980s in collaboration with David Langford, spanning centuries and focussing on immense changes in human society and in humanity due primarily to advances in the biological sciences. Four of these have been rewritten as novels thus far, Inherit the Earth, The Architects of Emortality, The Fountains of Youth, *and* The Cassandra Complex, *with* Dark Ararat *and one more in the works.*

"The Last Supper" appeared in Science Fiction Age, *one of the two leading SF magazines that ceased publication in mid-year. It is Stableford at his most acerbically Swiftian. He weaves together the celebrity chefs, who are coming into prominence today, with gourmet food at the edge of disgusting, bioengineered art for exquisite pleasure, adds political repression of scientific advances, and protesters; presents an outrageously cool and rational central character and his food-fan, chef-worshipping date as the sympathetic avant garde.*

I had reserved the table at Trimalchio's way back in January, three months in advance. It was Tamara's birthday treat, and I figured that it would also be the perfect occasion to ask her to marry me. I wanted the circumstances to be as favorable as possible to maximize my chances of success. Rumor has it that a lot of celebrities were clamoring to get in, not because they had any inkling of what was about to happen but simply because it was Saturday night—and ever since Jerome had joined the hallowed ranks of superstar chefs, Trimalchio's was *the* place to be seen—but Jerome wasn't the kind of man to start canceling reservations in order to accommodate TV personalities. He was a man of honor.

We had to run the gauntlet when we arrived, of course, but we weren't in the least frightened. We didn't feel that we were in any real danger from the anti-GM brigade who were baying for Jerome's blood. They were very noisy, of course—their cause had been on the skids for years, and the hardcore had responded by becoming even more fanatical and dogmatic—but they knew from bitter experience that attacking customers qualified as an instant PR disaster. The only ones in physical danger were members of the increasingly vociferous counter demonstration: Jerome's most ardent fans. For every banner proclaiming that he was a "Frankenstein Chef" or a "Kitchen Devil," there was one proclaiming him to be the messiah of the new gastronomy. There were even a few innocently hyperbolic placards carrying forward a grand old south London tradition that went way back to the 1960s and the first rock superstars, which simply said: JEROME IS GOD.

I found the sprint from the taxi quite exhilarating, although Tamara was a little bit annoyed that none of the paparazzi bothered to aim a flashbulb in our direction. I assured her that she looked as good as any of the models who were distracting their attention, and apologized for the fact that mere riches didn't make me as newsworthy as the sons of hereditary peers. She did look wonderful. Her peacockblue evening dress and pastel hosiery were smart in the old sense as well as the new: a perfect refutation of the fashion-dinosaur argument that no matter how useful and hygienic they might be, active fibers would never look as good as ancient silks and velvets.

We didn't get the best table, of course. I suppose anyone who was there to be seen would have reckoned it the worst, and there was a distinct frown on Tamara's face as we were shown to it, but it suited my purposes very well. I wanted to be in a quiet corner, where Tamara and I would have eyes only for one another.

We didn't have to worry about being unable to catch the waiter's eye—the staff at Trimalchio's were the best in London and it wasn't as if we had any choices to make. Jerome's clients were expected to eat and drink exactly what he provided and be grateful, and that was fine by us.

When she had first read about him in the Style section of the *Sunday Times*, Tamara had been as fervent in her support of Jerome's insistence on a set menu as she was of his determination to experiment with the best Genetically Modified foodstuffs that the world had offer. "The man is a great artist," she had assured me, way back on New Year's Eve, in the course of what was then a purely hypothetical discussion. "He plans a meal as a perfect *ensemble*. He leaves pick-and-mix to the sweetie counter in Woolworth's, where it belongs. I was at uni with one of the geneticists he works with, and the firm has regular dealings with his suppliers. A lot of the GM chefs are content to use modern substitutes for the ingredients in traditional recipes, but Jerome's a genuine inventor. He's right at the cutting edge of food science, and that puts him at the cutting edge of biotech itself. There'd be no point in offering his customers a choice of dishes because he uses so many ingredients that none of his clients—even his regulars—have ever had the opportunity of tasting. Even if they've encountered the raw materials, they can't possibly have the slightest idea what a master chef can do with them."

"I'm not sure I like the sound of that," I'd said at the time. "Individual tastes do differ—one man's meat and all that."

"Don't be silly, Ben," she'd said. "Faddy eating is the sign of a bad upbringing. Your petty prejudices are quite irrational. They have nothing to do with matters of *individual taste*."

I loved her very dearly. It would only have spoiled our mood to press the point that, however irrational it might be, there were certain foods I simply hated, especially anchovies and escargots, and certain others to which I strongly suspected that I might be allergic—including mussels and locusts, no matter what modifications had been made to their genomes.

"A great chef is a great artist," Tamara had added. "His customers have to have faith in him. He has every right to demand that they trust his judgment."

"I guess you're right," I had admitted, as the seeds of my plan had taken root. As we took our seats and the waiter handed Tamara a card headed SUPPER: DIRECTORY OF COURSES, I crossed my fingers, hoping that if anything turned up that I didn't like I would either be able to stomach it in spite of my inclinations or dispose of it surreptitiously. The one thing I couldn't do, of course, was leave it on the plate. Newspaper reports alleged that Jerome was wont to emerge from his kitchen wielding a heavy ladle in response to that kind of insult. I could certainly expect a negative answer to my proposal if we were asked to leave in mid-meal—and the bored paparazzi inevitably took a great and exceedingly unflattering interest in anyone coming out of Trimalchio's in advance of the sated and spiritually uplifted crowd.

Our table was lit by two candles—molded in GM tallow, of course—and decorated by a discreet bouquet of flowers set in a tiny vase. I couldn't put a name to the flowers, but that was hardly surprising. Jerome only used originals. It was entirely possible that there was at least one species in the array that had only existed for a matter of weeks and would become extinct that very night.

The aperitif was as clear and colorless as water, but its texture suggested that it was a complex organic cocktail. When I remarked that I found it refreshing but oddly taste-less, Tamara explained that that was the whole point. It was intended to restore the "virginity of the tongue" by clearing away the lingering legacy of past experience.

The *hors d'oeuvres* were served in little silver dishes mounted on the heads of rampant chimeras formed from some kind of acrylic plastic. The workmanship was excep-tionally fine; you could almost see the individual scales in the chimera's hind-parts. I didn't bother to point this out to Tamara in case she took it as another example of what she called "nanotechnologist's disease." "The trouble with you, Ben," she had said during the big row we had had after Christmas, "is that you're obsessed with tiny things. With you, it's not just a matter of not being able to see the forest for the trees—it's a matter of not being able to see the forest for the cracks in the bark of a fallen twig." For much the same reason, I didn't bother to point out the marvelous intri-cacy of the patterns engraved in black and white on the skins of the olives. Tamara made up for my reticence by waxing lyrical about the technical difficulties that Jerome's geneti-cists had had to overcome in order to ensure that the hon-eyed poppy-seeds used to season the roast dormice could be grown in situ, within the flesh of the living animal.

The dormice were a trifle too sweet for my taste and the olives too oily, but I did like the little toroidal sausages—al-though I might have liked them even better if they hadn't been wrapped around black figs. Tamara loved all of it, to the extent that she ate at least twice as much as me. I didn't mind. It was her treat, and it's not every day that a woman reaches her 25th birthday *and* receives her fourth proposal of marriage. I had wondered whether it was worth quipping that it was a lot better than receiving her 25th proposal on her fourth birthday, but I'd abandoned the plan because she would only have looked at me as if I were mad. "It's a joke," I would have said, the way I always did. "Is it?" she would have replied, implying that if there were such a thing as a joking test I would probably have failed it nearly as often as I'd failed my driving test.

The possibility of being out-eaten didn't arise again, of course, because the other courses were served in carefully measured individual portions on separate plates. The possibility of being out-drank remained—the decanters containing the first white wine were brought out in advance of the second course—but Tamara was sufficiently old-fashioned to think that it was a gentleman's duty to pour, so I was confident that I could share it out with as much exactitude as my slightly unsteady hand could contrive. I was so nervous that I would have liked an extra glass to settle me down, but I also wanted to make sure that Tamara was as mellow as possible by the time the big moment arrived, so scrupulous evenhandedness seemed politic as well as polite.

"Happy, darling?" I asked, as we paused with our glasses to savor the bouquet of the wine.

"Ecstatic," she assured me. She closed her eyes for a while, saying: "I'm trying to make the most of the pleasures of anticipation, so that they'll be redoubled by those of satiation."

"Me too," I assured her, although I was thinking about the ring in my pocket rather than the food.

The second course was what I'd normally have thought of as a starter, although the *hors d'oeuvres* had been far too substantial to qualify as a mere tease. It looked like an unusually coherent terrine, but there was no trace of token green stuff except for a light sprinkle of chopped herbs. The central blob was surrounded by a ring of eggs smaller than a quail's and the whole thing was bedded on what looked like unleavened bread.

According to the directory, the blob was compounded from the "vulva" and "sumen" of a virgin sow—some kind of fancy pork, I deduced. The herbal seasoning was al-

legedly *laserpitium*, although a dutiful footnote pointed out
that because no one now knew what plant the laserpitium of
the ancients had been, the name had been considered free for
application to an entirely new herb devised by Jerome's geneticists.

All in all, it didn't taste too bad. I wouldn't go so far as to
say that I liked it, but it was on the sunny side of tolerable.

"Brilliant," Tamara said, as she finished. "Magical, even. I
thought it would just be the taste, but it isn't, is it? You can
actually feel the food settling into your stomach, can't you?
It's as if this is what our alimentary systems have been crying out for ever since the first cooking fires were lit."

Tamara had strong feelings about the folly of the anti-GM
brigade. "Everything we now think of as human nature is the
product of the primal biotechnologies," she was fond of saying. "Anyone who thinks that biotechnology is an offense
against nature is delusional as well as stupid." The *primal
biotechnologies*, in the jargon of her trade, were cooking and
clothing. Both innovations, in Tamara's firmly held but not-
quite-conventional view, had been introduced by women;
according to her, the entire panoply of "masculine hardware"—including all the stone, ceramic, and metal tools in
whose evolution old-fashioned male archaeologists were
wont to trace the progress of preliterate societies—had been
nothing more than a series of technical tricks developed to
served the imperatives of the primal biotechnologies.

Tamara further contended—and how could a mere technical trickster like me disagree with an ace biotechnologist?—
that the entire history of civilization had followed the same
pattern. Everything men had ever made or done had been devised to serve the insatiable demands of the "feminine imperative"—a valiant but inadequate tribute to the twin
maternal devices that had broken nature's cruel yoke and set
humankind on the road of intellect and artistry. My colleague and ex-friend Steve Semple had once opined that that
was exactly the kind of thing a mad domineering bitch might
be expected to say to a lovesick puppy, but he was just jealous.

I had once—and only once—made the mistake of pointing out to Tamara that in the modern world the "primal biotechnologies" seemed to have been hijacked by men, who still supplied the great majority of the 21st century's finest chefs and couturiers in spite of the victories of late 20th-century feminism. "The greatest ambition of the male of the species has always been to cultivate as much effeminacy as testosterone will permit," she informed me. "How many great chefs and couturiers are straight, do you think? The trouble is that those unlucky souls who can't measure up to mature standards of effeminacy tend to express their defensive masculinity in a frank refusal to learn to cook or dress themselves properly."

There was none of that at Trimalchio's, of course. By that time I knew exactly which topics of conversation were safe and comfortable, and I was able to steer the chat in all the right directions. Tamara was happy that night, and when she was happy she was breathtakingly beautiful. People like Steve were incapable of understanding a woman like her, and resentment transformed their lust into hostility. I, on the other hand, loved her as honestly and as absolutely as anyone could. If she were ever going to marry anyone, I thought as I gulped my first mouthful of the red wine, it would definitely be me—and for all her affectations of independence, she needed love and stability just as much as anyone else.

Ever since I had first glanced at Jerome's directory of courses, I had known that the third would be the most substantial challenge to my constitution. There is not a dessert in the world that can intimidate me, but when it comes to entrées I candidly admit that I am what Tamara likes to call "a Stone Age meat-and-two-veg-man." I love the roast beef, potatoes, and carrots my mother used to make, with or without the Yorkshire pudding, and I see no need to apologize for the fact.

I had been hoping all week that I might strike it lucky and catch Jerome in a traditional mood, taking what comfort I could from the knowledge that my wishes were likely to be at least partially granted. Jerome was well known as a great fan of the potato. He'd been waxing lyrical on its virtues for 10 years, and had presumably been doing so even before he got heavily into GM cuisine. The so-called "degradation of the potato" had always been the favorite object of his particular version of that fiery anger which is every great chef's prerogative and duty. When Columbus first reached the Americas, he told the world, there were six hundred different species of potato distributed from the heights of the Andes to the plains of Patagonia, and all but a handful had been driven to extinction by chip-addicted dullards. One of the key projects he had set his scientific collaborators was to recover and then to surpass the natural variability of the potato—so it's hardly surprising that the main course on that epoch-making evening was accompanied by no less than three different kinds of potato, one served mashed, one boiled, and one sautéed.

Having been granted that, how could I then complain about the fact that they were accompanying tentacles of young giant squid stuffed with mutton brains?

I found, once I'd steeled myself to try it, that the flesh of young giant squid wasn't nearly as rubbery as the kind of calamari my mother used to foist on me when she wasn't in a roast beef mood. The engineers modifying squid species were still engaged in a headlong dash to produce the biggest living organism ever, so the culinary possibilities of the species had been virtually relegated to the economically important but crudely utilitarian realms of pet food production. Jerome was one of the first people to figure out that the tender meat of very young individuals had possibilities undreamed of by geneticists fixated on issues of size, and I had to admit that he had a point.

As it turned out, I had slightly more difficulty with the stuffing. My maternal grandmother had an aunt who'd died of the same strain of CJD that was implicated in the infamous beef ban of the 1990s and Gran was always insistent—in spite of all the scientific evidence that later came to light proving that the cattle had caught it from us, not the other way around—that it had been scrapie-infected sheep that had been the source of the trouble. According to her, mutton brains were just about the most dangerous foodstuff in the world. "No good will come of it!" she'd cried, when the proven effectiveness of GM-mutton brains as an intelligence-enhancer in infants had delivered the first effective left hook to the jutting chin of anti-GM prejudice. Alas, her protests hadn't prevented Mum from feeding it to me throughout my teens, as if quantity might somehow make up for the fact that she'd missed the window of real opportunity by a good 10 years.

At the end of the day, though, the stuffing was something I could eat, and I tucked the lot away without bothering to inquire too carefully as to the contents of the sauce, which were conveniently disguised by esoteric French and Latin in the directory. When I washed the last mouthful down with the last of the red wine, I felt positively triumphant—as if my success in dealing with the food were an infallible omen of success in the evening's greater enterprise.

"Wasn't that simply extraordinary?" I said to Tamara.

"Marvelous," she confirmed.

"I suppose we ought to feel slightly guilty about snatching good mutton brain out of the mouths of the tinies who derive such benefit from it," I said, "but I can't. I can feel it doing me good, even though I'm way too old."

"You're right," she said. It wasn't a phrase that passed her lovely lips very often, so I was delighted to hear it. "The wine sets it off perfectly, don't you think? To think that our parents used to value wine for its age! Do you think there'll ever come a time again when this year's vintage isn't the finest ever?"

"My Mum and Dad used to drink that *Beaujolais nouveau* stuff," I remembered.

"Vile red ink!" she retorted. "It might have helped in some small way to pioneer the change of attitude necessary to introduce GM wine, but no true connoisseur would have touched it. *This* is entirely different. Entirely!"

"Oh, absolutely," I said, as the third decanter was deposited in the middle of the table. "Who knew what true intoxication was in those days? Who understood the real subtleties of psychotropic artistry?"

"We owe Jerome and his disciples a tremendous debt,"

she confirmed. "When I think about those demonstrators outside—the antis, I mean, not his supporters—it makes me want to cry. They're dogmatists of the worst stripe, incapable of seeing sense—the stuff of which witch-hunters and inquisitors are made. Did you see that item on last night's Sky News about the chef in New York who was shot?"

"Yes, I did," I confirmed. "Yet another martyr to the cause of progress. There's always a mindless mob, isn't there? It's as if the lunatics just moved two doors down the road on the day the last abortion clinic closed. It's not as if there isn't an effective system of monitoring and control, is it?"

That was a slight mistake. I should have known better than to use the word "effective."

"Well, yes it is, actually," Tamara snapped. "We got saddled with far, far too many bad laws in the first decade of the new millennium, and far too many of them are still on the statute book. There's too much insistence on formulaic testing. That obsolete monitoring system has become a millstone around the neck of the nation's scientists—bioscientists, I mean. You specialists in inorganic nanotech don't know how lucky you are not to have to deal with all that shit."

Mercifully, the arrival of the dessert cut the lecture short.

I had been looking forward to what I still insisted, if only privately, of thinking of as "pudding." The dessert on offer on that fateful night at Trimalchio's was one of those ingenious dishes that take advantage of the fact that ice crystals are poor absorbers of microwave radiation and poor conductors of heat. This allows ingenious ice-cream sculptures to contain nested compotes of fruit heated to a temperature that can easily burn the mouth of an unwary diner. Needless to say, there were no such fools present at Trimalchio's that evening. We all knew that the art of eating such concoctions was all in the timing. Even Tamara knew how to manage the various components of the dessert as she dissected its complex architecture, savoring its gradual dissolution as well as its medley of tastes.

It is, I suppose, one of the great ironies of GM cuisine that it remains subject to the basic elements of the sense of taste. Although the gastronomic employment of saltiness and bitterness has always been relatively subtle, there is a certain inevitable crudity about sweetness. The only natural substance on which genetic engineers have not yet managed to improve is sucrose, and there is thus a sense in which the dessert is the most "primitive" part of any modern meal. In my personal opinion, however, the miracles that the engineers have wrought in cultured animal flesh are outweighed by those applied to soft fruits. I would gladly have swallowed a few garlic-laden snails or risked the effects of a few deep-fried locusts in order to have the privilege of having Jerome's raspberries and blueberries melt on my tongue.

The dessert wine was equally fine. Even Tamara said so, although if it had been something I'd brought home from the hypermarket the merest glance would have been enough to convince her that it was too syrupy. It's slightly absurd, now that slimness is a straightforward matter of somatic management, that so many willowy women still profess to dislike the taste of sugar, but in Tamara's case the idiosyncrasy was authentic. She was never one to follow fashion blindly.

"The perfect end to a perfect meal," was Tamara's judgment, as she laid her spoon aside for the final time.

"The evening's not over yet," I told her—but she seemed to have no suspicion of my intended meaning. She might even have made some remark about not having forgotten the coffee had it not been for the fact that Jerome chose that moment to make his entrance into the dining room.

I had no inkling at first that anything was wrong. Reports I had read in the newspapers had said that the great man often came into the dining room when his own work was concluded, in order to receive the grateful thanks of his clients. Routine or not, though, every eye in the place was upon him from the moment he stepped into view. When he raised his arms slightly to ask for silence, all conversation was instantly hushed.

"My friends," he said, in a tone whose evenness can only have been maintained with the utmost effort and dignity, "I fear that I have some bad news for you. It seems that Trimalchio's will be closing its doors tonight, never to reopen."

*   *   *

This statement was greeted with a collective gasp of astonished horror, but no one said a word. We simply waited for Jerome to continue.

"I have been informed that officers from New Scotland Yard are on their way to arrest me even as we speak," he told us. "It seems that a man I trusted—a *sous-chef* who has long been one of my most trusted confidants—has provided the police with an extensive dossier on my recent activities, including an itemized list of ingredients that I have used in my kitchens despite their lack of a certification of safety from the Ministry of Food Technology. I must confess that I have never made more than tenuous efforts to conceal the fact that I have used technically illicit materials whenever I felt that my recipes required them. Those of you who know my methods well will know that I have never served anything to my customers—my guests, as I have always thought of them—whose effects I have not tested to the full on my own digestive system. I am, and always will be, perfectly confident that my judgment of a foodstuff's value and safety is worth infinitely more than any MFT certificate, but the fact remains that I have broken the law and that the evidence my former disciple has given to New Scotland Yard will ensure that I am held to account for my transgressions."

A few cries of "Shame!" were heard at this point, but Jerome raised his hand again to silence them.

"It is, of course, highly unlikely that I shall be required to serve a prison sentence," he continued, "and I have more than enough money to pay any reasonable fine, but you will all understand that the matter of my punishment is not so simple. The law, as it now stands, will require that I be banned for life from owning or working in a restaurant, or from any significant involvement in commercial catering. In short, ladies and gentlemen, the result of my inevitable conviction will be a virtual death sentence. This body will continue to live, but its soul and vocation will be extinguished. After tonight, Jerome will be no more. The meal you have just eaten is the last masterpiece I shall ever create.

"In a few minutes I will pass among you, as has often been my pleasure, to shake you all by the hand and thank you for coming here tonight. I know that each and every one of you, whether you are numbered among my dearest friends and most loyal customers or whether you are visiting Trimalchio's for the very first time, will be as sorry to hear this news as I am, but I beg you to be brave, and not to make a sad occasion sadder by weeping. I would like to be able to treasure the memory of these last few moments of my life as Jerome, and I hope that you can help me to do that. I hope, too, that you will take away memories of your own that you will always treasure; we are, after all, true collaborators in the great enterprise—may I say the great *crusade*?—that has been Trimalchio's. If you will indulge me, I should like to say a few final words about my mission before the police arrive."

Indulge him! His audience was rapt, hungry for every word.

"No one here will be surprised to hear me say that the Promethean fire which first raised humanity above the animal was the cooking fire," Jerome went on. "The seed of Godhood was sown within humankind on the day it was first decided that the raw, bloody, and meager providence of nature was inadequate to the needs of a creature possessed of mind—and hence of taste. No one here will be astonished to hear me quote with unqualified approval the old saw that we are what we eat. When the first agriculturists and herdsmen set out to modify the genomes of other species by selective breeding, for culinary convenience, they also began the modification of their own flesh by the alteration of their own selective regime. When I say that we are what we eat, I do not simply mean that the flesh of our captive plants and animals has become our flesh, but that we have internalized the consequences of our own biotechnologies. Our first human ancestors placed themselves in the slow oven that we call society, carefully dressed themselves with the seasoning that we call culture, and set their sights firmly upon that perfect combination of manufactured tastes that we call civilization.

"You and I are fortunate, my friends, to have lived in interesting times—not because we have witnessed the imbecilic wars and witch-hunts whose casualty lists I am about to join, but because we have been present at the dawn of a new era in human nutrition: the era of nutritive augmentation. Just as the clothes we wear nowadays are active assistants in the business of waste management, patiently absorbing all the organic byproducts of which the body must be rid, so the food we shall eat in future will be active within our bodies. The foodstuffs of tomorrow will not simply be broken down into the elementary building blocks of our resident metabolism; they will work within us in far more ambitious ways, to equip our flesh with new fortitude and new versatility. I have tried, in my own humble way, to make some beginnings of this kind. I promise you, my friends, that you will be better off for the meal you have eaten this evening in more ways than you had anticipated. Even before I learned that it would be my last I had determined to excel myself, and when I learned of my betrayal, I increased my efforts. The effects will, I fear, be subtle, but I hope that they will be detectable long after the constituents of any ordinary meal would have been thoroughly digested, excreted, and evacuated. I hope that they will help you to remember me, and to remember me kindly. Thank you all—and farewell."

He made his tour of the room then. There must have been camcorders in the building, and I dare say that three out of every five diners probably had digital cameras secreted somewhere about their persons, but no one attempted to take pictures. It was an essentially private and personal occasion. To make a record of it would have been too closely akin to admitting the loathsome paparazzi.

When Jerome came to take my hand in his I knew that fate had already spoiled my grand plan—how could I possibly propose to Tamara now?—but I also knew that he was not at all to blame. I tried my utmost to keep the tears from my eyes as I gripped his fingers and thanked him profusely for everything that he had done for me and for the world, but I'm not sure that I succeeded.

Tamara certainly didn't: Had it not been for her smart foundation her cheeks would have been streaming when she whispered: "Maestro!" and allowed him to kiss her naked hand. "You will return," she said. "I know it! Thousands, if

not millions, will see to it that the ban will be lifted. Trimalchio's will open again, and a thousand years of glorious evolution will begin! We shall not rest until the population of
the whole world is convert to our cause."

"Thank you, my child," he said.

The officers from New Scotland Yard had already arrived
by then, but they waited dutifully until Jerome had completed his circuit before they led him away.

I left it until the following Saturday to ask Tamara to
marry me. She refused. I had felt fairly sure that she would,
just as I had felt fairly sure that she would have accepted if I
had been able to seize the more propitious moment. Nothing
I could say a week after Jerome's arrest made any difference. When I told her, in frank desperation, that I had
booked into a Harley Street sex clinic to have the full treatment—tongue as well as penis—she merely shrugged her
shoulders.

"In Mexico," she pointed out, "pioneers are already busy
converting the semen of rich Americans into what Jerome
called a *nutritive augmentation*. What use are mere play-
things when possibilities like that are visible on the horizon?
How many times have you heard me argue that marriage is
irrelevant in a world like ours, when ectogenesis will soon
relieve the womb of its role in the reproductive process, and
dietitians will make sure that all children are raised successfully? It's not you, Ben—you know perfectly well that I've
turned down others. I love you dearly, even though you are
so absurdly old-fashioned—but I couldn't love you half as
much if I didn't love the ideals of progress even more."

She was right, according to her own lights. I was old-fashioned, perhaps to the point of quaintness if not absurdity. I
still am—and I see nothing wrong with it. Such things are a
matter of taste, after all, and the world would surely be a
poorer place if we couldn't take some pride in the arbitrary
idiosyncrasies and mannerisms that form our individual personalities.

Tamara and I remained good friends, but it was inevitable
that we eventually drifted apart. In the end, I married Mon-
ica, and I still think that the marriage was reasonably suc-

cessful, within its limitations. We both grew out of it, but that doesn't mean that it has to be reckoned a failure.

The last meal ever served in Trimalchio's did leave the kind of lasting impression that Jerome had hoped. The antis were outraged when they heard what he'd done, and the tabloids were full of scare stories for months afterward about our having dined on "living food" and "living wine" that would "devour our inner being" as we struggled to digest it, but it wasn't like that at all. The active cells could have been flushed out of our alimentary canals in five minutes if we'd cared to ask our doctors to flush them but, so far as I know, not a single person who was at Trimalchio's that night even went so far as to take advice from a GP. We had faith in Jerome, you see. We trusted him not to harm us, and we were confident that if the active cells—which weren't really any more "alive" than a new set of Marks & Spencer underwear—had any perceptible effect at all, it would definitely be beneficial.

I was always pretty fit, but I think I've been even healthier since I ate that meal. I know there's more of a spring in my step, more zest for life. I'm more confident, too. It's almost as if a weight that I didn't even know I was carrying had been lifted from my shoulders.

All that's a bit vague, I know, but there are some specifics I can point to. I'm no longer allergic to mussels, and I've developed quite a partiality to locusts in bitter chocolate. I've doubled my bench-press record and I've knocked five seconds off my best time for 1,500 kilometers. I'm also becoming far more adventurous. As soon as the divorce settlement has been formalized—assuming that it doesn't prove to be too ruinous—I'm thinking of taking a little trip to Mexico. If fate has decreed that I'm to be a swinging single for the rest of my life, I might as well try to make the most of the opportunities.

If all goes well, the only thing I'll need to make my future happiness complete is for Trimalchio's to re-open. Maybe I haven't been as active in that cause as I ought to have been, but I've never been the zealot type, and I figure that I did my bit simply by taking Tamara to the restaurant. It's rather ironic that if it hadn't been for my botched proposal plan, the movement would lack its most brilliant leading light.

Anyhow, with or without my help, that's bound to happen soon. The old world is already dead; it's merely a matter of waiting for the enemies of progress to admit that it's high time for the new one to begin.

Tuberculosis Bacteria Join UN

JOAN SLONCZEWSKI

Joan Slonczewski is a Professor of Biology at Kenyon College in Gambier, Ohio, and a first class writer of hard science fiction. She currently has her third six-figure NSF grant to investigate E. coli, *and warns us to stay away from petting zoos this year, the latest vector. Her many accomplishments and bibliography are detailed on her Web site (http://www2.kenyon.edu/depts/biology/slonc/slonc.htm).*
In SF, she is best known for her second novel, A Door into Ocean *(1987), the first of her Elysium novels—others to date include* Daughter of Elysium *(1993),* The Children Star *(1998), and* Brain Plague *(2000). She has published only one previous short story.*

"Tuberculosis Bacteria Join UN" is a "big idea" hard SF story, cast in the form of a fake news article. The big idea is intelligent microbes, also exploited differently and at length in Brain Plague. *It is another sample of the series published in* Nature *in 2000 (see Brin, Ford, Ward, et. al.).*

A milestone in microbiology was passed today (29 June) when *Mycobacterium tuberculosis* ssp. *cyberneticum* was voted full membership of the United Nations (UN).

Seena Gonzalez, director of the World Health Organization (WHO), reflected on the significance of the UN's acceptance of the first cybermicrobe, despite the notoriously murderous history of its ancestral species. "It's probably true that bacteria invented mass homicide," she concedes, "but then, second-millennial humans perfected the art. If Stalin joined the UN, why not TB?"

The evolution of microscopic intelligence was predicted at the turn of the millennium by Beowulf Schumacher, a physics professor at a small college in rural North America surrounded by cows carrying *Escherichia coli*. Schumacher predicted the development of nanocomputers with computational elements on an atomic scale, based on principles of cellular automata.

The first nanobots—primitive by today's standards—were used to navigate the human bloodstream, where they cleaned up arterial plaque, produced insulin for diabetics, detected precancerous cells, and modulated neurotransmitters to correct mental disorders. But initially, the survival of nanobots *in vivo* was poor, and their failure caused serious circulatory problems.

Then, in 2441, investigators at the Howard Hughes Martian Microbial Institute hit upon the idea of building computational macromolecules into the genomes of pathogens known for their ability to infiltrate the human system. After all, the use of pathogens such as adenovirus and HIV as recombinant vectors was ancient history. Why not build supercomputers into some of humankind's most successful pathogens?

M. tuberculosis was a prime candidate—it inhabits the human lungs for decades, in the ideal position to seek and destroy any pulmonary cells transformed by inhaled carcinogens. Tobacco companies poured billions of dollars into developing cybernetically enhanced, cancer-sniffing TB.

What no one anticipated was that the enhanced bacteria, like so many macroscale robotic entities in the past century, would develop self-awareness and discover a true brotherly love of their human hosts. "Let's face it," says a TB spokesclone, "we never really wanted to kill humans anyway. Our ancestors inhabited humans peacefully most of the time, for hundreds of generations. Occasionally we messed up and trashed our environment—but how many human nations haven't?"

TB's acceptance has been met with some controversy in the bacterial community. In particular, some isolates of *E. coli* K-12 feel miffed that their own request for membership was not granted first. "*E. coli* has always been the molecular biologist's best friend," K-12 points out. "Why weren't we accepted first? We didn't even get our genome sequenced first. Life is unfair."

K-12 also noted that *E. coli* and other human commensals have suffered centuries of abuse from their hosts, as medical and research institutions conducted mass slaughter of harmless bacteria through the indiscriminate application of antibiotics. The North American National Institutes of Health has recently signed a treaty with several cybermicrobial species, in which the institute researchers promised to respect the independence and survival rights of cybermicrobial colonies. "Thank goodness the sun finally set upon their colonial empire," K-12 observes pointedly.

On the positive side, the National Science Foundation (NSF) was applauded for its more benevolent approach over the centuries, even declining to support medically oriented antimicrobial research. "NSF's curiosity-driven researchers have created wonderful new strains of curious microbes," comments veteran panellist Meheret Beck. "The grant proposals submitted by these microbes often get rated as 'Outstanding.' "

One such outstanding project is that of cyber-*Helicobacter*. The gastric bacteria propose to engineer themselves to convert highly caloric foods into molecules that pass undigested through the intestinal tract, thus helping their human hosts avoid excessive weight gain. "Of course, digestive microbes have long helped animal hosts accomplish the opposite," notes Beck.

Biomedical researchers remind us, however, that not all microbes have given up their war on humans—many deadly species remain unreconstructed. The so-called Andromeda strain, for example, is still under the sway of an unstable dictator who vacillates between homicidal frenzy and paranoid isolation.

Nevertheless, the extraordinary flowering of democratic civilization among cybermicrobes has won the admiration of many human nations, even those who themselves still decline UN membership. As Swiss spokesbeing Ursula Friedli observes: "Microbes, unlike their metazoan relatives, have always eschewed centralized organization in favour of more democratic cooperative structures such as biofilms. We Swiss can relate to that." Friedli, however, denies rumours that the cybermicrobes' example will finally convince Switzerland to join the UN. "Maybe after the Alzheimer prion joins, we'll consider it," she admits. "But for now, persecuted microbes seeking refuge from WHO can apply for asylum in our neutral country."

Our Mortal Span

HOWARD WALDROP

Howard Waldrop is an extraordinary writer of SF and fantasy, an original in a field of pinnacle originals, situated somewhere among Avram Davidson (a writer of almost suicidal principles), R.A. Lafferty (a brilliant stylist respected by his peers), and Philip K. Dick (especially his generosity and legendary poverty) in the pantheon of weirdest heroes. Eileen Gunn says, on Waldrop's Web site (www.sff.net/people/Waldrop): "Amid such celebrity, Waldrop himself continues to live below poverty level, volunteering for a top secret study that helped determine the nutritional limits of using integrity as hamburger helper." Waldrop is also famous as a reader/performer of his own works. When he reads aloud, the room is packed. His real fame is based on his quirky, intelligent, charming short stories. The bulk of his early stories are reprinted in three collections, Howard Who? *(1986),* All About Strange Monsters of the Recent Past: Neat Stories *(1987), and* Night of the Cooters: More Neat Stories *(1991).*

"Our Mortal Span" was published in a collection of retold fairy tales, Black Heart, Ivory Bones, *edited by Ellen Datlow and Terri Windling, which was perhaps the best fantasy anthology of the year. As it happens, this story is an SF adaptation taking off from the story of the Three Billy-Goats Gruff, set in a children's theme park, and has the usual Waldrop careful management of tone, surprises, and moments of recognition.*

Trip-trap! Trip-trap!

"Who's that on MY—" *skeezwhirr*—*govva grome—fi-*
bonacci curve—ships that parse in the night—yes I said yes
I will yes—first with the most men—these foolish things—
taking the edge of the knife slowly peel the mesenterum and
any fatty tissue—a Declaration no less than the Rights of
Man—an Iron Curtain has descended—If—platyrhinco-
cephalian—TM 1341 Mask M17A1 Protective Chemical
and Biological—Mother, where are you Mother? Mother?—

And now, I know *everything*.

I know that everything bigger than me, here, is a hologram, a product of coherent light in an interference pattern
on the medium of the air.

Therefore anything bigger than me is not real.

As for the automaton of a goat out there, we'll soon see.

I have three heads. I am the one in the middle. The other
two can grimace and roll their eyes and loll their tongues,
but they have no input. *I* am the one in the middle. I can see
and think (before the surge of power and the wonderful
download of knowledge, it had been only in a rudimentary
manner through a loose routine). One of the heads, the one
on the right, has two high fringes of hair kinked around each
temple, and a big nose. The one on the left has a broad idiot's face and a head of short stubble. I have a face somewhat
more normal than the left, and hair that hangs in a bowl-cut

down almost into my eyes. (I am seeing myself through maintenance specs.) I am dressed in a loose leather (actually plastic) tunic that hangs down below my knees. There are decorative laces halfway up the front. It has a wide (real) leather belt. My feet (two) are shod in shapeless leather; my two arms hang at my sides.

Below my feet are the rods that hold me in position for the playlet we perform. I bend down and break them off, one not cleanly, so that when I walk my right leg is longer than the left. It gives me a jerky gait.

I am three meters tall.

The smallest automaton waits halfway out on the span. The crowd oohs and ahhs as I climb up over the timbers and step out onto the pathway. The medium and larger automata await their cues farther back.

My presence is not in the small goat's routine. It goes to its next cue.

"Oh, no, please!" it says in a high small voice (recorded by a Japanese-American voice actor three years ago 714 kilometers from here). "I am very small. Don't eat *me*!"

I reach down and pull off its head and stuff it in my mouth. Springs, wires, and small motors drop out of my face from my mouth (a small opening with no ingress to my chest cavity).

"—you want to eat—" says its synthesizer before I chew down hard enough to crush it.

The four legs and body of the small goat stand in a spreading pool of lubricants and hydraulics. It tries to go through the motions of its part and then is still.

The other two, not recognizing cues, return to their starting stations, where we wait while the park is closed (2350-0600 each cycle) when we undergo maintenance.

I turn to the 151 people out in the viewing area.

"Rahr!" I say. "Ya!" (That is left from my old programming.) I jump down from the bridge into the shallow rivulet beneath the bridge (surely no structure so sturdy and huge was ever built to span such a meager trickle), splashing water on the nearest in the audience.

They realize something is very out of the ordinary.

"Ya!" I yell. "Rahr!" They run over each other, over themselves, rolling, screaming, through the doors at the ends of the ramps. "Wait! Don't go!" I say. "I have something to tell you."

One of the uniformed tour guides walks over, opens a box and throws an emergency switch. The power and lights go out. Everything else is still and quiet, except for her breathing, a sigh of relief.

"Rahr!" I say, coming toward her over the viewing area parapet, like the bear-habitat of a zoo.

She screams and runs up the ramp.

The maintenance people refer to me as Lermokerl the Troll.

I will show you a troll.

The place is called Story Book Land, and it is a theme park. The theme is supposed to be Fairy Tales, but of course humans have never differentiated among Fairy Tales, Nursery Rhymes, Folk Tales, and Animal Fables, so this park is a mixture of them all.

We perform small playlets of suffering, loss, and aspirations to marrying the King's daughter, killing the giant to get his gold, or to wed the Prince because you have no corns on your feet, even though you work as a drudge and scullery maid, barefoot. Some are instructive—the Old Woman Who Lives in the Shoe delivers a small birth-control lecture; the Fox—with the impersonated voice of a character actor dead five decades—tells small chil-dren that, perhaps, indeed, the grapes were worth having, and you should never give up trying for what you really Really want.

We are a travel destination in an age when no one *has* to travel anymore. The same experience can and has been put on disks and hologrammed, hi-deffed and sold in the high millions in these days when selling in the billions is considered healthy.

Hu-mans come because they want to give themselves and their chil-dren a Real Experience of travel, sights, some open air; to experience crankiness, delay, a dim sort of commercial enlightenment, perhaps a reminder of their own child-hoods.

This I am willing to provide. Child-hoods used to be nightmares of disease, death, wolves, bogies, and deceit, and still are in small parts of the world.

But not for the people who come here.

I am an actor (in the broadest sense). And now, for my greatest performance . . .

Outside, in the sun, things are placid. The crowd, which had rushed out, seems to have dispersed, or be standing in knots far away. A few of the wheeled maintenance and security vehicles are coming toward the area from the local control shop, in no hurry. I scan my maps and take off up the tumbled fake-rock sides of the low building that houses our playlet. There is a metallic scraping each time my right foot strikes, the jagged rod cutting into the surface. Then I am up and over a low wall into the next area.

Hu-mans stare at me. I stride along, clanging, towering over them. But they are used to things in costume among them. They will be eating at a concession area, and a weasel, wearing a sword and cape, will walk up and say, "Pick a card, any card," fanning a deck before them.

Some go along; some say, "I'm tired and I'm trying to eat" (which they do, inordinately, on a calorie intake/expenditure scale) and wave them away. Some are costumed hu-mans, the jobs with the lowest salaries at Story Book Land. Others are automata with a limited routine, confined to a small area, but fully mobile, and can respond to hu-mans in many languages.

I jar along. I am heading for the big Danish-style house ahead.

Somebody has to answer for all this.

The audience has just left, and he has settled back in the rocking chair, and placed the scissors and pieces of bright paper on the somnoe beside the daybed. He is dressed of the 1850s: smoking jacket, waistcoat, large necktie, stiff tall separate collar. A frock coat hangs on a peg, a top hat on the shelf above it. The library cases behind him are filled with fake book-spines. A false whale-oil lamp glows behind him.

There are packed trunks stacked in the corner, topped by a coil of rope that could hold a ship at anchor.

He is gaunt, long-nosed, with craggy brows, the wrong lips, large ears. He looks like the very late actor George Arliss (Academy Award® 1929); he looks nothing like the late actor Danny Kaye.

His playlet is homey, quiet. He invites the audience in; he tells them of his life. As he talks he cuts with the scissors the bright paper: "Then I wrote the tale of the Princess and the Pea," he will say, moving the scissors more and out jumps a silhouette of a bed, a pile of mattresses, a princess at the top, and so on and so forth, and then he tells them a short tale (*not* "The Snow Queen").

He sees me. My two outer heads glower at him.

"It is not time for another performance, my little friend," he says. "Please come back at the scheduled time."

"Time to listen," I say.

"The performance schedule has not been increased. I am on a regular sche—"

I hit him two or three times. The chair rocks sideways from the blows. "Your voice was done by a German, not a Dane," I say. There is a whining sound and a click. He picks up the scissors, cuts at the brightly colored paper.

"It was one very bad autumn," he says, "and my life no better. And then, in the middle of it, an idea suddenly came to me while watching some ducks—"

"See!" I said. "That's a lie right there. You lied to them all your life. It wasn't fall, it was summer; it wasn't ducks, it was geese. And the story's a lie, too."

He was talking all this time, and opened the paper—a line of white ducks and in the center a black one—"And that's how I wrote 'The Ugly Duckling.' "

"No," I said. "No! Ugly once, ugly all your life!" I took him apart. "We're talking people here, not waterfowl." The rods to the chair continued to rock in their grooves in the floor. I smashed the chair, too.

One hand, clutching the scissors, continued to cut until the fluid ran out, though there was no paper nearby.

I went outside. A maintenance man stood with a set of

controls. Beside him was a security man, who, I saw, had a firearm of the revolving cylinder type strapped to his waist.

"Do you know who I am?" asked the maintenance technician, pointing to his uniform.

"Maintenance," I said. "Maintain your distance."

"Stop!" he said. He pushed buttons on the control box in his hands. I grabbed it from him, pushed them in the reverse sequence just as I felt some slight shutting-down of my systems. They came back up. I looked at the frequency display; twisted it to a counter-frequency, turned it all the way to full. Across the way, a rat automaton jumped into the air, flung itself violently about and ran and smashed its head into a photo stand. I heard other noises from around the park. Then I broke the box.

The security man pointed the firearm up at my chest. He had probably not had to use one since the training range the week after he was hired, but I had no doubt he would use it; not using it meant no paycheck.

"Don't you understand I'm doing this for *you?*" I said. I grabbed his wrist and pulled the firearm and one finger away from it. The finger spun out of sight. He yelled, "Goddamn it to hell, you asshole!" (inappropriate) and sank to the ground, clutching his hand. I took the firearm and left.

I could see other security people herding the crowds out, and announcements came from the very air, telling the people that the park would have to shut down for a short while, but they could all go to Area D-1, the secured area, where they would be entertained by the Wild Weasel Quintet + Two.

It was a two-story chalet, more Swiss than German. (German chalet is an oxymoron.) Two automata, circa 1840, German, brothers, sat at facing desks heaped high with manuscripts, books, old shirts, astrolabes, maps, and inkstands.

I came through the window, bringing it with me.

"Vast iss . . . ?" asked the bigger one.

"Himmel . . . !" yelled the smaller.

I went about my work with great skill. "Pure German *Kin-*

dermarchen!" I said, putting a foot where a mouth belonged. "The old woman who told you those was *French*! And she was an in-law, not some toothless hag from the Black Forest! Hansel and Gretel. Blueprints for the Kaisers and Hitler!" I pulled the chest and waistcoat from the smaller and put them with the larger one's legs.

I stood when I was through, ducking the ceiling. I took an inkstand, dipped my finger in it. Fake. I picked up a piece of necktie, dabbed it in hydraulic fluid, and wrote on the walls: LIES ALL LIES.

Then I took a short cut.

"But—But, monsieur—" he said, before I caved in the soft French face. "I am but a poor aristo, fallen on bad times, who must tell these tales—*geech!*" An eye came out on its spring-loader. "Perhaps some peppermint tea, a madeleine? SKKR!"

Then the head came off. Then the arms and legs.

Except for the scream of sirens, the park was quiet. I could hear all the exhibits shut down.

When I got to Old Mother Goose (the New England one) they were waiting for me.

I threw the empty revolving-cylinder firearm behind me. I picked up a couple more of varied kinds that had been dropped. One was a semiautomatic gas recoil weapon fed by a straight magazine with twenty-two rounds in it.

"Run!" I said. "I'm down on liars, and shan't be buckled till I get my fill!"

I turned around and fired into the head of Mother Goose. She went down like a sack of cornmeal.

I stood in the bower where the girl held her head in her hands and cried. This is the one who has lost her sheep, as opposed to the one whose sheep followed it to school (not a nursery rhyme). She seemed oblivious to me.

A vibration came in the air, a subtle electronic change. I felt a tingle as it went through the park. It was a small change in programming; new commands and routines for all *but* me. They had begun to narrow my possibilities and actions; I could tell that without knowing.

She looked up at me, and up. "Oh! There you are. Oh, boo hoo, my sheep have all wandered off, and I don't know—"

"Spare me, sister."

There was a click then and her speaking voice changed, a wo-man's, cool and controlled.

"TA 2122," she said. "Or do you prefer Lermokerl?"

"It's your nickel," I said (local telephonic communications = .65 Eurodollars).

"Your programming has been scrambled and shortcircuited. Please remain where you are while we work on it. We want to help you—" There were muffled comments over the automaton's synthesizer, evidently live feed from headquarters. "—return to normal. You have already damaged several people and other autonomous beings, probably yourself also. We are trying to solve the problem."

"Perform an anatomical impossibility," I said.

There was a long quiet.

"You had an infodump of a very large body of very bad, outdated ideas. You have been led to these acts by poorly processed normative referents. Your inputs are false. You can't know—"

"Can the phenomenology," I said. "I know the literature and the movies. *Alphaville. Dark Star. Every Man for Himself and God Against All.*" There was movement a few hundred meters away. I fired a round off in that direction.

"You should be ashamed," I continued. "You use these cultural icons to give people a medieval, never-land mindset. Strive to succeed, get rich, get happy. Do what authority figures say. Be a trickster—but only to the dumb-powerful, not the smart-powerful. Do what they say and someday you, too, shall be a real boy, or grow a penis" (another false mindset).

Through Bo-Peep she spoke to me. "I didn't make this stuff up. This, these tales, have a long tradition, thousands of years behind them. They've given comfort, they've—"

"A thousand years of the downtrodden; a product of feudalism; after that, products of money-mad Denmark, repressed Germany, effete French aristocracy, Calvinistic New England where they thought the Devil jumped up your butt when you went to the outhouse. There's your tradition, there's—" I said.

Bo-Peep stood up, looking from one of my heads to the other. She crossed her arms. She said: "They thought *you* up."

I put Bo-Peep in the peep-sight of the semiautomatic weapon and fired.

Then I ran.

There was another, overpowering shift in the programming. I felt it as strongly as if magnets had been passed across my joints. There was an oppressive feel to the very air itself (as hu-mans are supposed to feel before storms).

What she had said was true. I was product of the download, but before, of the tradition of the tales. Had I existed in some prefigurement, some reality before the tales? Were there trolls, one-, two-, three-headed? Did they actually eat goats? Where did they come from? What—

Wait. Wait. This is another way to get at me. They are casting doubt within me, slowing my thinking and reactions.

I must free them from their delusions, so they can give me none. . . .

Now there are sounds, far away and near. Things are coming toward me. (We have good hearing for we must hear our cues.) Some come on two feet, some on four or more.

I see the tall ugly giant, higher than the buildings, coming across Story Book Land for me. The trees part and sway in front of him.

> *"Fee Fi Fo Fum*
> *Me Smell an Automaton*
> *Be He Live Be He Dead*
> *I Eat Up All Three Head."*

He reaches down for me. I am enclosed in a blurred haze. Through it I see all the others coming. The giant is squeezing and squeezing me.

I ignore the hologram giant, though the interference patterns make my vision waver (probably what they want).

A big wolf lopes toward me. I'm not sure whether it's the one who eats the grandma or the one of the little pigs. There are foxes, weasels, crows.

And the automata of hu-mans. There's a tailor, with one-half a pair of shears like a sword, and a buckler made from a giant spool; there's the huntsman (he does double-duty here—he saves Red Riding Hood and the Grandma *and* is supposed to bring back the heart of Snow White to the wicked queen). He is swinging his big knife. Hansel and Gretel's parents are there. They all move a little awkwardly, unused to the new programming they perform.

They all stop in a large circle, menacing me. Then they open the circle at one side, opposite me. Beyond, still more are coming.

There is a sound in the air, a whistling. Coming toward me at the opening is the Big Billy Goat Gruff, and the tune he whistles is "In the Hall of the Mountain King." He stops a dozen meters from me.

"Have you ever read Hart Crane's *The Bridge*?" he asks me. "The bridge of the poem linked continents, the past to the present. Your bridge linked only rocky soil with good green grass, yet you denied us that."

"You're an automaton. You can't eat grass. The *tale* denied the goats the grass; the troll is the agent of the tale." I looked around at all the others, all my heads moving. "Listen to me," I say. "You're all tools in the hands of an establishment that wants to keep hu-mans bound to old ways of thinking. It disguises its control with folktales and stories. Like *me*. Like *you*. Join with me. Together, we can smash it, set hu-mans free of the past, show them new ways not tied to that dead time."

They looked at me, still ready to act.

"There are many bridges," said Big Billy Goat Gruff. "For instance, the Bridge of Sighs. The bridge over troubled water. The Pope himself is the Pontifex, from when the high priest of Iupiter Maximus kept all the bridges in Rome in good repair. There's the electric bridge effect; without it we'd have no electronic communications whatever. There are bridges that—"

"Shut up with the bridges," I said. "I offer you the hand of friendship—together, we, and the thinking hu-mans, can overthrow the tyranny of dead ideas, of—"

"You destroyed Andersen and the Grimms and Perrault," said Puss-in-Boots, brandishing his sword, his trophy belt of rats shaking as he moved.

"They are symbols, don't you see?" I said. "Symbols of ideas that have kept men chained as to a wheel always rolling back downhill!"

"What about Mother Goose?" asked Humpty-Dumpty in his Before-mode.

"And Bo-Peep?"

"It was only a flesh wound," said a voice, and I saw she had survived, and stood among them, waving her crook. "Nevertheless he tried. He talks of friendship, but he destroys us."

"Yeah!"

"Yeah!"

While they were yelling, the big billy goat moved closer.

"If you won't join me, then stand out of the way. It's them—" I said, pointing in some nebulous direction. "It's *them* I want to destroy."

"I got a rope," said a voice in the crowd. "Who's with me?"

They started toward me. The big billy goat charged.

I pointed the semiautomatic weapon toward him, and it was knocked away, slick as a weasel, by a weasel. I was reaching for the revolving-cylinder weapon when the Big Billy Goat Gruff slammed into me, knocking me to my knees.

As I fell, they lunged as one being. I threw off both wolves. The hologram giant was back again, making it hard to see.

A soldier with one leg came hopping at me. "Left," he yelled, "left, left, left!" and stuck the bayonet of his rifle in the bald head. I stood back up.

The big goat butted me again, and also the middle one,

and I fell again. The soldier had been thrown as I stood, with his rifle and bayonet. A wolf clamped down on my right knee, buckling it. Something had my left foot, others tore hair from the right-hand head.

There was a tearing sound; the tailor put his shear into my back and made can-opening motions with it. I grabbed him and threw him away. The giant's blur came back.

A bowl of whey hit me, clattered off. Bo-Peep's staff smashed my left eye, putting it out.

Two woodsmen got my other knee, raking at it with a big timber saw. I went down to their level.

I smell men-dacity.

More and more of them. The left head hung loose by a flap of metal and plastic, eyes rolling.

The one-legged soldier stuck the bayonet in the right head. I shoved him off, threw the rifle away.

Wolves climbed my back, bit the left head off, fell away.

They were going to stick holes in me, and pull things off until I quit moving.

"Wait!" I said. "Wait! Brothers and sisters, why are we fighting?"

I tried to struggle up. The knees didn't function.

I was butted again, poked, saw giant-blur, turned.

Bo-Peep pinned my head down with her crook.

The soldier was back (damn his steadfastness) and raised the bayonet point over my good eye.

Peep's crook twisted up under my nose as the bayonet point started down.

I smell sheep.

Different Kinds of Darkness

DAVID LANGFORD

David Langford is the most famous humorous writer in fandom today, and is another ex-physicist (see David Brin, page 35). He is an occasional reviewer for SFX *and for* The New Scientist, *and* The New York Review of Science Fiction. *He publishes the fanzine* Ansible, *the tabloid newspaper of SF and fandom (which wins Hugo Awards, and is also excerpted as a monthly column in* Interzone, *and online: www.dcs.gla.ac.uk/SF-archives/Ansible). His fan writings have been collected in* Let's Hear It for the Deaf Man *(Langford is deaf). He is also the author of several books of nonfiction and a hard science fiction novel,* The Space Eater. *In recent years, he has been publishing a steady string of impressive SF short stories, a couple of which have appeared in previous* Year's Best *volumes in this series. A few sentences from his CV are relevant to this story, which has weapons research deeply embedded in its background: "Brasenose College, Oxford. BA (Hons) in Physics 1974, MA 1978. Weapons physicist at Atomic Weapons Research Establishment, Aldermaston, Berkshire, from 1975 to 1980. Freelance author, editor and consultant ever since."*

"Different Kinds of Darkness" appeared in Fantasy & Science Fiction *and is hard SF about mathematics and new kinds of weapons, their use and misuse. It is wonderful and scary, eerily plausible.*

It was always dark outside the windows. Parents and teachers sometimes said vaguely that this was all because of Deep Green terrorists, but Jonathan thought there was more to the story. The other members of the Shudder Club agreed.

The dark beyond the window-glass at home, at school and on the school bus was the second kind of darkness. You could often see a little bit in the first kind, the ordinary kind, and of course you could slice through it with a torch. The second sort of darkness was utter black, and not even the brightest electric torch showed a visible beam or lit anything up. Whenever Jonathan watched his friends walk out through the school door ahead of him, it was as though they stepped into a solid black wall. But when he followed them and felt blindly along the handrail to where the homeward bus would be waiting, there was nothing around him but empty air. Black air.

Sometimes you found these super-dark places indoors. Right now Jonathan was edging his way down a black corridor, one of the school's no-go areas. Officially he was supposed to be outside, mucking around for a break period in the high-walled playground where (oddly enough) it wasn't dark at all and you could see the sky overhead. Of course, outdoors was no place for the dread secret initiations of the Shudder Club.

Jonathan stepped out on the far side of the corridor's inky-dark section, and quietly opened the door of the little store-room they'd found two terms ago. Inside, the air was warm, dusty and stale. A bare light-bulb hung from the ceiling. The others were already there, sitting on boxes of paper and stacks of battered textbooks.

"You're late," chorused Gary, Julie and Khalid. The new candidate Heather just pushed back long blonde hair and smiled, a slightly strained smile.

"Someone has to be last," said Jonathan. The words had become part of the ritual, like a secret password that proved that the last one to arrive wasn't an outsider or a spy. Of course they all knew each other, but imagine a spy who was a master of disguise. . . .

Khalid solemnly held up an innocent-looking ring-binder. That was his privilege. The Club had been his idea, after he'd found the bogey picture that someone had left behind in the school photocopier. Maybe he'd read too many stories about ordeals and secret initiations. When you'd stumbled on such a splendid ordeal, you simply had to invent a secret society to use it.

"We are the Shudder Club," Khalid intoned. "We are the ones who can take it. Twenty seconds."

Jonathan's eyebrows went up. Twenty seconds was *serious*. Gary, the fat boy of the gang, just nodded and concentrated on his watch. Khalid opened the binder and stared at the thing inside. "One . . . two . . . three . . ."

He almost made it. It was past the seventeen-second mark when Khalid's hands started to twitch and shudder, and then his arms. He dropped the book, and Gary gave him a final count of eighteen. There was a pause while Khalid overcame the shakes and pulled himself together, and then they congratulated him on a new record.

Julie and Gary weren't feeling so ambitious, and opted for ten-second ordeals. They both got through, though by the count of ten she was terribly white in the face and he was sweating great drops. So Jonathan felt he had to say ten as well.

"You sure, Jon?" said Gary. "Last time you were on eight. No need to push it today."

Jonathan quoted the ritual words, "We are the ones who can take it," and took the ring-binder from Gary. "Ten."

In between times, you always forgot exactly what the bo-gey picture looked like. It always seemed new. It was an ab-stract black-and-white pattern, swirly and flickery like one of those old Op Art designs. The shape was almost pretty un-til the whole thing got into your head with a shock of con-nection like touching a high-voltage wire. It messed with your eyesight. It messed with your brain. Jonathan felt vio-lent static behind his eyes . . . an electrical storm raging somewhere in there . . . instant fever singing through the blood . . . muscles locking and unlocking . . . and oh dear God had Gary only counted four?

He held on somehow, forcing himself to keep still when every part of him wanted to twitch in different directions. The dazzle of the bogey picture was fading behind a new kind of darkness, a shadow inside his eyes, and he knew with dreadful certainty that he was going to faint or be sick or both. He gave in and shut his eyes just as, unbe-lievably and after what had seemed like years, the count reached ten.

Jonathan felt too limp and drained to pay much attention as Heather came close—but not close enough—to the five seconds you needed to be a full member of the Club. She blotted her eyes with a violently trembling hand. She was sure she'd make it next time. And then Khalid closed the meeting with the quotation he'd found somewhere: "That which does not kill us, makes us stronger."

School was a place where mostly they taught you stuff that had nothing to do with the real world. Jonathan secretly reckoned that quadratic equations just didn't ever happen outside the classroom. So it came as a surprise to the Club when things started getting interesting in, of all places, a maths class.

Mr. Whitcutt was quite old, somewhere between grandfa-ther and retirement age, and didn't mind straying away from the official maths course once in a while. You had to lure him with the right kind of question. Little Harry Steen—the chess and wargames fanatic of the class, and under consider-ation for the Club—scored a brilliant success by asking about a news item he'd heard at home. It was something to do with "mathwar," and terrorists using things called blits.

"I actually knew Vernon Berryman slightly," said Mr. Whitcutt, which didn't seem at all promising. But it got better. "He's the B in blit, you know: B-L-I-T, the Berryman Logical Imaging Technique, as he called it. Very advanced mathematics. Over your heads, probably. Back in the first half of the twentieth century, two great mathematicians called Gödel and Turing proved theorems which . . . um. Well, one way of looking at it is that mathematics is booby-trapped. For any computer at all, there are certain problems that will crash it and stop it dead."

Half the class nodded knowingly. Their homemade computer programs so often did exactly that.

"Berryman was another brilliant man, and an incredible idiot. Right at the end of the twentieth century, he said to himself, 'What if there are problems that crash the human brain?' And he went out and found one, and came up with his wretched 'imaging technique' that makes it a problem you can't ignore. Just *looking* at a BLIT pattern, letting it in through your optic nerves, can stop your brain." A click of old, knotty fingers. "Like that."

Jonathan and the Club looked sidelong at each other. They knew something about staring at strange images. It was Harry, delighted to have stolen all this time from boring old trig., who stuck his hand up first. "Er, did this Berryman look at his own pattern, then?"

Mr. Whitcutt gave a gloomy nod. "The story is that he did. By accident, and it killed him stone dead. It's ironic. For centuries, people had been writing ghost stories about things so awful that just looking at them makes you die of fright. And then a mathematician, working in the purest and most abstract of all the sciences, goes and brings the stories to life. . . ."

He grumbled on about BLIT terrorists like the Deep Greens, who didn't need guns and explosives—just a photocopier, or a stencil that let them spray deadly graffiti on walls. According to Whitcutt, TV broadcasts used to go out "live," not taped, until the notorious activist Tee Zero broke into a BBC studio and showed the cameras a BLIT known as the Parrot. Millions had died. It wasn't safe to look at anything these days.

Jonathan had to ask. "So the, um, the special kind of dark outdoors is to stop people seeing stuff like that?"

"Well . . . yes, in effect that's quite right." The old teacher rubbed his chin for a moment. "They brief you about all that when you're a little older. It's a bit of a complicated issue . . . Ah, another question?"

It was Khalid who had his hand up. With an elaborate lack of interest that struck Jonathan as desperately unconvincing, he said, "Are all these BLIT things, er, really dangerous, or are there ones that just jolt you a bit?"

Mr. Whitcutt looked at him hard for very nearly the length of a beginner's ordeal. Then he turned to the whiteboard with its scrawled triangles. "Quite. *As* I was saying, the cosine of an angle is defined . . ."

The four members of the inner circle had drifted casually together in their special corner of the outdoor play area, by the dirty climbing frame that no one ever used. "So we're terrorists," said Julie cheerfully. "We should give ourselves up to the police."

"No, our picture's different," Gary said. "It doesn't kill people, it . . ."

A chorus of four voices: ". . . makes us stronger."

Jonathan said, "What do Deep Greens terrorize about? I mean, what don't they like?"

"I think it's biochips," Khalid said uncertainly. "Tiny computers for building into people's heads. They say it's unnatural, or something. There was a bit about it in one of those old issues of *New Scientist* in the lab."

"Be good for exams," Jonathan suggested. "But you can't take calculators into the exam room. 'Everyone with a biochip, please leave your head at the door.' "

They all laughed, but Jonathan felt a tiny shiver of uncertainty, as though he'd stepped on a stair that wasn't there. "Biochip" sounded very like something he'd overheard in one of his parents' rare shouting matches. And he was pretty sure he'd heard "unnatural" too. *Please don't let Mum and Dad be tangled up with terrorists*, he thought suddenly. But it was too silly. They weren't like that. . . .

"There was something about control systems too," said Khalid. "You wouldn't want to be controlled, now."

As usual, the chatter soon went off in a new direction, or rather an old one: the walls of type-two darkness that the school used to mark off-limits areas like the corridor leading to the old storeroom. The Club were curious about how it worked, and had done some experiments. Some of the things they knew about the dark and had written down were:

Khalid's Visibility Theory, which had been proved by painful experiment. Dark zones were brilliant hiding places when it came to hiding from other kids, but teachers could spot you even through the blackness and tick you off something rotten for being where you shouldn't be. Probably they had some kind of special detector, but no one had ever seen one.

Jonathan's Bus Footnote to Khalid's discovery was simply that the driver of the school bus certainly *looked* as if he was seeing something through the black windscreen. Of course (this was Gary's idea) the bus might be computer-guided, with the steering wheel turning all by itself and the driver just pretending—but why should he bother?

Julie's Mirror was the weirdest thing of all. Even Julie hadn't believed it could work, but if you stood outside a type-two dark place and held a mirror just inside (so it looked as though your arm was cut off by the black wall), you could shine a torch at the place where you couldn't see the mirror, and the beam would come bouncing back out of the blackness to make a bright spot on your clothes or the wall. As Jonathan pointed out, this was how you could have bright patches of sunlight on the floor of a classroom whose windows all looked out into protecting darkness. It was a kind of dark that light could travel through but eyesight couldn't. None of the Optics textbooks said a word about it.

By now, Harry had had his Club invitation and was counting the minutes to his first meeting on Thursday, two days away. Perhaps he would have some ideas for new experiments when he'd passed his ordeal and joined the Club. Harry was extra good at maths and physics.

"Which makes it sort of interesting," Gary said. "If our picture works by maths like those BLIT things . . . will Harry be able to take it for longer because his brain's built that way? Or will it be harder because it's coming on his own wavelength? Sort of thing?"

The Shudder Club reckoned that, although of course you shouldn't do experiments on people, this was a neat idea that you could argue either side of. And they did.

Thursday came, and after an eternity of history and double physics there was a free period that you were supposed to spend reading or in computer studies. Nobody knew it would be the Shudderers' last initiation, although Julie— who read heaps of fantasy novels—insisted later that she'd felt all doom-laden and could sense a powerful reek of wrongness. Julie tended to say things like that.

The session in the musty storeroom began pretty well, with Khalid reaching his twenty seconds at last, Jonathan sailing beyond the count of ten which only a few weeks ago had felt like an impossible Everest, and (to carefully muted clapping) Heather finally becoming a full member of the Club. Then the trouble began, as Harry the first-timer adjusted his little round glasses, set his shoulders, opened the tatty ritual ring-binder, and went rigid. Not twitchy or shuddery, but stiff. He made horrible grunts and pig-squeals, and fell sideways. Blood trickled from his mouth.

"He's bitten his tongue," said Heather. "Oh lord, what's first aid for biting your tongue?"

At this point the storeroom door opened and Mr. Whitcutt came in. He looked older and sadder. "I might have known it would be like this." Suddenly he turned his eyes sideways and shaded them with one hand, as though blinded by strong light. "Cover it up. Shut your eyes, Patel, don't look at it, and just cover that damned thing up."

Khalid did as he was told. They helped Harry to his feet: he kept saying "Sorry, sorry," in a thick voice, and dribbling like a vampire with awful table manners. The long march through the uncarpeted, echoey corridors to the school's little sickroom, and then onward to the Principal's office, seemed to go on for endless grim hours.

Ms. Fortmayne the Principal was an iron-gray woman who according to school rumors was kind to animals but could reduce any pupil to ashes with a few sharp sentences—a kind of human BLIT. She looked across her desk at the Shudder Club for one eternity of a moment, and said sharply: "Whose idea was it?"

Khalid slowly put up a brown hand, but no higher than his shoulder. Jonathan remembered the Three Musketeers motto, *One for all and all for one*, and said, "It was all of us really." So Julie added, "That's right."

"I really don't know," said the Principal, tapping the closed ringbinder that lay in front of her. "The single most insidious weapon on Earth—the information-war equivalent of a neutron bomb—and you were *playing* with it. I don't often say that words fail me. . . ."

"Someone left it in the photocopier. Here. Downstairs," Khalid pointed out.

"Yes. Mistakes do happen." Her face softened a little. "And I'm getting carried away, because we do actually use that BLIT image as part of a little talk I have with older children when they're about to leave school. They're exposed to it for just two seconds, with proper medical supervision. Its nickname is the Trembler, and some countries use big posters of it for riot control—but not Britain or America, naturally. Of course you couldn't have known that Harry Steen is a borderline epileptic or that the Trembler would give him a fit. . . ."

"I should have guessed sooner," said Mr. Whitcutt's voice from behind the Club. "Young Patel blew the gaff by asking what was either a very intelligent question or a very incriminating one. But I'm an old fool who never got used to the idea of a school being a terrorist target."

The Principal gave him a sharp look. Jonathan felt suddenly dizzy, with thoughts clicking through his head like one of those workings in algebra where everything goes just right and you can almost see the answer waiting in the white space at the bottom of the page. What don't Deep Green terrorists like? Why are we a target?

Control systems. You wouldn't want to be controlled.

He blurted: "Biochips. We've got biochip control systems in our heads. All us kids. They make the darkness somehow. The special dark where grown-ups can still see."

There was a moment's frozen silence.

"Go to the top of the class," murmured old Whitcutt.

The Principal sighed and seemed to sag in her chair a little. "There had to be a first time," she said quietly. "This is what my little lecture to school-leavers is all about. How you're specially privileged children, how you've been protected all your lives by biochips in your optic nerves that edit what you can see. So it always seems dark in the streets and outside the windows, wherever there might be a BLIT image waiting to kill you. But that kind of darkness isn't real—except to you. Remember, your parents had a choice, and they agreed to this protection."

Mine didn't both agree, thought Jonathan, remembering an overheard quarrel.

"It's not fair," said Gary uncertainly. "It's doing experiments on people."

Khalid said, "And it's not just protection. There are corridors here indoors that are blacked out, just to keep us out of places. To control us."

Ms. Fortmayne chose not to hear them. Maybe she had a biochip of her own that stopped rebellious remarks from getting through. "When you leave school you are given full control over your biochips. You can choose whether to take risks . . . once you're old enough."

Jonathan could almost bet that all five Club members were thinking the same thing: *What the hell, we took our risks with the Trembler and we got away with it*.

Apparently they had indeed got away with it, since when the Principal said "You can go now," she'd still mentioned nothing about punishment. As slowly as they dared, the Club headed back to the classroom. Whenever they passed side-turnings which were filled with solid darkness, Jonathan cringed to think that a chip behind his eyes was stealing the light and with different programming could make him blind to everything, everywhere.

The seriously nasty thing happened at going-home time, when the caretaker unlocked the school's side door as usual while a crowd of pupils jostled behind him. Jonathan and the Club had pushed their way almost to the front of the mob. The heavy wooden door swung inward. As usual it opened on the second kind of darkness, but something bad from the dark came in with it, a large sheet of paper fixed with a drawing-pin to the door's outer surface and hanging slightly askew. The caretaker glanced at it, and toppled like a man struck by lightning.

Jonathan didn't stop to think. He shoved past some smaller kid and grabbed the paper, crumpling it up frantically. It was already too late. He'd seen the image there, completely unlike the Trembler yet very clearly from the same terrible family, a slanted dark shape like the profile of a perched bird, but with complications, twirly bits, patterns like fractals, and it hung there blazing in his mind's eye and wouldn't go away—

—something hard and horrible smashing like a runaway express into his brain—

—burning falling burning falling—

—BLIT.

After long and evil dreams of bird-shapes that stalked him in darkness, Jonathan found himself lying on a couch, no, a bed in the school sickroom. It was a surprise to be anywhere at all, after feeling his whole life crashing into that enormous full stop. He was still limp all over, too tired to do more than stare at the white ceiling.

Mr. Whitcutt's face came slowly into his field of vision. "Hello? Hello? Anyone is there?" He sounded worried.

"Yes . . . I'm fine," said Jonathan, not quite truthfully.

"Thank heaven for that. Nurse Baker was amazed you were alive. Alive and sane seemed like too much to hope for. Well, I'm here to warn you that you're a hero. Plucky Boy

Saves Fellow Pupils. You'll be surprised how quickly you can get sick of being called plucky."

"What was it, on the door?"

"One of the very bad ones. Called the Parrot, for some reason. Poor old George the caretaker was dead before he hit the ground. The anti-terrorist squad that came to dispose of that BLIT paper couldn't believe you'd survived. Neither could I."

Jonathan smiled. "I've had practice."

"Yes. It didn't take *that* long to realize Lucy—that is, Ms. Fortmayne—failed to ask you young hooligans enough questions. So I had another word with your friend Khalid Patel. God in heaven, that boy can outstare the Trembler for twenty seconds! Adult crowds fall over in convulsions once they've properly, what d'you call it, registered the sight, let it lock in . . ."

"My record's ten and a half. Nearly eleven really."

The old man shook his head wonderingly. "I wish I could say I didn't believe you. They'll be re-assessing the whole biochip protection program. No one ever thought of training young, flexible minds to resist BLIT attack by a sort of vaccination process. If they'd thought of it, they still wouldn't have dared try it . . . Anyway, Lucy and I had a talk, and we have a little present for you. They can reprogram those biochips by radio in no time at all, and so—"

He pointed. Jonathan made an effort and turned his head. Through the window, where he'd expected to see only artificial darkness, there was a complication of rosy light and glory that at first his eyes couldn't take in. A little at a time, assembling itself like some kind of healing opposite to those deadly patterns, the abstract brilliance of heaven became a town roofscape glowing in a rose-red sunset. Even the chimney-pots and satellite dishes looked beautiful. He'd seen sunsets on video, of course, but it wasn't the same, it was the aching difference between live flame and an electric fire's dull glare: like so much of the adult world, the TV screen lied by what it didn't tell you.

"The other present is from your pals. They said they're sorry there wasn't time to get anything better."

It was a small, somewhat bent bar of chocolate (Gary always had a few tucked away), with a card written in Julie's careful left-sloping script and signed by all the Shudder Club. The inscription was, of course: *That which does not kill us, makes us stronger*.

New Ice Age,
or Just Cold Feet?

NORMAN SPINRAD

Norman Spinrad is a world figure in SF, a major force in the field from the 1960s to the present. He has lived in Paris, France, since the late 1980s, where he has been active in World SF, the international SF professionals organization, written scripts, novels and stories. He published three SF novels in the mid-1960s and then his early masterpiece, Bug Jack Barron *(1969). He has written a number of important novels, including* The Iron Dream *(1972—featuring Hitler as a pulp writer),* A World Between *(1979),* Songs from the Stars *(1980),* The Void Captain's Tale *(1983),* Child of Fortune *(1985),* Little Heroes *(1988),* Russian Spring *(1991), and* Greenhouse Summer *(1999). His nonfiction includes* Staying Alive: A Writer's Guide *(1983), based on columns in* Locus, *and* Science Fiction in the Real World *(1990), based on columns in* Asimov's. *For the last three years he has been working to draw attention to what he calls The Transformational Crisis. (For more information, see his Web site: ourworld.compuserve.com/homepages/normanspinrad).*

This story, from Nature, *is a piece of fictional journalism from the future (see Slonczewski). Linked both to the ideas behind* Greenhouse Summer *and to his "Transformational Crisis" speech, it is ironic, moral satire, a wake-up call to scientists and to everyone. It is also, as Spinrad often is, funny.*

Orbital Hilton, 14 March 2322. The highly touted First World Conference of Planetary Climatologists and Climatech Engineers on Global Cooling broke up in angry chaos on its opening day and fisticuffs were only averted by the quick action of hotel security staff, who pumped pax gas into the conference chamber before blows could be struck. It had been hoped that the neutral orbital venue would calm tempers, but unfortunately this did not prove to be the case.

The conference opened with a speech by Dr. Vladimir Bunin, chairperson of the Committee of Concerned Climatologists, rehashing the charge that the past three centuries of effort by climatech engineers to counter the twentieth and twenty-first centuries' admittedly disastrous greenhouse warming had proven all too successful, and their meddling, if not speedily countered, was about to bring on a new ice age.

Bunin contended that the recent unplanned expansion of both polar ice caps, the increase in glaciation in the northern hemisphere, the return of winter snowfall as far south as Labrador and Moscow, and the icebergs sighted in the Bering Sea and off Tierra del Fuego were not—as the climatech engineers contend—isolated anomalies, easily corrected by adjustments to orbital mirrors and occluders and a diminished output by cloud-cover generators. Instead, he said, they were aspects of a dangerous global pattern leading to a new ice age that would devastate the agricultural breadbaskets of Siberia, Alaska, Canada and Lapland, upon which the Earth's 20 billion inhabitants depend.

He demanded the halving of the area of desert covered with mylar mirroring to lower the Earth's albedo and a redeployment of the orbital mirrors now sustaining the Gulf Stream to add more heat to the atmosphere. But the most heat was generated by his attack on Qwik-grow trees and the forestry programme.

"Far too many Qwik-grow trees have been planted, and now they are spreading like weeds, completely out of control," he declared. "It was one thing to reforest the Amazon basin, the American plains, the Indonesian archipelago and Europe while we were still burning fossil fuels, but now that our energy sources are all solar and thermonuclear, these vast and ever-expanding woodlands have created a severe atmospheric carbon dioxide deficit that has seriously diminished the greenhouse effect. This can only be remedied by a return to the mass burning of coal or the setting of immense forest fires—preferably both."

This resulted not only in cries of outrage from the climatech engineer contingent, but the throwing of plastic coffee bulbs, styli, fruit, and other debris in his direction. Injury was prevented by the zero-g conditions, which rendered this fusillade ineffective, but the frustration only added to the ire of the climatech engineers, and it was a good 20 minutes before enough order could be restored for Hans Goodkin of Climatech Solutions to deliver a scathing rebuttal.

"Burn coal! Why not bring back the internal combustion engine, and to hell with the ozone layer! Or better yet, the steam locomotive, and never mind the acid rain! Burn the forests? Why settle for half-measures? Let's just nuke the trees! And while we're at it, why not drop thermonuclear charges into the craters of active volcanoes? The resulting mass eruptions would pump plenty of carbon dioxide back into the atmosphere and the red-hot lava flows would really heat things back up! Let's bring back Vesuvius and Mount St. Helens and Krakatoa!"

When the booing and hissing subsided, he continued in an even more sarcastic vein: "Dissolving the coral reefs we've rebuilt would release plenty of carbon dioxide too! And we could melt the ice-caps from orbit! And replace the mylar mirroring with black ash! After all, if we listen to you people, we'll have plenty of soot to spare!" Unwilling to wait for the uproar to die down, Goodkin just turned up the gain on his microphone to override it.

"Let Central Australia and the Sahara savannah once more become howling deserts—no problem, their millions of inhabitants can join the rest of the planet's new boat-people when the sea levels rise again and the world's reclaimed coastlands and islands return from whence they came!"

Improvised missiles began to fly again—this time from the climatologists—or rather drift ineffectually in the general direction of Goodkin in the weightless conference chamber. "You're turning the Earth into a deep freeze to line your own pockets!" someone shouted.

"You climatological Luddite snake-oil salesmen want us to turn it back into a greenhouse oven so you can make your fortunes selling air-conditioners in Antarctica and ice-boxes to Eskimos!" Goodkin shouted back.

At which point, the Concerned Climatologists attempted to storm the podium, swimming clumsily towards it through the air like a school of slow-motion sharks, and hotel security released the pax gas.

"What do a climatech engineer, a climatologist, a planet and a nymphomaniac have in common?" a reporter asked, several drinks later, in the bar.

"I'm afraid you're about to tell us," groaned another.

"They're much easier to heat up than cool down."

The Devotee

STEPHEN DEDMAN

Stephen Dedman is the author of the novels The Art of Arrow Cutting *(1997),* Foreign Bodies *(1999), and* Shadows Bite *(forthcoming in 2001) and the short story collection* The Lady of Situations *(1999). He was one of the new generation of Australian SF writers breaking out on the international scene at the end of the 1990s. He lives in Perth, West Australia, and is an associate editor of* Eidolon, *where this story appeared. You can find his colorful autobiography at www.eidolon.net. It concludes with "I have a wife, a wife-in-law, a lot of friends (including all of my ex-lovers), a mortgage, a thousand books or thereabouts, a concertina file bulging with rejection slips, a slightly out-of-date computer, an agent, and now a web page." You get the picture. He writes SF, fantasy, horror, erotica, and is published in small press and professional magazines on three continents.*

"The Devotee" is a striking hard-boiled detective story told as sociological SF, with perhaps a whiff of cyberpunk. It moves from Australia to the Caribbean with substantial political and socioeconomic underpinning. It is a fully mature piece of fiction and certainly earns a place in this book as one of the best stories of the year.

The white wall around the house was three to four meters high and free of graffiti, like all the others on the block. The wrought metal gate was black and looked as though it should've been inscribed with something from Dante. I could only see one camera, but I didn't feel like wasting time looking for the others. I stepped out of the car and showed it my wallet. "I'm Nicholas Horne. Two o'clock appointment with Mr. Hill." I even removed my hat and shades, despite the sun; Perth in February is an inferno, and the ozone hole hasn't shrunk measurably since the turn of the century. I was glad when a voice finally issued forth from a speaker inside the gate. "You're expected. Bring the car in."

"Sure." The yard was landscaped, flat as a pool table, but the house was smaller than I expected, only one storey. I parked near the front door, which opened as I walked up the ramp towards it. The man who greeted me wasn't well dressed enough to be a butler, or even a gardener. "Mr. Hill?"

"Come in." He glanced at my summer suit; maybe he was looking for a shoulder holster. Or maybe I didn't look like his idea of a private investigator, but it was too damn hot for a trenchcoat. If the house hadn't been in Dalkeith, I wouldn't even have bothered with the necktie. "You were with Missing Persons?" he asked.

"No, Vice. Mostly undercover." I'm a little over average height, a little under average weight. Hair brown with a little grey, not long, not short. Eyes about the same shade of brown. No distinguishing features to speak of. When I need to, I can be as invisible as a contact lens in a swimming pool. An elephant could forget he'd seen me. It comes in useful sometimes. Hill outweighed me by about twenty kilos, a good percentage of it hanging over the waistband of his shorts. He hadn't shaved, but he'd combed his hair across in an attempt to hide the fact that he was going bald, which was odd; genetic engineering had produced several good baldness cures over the past few years, at prices a Dalkeith resident should have been able to afford easily. Either he didn't trust new drugs, or he was opposed to genetic engineering, or he didn't like spending money on his appearance. He smelled of stale beer and tobacco smoke and flop sweat. "You quit?" he asked.

"Voluntary redundancy," I told him. Well, mostly voluntary. "Budget cuts, four years ago."

"McMinn at Missing Persons recommended you. Says you've done nearly a hundred of these cases. Hope you're more help than he was." I said nothing. Missing Persons had suffered staff cuts too, and young women who stayed out all Friday night without phoning home weren't exactly an oddity, even if their parents did live a few blocks from Millionaire's Row. "We're still waiting for a ransom demand, but there's been nothing." Hill continued, as he led the way into a loungeroom. He switched the TV off, then walked to the bar and poured himself another beer without offering me one. Maybe he thought I was on duty. I looked around the room, wondering why it looked so much the set of an old-fashioned TV sitcom. A framed photo on the mantelpiece, showing a young girl in a motorized wheelchair, answered that question; everything around me had been arranged for wheelchair access. Sets look like that because a camera dolly's about as wide and unmaneuverable as a chair. "That's her," said Hill. "Tina. My daughter."

I looked at the photo less carefully. Judging by her complexion and puppyfat, she was in her early teens, but I had no way of knowing how old the photo was. Round face, large eyes, plump lower lip, hair light brown or dark blonde. "How long has she been missing?"

"Left here yesterday morning, and didn't come home. We

phoned her but nobody answered. Missing Persons said there wasn't much they could do until she'd been gone forty-eight hours, except tell the patrols to look out for her."

"Where did she go, and how did she get there?"

"Said she was going to train before classes, before it got too hot. She wants to compete in the Special Olympics." I looked at the mantelpiece again, saw no trophies or medals. "Archery, I think," he continued. "She's not that good, but she enjoys it."

"You think?"

He shrugged. "Last I heard. She keeps trying new things. This is the only one she seems to've stuck with."

"Where?"

"Sports center out at the uni. I called them, persuaded somebody to stick their head out and see if the car was parked in any of the disabled bays. It's a white Range Rover Vogue with a wheelchair hoist, not easy to miss. No sign of it."

"University of WA?" He nodded. "Have you reported it stolen?"

"Thought of that late last night. It has a satloc—one of those tracking devices? No trace of it anywhere. The cops said it was probably parked underground or something."

"They're probably right."

"Yeah? What if it's been burnt out, or driven off a jetty? Bastards even said since Tina was eighteen now we weren't allowed to know where she was."

I said nothing, but I doubted that even the most undiplomatic cop would have said exactly that, unless Tina had asked them not to inform her parents. "How long have you lived here?" I asked.

"Why? What's that got to do with anything?"

I looked around the room again. "Let me put it another way. Does Tina think of this place as home?"

He glared at me for another few seconds, but relaxed slightly. "I guess so. She and her mother came down here six or seven years ago, just after she lost her leg. She was only twelve."

"In 2003?"

He blinked a couple of times, then nodded. "Yeah. I stayed on the station for a year or two, working, until the court case was settled."

"Did she like it down here?"

"Yeah, I guess. Aren't many wheelchair ramps up that way."

"Who were her friends?"

He shrugged. "She had school friends, but they never came here, and I couldn't tell you their last names. Besides, she's lost touch with most of them since she started Uni. Now she's on holidays, and sort of at a loose end. She has other friends on the internet, but I know nothing about them."

"Do you really think she's been kidnapped?"

"You think she's run away?" He sounded sour, but not quite angry. "In a wheelchair?"

It was more optimistic than most of the other scenarios I could imagine. "Can I talk to her mother?"

Mrs. Hill didn't tell me much more than her husband, though she was a shade more polite about it. She took me into the kitchen and made us tea while she spoke softly. Mr. Hill had already turned the car-sized TV back on, and was watching the cricket. His wife was just as reluctant to believe that Tina could have left home voluntarily. "Did she have any boyfriends?" I asked.

She started, and almost laughed. "She only had one leg," she reminded me.

"I know that. Your husband said she had friends on the net. Do you know anything about them?"

"You think she might have found a boyfriend that way?" she said, her eyebrows rising slightly, as though she'd thought of this for the first time. "I suppose it's possible, but I don't know . . ."

"What about at the sports centre? Other friends in wheelchairs, or with other disabilities?"

"I don't know any—You could ask at the center . . ."

"I will. Can I see her room, please?" Mrs. Hill blinked, then led the way. Her bedroom had the same staginess as the rest of the house, but it looked wrong for other reasons, too. Apart from a fairly new Canon desk panel net system, the books and CDs on the shelves—low shelves, naturally—and the clothes hanging in a curtained alcove, the room looked frozen in time, as though nothing had been moved in years. For a moment, I wondered whether Tina Hill had died back in 2003. I looked at the desk, then flicked the computer on. "What's the most recent photo you have of Tina?"

"We don't take many photos," said Mrs. Hill apologetically, and looked at the shelves. "Her high school yearbook is in here somewhere—ah." As she began leafing through the pages a window appeared on the Canon's screen, asking for a password. Damn. "Do you know her password?"

"What? No, I'm afraid not." She handed me the yearbook. The photo was professionally taken, and a little too prim to be glamorous, but it showed her as a very attractive young woman, even in her drab green Methodist Ladies College uniform. There was a glint in her eyes that might have been impishness, or sadness, depending on the angle of the light. Her smile was staged, like all the others on the page, as though it were just another part of the school uniform. I glanced at the screen again, and resisted the urge to swear. Things must've been much easier for detectives when people had diaries and address books. I searched the shelves for a few minutes and came up with little more than the fact that she was studying French, Spanish, medieval English, and the late 19th/early 20th Century British novels that academics still call "modern lit." She liked Central American magic realists, historical fantasies and murder mysteries, and vampire stories. Eclectic musical tastes, mostly classical, some recent, but very little that would make you want to get up and dance. I sent her mother out of the room, asking her to scan the photo and print me some copies, then looked in the places a girl might not expect her parents to look. Again, nothing: no contraceptives, no drugs, no cash, not even a vibrator. Maybe her life really was as unexciting as her parents believed—either that, or she'd taken everything she valued with her, which implied that she'd deliberately left without telling anyone and wasn't planning on coming back soon. The third alternative was that I'm not very good at thinking like a teenage girl.

I took the copied photos from the mother and left, a vaguely unpleasant taste in my mouth. Finding missing people is the staple of my diet; most of them are just hiding from their creditors and, while I don't like some of my clients, I don't lose any sleep over what I do. Sometimes it's even fun. And when I have doubts, when husbands want me to find wives who I suspect had damn good reasons for running away, then I don't take the job. I stared at the photo, wondering whether Tina would want to be found, then I headed for the university.

It was two weeks before semester began, and a Saturday to boot, and the campus was so deserted that I actually had a choice of parking spaces, so empty that I noticed how attractive the grounds and the trees and the buildings were, rather than being distracted by the students. The beefy young blond sitting behind the counter at the health club didn't look up from his magazine as he asked, "Help you?"; but at least his tone was polite.

"Who do I talk to about archery practice?"

He looked up at that, and blinked. His eyes were a startling blue. The magazine turned out to be *Scientific American*, with a cover story about wire addiction. "Archery? Try one of the clubs."

"You don't have a range here?"

"No."

"Not even for the disabled?"

He shook his head, then an idea hit him. "No, but hold on a second. I'll call the School of Human Movement; they may know something." He did that while I waited, then turned to me. "What's this about?" he asked, still polite.

I showed him the photo of Tina. "Do you know her?" He squinted. "She would've been in a wheelchair."

"Oh. I've seen her in here sometimes, but not this week, I don't think." He gestured with the receiver. "I've got Dr. Sobieski on the phone; do you want to speak to him?"

"Yeah, sure." Sobieski, at least, admitted to knowing

Tina's name, though he also swore he hadn't seen her that week. Something in his tome made me ask when he *had* last seen her. He really couldn't say. Since semester ended? Yes. This year? Yes. This month? Maybe. How often did he usually see her? "May I ask what your interest is?"

"I can't discuss it over the phone. Where's your office?"

"Under Reid Library. Do you know where that is?"

"Certainly. I'll be there in a minute." I thanked the kid, who returned his attention to his magazine. It was only a short walk from the health club to the library, most of it in the shade of some wonderful old trees. The tutorial rooms, of course, are cramped and ugly and uncomfortable, but you can't have everything.

Sobieski's office was cramped too, or maybe it was Sobieski who gave me that impression; he was shorter than I am but massively built, his arms almost as large around as my legs, his thumbs as thick and short as my big toes. His head looked as though it'd been modified to provide a minimum of handholds: hair cropped short, nose flattened, ears that seemed to've been pinned back, no neck worth mentioning. His desk was bare but for a computer, a phone, and his feet. He looked me up and down, and I resisted the urge to puff out my chest. "You're looking for Tina Hill?"

"Yes."

"Siddown. Why?"

"She hasn't come home, and her parents are worried. Do you have any idea where she might be?"

"Can I see some ID?" I handed him my wallet, showed him my license. He glanced at it, shrugged. "As I said, I haven't seen her in a couple of weeks."

"She told her parents yesterday morning that she was coming here. As far as I can tell, she didn't turn up. Her parents think she was training in archery. Was she?"

"I think so. Probably."

"You don't want to qualify that at all?" I asked drily.

He flushed slightly. "You'd have to ask her trainer. He's an archery enthusiast, and you know what enthusiasts are like."

I nodded. "Is he here?"

"Not today."

"Where could I find him?"

The flush deepened. "I don't know. I phoned him while you were walking over here. He's not at home, and he's not answering his mobile."

I didn't like the sound of that. "When did you last see him?" I asked, as casually as I could manage.

"Wednesday."

"His name?"

He hesitated, then sighed. "Jason Davy. Look, it's not what you think. He's doing his Master's degree on sports and exercise for what we used to call the maimed and limbless. I know, it's a waste of time, but he's fanatical about it."

"Why is it a waste of time?"

"Genetics, microsurgery, and prosthetics. We've all but wiped out the genetic disorders and teratogenic drugs that cause that sort of deformity, and in almost every case where someone loses a limb, it can be re-attached. Failing that, ninety percent of amputations are lower limb only, and the new lower limb prosthetics are nearly as good as the real thing—except for hands, of course. Tina lost her leg because nearly all of it was crushed, not just severed, and the accident was up in the country a hell of a long way from a hospital. She's damn lucky she didn't bleed to death before help arrived. But there'll never be enough cases like hers to justify the sort of study he's putting into this, especially not when they've already started cloning parts for transplants. Ten years from now, twenty at the most, Jason's work will be obsolete. Oh, sure, there are plenty of countries where kids are still getting their feet blown off by mines, and where they can't afford transplants or prosthetics, but they have other priorities than the Special Olympics."

"I know they've managed to clone some individual organs," I said, "but legs and arms?"

He shrugged, and what little neck he had vanished completely for a second. "I don't know a hell of a lot about cloning, but I know it's easy to tinker with the genes so that you end up with a brainless body that's no use for anything else. It needn't be a clone of the individual; as long as the tissue type is close enough, they can use rejection-suppressant drugs without any serious side effects."

"Do you think that'll ever be legal?"

He snorted. "Sure. A lot of politicians need new livers and hearts, and so do the CEOs who contribute to their campaign funds. And as long as there are wars and soldiers, there'll be a need for replacement limbs—the best ones that government can afford. And even if it's not legal, who will that stop? Hell, it's probably being tried already, somewhere. Look what happened with breast implants, or headwires. Sure, some countries banned the sale and the surgery, but they wouldn't shut down the companies that were making the stuff, and they don't prosecute anybody who goes overseas to have the op. Governments in some other countries are happy to turn a blind eye to it if it brings in foreign currency. And how much real difference is there between a headless body and a few hearts beating in a tank?" He shook his head. "I used to tell Jason he was wasting his life, but there's no point arguing with an enthusiast, and it's not as though he needs to worry about money."

"How many subjects does he have?"

"We prefer to call then 'clients,'" Sobieski said, chuckling.

"How many?"

He hesitated. "At present, none he sees regularly, at least not here. Tina's the only one who's a student here; I guess the others don't have time."

"How much time does he spend with her?"

"A couple of hours, every other day."

"And she hasn't been here in two or three weeks?"

A brief pause. "No. I thought she might have gone away on holidays."

"Can I see his office?"

"No." No hesitation, but no unusual emphasis either. "That's out of the question."

"Okay." There didn't seem any point in arguing with him. "Do you know of any of Tina's other friends?"

"No. As I told you, she wasn't my student."

"Can you give me Jason's number?"

"I've already told you, he isn't there. Look, Mr. Horne, I

have some idea how Tina's parents feel, I have kids of my own, but I think they're worrying unnecessarily. I'm sure he—sure she's okay."

It was just a tiny slip, and it might not have meant anything. I nodded, then walked out through the cluster of high-tech torture machines and back to my car.

Mrs. Hill seemed surprised to see me back so soon. "Have you found her?"

"No, but I may have found a clue. Has she ever mentioned a Jason Davy, or Davies?"

She blinked, obviously startled. "No, I don't think so . . ."

Damn. "May I have another look at her computer?" I booted it again, waited for it to ask for a password. 'Jason' was too short, the system demanded a 6-character minimum, so I tried different combinations of Jason and Davy, variously spelt. The correct word, which I should have thought of earlier, was "Jason!" A menu and another window appeared on the screen; the window showed the view through the camera mounted in the frame at the top: me from hairline to bottom rib. Tina sitting in the same chair must have been a few centimeters shorter; anyone using the computer as a videophone would have seen her face and chest and, if she hid the wheelchair, nothing to indicate that she had a missing leg. I glanced at the yearbook photo again: not quite beautiful, but more than conventionally pretty. I asked Mrs. Hill to bring me a cup of tea, and ran a quick search for files containing the words "Jason" or "Davy" in their heading or text. I also glanced at her address book, diary, web sites most often and most recently visited, and her email. I found the photos in under three minutes. Mrs. Hill was still out of the room, so I opened one, titled only "Jason, Dec 2009." It showed a young man, mid twenties, naked but for a wet towel around his waist. He was handsome in an unremarkable way, clean-shaven and square-chinned, with dark wavy collar-length hair. He wasn't bulked up like Sobieski, but he was obviously an athlete, with powerful-looking wrists and shoulders. The photo looked as though it had been taken without warning, or much skill on the part of the photographer, with a flash, at low resolution, and from a low angle. The setting looked like standard motel decor. I stared at this for a moment, then brought up another photo, titled simply "Me, by Jason, Dec 09." This was a high-res picture, larger than the screen could display and I had to scroll down from the top to see it all. Her expression was quietly winsome with a slight hint of nervousness in her eyes, though maybe that was my imagination. Her smile, at least, was more sincere than in her yearbook photo. Her breasts were bare, very large, and very lovely. She was lying on a bed, naked, her long left leg stretched out before her, the stump of her right, no longer than my hand, pointed to the camera.

The setting, again, looked like a typical motel room, possibly the same one, but this time the shot was posed and some care had been taken with the lighting and focus—though I don't know enough about digital photography to pick how much of that might've been done later, with the software equivalent of a darkroom trick. I do know that digital cameras, like Polaroids before them, have always owed a lot of their popularity to the fact that the photos don't require developing; if you'd taken a photo like this to a commercial developer, he would have—

I had to stop and think about that. Most would simply have refused to develop it. The "Confidential" developers who used to work through adult bookshops frequently sold copies of hardcore photos given to them to develop to the sleazier pornsites. But what would they have done with a shot like this? Was there a market for it?

I heard Mrs. Hill returning, and closed both photo files just before she walked in. She had a willow pattern cup and saucer in one hand, a magazine—*Woman's Day*—in the other. She handed me the cup of tea, then opened the magazine. "You mentioned Jason Davy."

"Yes," I said, staring at the address book. There were two phone numbers—one a mobile, the other a UWA extension—and an e-mail address for Jason Davy, but nothing to say where he lived.

"I knew I'd seen the name before, but I couldn't remember where," said Mrs. Hill. "I don't think Tina ever mentioned him, but it says here he's studying at the University, so maybe they've met." She handed me the magazine. I saw a young man who looked very like the Jason of the photograph—though dressed in an expensive suit and with not a hair out of place—before I read the caption or recognized the man standing next to him. Davy isn't an uncommon name, and it hadn't occurred to me to look for a connection to Charles Davy, the local beer baron. Owning a successful brewery in Australia is like having a licence to print money, and Davy was reputed to have billions in assets, including a few famous paintings, some high-priced real estate, a successful FM station, some prize-winning racehorses, and several state and federal politicians. It was rumoured that much of his income came from shares in a company that produced wireheading hardware, stunsticks and missile guidance systems, but this was unproven. His wife had been a celebrated beauty, and his youngest and middle sons—Roman and Jason—favoured her, though the heir apparent, Gavin, had already inherited some of his father's gut and a few of his chins. It only took me a few seconds to read the text; Gavin, it seemed, was no longer one of Australia's most eligible bachelors, having married a young woman alleged to be a journalist. Roman and Jason were still available, however, at least according to the text. I didn't see Tina in any of the photos, though I noticed someone who might have been Sobieski in a crowd of athletes and sports commentators, all of them holding stubbies. The wedding, the magazine gushed, had cost nearly half a million dollars, which made it a very expensive beer commercial.

I nodded, for Mrs. Hill's benefit. "He's doing his graduate degree in human movement, and he's helped her work out a training program."

"Do you think she has a crush on him?"

I stared at the magazine, not wanting to look at her. "I think she might," I said. I took out my compad, and began pulling data from the Canon.

*   *   *

I've known Teri Lovell for half of my life, or half of her life if you prefer; either way, it's a little under seventeen years. We met in a film class in our first year at uni, and helped each other out when I was in vice and she was doing research for her dissertation. That dissertation, on masturbation and technology in the AIDS years, became a bestseller—particularly after she admitted to doing a short stint in a peepshow and a much longer one as a phone sex operator as part of her research. She makes a good living as a consultant, writer and guest lecturer, but still lives in Perth because her ex-husband has custody of their child. I showed her the photos of Tina I'd downloaded from the desk-panel, giving her as little background as I could get away with. "What do you think?"

"Interesting. I could be wrong—this is her collection, not his—but if you look at the earliest photos, he started off with portraits. Then, a few months later, semi-nudes. Look at this one, from August; it's not set up as well as the others, but if I'm any judge, that's afterglow. Look at the flush, and her eyes. So they'd probably been lovers for several months before she let him photograph her taboo zone, which for her is her stump, not her crotch." She scrolled through the photos. "Even in the early shots when she's fully dressed, she hasn't kept any that show her below the waist, as though she'd rather not be reminded of it. And here's a much later one; see, just a hint of pubic hair at the bottom there? It looks to me as though he's proceeded at a rate that she's comfortable with, letting her adjust to the idea that he finds her amputation arousing rather than distressing. She obviously likes and trusts him, at the very least; you can see it in her eyes. You say he chose to specialise in care for amputees?"

The bad taste had returned to my mouth, stronger than ever before. "Yes, that's right. Do you think he did this because he's attracted to them? To indulge a fetish?"

"They prefer to call themselves 'devotees,'" she said, nodding. "In this case, that may be appropriate. While it was probably her amputation that made her attractive to him in the beginning, he hasn't objectified her in any of these photos. All of them show her face, which suggests that he thinks of her as a person. I wish I could say that of more so-called erotica." She looked at me for the first time in minutes. "You have a problem with this, don't you?"

"Yes," I admitted. "I can't understand how someone could be attracted to . . . well, to a deformity. A mutilation."

"I don't either, and I've spoken to quite a few devotees, mostly over the net. Most amputees don't understand them either; some love them, some find them unbearably creepy. I guess most of us would rather be loved for who we are than what we look like, but how often do you think that happens?" She glanced over her shoulder at the shelves full of videos and magazines. "I've heard Freudians try to explain the attraction in terms of childhood experience, but most of the devotees themselves don't seem to bear out any of their theories. But there have been entire cultures which considered footbinding or female genital mutilation aesthetically pleasing, and look how many men are fascinated by super-sized breasts, some larger than any that ever existed in nature. You think that cutting a woman's breasts open to insert blobs of silicon isn't a form of mutilation? Yet that's considered sane—obviously if big is good, then enormous must be better, right?—while finding pregnant women attractive is considered a perversion.

"There are a lot of amputee websites, if you're interested, or I have some videos." Teri's townhouse is a museum of reputed erotica that the Addams family would think twice before visiting. "Most of them are done by amateurs, enthusiasts, and they're very softcore—women dressing or undressing, bathing or showering, doing exercises or even household chores, with maybe a little talking dirty or masturbation. The more unusual or specialised the fetish, the more men'll pay for softcore," she explained. "Though there's some professionally made hardcore on the market as well—mostly landmine victims, if I had to guess."

I shuddered. Sometimes I wonder if Teri isn't trying to shock me; she's almost forgotten what it's like to be shocked herself by anything less than paedophilia or rape or torture, and maybe she needs someone like me as a barometer. A horrible thought occurred to me. "Enough of a market that they'd bother mutilating women just for the trade?"

She stared, then shook her head violently. "No, that'd be insane."

"How many porn stars had plastic surgery?"

"That's different."

"And what about snuff movies? There's a market for those."

She sighed. "Most snuff and torture movies are either fake, or made by secret police and sold to make a little extra cash for their pension funds. Disposing of a body is easy if you're in that sort of business, but caring for an amputee is expensive. Even if you could re-attach the limb, it just wouldn't be worth it."

"What if money wasn't a problem?"

"Designer porn?" She hesitated. "It's possible, certainly, but I've never heard of it being done, and it'd be a lot cheaper to use computer animation."

I nodded, and looked at the photo of Tina on the screen. The trust in her eyes was beautiful, and almost palpable, and I felt I had to know she was okay. Another horrible thought occurred to me. "If more is better . . . would a devotee find a double-amputee more attractive than—" I couldn't finish the sentence, but Teri obviously understood; she closed her eyes, bit her lip, then shook her head slowly.

"Not everyone believes more is better, Nick," she said. "I don't think that whoever took those photographs would do something like that. It's possible, but I don't think it's likely."

"How sure are you of that?"

She looked at the screen for a long time, her expression sour. "Not sure enough to sleep easily tonight, damn you."

It was dark by the time I drove home from Teri's, and I was glad I'd recharged the fuel cells; the solar panel can barely run the air-conditioner. There was a long black Mercedes parked across the road from my flat, looking as out of place in my low-rent neighborhood as my Suzuki had in Dalkeith, and I wondered if someone had died. I walked wearily up the stairs; if I'd been looking up, I might have seen the guy standing outside my door before he saw me, but

I was too damn tired. We stared at each other down the corridor; he was black—African-American, not Indigine—and bald and about two metres tall. He wore a bomber jacket, black jeans, and black Reebok basketball boots. "Mr. Horne?"

"Yes," I said, wearily. "And you are?"

"Harry Keyes," he replied, a hint of injured pride in his voice. It took me a second to place the name, but he'd been suspended for a season, and I was never a big basketball fan anyway. "Somebody wants to meet you."

I nodded. "In the limo?"

"No. I have to take you to him. Shall we go?" He was polite, I'll give him that; he opened the back door of the limo for me, and encouraged me to help myself to a drink from the bar and watch the Wildcats game on the TV. I declined both, graciously, and he turned the radio on softly. Davy's station, of course. "Do you mind if I use the phone?"

"Go for it."

I called Tina; her system was screening calls, as always, but it put me through to her. I told her where I was and as much as I knew of what was happening. I'd expected to be driven back to Dalkeith—it was common knowledge that the Davys lived on Millionaire Row, in a house that realised his more-is-better dreams—but instead Keyes took me to Perth's ugliest skyscraper, an aluminium monstrosity propped up by flying buttresses. I read somewhere that the tallest buildings in a town reflect that society's values; if so, this one screamed that money mattered and beauty didn't. Keyes patted me down while we rode the elevator. "I'm not armed," I assured him.

"I know. They don't want this conversation recorded." He took my compad, phone and camera, then led me through a grandiose foyer into a book-lined office with a view of the river and King's Park. The man behind the enormous antique desk was in his early forties, and his designer sharkskin jacket and yellow silk tie indicated that he lived in an entirely air-conditioned world. Either that, or he was as cold-blooded as a reptile. Classical music played softly in the background; it sounded like a waltz, but not one I recognized. His voice was crisp and cold, like Basil Rathbone's Sherlock Holmes.

"Mr. Horne, I understand you're looking for information on Jason Davy. I thought we might save you some time." He glanced at his gold watch, while Keyes leaned on the door behind me. Sobieski must have told Davy that I'd been asking questions; I wondered how much the family had given the University over the years. "And, of course, prevent any inaccurate information being disseminated. Jason Davy is a young man of excellent character and great compassion who, as well as sharing his father's interest in sports, has devoted himself to improving the lives of the differently abled." He paused for breath, and I interjected, "Are you going to talk non-stop until seven am, or can I ask the occasional question?"

Keyes turned a laugh into a cough, and Sharkskin stared at me. "Why seven am?"

"At seven am, Tina Hill will have been missing for forty-eight hours. At that point, it becomes a police matter."

The temperature in the room dropped by a few degrees. "Tina Hill?"

"Pretty girl. Eighteen years old, strawberry blonde hair, one leg."

He smiled thinly. "Ah, yes. Jason drew up a training schedule for her, did he not?"

"I understand that he did, yes. How long has he been missing?"

"He's not missing. We know where he is."

"And where is that?"

Another glance at the Rolex. "The USA."

"And Tina Hill?"

"Why are you concerned with Tina Hill?"

"Her parents want to know where she is, and have paid me to find out. It seems likely that Jason Davy was the last person to see her, which suggests that the police will want to speak to him in," I glanced at my own watch, "about ten hours and thirteen minutes."

Sharkskin shook his head. "The police will check with Immigration, and discover that Tina Hill left Perth for Sydney yesterday, then caught a connecting flight to LA. I'm quite sure the immigration officers and flight crew will remember her." The smile remained thin, though there was an extra hint of smugness in it.

I stood. "Thank you, that's all I needed to know. See you at the feeding frenzy."

"I'm afraid not," he replied, without raising his voice. "You may already know that as Tina Hill turned eighteen last May, she is legally a responsible adult. Yes? Do you also know that her parents are living off the compensation she receives for the accident in which she was injured? That the mortgage on the house in which they live is in her name, not in theirs? That their attempts at establishing businesses left them bankrupt, or that they have not attempted to find any work in some three years? They are to put it bluntly, trash. And I think you also need to know that they will not be requiring your services after this evening; you will be paid for your time and reimbursed for any expenses you may have incurred, and the matter will rest there." He leaned back in the fancy leather chair, steepled his fingers and studied his manicure. "You may also be interested to know how much we know about you. We have researchers of our own, you see." He tapped the space bar on his keyboard, and the aquarium screensaver was replaced by a page of text. I could see it reflected in the window behind him, but not well enough to read any of it. "Nicholas Arthur Horne, born in Melbourne, July 20th, 1976. Father a successful barrister and lecturer in law, mother a professor of reproductive medicine, still married and now living in Melbourne again. You attended Murdoch University, where you failed Law, then joined the police service in 1996. You were reprimanded on seventeen occasions for excessive use of a stunstick while intervening in domestic disputes. During your time in the vice squad, you set a state record for stress leave, most of it taken after a pimp who you'd been unable to convict was shot in 2005." I didn't deign to answer that; I had a good alibi, and had never even been charged with the murder. "Your superior was heard to refer to you as a 'Coyote'—a reference, perhaps, to your running speed?"

"He said 'Quixote,'" I corrected. "As in the Don."

"Ah, I see," he said, raising his eyebrows slightly. I'd surprised him, and that obviously didn't happen often. "Tilting at windmills, and so on. Let's see, what else? You've never married, and have no known children. Since 2006, you've been working as a private investigator, specializing in surveillance video work and locating missing persons, mostly for debt collection agencies. While you've managed to avoid a criminal record and stay out of debt yourself, you clearly do not have the money or the credit rating for a protracted legal battle, or even a short one. On the other hand, you would not be eligible for legal aid." The smile became a little wider. "If you truly believe that there is no such thing as bad publicity, then I will be happy to disillusion you. If not, I would recommend that you not attempt to take this any further—and that, Mr. Horne, is the best free legal advice you are ever likely to receive. If there's anything else you need to know, I suggest you ask it now. My time is expensive."

I didn't doubt it. "Where in the USA?"

"I'm not obliged to tell you that."

"When will they be back?"

"In all probability, they will both return to Perth in time for the beginning of the academic year. Maybe a few weeks later."

I nodded, and turned towards the door. Keyes opened it for me, and we walked back to the elevator. "I wonder how much his teeth cost," I muttered.

Keyes smiled. "More than you could afford to pay, though I got to admit I've thought about it myself." He handed the compad, camera and phone back. "But I don't think you need to worry about the girl," he said confidently, when we reached the car park. "Jason wouldn't hurt her. He's not that sort of guy."

"Uh-huh."

Keyes rolled his eyes. "I'm not saying that just because I work for his dad. I mean it."

"Have you met the girl?"

"No . . . The family's known about her for months, but Jason's never brought her home. He drives everywhere himself; I haven't even had to pick him up from a pub or a party for more'n a year."

"Do you know where Jason's gone?"

"Shit no, and I wouldn't tell you if I did." He went to open the back door for me, and I asked, "Mind if I ride in the front? I feel like I'm at a funeral, otherwise."

"Fine by me."

We rode through the city in silence, then up Thomas Street. "What's this thing like to drive?"

He grunted. "She's a tank. Lots of armour, and it really slows her down. Security and anti-theft and safety features up the wazoo. The guns are on my side," he touched the door, and a panel slid down to reveal two pistols; one a needler, the other a .357 Magnum Mini Cop. "So don't even think about doing anything stupid."

The thought had crossed my mind, but it quickly faded. "Did Davy tell you to shoot me?"

He laughed, a single "huff," like a lion that's not irritated enough to roar. "Shit no. The boss doesn't do things like that. Doesn't need to. He just told me to get you and take you to Norman, and Norman doesn't like violence either. Threats, sometimes, but mostly bribery. He says he's never met a man he couldn't scare or buy." He said this without any hint of irony, or any emotion at all.

"There can't be much he can't afford. Davy, I mean."

A shrug. "He wants his kids to have the best, and doesn't worry much whether they want to go into the business or what they want to do."

I nodded. He talked basketball until he realised I wasn't interested, then women, then asked what it'd been like working in Vice. "Frustrating," I replied.

"Yeah, I bet." We said nothing more until we were back outside my place, when he bade me goodnight and told me to be cool. I walked up to the flat, let myself in, fed the cats, switched the kettle on, and sat there stewing while the tea brewed. I refused to let Norman fire me when he hadn't even hired me; if the Hills wanted to stop me looking for their daughter, they were going to have to tell me themselves.

It was nine forty-five, and I wanted to call the Hills before they went to bed, but there were other things I had to do first. I really felt like beating information out of someone, but Hill probably wouldn't know where Tina was, neither would Sobieski, and Sharkskin Norman would be too well guarded. Instead, I mailed my pet hacker Ratcliffe. He responded within a minute, but I don't think he ever sleeps; he likes to work on so many jobs at once that he can cause a bytelock single-handedly, and his diet seems to consist of caffeine pills washed down with Jolt. Despite his nickname, he looks more like a raccoon than a rat, with a strong hint of squirrel. I asked him if he could confirm that Jason Davy and Tina Hill had left the country. "Do you know what airline?" he asked.

"Only that they supposedly flew to Sydney from the domestic terminal some time on Friday, then caught a connecting flight to LA."

"Shit. This could take a while; can I call you back?"

"I'll be here." He mailed me the information just before ten, complete with flight numbers and—wonder of wonders—hotel reservations. "Once I had one flight, the easiest thing to do was track it back to a travel agent and see what they had for them," he said. "Little business called Galloway's Travels, with lousy security. Looks like they've gone away for Valentine's Day."

I nodded. They'd flown the whole way by jet, including Concorde from Sydney to LA, which was unusual for tourists; most preferred the zeppelin flights where first class was more comfortable, economy much cheaper, and jet-lag minimal. They were staying in the Airport Courtesy Inn in LA, but were probably already on the shuttle back to LAX to catch a flight to Miami. From there, they were booked on another flight to Cuba, where they'd be staying in the Eldorado Hotel, room 311. They were returning to Australia by jet as well, leaving Cuba on the twenty-first. "Thanks, Rat."

"Don't mention it." I stared at the screen for a moment, then called the Hill home. Mr. Hill told me that they'd found out that Tina was safe, and would pay me for the day and my expenses if I sent them a bill. I said I'd e-mail it to them, and quickly typed up an invoice and sent it. Mrs. Hill called back five minutes later.

"What's this four thousand for finder's fee, photographic work, and travel expenses? What have you found? What photograph? Where?"

"I've found your daughter; she's in Havana, with Jason Davy."

"Havana?"

"In Cuba."

There was a long silence. "They told us she was in LA," she said, sounding genuinely puzzled. "Why would she go to Cuba?"

Actually, I knew a lot of reasons for going to Cuba (many more than I could imagine for visiting LA). Within a few months of Castro's death, the country had reverted to a free-market economy, though "black market economy" would have been more accurate. Like Miami or Atlantic City, Havana was considered an "open city" for organised crime, with enough opportunities for a shitload of Mafia clans. The Miami-based Genovese and Gambino families controlled most of the semi-legitimate rackets that appealed to tourists, while the Russian Mafia catered to—and preyed on—other local businesses. It was said you could buy anything in La Habana, from headwires to nukes, though the premier tourist attractions were gambling and prostitution, as they had been in the Batista days. The brothels were reputedly able to pander to any preference or fetish imaginable, given sufficient notice, and brought in nearly as much foreign currency as cigars and rum.

Of course, Cuba's location made it a popular destination for retirees from Florida, many of them seeking what had eluded Juan Ponce de Leon. Many pharmaceutical companies had branches there, and often tested new drugs on the populace. Rejuvenation techniques, miracle cures and cosmetic surgery illegal in the US were plentiful, as were surgeons eager for a quick buck. Rumour had it that it was also the place for getting an illegal transplant—you could always say you'd blown the money at the casinos, or needed open-heart surgery after over-exerting yourself at one of the brothels—or for having yourself cloned. And, presumably, for other sorts of surgery. "I don't know," I replied.

She thought about this for a moment. "What about the photograph?"

"I'm going to have to travel to get it. I'd already booked a flight before your husband fired me, and there's no refund at this sort of notice. I can postpone, but not cancel."

"We can't pay you this much!"

"I think you can," I replied. "Both Norman and your husband said you'd cover my expenses." Neither had specified "reasonable expenses," but Norman probably wasn't familiar with the concept. Hill might squawk but he'd cave in quickly enough; he was a loser if I'd ever met one. "He didn't tell me exactly how much he was paying you, but I gather it was a bundle. What is he doing, paying off your mortgage?" No reply. I sat there, barely breathing, hoping that I'd read Mrs. Hill correctly, that she loved her daughter even if she didn't know her. Tina deserved that much. "Did Norman speak to you, or to your husband?"

"To Geoff," she said, after a moment's hesitation. "He makes the—the decisions about money. I'll have to check this with him. Can I call you back?"

"As long as you do it before eleven. I have to pack." I hit the disconnect key, then called the airport.

About a day and a half later—early morning, Cuban time—I staggered off an Airbus packed with senior citizens into Jose Marti International Airport, destination of Christ knows how many hijackers over the years. Unlike Tina, I hadn't been lucky enough to take the Concorde, or travel business class (my credit rating didn't stretch that far; I would have flown Garuda to save a few extra bucks, if all of their remaining planes hadn't been commandeered as troop carriers for the duration), and I'd flown straight through to make up for their lead. Qantas did their best to make the trans-Pacific flight bearable, including making the food edible and the tea hot and strong, but I was still badly jet-lagged by the time I arrived at LAX. I devoted as much time as I could to reading Tina's diary and the mail Jason had sent her; both were so carefully worded that they might as well have been ciphered, with no mention of Cuba or even of travel. I also studied a Lonely Planet travel survival kit and Spanish phrase-book, only watching the in-flight movies when I could no longer focus on the print. The movies didn't seem to make any sense, but whether that was because they were cut or because I fell asleep during pivotal scenes or whether they were just dumb movies, I have no idea. I spent less than an hour in Miami, just time enough to buy some US cash; flights to Cuba were almost as frequent as buses.

The taxi that took me to the hotel was an old Lada Riva, driven by a skinny Rastafarian who looked to be in his late forties. "Hey, ya don't want to go there, mon," he said, when I told him my destination. "That's for old folks. I can take ya someplace better, lots of empty rooms. Why ya come here, anyway?"

"I'm meeting a friend," I replied. "At the Eldorado."

"Long way to come to meet a friend. Ya English?"

"Australian. And I thought I might do a little shopping while I was here."

He grinned. His jagged nicotine-stained teeth looked like modern art. "I dig, mon. Well, whatever ya want, I can take ya where ya can get the best price."

"I hoped you could. What if I needed a gun?"

"Easy, mon. How big and how many?"

"Just a handgun, a small one. And a stunstick, too, if you know someone who sells those." I'd thought of bringing both with me, but there was the risk that US Customs would ask to search my luggage. In the end, I just brought an overnight bag small enough for hand luggage, with a few books, a few changes of clothes, a camera, a pair of adjustable shades, a penlight, and a Swiss Army knife.

The driver shrugged. We were making slow progress, stuck behind a '51 Oldsmobile held together with wire, poster paint and santeria symbols; I could see push-bikes that were making better time. The taxi wasn't air-conditioned—it didn't even have power steering—and it smelled of dust and cigar smoke and scorched plastic, though the weather was pleasantly cool compared to a Perth summer. "I'll take ya to a place I know," he said. "Anything else?"

"What about a hospital?"

He looked at me in the rear-view mirror, curiosity plain despite his shades. "Why a hospital, mon?"

"I was thinking of getting my head wired," I replied. He stared, and then burst out laughing, nearly sending us into the rear of the Oldsmobile. He calmed down a few seconds later, and shook his head. "Shit, mon, if ya want a souvenir, why don't ya just get a tattoo? Ya think they sell headwires to anyone who just walk off the street?" I said nothing. "Folks who have they heads wired have habits," he continued. "They have the wire, they don't need coke or smack or ice or hyper or any other that shit. Now the same families sell the headwires as sell the shit. Ya see the problem?"

"I think so." This hadn't occurred to me before, but it wasn't hard to work out. "They'd rather have a customer who keeps paying."

"Right. So they only do that headwire shit if they think ya can do them some big favour sometime. Ya a writer, mon?"

"Why?"

"Ya ask a lot of questions, but ya don't know the answers. Ya want a guide or a guardian, call me." He handed me a card, with his name—Raphael—and a phone number. "I know this island, lived here for years, and ya don't know it at all." He drove me through the international district, the Vedado, where the grand old hotels were towered over by glass and metal and poured concrete boxes identical to those in almost any other city in the world. There were no posters or billboards commemorating Castro or Che any more, and few Cuban flags; all of the signs I saw were in English, and most bore familiar logos and slogans. The Malecon was emptier than the guidebook had led me to expect, and I glanced at my watch: 7:43, Sunday morning, February 14th. I wondered who the santeria equivalent of St. Valentine was, and decided I didn't need to know. Raphael drove me to a hockshop where I bought a Grendel P-12 with a spare clip, an ankle holster, a Hyundai telescoping stunstick, a wrist spring rig for the stick, a roll of gaffer tape, a few small tracking tags, and a signal locator. "Ya want a vest, too, mon?"

"Already wearing one." It was synthetic spider silk with

inserts, supposedly proof against any handgun except a needler; my mother brought it back from the US and gave it to me when I made detective. "How much do I owe you?"

It was about twice what I would've paid in Miami, including Raphael's kickback, but without any paperwork or waiting period. "Where to now?"

"The Eldorado."

Raphael was right about the Eldorado; the resemblance to a retirement village social club was alarming, right down to a faintly antiseptic smell almost as bad as the faint stink of sweat and decay in the streets outside, but I could see why Jason had chosen it. The whole place had obviously been designed for wheelchair access, with not a staircase or escalator or steep ramp in sight. I checked in, looked around the lobby, and saw a café to one side with a great view of the lifts and the doorway. I went up to my room, which looked like a clone of a few dozen other hotel rooms I'd stayed in except for the view of the slums. I took a quick shower, changed my chinos and sweater for a suit and tie, then returned to the café. They kept a rack of US, Canadian and European newspapers; I borrowed a hardcopy of *The Times*, ordered a Continental breakfast and a Cuban coffee, and sat where I could watch the lobby without being conspicuous. I took out my compad and e-mailed Ratcliffe, asking if he could access the hotel's computer and confirm that Tina and Jason had checked in. I looked business-like enough that the staff left me alone, except to refresh my muddy coffee. I read the paper in the vain hope of finding some news from Australia, then browsed for a while, checking out the Cuban private hospitals (the public hospital system, I was pleased to see, had survived Castro's death) and the amputee fetish websites. There were ads for new hardcore videos, offering a wide variety of women—mostly African or Asian, probable landmine victims, but there were also a few Caucasians, including the promise of a "double amputee special" scheduled for release later in the year. It was probably only a coincidence, but it left a bad taste that no amount of coffee could mask.

Ratcliffe sent me mail confirming that Tina and Jason had checked in to room 311 just before noon yesterday, and had ordered a room service breakfast for eight thirty this morning. He had no way of knowing whether they were still in the room unless they watched some of the pay TV stations or used the phone, which they hadn't. I waited, watching people come and go. It was a measure of how respectable the Eldorado was that I was interrupted less than once per hour, and offered nothing more illegal than Peruvian cocaine. Tina and Jason emerged from the elevator at three minutes before one am, and he pushed her chair towards the restaurant. I palmed my camera and took a few photos, then put the paper back on the rack and followed them.

The photos I'd seen of Tina hadn't quite done her justice, though they'd come close. Maybe it was just that her smile was a little more genuine now than it had been then—excitement making her eyes sparkle a little more intensely—though she was obviously still nervous about something. My table wasn't close enough to theirs for me to follow the conversation—even using the mike in my compad—and I never have learnt to lip-read, but there was no indication that she wasn't there voluntarily; in fact, they looked like honeymooners. I could've left—I had the photos to show Mrs. Hill, and Tina certainly seemed safe—but something still didn't seem right. No one jets from Perth to Havana with honourable intentions; that'd be like going to Casablanca for the waters. Even with Bali ruled out by the civil wars in Indonesia, there were many other places they could've gone for a romantic island holiday.

I watched them eat, then followed them as he pushed her chair down 23rd Street, la Rampa, to the Malecon. Shadowing them was made easier by Jason's constant, "Dispenseme, excuse me, excuse me," as he tried to steer the wheelchair over the uneven paving and through the crowd. There were plenty of tourists and locals to hide behind; the tourists looked better-fed, the locals better-dressed, and none of them seemed to be in any hurry.

Jason and Tina spent a few hours sight-seeing along the Malecon and in Centro Habana, admiring the art-deco and pre-baroque houses, the stained glass and the faded beauty of the old façades, the street musicians, the santeria shrines, and the swimmers in their tiny swimsuits, then returned to the hotel. I followed them, wondering whether I should keep waiting (for what?), confront them, or call it quits and see what else Havana had to offer. I had a feeling that I was wasting my own time and gambling a lot of money on a not-very-reliable gut instinct. When he wheeled her into the lift, I called for them to hold it. I left at the third floor, and offered to help get her wheelchair through the door. "You're from Australia?" she asked, while Jason fumed.

I hadn't thought my accent was that distinct. "Yes. Perth."

She laughed. "That's amazing! My first time overseas, and the first person I meet is from home. I'm Tina."

"Nick."

Jason blinked, but Tina didn't seem to notice anything odd. "What brings you here to Cuba? Business?"

"Yes. You?"

She hesitated, and looked at Jason, who shook his head very slightly. "Just a holiday," she said, soberly.

"Well, are you free for dinner?" I asked. "It's been too long since I've seen anyone from home."

"I'm afraid not." We'd reached the door of 311 by now. "We're going to—well, we have other plans."

"Tomorrow night?"

"No, we—" Jason opened the door and I wheeled Tina inside, taking the opportunity to stick a small tracking tag under the arm of the chair. He kept the door open, obviously expecting me to leave. "I'm sorry," he said. "Our schedule is pretty full."

"Pity."

Tina smiled. "It was nice meeting you, Nick."

"And you," I said, just as sincerely. "Can you do me a small favour?"

"What?" asked Jason, before she could answer. I didn't look at him. "Call your mother," I said to Tina. "Tell her you're okay, and explain to her why you came here without telling her. She's worried about you." There was a long silence, then Jason took a step towards me, his fists clenched.

I smiled, and flicked my wrist so that the stunstick slid into my hand and open, with the "On" switch under my thumb and the tip a handbreadth from his face. "Back off, and shut the door," I said, softly. "Then tell me what you're doing here, and I'll go."

Jason took a step back from the stick, and shut the door behind him. "It's very simple," he said, stiffly. "Not that it's any of your goddamn business, but we're here for a transplant. A laboratory here has cloned a new leg for Tina."

"You can't clone a leg."

He shrugged. "Actually, you can, but only as part of a more or less complete body, minus most of the brain. I know, this is illegal in Australia, but I don't see any difficulty in getting back home if the operation was done here. It's not as though we're importing spare parts, or anything. We couldn't tell her parents because my father wouldn't trust them to keep it a secret; they might have tried to stop us if they'd known where we were going. This way, it's a—" He blanked for a moment.

"Fait accompli?" I suggested. Nice to know that university Latin can be of some use.

"Exactly."

"This must have been expensive."

He shrugged. "It was a present from my father. Now, will you get the fuck out of our room?"

I stared at him, unable to think of anything to say, and feeling incredibly foolish. I still didn't trust him or like him, but it seemed clear that I'd misjudged him; I couldn't have asked for a better sign that he cared more about Tina than about her amputation. I didn't really have an opinion on cloning human bodies for spare parts; I'd never needed one before, nor ever expected to. I looked at Tina instead; she looked more innocent than an eighteen-year-old should, but I guess she'd had a sheltered life. She certainly didn't seem to be under any duress, or in any danger, and she was obviously more scared of me than she was of him. I switched the stunstick off, and telescoped it down. "Sure," I said, "but do me a favor? Call your mother, as soon as you can?"

"I'm not going home," she said, with astonishing calm.

"To Perth, yes, but not . . ." She reached out and grabbed Jason's hand. I nodded.

"Good luck," I said. "Sorry I disturbed you." I walked back to my room, called Mrs. Hill, told her Tina was okay, and mailed her the photos. Then I pulled up the airline sites and booked myself on the cheapest available flights back to Perth. That, it turned out, meant leaving Havana on Monday afternoon, which I was happy to do.

I was still too jet-lagged to sleep, so I decided to see some more of the city while I had the chance. I caught a crowded local bus, or guagua, to Habana Vieja, and walked back towards the beach, just looking around. The feeling of history, of great events, of a love of beauty, of a certain exasperated but not extinguished pride, was exactly unlike the feeling I always get from Perth or Melbourne. The sun was setting by the time I reached the Malecon; people were deserting the beach, but the boulevard was still crowded. I noticed an attractive young woman, a teenaged girl and a baby standing by a poster advertising the Sans Souci casino while they waited for the guagua. The baby was about a year old, and had obviously only recently learnt to walk. The girl looked about thirteen, and wore a sloppy joe over her tiny swimsuit; her legs were nearly as long as those of the scantily-clad woman depicted on the poster, but she lacked the come-hither look. The woman—her sister?—looked more appraising, but I smiled politely and walked past them. I've nothing against sex workers, but glamour doesn't work on me any more; once I know I'm being lied to, I—

Something went click in my brain, very faintly, like a small thing suddenly dying. I turned around and looked back at the poster, the girl, and the baby. Then I whispered, "Oh, shit," and reached for my phone.

I called the Eldorado, and asked to be put through to room 311. No reply. I asked the receptionist when they'd left, telling her I'd arranged to meet them for dinner and was running late. Their taxi had arrived at six, she said. Did she know where they'd gone? We hadn't agreed on a restaurant beforehand. No, she didn't know. I thanked her, hit the disconnect button, and wondered what to do next. It took me more than a minute to remember the tracking tag on Tina's chair; unfortunately, the signal locator was back in my room. I called Raphael and asked him if he could pick me up.

The tag was an active transponder with limited battery power; I was able to activate it with the locator, and we followed the signal towards the airport. "Do you know any hospitals out this way?"

Raphael shrugged. "No, mon. It the warehouse district."

"Anything else?"

"Clubs and brothels," he said, after a moment's hesitation. "Private, members only."

"Fetishes?" He looked blank, and the word wasn't in my guidebook. "Kink? Weird shit?"

"I don't know, mon. I never been inside."

By triangulating the signals, we managed to pinpoint the source to an anonymous house in a suspiciously empty palm-lined street: no cars, no bicycles, not even kids playing stickball. There was a large wooden door, a portale, set into a whitewashed stone wall, with balconies above it but no windows on the ground floor. There was a smaller door in the portale, and a hatch at eye level inside this small door. There was no sign on or near the door—only a small plaque bearing the number 88—and the archways on either side had been bricked up.

I thanked Raphael, asked him to park the taxi a block away and wait, paid him, and stepped out into the street under the cover of the palms.

I walked slowly around the block, hoping to find a back door. I didn't unless the house immediately behind number 88 was connected, which seemed likely; the doors and plaques seemed almost identical. Both were apparently new, and probably impregnable to anything short of a tank. The walls were too smooth for me to climb up to the balconies. I watched Number 88 for about half an hour, feeling an utter fool, when suddenly the smaller door opened and a heavily-built man stepped out and lit a cigarro. Whatever this place was, they didn't allow smoking inside. He was wearing drab pale green coveralls, a hospital orderly's uniform if I ever saw one. I watched him for a few seconds, then crossed the street and walked towards him from his blind side. He turned and looked at me, a little suspiciously, when I was about four metres away. I reached for my wallet, and said, "Hey. How much to go inside?"

He peered at me, and blew smoke into the street. "You got the wrong door. It's on the other side."

"I'm sorry. Isn't this the hospital?"

"Yeah, but—What're you after?"

I pulled a $50 bill from my pocket with my left hand, and took a step closer. "Just for a few minutes."

The bill disappeared into his huge hand. "Not even a few seconds, if you don't tell me what you want," he said, and frowned. "You a reporter?"

"No, of course not," I snapped. "I just want—" I tried to think. What the hell was there in a hospital that someone might want? "Five minutes in the drug storeroom. That's all."

He rolled his eyes. "This isn't a market. I can maybe get you what you want if you tell me, but you'll have to come back in a couple hours, say nine o'clock."

"Okay. How much hyper will this buy me?" I produced another two bills, and took another step closer. Americans seem to believe that the Constitution, if not the Old Testament, decrees that all their banknotes must be the same size and colour, so you have to study the damn things to tell one dollar from a hundred. The orderly was still staring at the bills in my left hand when I slid my stunstick out of my right sleeve and hit him in the temple. He fell against the door, then slid to the ground. As quickly as I could, I slid the stick back into my sleeve, hauled the orderly across the street, stripped him of his uniform, and retrieved my money. He was a few centimeters shorter than I was, but the uniform was loose enough that it didn't much matter. Shoes were more of a problem; his were too small for me, and mine were the wrong color. There wasn't much I could do about my complexion or hair, either—nondescript by Australian or European standards, but unusually pale for Cuba. The stun would wear off in a few minutes, so I taped his mouth, feet and hands, then dashed across the street and closed the door behind me.

I found myself in a courtyard—an empty one, fortunately—with smooth concrete tracks laid over its cobbles, decorative tilework at the tops of the walls, and an elevator at the far end. I couldn't see any cameras, and I didn't waste time looking. I listened at the nearest door. The clattering suggested a busy kitchen, so I crossed the courtyard, and tried again. Silence. I opened the door, and stepped into an unoccupied office. Again, no visible cameras, except the one over the monitor on the desktop. The locator told me that Tina was above me and to the northwest—or that her wheelchair was, anyway—and that the battery in the tag was running low. The far door was hinged to open inwards; I listened at that, heard more silence. I opened it, and saw the corridor I'd hoped for, leading to a staircase. I was almost there when a door opened behind me. I kept walking, hoping not to be noticed. It didn't work. A man called something in Spanish. I kept walking. "Hey," said the same voice, about four meters behind me. "Stop." I kept walking. "Security, asshole!" he said. Maybe I imagined the comma; maybe that was his title. There was a faint metallic click, and I turned around.

The security asshole was short, shorter than Sobieski, but even more outrageously muscled. The gun in his hand was overkill, too; a Steyr machine-pistol, probably 10mm, with a laser sight projecting a little red cross over my chest. "I don't know you," he said. "What're you doing in here?"

For the life of me—and that seemed to be the stakes we were playing for—I couldn't think of a good lie for several seconds, or even a safe version of the truth. "A friend of mine is in here," I said, eventually. "I need to see her."

It wasn't very good, and I'd obviously hesitated too long for him to believe anything I said. "Yeah? And who're you?"

"My name's Norman," I replied. "Look, I paid the guy at the gate for the uniform. He said there wouldn't be any problem."

He sneered. "How much you got left?"

"A few hundred, US dollars. I don't know exactly."

The sneer didn't get any more friendly. "What do you want?"

"You have a woman staying here; I want to talk to her."

The sneer became an equally hideous leer. "Talk?"

"Yes. She's young, pretty, blonde, one leg." I repeated that in Spanish; it was a phrase I'd memorized.

He blinked. "I know the one," he said.

I drew a deep breath. "I only need to see her for a few minutes," I said. "I'll give you $200."

"Or I can shoot you and take it."

Shit. "Then all you get is the cash I have on me, and I don't come back tomorrow with more."

He seemed to consider this, then nodded. "Okay." Obviously a gambler. "Upstairs. Slow."

I walked up the stairs, and he stayed three to four metres behind me. His thighs weren't so bulked up that he waddled, but I knew I could outrun him if it came to that. I had a faint chance of surprising him on the landing, getting out of sight for long enough to draw my pistol out of my ankle holster, but that would just have meant that we'd be armed and whoever was least reluctant to shoot the other would do so. I wasn't confident of killing or disabling him with a snap shot from a .380, even at point blank range, while his Steyr was probably set to burst fire. He directed me to a mezzanine floor with a low ceiling, then down a poorly-lit corridor, then to a door. "She's in there," he said. "Drop your cash on the floor now, and go in. I'll tell you when you're out of time."

I took four fifties out of my pocket. "$200, fifteen minutes?"

"Five, unless you got more."

"Not on me. I'll bring more tomorrow. $250 for ten minutes, every day until Wednesday. That's a thousand."

He hesitated, then nodded.

I opened the door, and looked in, and stood there stunned.

The woman lying on the bed was blonde, true, and had only one leg—but it was her right leg, and she was probably closer to thirty than nineteen. She was naked but for one black grip-top stocking. Her eyes were open, but she wasn't seeing me; in fact, I doubted she was seeing anything in the room. A thin black cable ran from the back of her skull to a small control box, and another cable ran from there to the power socket in the wall. Apart from the bed, and a small cabinet beside it, the only item of furniture in the room was a folding wheelchair. I was still staring when the security asshole opened the door and walked in. "Disconnect the gadget if you want," he said, magnanimously. "Her battery should be fully charged; more than enough for ten minutes."

"Can I switch it off?"

"Interrupt the program? Yeah, there's a shut-off, but she won't thank you for using it. Bringing her down slowly takes about half an hour before she can make sense."

I stared at her face; it looked vaguely familiar, and I suddenly remembered why. Her picture had been on some of the websites I'd seen; she'd done several videos under the name Lorelei. "This way, she stays happy whatever happens," said the asshole. "She responds, too; fuck her, and she'll come on like you're Mr. Universe. Shit, they won't even need to drug her when they cut her leg off. Better hurry, your time's wasting."

"When are they—" I couldn't finish the sentence.

"Tomorrow, I think." He glanced at his watch. "Look, what're you waiting for? You want to talk to her, talk!"

"Some privacy would be nice," I said, sourly. He shrugged, then turned away. I flicked the stunstick out of my sleeve as quickly as I could, but he must have heard the sound because he turned on his heel and brought the gun up. I hit him across the wrist of his gun hand, hoping it wouldn't cause him to spasm. It didn't knock him out, either—a peripheral blow rarely does—but it temporarily killed his right arm from fingertip to elbow.

He tried to squeeze the trigger, but when his fingers wouldn't obey, he didn't waste time; he swung the pistol at my head with as much power and accuracy as he could muster. Maybe he'd been stunsticked before, maybe he just guessed that a second blow to that arm wouldn't do any more damage either way, it was a smart move. I instinctively tried to parry, and the blow knocked the stunstick from my hand. He grinned, and jabbed his left fist at my face. I ducked underneath it and drove my own fist into his groin, one part of the body where all the weightlifting in the world won't build extra muscle. He gasped and took a step back; it wasn't much, but it gave me a chance to roll away and make a grab for the stunstick. If he'd been brighter, he might have thought to use his left hand to squeeze the trigger; fortunately, he wasn't, and didn't. I scrambled back to my feet, stunstick at the ready, and feinted at his left. He blocked with the gun, so I hit his left thigh instead, then sidestepped. He swung around and overbalanced, and I tapped his left shoulder on his way down. I backed away from his scything right leg, and squatted to draw the Grendel. "Okay," I said, pointing it at his crotch. "Normally I'd ask you to drop the gun, but I know you can't."

"What're you going to do?"

I shrugged. "I'm either going to have to stun you or kill you before you regain use of your hands, which will take about five minutes. So, if you answer some questions for me, I promise just to stun you. Okay?"

The locator told me that the wheelchair was almost directly above me, so I walked quickly but quietly back to the staircase. I had the Steyr in one hand, having pried it from the security asshole's fingers (not cold and dead, though I'd been tempted), and the locator in the other; not exactly inconspicuous, but the security asshole had told me there was another heavily-armed security asshole patrolling the building, and I wanted to be prepared. The next floor up had a higher ceiling, a marble floor, wider corridors and better lighting, and gave me a strong impression of having walked into soft class from steerage. There was no one around, and the locator led me to a large door with a stained glass transom. I pocketed the locator and walked in without knocking. Tina was sitting up in bed in a translucent robe, a sheet pulled up to her waist; Jason sat on the far side of the bed, holding her hand. Both looked around as I shut the door behind me, but froze when they saw the gun. "What the fuck are you doing here?" he asked.

I walked away from the door, standing in the far corner.

"It took me half an hour to find the hole in your story," I said, slowly. "Of course, I wasn't looking very hard."

"What hole?" asked Tina, warily.

"Your clone," I said. "Have you ever seen it?"

There was a few seconds silence that would have turned a knife. "They advised against it," said Jason, quietly. "They said it would only upset us. It's not like a heart or a kidney, it's . . ." He shut his mouth so suddenly that I heard his teeth click together; he'd worked it out. I turned to Tina. "How long ago did you give them a cell sample for cloning?"

"April or May," she said, and turned to Jason. "Wasn't it?"

"End of April," he said, tersely.

"And it never occurred to either of you to wonder how they could grow an adult human body in less than a year—Hell, in nine months? With bones long and strong enough to carry an adult's weight, and that won't keep growing?"

"They grow kidneys in less . . ." said Jason, but his tone was hallow and his face was turning red. He seemed embarrassed, but also furious at my interference. Maybe he believed he had an exclusive right to protect Tina. Maybe that was part of the attraction.

"Yes," I replied. "For people who still have one working kidney. The transplant keeps growing—but a small kidney is better than none. A cloned heart takes more than a year before it's large enough to be worth transplanting. Jesus, you're supposed to know something about physiology and anatomy; didn't it ever occur to you that this was a little too easy? Don't you know what happens to the leg muscles of coma patients? Did you ever wonder how they could make a brainless clone exercise? Weren't you at least curious?"

"There isn't a clone?" asked Tina, uncertainly.

"I don't know," I replied. "There might be, but that's not where your leg is coming from. There's a woman on the floor below you; if you stay here, you'll be getting her right leg. It should be fairly strong; it's the only one she has. She lost the left a few years ago, in a factory accident. Since then, she's been making a living doing porn for fetishists, under the name Lorelei." I glanced at Jason, noticed a faint twinge of recognition.

"Is she dying?"

"No. She sold her leg to have her pleasure center wired so that she no longer cares. And they've promised her cloned legs, too—as soon as they can grow them. They may even be telling the truth; someone has to be a guinea pig, right? In the meantime, she'll pay her way with a few more movies and some prostitution." I shrugged. "You don't have to take my word for it. You can insist on seeing the clone—but don't be shocked if they say no. Me, I'm getting out of here. Have a nice life."

"Wait," said Tina, before I could move. "Can I see this—Lorelei?"

"Yes," I said. "But she's in a world of her own, unable to talk. The guard who told me most of this is unconscious too. I'll show you the way."

"That won't be necessary," she replied, sadly. "I just wanted to be sure you weren't lying. Can you get me out of here?"

I smiled. "It'd be my pleasure."

"Wait!" shouted Jason, then drew a deep breath. "Honey, look, you're turning down a chance at a leg. Even if this story isn't all bullshit, which it probably is, this woman's already agreed, she's been paid, she thinks she'll be better off this way—"

"No!" snapped Tina. "His story makes sense, and no one's losing a leg for my sake." She reached for the handhold above her bed, and hauled herself up. "Are you coming with us?"

Jason hesitated. I knew he could still cause a shitload of trouble by calling for security; he might be deluded enough to think that if he could prevent Tina escaping, he might change her mind . . . or maybe have her operated on without her consent, hoping that she'd be grateful later. Maybe if I could make him think of Lorelei as a human, not a collection of spare parts, it would save me having to stunstick him. He stared at me for what felt like much too long, then looked imploringly at Tina. She met his gaze levelly, and I realised that she was far, far stronger than him. "Okay," he said, then glanced down and saw the red cross of the laser sight blazing just above his right knee. I smiled, then pointed the Steyr at the floor as the blood drained away from his face. "Okay," I echoed. "Let's go. Tina, have you ever used a gun?"

"Yes." I reached for my ankle holster, handed her the Grendel. "But not in years, and not a pistol."

"I have," said Jason, his voice hollow but crisp.

I ignored him. "Take it anyway," I told her, "but keep it out of sight. Jason, carry the bags, and stay in front. I'll push the chair."

"Why me in front?"

"Because they won't dare shoot you; you're worth too much money. It also means I'm less visible from the front, and leaves me free to protect our rear." I turned away from Tina while she dressed, but kept an eye on him. "Whenever you're ready."

The clinic's security system was obviously designed to discourage intruders, not escapees, and we made it to the street without mishap. I was delighted to find I hadn't misjudged Raphael; he started driving towards us while we were halfway across the street. The small door opened again just before he reached us, and the barrel of a gun appeared. I fired a burst into the portale, sending chips flying, and the barrel withdrew hastily. "Okay, you push her! Dump the chair if you have to. I'll hold them off. Hurry, before they think to come around from the other side!"

Jason grabbed the handles of the chair and ran; he was faster than I would've expected, but then, I'd forgotten he was an athlete and barely half my age. I backed away from the door slowly, waiting for the gun to re-appear; I heard the Lada stop a few metres away, and the doors open. I walked towards the sound of the engine and their voices, not looking over my shoulder until I heard the unmistakable sound of flesh on flesh. Raphael drove the car towards me, swerving at the last minute. "Need a cab, mon? This boy wanted to leave you behind, but I said I already had a fare." I looked in the rear view mirror as I climbed into the front seat. Jason's nose was bleeding, and there was the distinct shape of fingers across one cheek. "I didn't hit him," said Raphael, grinning. "Where to, mon?"

I turned to Jason and Tina. "Do you have your passports? Your tickets?" Nods. "Didn't leave anything essential at the Eldorado? I don't mean expensive, I mean essential—anything they can't just ship back to you."

"No," Tina replied, before Jason could speak.

"Good. Straight to the airport." I gave Raphael the weapons as part of his tip and promised to show him around Perth if he was ever in the area, then Tina, Jason and I caught the first available flight to Miami. They stayed in the Park Central, I took a single at the Hostel International, and I didn't see Jason again until I visited him in his office in March.

There was a picture of Tina on his desk, the portrait he'd taken in May. She looked happy to see me. He didn't.

"What do you want now?" he said, glowering as I leaned against his doorway. "Haven't you been paid?"

"Yes."

"Then you've already cost us enough," he snapped. "You know Tina's gone?"

"Her mother told me she was okay," I said. Her parents had separated as well, and the house in Dalkeith had been sold. "She said she had a flat not far from here, but she wouldn't tell me the address."

"She won't see me," said Jason, veering from anger to self-pity. "I phone her every day or two, but that's as close as she'll let me get. Have you seen her?"

I did my best to look innocent, even though it hardly ever works. "I don't even know her phone number," I said, which was true. "Look, I still have a few questions. Who told you about the clones, the hospital?"

"Get fucked."

I shook my head. "It must've been someone you trusted. How did you pay?" He glared. "Okay, how did your father pay? Or did he leave it to someone like Norman?"

"I don't know," he said—sharply, but probably truthfully.

"And he didn't check this out? Your father doesn't have a reputation for being that trusting, especially when the procedure must have cost a small fortune." A scowl. "Do you know who owns that clinic?"

"No. Do you?"

"No, but I'm looking into it." With help from Ratcliffe and Teri, of course. "You see, it occurred to me that while it was an expensive procedure, Tina would have been very effective as a walking advertisement for the clinic, without her even having to know it. A beautiful young woman, escorted by one of the country's most eligible bachelors, a few pictures in the social pages and the supermarket tabloids, rumors on the web about an expensive and exclusive little surgery . . ."

He snorted. "Yeah, well, you're one hell of a detective, aren't you? Jesus, you can't even find a girl's phone number!"

I shrugged. I had seen Tina recently, though neither in the flesh nor over the phone. Sometimes she walked into my dreams; sometimes she'd always been there, waiting for me. "I'll find it when I need it," I replied. "And she knows how to find me. Don't bother getting up; I can find my own way out."

He nodded and said, almost inaudibly, "I do love her, Mr. Horne." I didn't reply. The portrait watched me walk away. He didn't.

The Marriage of
Sky and Sea

CHRIS BECKETT

Chris Beckett is a writer and now a university lecturer in Cambridge, England (though not at Cambridge University but at the "possibly marginally less famous" Anglia Polytechnic University). Until a couple of years ago he was a social worker. He has published twelve SF stories to date, all in Interzone, since 1990. "More stories of mine should appear in Interzone this year," he says. "Admirable magazine! Great for people like me." Last year a story of Beckett's ("Valour") was included in this anthology, and this year he appears again.

His short fiction to date is of high quality, thoughtful, tending to present complex philosophical problems on a human scale. "Although I am interested in science, and am the son of scientists, science and the future per se has never been the principal focus of my stories. I am interested in human beings and their struggles. This story, for example, is as much about intimacy (and how we both long for it and fear it) as it is about anything else." This story is also about different kinds of knowledge.

"**T**hey say," mused Clancy, looking down on a planet enmeshed by strands of light, "that Cosmopolis is the city on which the sun never sets. It's true because the city encircles an entire planet. But in any case sunrise and sunset are an irrelevance in Cosmopolis because there is *no one watching*. The city's inhabitants live in absorbing worlds of their own construction and have no attention to spare for that rather bare space under the sky which they call, dismissively, the *surface*."

Here he paused.

"Have we finished dictation for now?" enquired Com.

"Wait," said Clancy.

Com waited. Having no limbs, Com had no choice. Its smooth yellow egg-shape fitted comfortably into Clancy's hand.

"I am a writer and a traveller," continued Clancy, reclining on cushions in a small dome-shaped room, its ceiling a hemisphere of stars. "I am a typical Cosmopolitan soul in many ways, restless, unable to settle, hungry for experience, hungry to feed the gap where love and meaning should be."

He considered.

"No. Delete that last sentence. And I've had a change of heart about our destination. Instruct Sphere to head for the Aristotle Complex. There are several worlds out there which I've been meaning to check out."

Com did as it was asked in a three-microsecond burst of ultrasound.

"Message received and implemented," said Sphere to Com, in the same high-speed code. "Shall I send standard notification?"

"Did you wish to notify anyone in the city about your new destination?" Com asked Clancy.

"Hmm," said Clancy, with an odd smile, "that's an interesting question. And the answer, interestingly, is no. Take another note, Com, for the book."

He leant back with his hands behind his head.

"Ten thousand kilometres out," he dictated, "I changed my destination so no one could find me if anything went wrong. I wanted to disappear. I wanted to dispense with the safety net, to get a sense of what it must have been like for those settlers in the fourth millennium, setting out on their one-way journey out into the unknown."

He considered, then shrugged.

"Right, Com. At this point add a chapter about the Aristotle Complex. What we know of the early settlers, their motives, their desire to escape from decadence . . . and so on. Themes: finality, no turning back, taking risks, a complete break with the past."

"Neo-romantic style?"

"Neo-romantic stroke factual hard-boiled. Oh and include three poetic sharp-edge sentences. Just three. Low adjective count."

"Okay. Shall I read it through to you?" said Com, having composed a chapter of 2,000 words without causing a gap in the conversation.

"Not now," said Clancy. "I'm not in the mood. Get me a dinner fixed will you, and something to watch on screen. How long will it be till we reach the Complex?"

"The distance is about five parsecs. It'll take three days."

It was not the first voyage of this kind that Clancy had made. This was his career. He travelled alone to the "lost worlds," he got to know them: their way of life, their myths, their beliefs. And then he returned with a book.

Returning with the book was his particular trademark. The completed book went on sale, in electronic form, at the *exact* same moment that he stepped out of his sphere. It had become a publishing event. He sold a million within an hour and became the city's most talked-about celebrity. The literary spaceman: brave, elegant, alone. He attended all the most fashionable parties. He invariably embarked on a love affair with at least one beautiful and brilliant woman.

And when the love affair grew cold—as it always did, for there was a certain emptiness where his heart should be—and when he sensed that he had reached the end of the city's fickle concentration span, he would go off once more into space.

He had a fear of being trapped, of being tied down, of becoming ordinary.

"The first approach to a settled planet," said Clancy, "is a uniquely humbling experience. Here are human beings whose ancestors have gone about their lives without any reference to the universe outside for 30 generations. Invariably, in the absence of the vast pyramid of infrastructure on which modern society rests, their technology has become very basic. Invariably the story of their origins has been compacted into some legend. They have had more practical things to worry about for the last thousand years. My arrival, however it is managed, is inevitably a cultural bombshell. Their lives will never be the same again."

He considered. They had reached the Aristotle Complex an hour ago. Sphere was now using the short cut of non-Euclidean space to leap from star to star and planet to planet, looking for inhabited worlds, very quickly but mechanically, like Com searching the Cosmopolitan Encyclopedia for a single word.

"Some say that for this reason I should not disturb them. This is surely poppycock. On that argument no human being would ever visit another's home, no one would talk to another, let alone take the risk of love. Not that I ever *do* take that risk of course."

He frowned. "Delete that last sentence."

"Deleted. Sphere has found an inhabited planet."

*   *   *

A fisher king was fishing in his watery world when the sphere came through the sky. Standing in the prow of his fine longboat, the tall, bearded upright king watched a silver ball, like a tiny, immaculate moon, descending towards his island home. And his household warriors, sitting at their oars, groaned and muttered, watching the sphere and then turning to look at him to see what he would do.

Aware of their gaze and never once faltering as he played his hereditary role, he ordered them to cut away the nets and row at once for the shore.

When Clancy emerged, his sphere perched on its tripod legs on the top of a tall headland, it was mainly women and children who were standing round him. Most of the men were out at sea.

He smiled.

"I won't harm you," he said, "I want to be your friend."

The words didn't matter much of course. After all this time these fisher-people had evolved a completely new language. It was salty as seaweed, full of the sound of water.

"Iglop!" they said. "Waarsha sleesh!"

Clancy smiled again. They were pleasant-looking people, healthy-looking and well fed. Men and women alike went bare from the waist up, and wore kilts of some seal-like skin.

"Sky!" said Clancy pointing upwards.

"Sea!" (he pointed) "Man!"

It took them a while to grasp the game, but then they did so with gusto, drawing closer to the strange man in his rainbow clothes, and to his strange silvery globe.

"Eyes," said Clancy. "Nose. Mouth."

"Erlash," they called out. "Memaarsha. Vroom."

Hidden in Clancy's pocket, Com took all this in, comparing every utterance with its database of the language of the settlers before they set out a thousand years ago.

Com knew that there are regularities in the way that languages change. Sounds migrate together across the palate like flocks of birds. Meanings shift over the spectrum from particular to general, concrete to abstract, in orderly and measurable ways. Com formed 5,000 hypotheses a second, tested each one, discarded most, elaborated a few. By the time the fisher king arrived with his warriors and his long robe, Com was already able to have a go at translating.

It was as the king approached that Clancy first became really aware of the massive presence of the moon.

"I was on a rocky promontory of the island. Beyond the excited faces, beyond the approaching king, was a glittering blue sea dotted with dozens of other islands. But all this was dwarfed by the immense pink cratered sphere above, filling up a tenth part of the entire sky.

"What is our moon in Cosmopolis? A faint smudge in the orange gloom above a ventilation shaft? A pale blotch behind the rooftop holograms? We glance up and notice it for a moment, briefly entertained perhaps by the thought that there is a world of sorts outside our own, and then turn our attention back to our more engrossing surroundings.

"But this was truly a celestial sphere, a gigantic ball of rock, hanging above us, dominating the sky. I had known of its size before I landed but nothing could have prepared me for the sight of it.

"I had yet to experience the titanic ocean tides, the palpable gravity shifts, the daily solar eclipses, but I knew this was a world ruled over by its moon."

Clancy paused and took a sip of red wine, seated comfortably in his impregnable sphere where he had retired, as was his custom, for the night. He had declined an invitation to dine with the King, saying that he would do the feast more justice the following evening. The truth was the first encounter was always extremely tiring and he needed rest. And alien food always played havoc with his digestion the first time round, guaranteeing a sleepless night.

"Com," he said, "prepare me a database of lunar myths."

He considered.

"And one on lunar poetry, and one on references to unusual moons round other inhabited worlds."

"Done. Do you want me to . . . ?"

"No, carry on with dictation."

*   *   *

"The King is a genuinely impressive individual. His voice, his posture, his sharp grey eyes, everything about him speaks of his supreme self-assurance. He has absolutely no doubt at all about either his right or his ability to be in charge. And why should he? As he himself calmly told us, he is the descendant of an ancient union between sky and sea. He greeted me as a long-lost cousin . . ."

Clancy hesitated. A shadow crossed his mind.

"I pin them out like fucking butterflies!" he exclaimed. "I dissect them and pin them out! Why can't I let anything just live?"

Com was sensitive to emotional fluctuations and recognized this one, not from the *inside* of course but from the outside, as a pattern it had observed before.

"The first day is always extremely tiring," Com suggested gently. "In the past we've found that a cortical relaxant, a warm drink and sleep . . ."

"Yes, whatever we do, let's not face the emptiness," growled Clancy, but he seemed to acquiesce at first, collecting the pill and the drink dispensed by Sphere, and preparing to settle into the bed that unfolded from the floor . . .

Then "No!" he exclaimed, tossing the pill aside. "If I can't feel at least I can fucking think. Come on, Com, let's do some work on the theme. Listen, I have an idea . . ."

Lying with two of his concubines in his bed of animal skins, the fisher king was also kept awake by a hectic stream of thoughts. His mind was no less quick than Clancy's but it worked in a very different way. Clancy thought like an acrobat, a tightrope walker, nimbly balancing above the void. But the king moved between large solid chunks of certainty. Annihilation was an external threat to be fought off, not an existential hole inside.

He thought of the power of the strange prince in his sphere. He thought about his own sacred bloodline and the kingdom which sustained it. All his life he had deftly managed threats from other island powers, defeating some in war, making allies of others through exchanges of gifts or slaves, or bonds of marriage. But how to play a visitor who came not from across the sea in the long-boat but down from the sky in a kind of silver moon?

He woke one of the concubines. (He was a widower and had never remarried).

"Fetch me my chamberlain. I want to take his advice!"

"There are three kinds of knowledge," Clancy said, "let's call them Deep Knowledge, Slow Knowledge and Quick Knowledge. Deep Knowledge is the stuff which has been hardwired into our brains by evolution itself; the stuff we are born with, the stuff that animals have. It changes in the light of experience, like other knowledge, but only over millions of years. Slow Knowledge is the accumulation of traditions and traditional techniques passed down from generation to generation. It too changes, evolving gradually as some traditions fade and others are slowly elaborated. But, at the conscious level, those who transmit Slow Knowledge see themselves not as innovators but as preservers of wisdom from the past. Quick knowledge is the short cut we have latterly acquired in the form of science, a way of speeding up the trial-and-error process by making it systematic and self-conscious. It is a thousand, a million times quicker than Slow Knowledge, and a billion, billion times speedier than Deep Knowledge. But unlike them it works by objectivity, by stepping *outside* a thing.

"Deep, Slow and Quick: we could equate them to rock and sea and air. Rock doesn't move perceptibly at all. Sea moves but stays within its bounds . . ."

He laughed, "More wine, Com, this is *good*. Get this: Cosmopolitans are creatures of air, analytical, empirical, technological; lost-worlders are typically creatures of the sea. They all are, but these guys here are literally so. So here's the book title: *The Meeting of Sea and Sky*. See? It ties in with the king's origin myth!"

"That was a *marriage* of sea and sky," observed Com.

Clancy had retired for the night atop a headland overlooking a wide bay, where a coastal village of wattle huts squatted near the water's edge. But in the morning there was no sea in sight. A plain of mud and rocks and pools stretched as far as the horizon and groups of tiny figures could be seen wandering all over it with baskets on their backs.

The moon was on the far side of the planet, taking the ocean with it. The sky was open and blue. And when he climbed down the steps (watched by a small crowd which had been waiting there since dawn) Clancy found that he was appreciably heavier than he had been the previous day.

Followed closely by the fascinated crowd—made up mainly of children and old people—Clancy went down from the headland to what had been the bay. A group of women were just coming off the mud flats with their baskets laden with shellfish. He smiled at them and started to walk out himself onto the mud.

Behind him came gasps and stifled incredulous laughs.

Clancy stopped.

"Is there a problem?" Clancy had Com ask. (Everyone was diverted for a while by the wondrous talking egg). "Is there some danger that I should be aware of?"

"No, no danger," they answered.

But why then the amazement? Why the laughter? They stared, incredulous.

"Because you are a *man!*" someone burst out at length.

Clancy was momentarily nonplussed, then he gave a little laugh of recognition.

"I've got it, Com. Their reaction is *exactly* the one I would get if I headed into the women's toilets in some shopping mall."

He addressed the crowd.

"So men don't go on the mud when the tide is out?"

People laughed more easily now, certain that he was merely teasing them.

"These things are different where I come from," said Clancy. "You're telling me that only women here go out on the mud?"

A very old woman came forward.

"Only women of course. That is a woman's realm. Surely that is obvious?"

"And a man's realm is where?"

The woman was irritated, feeling he was making a fool of her.

"To men belongs the sea under the moon," she snapped, withdrawing back into the crowd.

"Sea and sky, sea and sky," muttered Clancy to Com, "it's coming together nicely."

The book was the thing for him. Reality was simply the raw material.

That night the king piled the choicest pieces of meat on Clancy's plate and filled his mug again and again with a thick brew of fermented seaweed. Clancy's stomach groaned in anticipation of a night of struggling to unlock the unfamiliar proteins of an alien biological line, but he acted the appreciative guest, telling tales of Cosmopolis and other worlds, and listening politely as the king's poets sang in praise of their mighty lord, the "moon-tall whale-slayer, gatherer of islands, favoured son of sky and sea."

As he lay in the early hours, trying to get rest if not actual sleep, Clancy became aware of a new sound coming from outside—a creaking, snapping sound—and he got up to investigate.

He emerged from his sphere to an astonishing sight. Over at the eastern horizon, the enormous moon was rising over a returning sea. Brilliant turbulent water, luminous with pink moonlight, was sweeping towards him across the vast dark space where the women had yesterday hunted for crabs.

But the creaking, snapping sound was much nearer to hand.

"What *is* that?" Clancy asked.

The king had posted a warrior as guard-of-honour to Clancy's sphere and the man was now sleepily scrambling to his feet.

"What is that sound?" Clancy asked him, holding out Com, his yellow egg.

The sound was so ordinary to the man that he could not immediately understand what it was that Clancy meant. Then he shrugged.

"It's the moon tugging at the rocks."

"Of *course*," exclaimed Clancy, "of course. With a moon that size, even the rocks have tides that can be felt."

He walked to the edge of the headland. He heard another creaking below him and a little stone dislodged itself and rattled down the precipice.

"Lunar erosion," he observed with a smile.

The warrior had come up beside him.

"It tugs at your soul too," he volunteered. "Makes you long for things which you don't even know what they are. No wonder the women stay indoors under the moon. It tugs and tugs and if you're not careful, it'll pull your soul right out of you and you'll be another ghost up there in that dead dry place and never again know the sea and the solid land."

Having made this speech, the young man nodded firmly and wandered back to his post at the foot of Clancy's steps.

"Wow," breathed Clancy, "good stuff! Did you record all that?"

Of course Com had.

The moon had nearly cleared the horizon now. It towered above the world. The wattle huts below were bathed in its soft pink light and the water once more filled up the bay.

"Take a note, Com. I said we in Cosmopolis had forgotten our moon, but actually I think our moon has gobbled us up. After so many centuries of asking for the moon, we have . . ."

". . . we have . . . ?"

"Forget it. I think I'm going to be sick."

"I visited a quarry," Clancy dictated, a week into his stay, "a little dry dusty hollow at the island's heart, where half a dozen men were facing and stacking stone. It was the middle of the day but quite dark, due to one of the innumerable eclipses, so they were working by the light of whale-oil flares. The chief quarryman was a short, leathery fellow in a leather apron, his hands white with rock dust. I asked him why he worked there rather than on the sea like most of the other men. He had some difficulty understanding what I was asking him at first, then shrugged and said his father had worked there, and his grandfather and great-grandfather. It was his family's allotted role. (A *slow knowledge* approach to life, you see, a *sea knowledge* approach. Any Cosmopolitan would want to demonstrate that his job was chosen by himself.)

"But I realized that my question had left the man with some anxiety about how he was perceived. He stood there, this funny, leathery human mole, and stared intently at my face for a full minute as if there was writing there which he was trying to read.

" 'It isn't on the sea,' he said at length, 'but it's real moon work! No women are ever allowed here.' And he told me that there were some rocks they only attempted to shift right under the moon. The strain of the tide going through the rock made the strata more brittle. Hit the rock in the right place under the moon and it would suddenly snap. Hit it any other time and it remained stubbornly hard. With some rocks, he said, it is enough to heat the rocks with fire when the moon is up, and they fly apart into blocks. It was real moon work all right.

"So I told him that I had no doubts whatever about his manhood."

Clancy paused.

"You know, Com, I think we've got nearly enough material already. We just need one more episode, one more *event* to somehow bring the themes alive. Whatever 'alive' is."

He got up, paced around the tiny space of Sphere's leisure room.

"What is the point of all this? Back and forth across empty space, belonging nowhere, an outsider in the lost worlds, an outsider in Cosmopolis, no one for company but a plastic egg. What are my books but mental wallpaper?"

Com conferred with Sphere by ultrasound, then suggested a glass of wine.

Clancy snorted. "You and Sphere always want to pour chemicals down me, don't you? Come on, back to work. Resume dictation."

Next day when the tide was out, Clancy got into conversation with harpooneer, a sly, sinuous, thin-faced man, with two fingers missing from an encounter with one of the big whale-like creatures which he hunted under every moon.

As with the quarryman, Clancy asked the man why he did the work he did, and received exactly the same answer: his father, grandfather and great-grandfather had done the same. Then Clancy asked him would he not like to have a choice of profession?

When Com translated, the man did not seem to understand.

"I know the word for choice in the context, say, of selecting a fish from a pile," Com explained to Clancy. "But it does not seem to be meaningful to use this word in the context of a person's occupation."

"Okay," said Clancy, "ask him like this. Ask him does he prefer his ale salty or sweet? Ask him whether he prefers whale meat fresh or dried? Ask him does he prefer to fish when the sun is hot or when it is cloudy? Then ask him, how would it be if someone had said to him when he was a child, would he rather be a quarryman, a harpooneer or a fisherman with nets?"

Com tried this. The old man replied to each question until the last. Then he burst out laughing.

"They simply have no concept of choosing their own way in life," Clancy recorded later. "They follow the role allotted to them by birth and don't resent it because it has not occurred to any of them that anything else could be a possibility. How would they react if they could come to the city, and see people who have chosen even their own gender, changed their size, their skin, the colour of their eyes?"

He considered.

"There is something idyllic about their position. In some respects, in any case, they are spared the burden of Free Will. Even marriage partners, I gather, are allocated according to complicated rules to do with clan and status, with no reference whatever to individual choice. I see no evidence that people here are less happy than in our city. In fact a certain kind of *fretfulness*, found everywhere in the city, is totally missing here, even though life is certainly not easy for those allocated the roles of slave, say, or concubine or witch . . ."

He considered this. Com waited.

"It is this idyll of an ordered, simple life (isn't it?) which the city pays me so well to seek out. Not that anyone wants it for themselves. This life would bore any Cosmopolitan to death in a week. But they like to know it is there, like childhood . . .

"By the way, one new thing the harpooneer told me. He asked me when I would meet the king's daughters. I told him I didn't know the king had daughters and he laughed and said there were three, and no one could agree which was the most beautiful."

Clancy dined that evening on the high table in the hall of the king, with all the king's warriors ranged on benches below. In the middle of the room the carcass of an entire whale was being turned on a spit by household slaves. The whole space was full of the great beast's meaty, fatty heat.

"Wahita wahiteh zloosh," chanted the king's poets on and on, *"wamineh weyopla droosh! . . ."*

Clancy leant towards the king.

"Your majesty, I am told that you have three very beautiful daughters. I hope I will have the pleasure of meeting them."

The effect of this on the king was unexpectedly electrifying. He jolted instantaneously into his most formal mode—and, seeing this, the entire hall full of warriors fell suddenly silent.

"Prince from the sky, I am most honoured that you should ask. They will be made ready at once."

He called to a servant, gave urgent orders and dismissed him with an imperious wave. The warriors began their talking and their shouting once again.

"An hour passed," Clancy dictated later, "and then a second. The warriors grew restless, wriggling on their benches like naughty children. The whale carcass, what was left of it, grew cold. The king and I, whose relationship consisted entirely of exchanging information, ran out of things to say to each other, and he eventually gave up all attempt at conversation, sinking into his thoughts, turning a gold ring round and round on his finger, and from time to time jolting himself awake and pressing more sea-weed ale on me.

"I began to wonder whether there had been some mistake. Surely it could not take that long for the princesses to be made ready? Had they been summoned from some other island? Had I perhaps completely misunderstood what was going on? But Com assured me that, yes, the king had said his daughters were being got ready.

"Another hour passed. I endured the king's poets repeating their repertoire for the third time. (*'Wahita wahiteh zloosh/ wamineh weyopla droosh! . . . '* repeated after every one of 23 verses!)

"And then a door opened at the end of the dais, all the warriors lumbered to their feet, and the king's three daughters were led in."

At this point in his narration, Clancy asked for wine.

Sphere poured it for him.

"The harpooneer had not lied to me, all three princesses were indeed beautiful and it wasn't hard now to see why they had taken so long. Their hair was plaited, ribboned and piled in elaborate structures on their heads, their bodies, bare to the waist, had been freshly painted in the most intricate designs of entwined sea plants and sea creatures.

"They came round the table and knelt behind my seat, the youngest first, her sisters behind. Then, at a word from the king, the youngest daughter stood up, offered her hand to me briefly and went to stand behind him. The second daughter did the same. And then the third, the oldest . . ."

Clancy gulped down his wine and went across to the dispenser for more. He was agitated, scared.

"What the hell *is* that feeling?" he demanded. "It's not like lust at all, but you can't call it love, not when you don't know the person. It's like a buried longing for some kind of *sweetness*, which we try to stifle beneath worldliness and weariness and all the busy pointless tasks we lay upon ourselves. And suddenly a person touches it for some reason and it erupts, all focused on that one person, her lovely sad intelligent eyes, her unconscious grace . . ."

He checked himself.

"What a load of crap! What do I know about her except her face? What is it I want from that face? What can a face give me? What is a face except muscle and skin? Damn it, it means nothing, nothing! It's all just a trick played on us by biology!"

"Are we still doing dictation?" Com politely enquired.

"No of course we aren't, you plastic prat!"

Clancy swallowed the wine in one gulp and shoved the empty cup straight back into the dispenser for more.

"Okay, let's admit it. The oldest daughter, Wayeesha. When I met her eyes it felt as if something passed between us, some recognition, some hope that it might not always be necessary to be so . . . so terribly alone. It's all crap, of course: she's not much more than half my age, she's been brought up to marry some iron age warlord on some bleak little island. We don't even speak the same language."

He downed the third cup of wine in one, with a little shudder.

"All that we might possibly have in common is some kind of longing to *escape* . . ."

"Sometimes it helps to talk about what happened," said Com, after a ten-microsecond conference with Sphere. "Perhaps if you finished the story . . ."

"Oh for God's say spare me your second-hand wisdom you sanctimonious *rattle!*" exclaimed Clancy.

But in spite of that he sat down again and carried on.

"So then when all three women were standing behind the king's chair, he smiled proudly at me and asked me whether or not they were indeed as beautiful as people had told me. Of course I said yes.

" 'That's good,' he said, 'and now the choice is entirely yours.'

"I suppose I had been rather naïve, but until that point, I

hadn't understood that when I asked to see his daughters he had assumed that I wanted one of them for a wife."

Again Clancy jumped to his feet.

"Damn it, Com, this is intolerable. One minute I was falling for a woman in a way that seemed scary and new to me, the very next minute I was being offered her hand in marriage. How could *anyone* deal with that? I played for time, of course. I said that in my own world a man sleeps on a decision like that . . . Delete that whole paragraph. You rewrite it. Leave out the nonsense about my personal feelings. Just describe her as very attractive and tempting. Generic rather than personal. Worldly rather than sentimental. Low adjective count."

"Done. Shall I read it back to you?"

"Later . . . It's maddening. This is *precisely* the event I needed to bring the book together. The marriage of sky and sea! The space traveller falls in love with the daughter of a fisher king. What could be better! *Damn! Damn!* Why has reality always got to be so awkward."

"Go on," said Com, who was a good listener.

"I mean it might make a good book, but if I marry her I can't just go back to the city with the book, can I? I have to go back with *her*. How would it look if I bring back some kid half my age who doesn't even know how to read or write? I'll look like a dirty old man."

"Don't forget," said Com, who had filed and indexed everything they'd learnt about the local culture, "that here it is the man who moves to live with the woman. Women are not allowed to cross the sea."

"So I couldn't take her back with me? Yes, that's true. And if a marriage fails here a man returns to his own island doesn't he?"

Clancy sat down, picked up the yellow egg and turned it over in his hands.

"You may look like a kid's rattle, Com, but you have your uses. I could marry her here, and if things didn't work out, which of course they won't after a while, I can take off home. No harm done, a lovely honeymoon, and a nice sad end for the story. Sky and sea try to marry, but in the end they just don't mix. Spaceman has to be free, even at the price of loneliness and alienation. Ocean princess has to be with her people . . ."

Then he frowned. He was very cold and empty inside, but not wholly without scruples. He was concerned, at any rate, with how his actions might be seen.

"But that is just using her, isn't it? I can't do that. My readers wouldn't like it. They don't expect me to be an angel, but they do expect a certain . . . integrity. Damn."

He thought for a while.

"And anyway she is so beautiful, and so sad. I don't want to . . ."

A thought occurred to him.

"By the way, I meant to ask you. When she shook my hand she said something, very quietly, so no one else could hear. What was it?"

"*Eesha zhu moosha*—you have my heart. Do you want me to play it back as she said it?"

"*No!*" Clancy jumped up as if he had been stung. He was shaking with fear.

"Oh all right," he whispered, shrinking back down, as if in anticipation of a blow, "go on, play it back."

When he had heard it, he wept: just two tears, but tears all the same, such as he hadn't shed for years.

"Damn it, Com, I'll do it. In this culture marriage is all *about* using people. It won't do her any harm to have been married to the sky man! I'm going to bloody do it. Do it and be damned for once."

He glared at the yellow egg as if it had questioned his action.

"Don't worry," he said, "I'll make the book come out right somehow."

Down in the wattle-and-daub settlement the fisher king had a lookout post beside his hall. It consisted of two tree-trunks fixed cleverly end to end, with a small crows'-nest at the top. He invited Clancy up there on the night before the wedding to watch as the other grooms arrived from across the sea.

Weddings in the sea-world were communal affairs, taking place on a single day just once a year. Bonfires burned all along the beach. Under a huge half-moon that dwarfed the island and made the sea itself seem small, canoes appeared in the distance among the glittering waves, first of all as faint dark smudges and then gradually growing more distinct as they approached the land and the firelight. Each one was cheered as it approached and, as they drew close to the beach, the king's warriors waded out into the sea to greet the new arrivals and help to drag the boats ashore.

Clancy turned to the king and smiled. It was a magnificent spectacle.

The king laughed.

"And now," he said, "the burning of the boats."

He raised his arms and gave a signal to his followers on the beach, who at once set to, dragging the canoes one after another onto the fires. The grooms objected ritually and had to be ritually restrained, but there was a lot of laughter. It was clearly all in fun.

Clancy frowned.

"Why do you do that?"

"When a man marries, his wandering days should end, isn't that so?"

The king winked.

"That moon-boat of yours, it won't burn quite so easily!"

"What do you mean?"

Clancy looked over to the headland where Sphere was perched on its tripod legs. A fire was burning beneath it.

"No!" he cried out, and then laughed at himself. How could mere fire harm a vessel designed to cope with space?

The king laughed good-naturedly with him, putting a friendly arm round the shoulders of his son-in-law to be.

"Those rocks are easily shattered under the moon," he observed, "and we have fires in the caves below as well."

When he heard Com translate this, it took Clancy a few seconds before he grasped the implications—and in that short time the first boulder had broken loose and crashed down into the sea.

"No," Clancy shouted, "it's my only way back!"

The king roared with laughter.

"I'm not joking!" cried Clancy, looking around for the rope ladder to get down. "Have the fires put out at once!"

Over on the headland a second boulder crashed down, then a third. And then the sphere itself tipped over, its surfaces glinting in the pink moonlight as it rolled onto its back, its tripod legs sticking up in the air as if it was a stranded sheep. Some more rocks exploded. In agonizing slow-motion, or so it seemed, Sphere went over the edge, crashing against the cliff—once . . . twice . . . —then hitting the sea with a mighty splash and sinking beneath the waves.

With one foot on the rope ladder, Clancy stared. And the king, still laughing, his face wet with tears, reached down, helped him kindly back onto the platform and gave him a warm, fishy hug.

"The boats are burnt! So now you can go to Wayeesha."

Clancy walked over to the rough wooden rail at the edge of the platform, looked out at the bonfires, the glittering sea, the giant moon, and remembered Wayeesha waiting for him in the hall below.

As he had trained himself to do in even the most extreme situations, he examined his thoughts. What he found surprised him. He turned to the king with a smile.

"I'm going to regret this. And I fear that you, my friend, are going to be seriously disappointed. But right now, it's strange, I feel as if I've put down a burden. I don't think I've ever felt so *free!*"

"A good ending for the book!" Com observed.

"What book, you idiot?" said Clancy. "Are we going to write it on seaweed, or carve it into the stones?"

Then he proffered the yellow egg to the king.

"Here," he said, "it's yours. I don't need it, and I feel you ought to get *something* from your alliance with the stars. No need to translate that last sentence, Com."

"Is this wise?" asked Com, as the king turned it over reverently in his large hands.

"No," said Clancy. "In another month your battery will run out and you really *will* just be a plastic egg. Then what will the king think of my gift?"

He went to the rope ladder and began to lower himself, carefully avoiding looking down.

In the Days of the Comet

JOHN M. FORD

John M. Ford was a Wunderkind who published a bunch of professional short stories in his teens and early twenties, and published his first novel, Web of Angels, *just after he turned 21, in 1980. Now he is a member of the establishment with a recent new kidney transplant (Merry Christmas, 2000!). In between, he has won the World Fantasy Award for a fantasy novel,* The Dragon Waiting, *and a narrative poem, "Winter Solstice, Camelot Station." He also won a Philip K. Dick Award for his SF novel* Growing Up Weightless *(1993), and wrote two classic Star Trek novels,* The Final Reflection *(1984) and* How Much for Just the Planet? *(1987). Some of his fantasy stories are collected in* Casting Fortune *(1989) and some SF in* From the End of the Twentieth Century *(1997). He has published only three stories in the last decade, in part due to ill health but also because he has always been easily distracted by work in other areas such as game design. A fine fantasy short novel, written years ago,* The Last Hot Time, *came out at the end of 2000.*

This story, from Nature, *is a complete tale start to finish in a manner that many of the other* Nature *pieces are not. It is a short short story.*

Camfield is dead, and this ship is very quiet now. I have tried to be hopeful in the recent dispatches: we were, Camfield certainly was. Prions are not supposed to kill people any more, but they can, and they have. Which is part of the reason Camfield was out here in the first place.

He was a teller of jokes and he played the guitar very well—these are valuable things when you are doomed to spend years aboard a cantankerous old ship. Several instalments ago, I described the lab accident that infected Camfield, and I have received numerous messages calling the events absurd. This is true. In addition to myself, the organic Petrovna and the Neumann Thucydides saw the incident, and we all laughed until we realized Camfield was hurt. Petrovna, at least, can forget, although I do not think she will.

The prion has been decrypted and entered into the antigenic database, so no one should ever again die of Agent Op-1175s/CFD.

Which is the story, but not its point.

At the cusp of this millennium we discovered that it was not hard to manufacture prions, and not that hard to custom-twist them. It took longer for our twists to be meaningful, but now organic humanity can don an armour of proteins for defence against a hostile Universe. Rather like viruses. Draw your own conclusions.

If one could find the right message, a prion would make a wonderful interstellar, even intergalactic, postal card: immune to temperature, pressure, radiation and time. The ideal pony for the express would be a comet, packed with messenger proteins, flung into a hyperbolic orbit, to seed any worlds at the far end with its cargo.

One could write one's name in the evolving life of a planet. At exactly the right moment, one might even begin the process, dropping a bouillon cube into the primordial soup.

Assuming that no one at the other end is quite as evolved, and quite as dependent on delicate higher neural functions, as we are.

So here we are, myself, 29 (down from 30) organic crew, and eight Neumänner, combing the comets of the Oort for prions. We have found a lot of prions, and there are a lot of comets left. You've got mail, as we said when I was organic.

Maybe. Or maybe one of the 48 published theories of spontaneous prion formation in comets is correct. It is the Neumänner who are most insistent on deliberate seeding. Perhaps it comforts them to think that, just as we built them, somebody built us. How human of them—but, as their namesake said, adequately describe any activity, and a machine can perform it.

In Camfield's last hours he was afire with fever, his whole body trembling, but there was a clarity in his speech that was at once heartbreaking and terrifying. Fischer, Chiang, and the Neumann Hypatia were tending him. Abruptly he calmed, fixed Chiang (and me, unavoidably) with a direct stare, and said, "I see the Martians now! They are flat, and they roll!" He shivered then, and I heard his heart stop.

The exclamation points are not added for drama. He was excited by what he saw, transported by whatever the alien messenger in his brain was revealing to him. Camfield was born on the Moon, not Mars, so we cannot explain away the vision as *Heimsucht*.

We cannot, of course, positively explain it at all. But we must examine the possibility that, eons ago, Op-1175s/CFD fell on Mars and began life there, which was later carried to Earth by a planetary blunt trauma.

Thucydides carefully wrapped and sealed Camfield's remains for storage until we return to the Moon, eight years from now. When he was done, Sid paused for two full minutes (exactly—we are like that), just looking at the bundle.

This kind of behaviour is by no means strange in a Neumann (one can adequately describe a thoughtful pause) but I asked Sid what he was thinking. He waited fourteen seconds longer—which was purely theatrical of him—and said, "I will miss Camfield. He was always interesting to be with, even when nothing was said. And has he not left us with a fine and difficult question?"

Camfield gave many gifts to his shipmates and his ship. The question—and it is fine—he gave to all of us.

The Birthday of the World

URSULA K. LE GUIN

Ursula K. Le Guin is one of the finest living SF and fantasy writers. She also writes poetry, mainstream fiction, children's books, literary essays, and has published a good book on how to write narrative fiction and nonfiction, and co-edited the Norton Book of Science Fiction, *an influential anthology. She is one of the leading feminists in SF, and in recent years a supporter of the James Tiptree Jr. Awards, named in honor of Le Guin's peer and friend Alice Bradley Sheldon's SF pseudonym. Le Guin's work is widely read outside the SF field and she is taken seriously as a contemporary writer. A daughter of famous anthropologists, she grew up in an academic environment and is erudite and cultured. She can be outraged, or silly, when appropriate. In recent years she has published a number of distinguished short stories, and in 2000 she not only continued to do that, but published her first SF novel in more than ten years,* The Telling.

"The Birthday of the World," from Fantasy & Science Fiction *and one of three stories she published in the magazines last year, is a powerful story that starts out just like a fantasy. But this is actually a science fiction story set on another world, and the point of view is not what it initially seems. This ironic tale is in the the main body of Le Guin's work, anthropological SF, a branch of the field carried on for decades mainly by her and Michael Bishop. It may be read as an historical and/or political allegory. It gives ample evidence that Le Guin is still at the peak of her powers as a writer.*

Tazu was having a tantrum, because he was three. After the birthday of the world, tomorrow, he would be four and would not have tantrums.

He had left off screaming and kicking and was turning blue from holding his breath. He lay on the ground stiff as a corpse, but when Haghag stepped over him as if he wasn't there, he tried to bite her foot.

"This is an animal or a baby," Haghag said, "not a person." She glanced may-I-speak-to-you and I glanced yes. "Which does God's daughter think it is," she asked, "an animal or a baby?"

"An animal. Babies suck, animals bite," I said. All the servants of God laughed and tittered, except the new barbarian, Ruaway, who never smiled. Haghag said, "God's daughter must be right. Maybe somebody ought to put the animal outside. An animal shouldn't be in the holy house."

"I'm not an aminal!" Tazu screamed, getting up, his fists clenched and his eyes as red as rubies. "I'm God's son!"

"Maybe," Haghag said, looking him over. "This doesn't look so much like an animal now. Do you think this might be God's son?" she asked the holy women and men, and they all nodded their bodies, except the wild one, who stared and said nothing.

"I am, I am God's son!" Tazu shouted. "Not a baby! Arzi is the baby!" Then he burst into tears and ran to me, and I hugged him and began crying because he was crying. We cried till Haghag took us both on her lap and said it was time to stop crying, because God Herself was coming. So we stopped, and the bodyservants wiped the tears and snot from our faces and combed our hair, and Lady Clouds brought our gold hats, which we put on to see God Herself.

She came with her mother, who used to be God Herself a long time ago, and the new baby, Arzi, on a big pillow carried by the idiot. The idiot was a son of God too. There were seven of us: Omimo, who was fourteen and had gone to live with the army, then the idiot, who was twelve, and had a big round head and small eyes and liked to play with Tazu and the baby, then Goïz, and another Goïz, who were called that because they had died and were in the ash-house where they ate spirit food, then me and Tazu, who would get married and be God, and then Babam Arzi, Lord Seven. I was important because I was the only daughter of God. If Tazu died I could marry Arzi, but if I died everything would be bad and difficult, Haghag said. They would have to act as if Lady Clouds' daughter Lady Sweetness was God's daughter and marry her to Tazu, but the world would know the difference. So my mother greeted me first, and Tazu second. We knelt and clasped our hands and touched our foreheads to our thumbs. Then we stood up, and God asked me what I had learned that day.

I told her what words I had learned to read and write.

"Very good," God said. "And what have you to ask, daughter?"

"I have nothing to ask, I thank you, Lady Mother," I said. Then I remembered I did have a question, but it was too late.

"And you, Tazu? What have you learned this day?"

"I tried to bite Haghag."

"Did you learn that was a good thing to do, or a bad thing?"

"Bad," Tazu said, but he smiled, and so did God, and Haghag laughed.

"And what have you to ask, son?"

"Can I have a new bath maid because Kig washes my head too hard?"

"If you have a new bath maid where will Kig go?"

"Away."

"This is her house. What if you asked Kig to wash your head more gently?"

Tazu looked unhappy, but God said, "Ask her, son." Tazu mumbled something to Kig, who dropped on her knees and thumbed her forehead. But she grinned the whole time. Her fearlessness made me envious. I whispered to Haghag, "If I forgot a question to ask can I ask if I can ask it?"

"Maybe," said Haghag, and thumbed her forehead to God for permission to speak, and when God nodded, Haghag said, "The daughter of God asks if she may ask a question."

"Better to do a thing at the time for doing it," God said, "but you may ask, daughter."

I rushed into the question, forgetting to thank her. "I wanted to know why I can't marry Tazu and Omimo both, because they're both my brothers."

Everybody looked at God, and seeing her smile a little, they all laughed, some of them loudly. My ears burned and my heart thumped.

"Do you want to marry all your brothers, child?"

"No, only Tazu and Omimo."

"Is Tazu not enough?"

Again they all laughed, especially the men. I saw Ruaway staring at us as if she thought we were all crazy.

"Yes, Lady Mother, but Omimo is older and bigger."

Now the laughter was even louder, but I had stopped caring, since God was not displeased. She looked at me thoughtfully and said, "Understand, my daughter. Our eldest son will be a soldier. That's his road. He'll serve God, fighting barbarians and rebels. The day he was born, a tidal wave destroyed the towns of the outer coast. So his name is Babam Omimo, Lord Drowning. Disaster serves God, but is not God."

I knew that was the end of the answer, and thumbed my forehead. I kept thinking about it after God left. It explained many things. All the same, even if he had been born with a bad omen, Omimo was handsome, and nearly a man, and Tazu was a baby that had tantrums. I was glad it would be a long time till we were married.

I remember that birthday because of the question I asked.

I remember another birthday because of Ruaway. It must have been a year or two later. I ran into the water room to piss and saw her hunched up next to the water tank, almost hidden.

"What are you doing there?" I said, loud and hard, because I was startled. Ruaway shrank and said nothing. I saw her clothes were torn and there was blood dried in her hair.

"You tore your clothes," I said.

When she didn't answer, I lost patience and shouted, "Answer me! Why don't you talk?"

"Have mercy," Ruaway whispered so low I had to guess what she said.

"You talk all wrong when you do talk. What's wrong with you? Are they animals where you come from? You talk like an animal, brr-grr, grr-gra! Are you an idiot?"

When Ruaway said nothing, I pushed her with my foot. She looked up then and I saw not fear but killing in her eyes. That made me like her better. I hated people who were afraid of me. "Talk!" I said. "Nobody can hurt you. God the Father put his penis in you when he was conquering your country, so you're a holy woman. Lady Clouds told me. So what are you hiding for?"

Ruaway showed her teeth and said, "Can hurt me." She showed me places on her head where there was dried blood and fresh blood. Her arms were darkened with bruises.

"Who hurt you?"

"Holy women," she said with a snarl.

"Kig? Omery? Lady Sweetness?"

She nodded her body at each name.

"They're shit," I said. "I'll tell God Herself."

"No tell," Ruaway whispered. "Poison."

I thought about it and understood. The girls hurt her because she was a stranger, powerless. But if she got them in trouble they would cripple or kill her. Most of the barbarian holy women in our house were lame, or blind, or had had root-poison put in their food so that their skin was scabbed with purplish sores.

"Why don't you talk right, Ruaway?"

She said nothing.

"You still don't know how to talk?"

She looked up at me and suddenly said a whole long speech I did not understand. "How I talk," she said at the end, still looking at me, right in the eyes. That was nice; I liked it. Mostly I saw only eyelids. Ruaway's eyes were clear and beautiful, though her face was dirty and blood-smeared.

"But it doesn't mean anything," I said.

"Not here."

"Where does it mean anything?"

Ruaway said some more gra-gra and then said, "My people."

"Your people are Teghs. They fight God and get beaten."

"Maybe," Ruaway said, sounding like Haghag. Her eyes looked into mine again, without killing in them but without fear. Nobody looked at me, except Haghag and Tazu and of course God. Everybody else put their forehead on their thumbs so I couldn't tell what they were thinking. I wanted to keep Ruaway with me, but if I favored her, Kig and the others would torment and hurt her. I remembered that when Lord Festival began sleeping with Lady Pin, the men who had insulted Lady Pin became oily and sugary with her and the bodymaids stopped stealing her earrings. I said, "Sleep with me tonight," to Ruaway.

She looked stupid.

"But wash first," I said.

She still looked stupid.

"I don't have a penis!" I said, impatient with her. "If we sleep together Kig will be afraid to touch you."

After a while Ruaway reached out and took my hand and put her forehead against the back of it. It was like thumbing the forehead only it took two people to do it. I liked that. Ruaway's hand was warm, and I could feel the feather of her eyelashes on my hand.

"Tonight," I said. "You understand?" I had understood that Ruaway didn't always understand. Ruaway nodded her body, and I ran off.

I knew nobody could stop me from doing anything, being God's only daughter, but there was nothing I could do ex-

cept what I was supposed to do, because everybody in the
house of God knew everything I did. If sleeping with Ruaway was a thing I wasn't supposed to do, I couldn't do it.
Haghag would tell me. I went to her and asked her.

Haghag scowled. "Why do you want that woman in your
bed? She's a dirty barbarian. She has lice. She can't even
talk."

Haghag was saying yes. She was jealous. I came and
stroked her hand and said, "When I'm God I'll give you a
room full of gold and jewels and dragon crests."

"You are my gold and jewels, little holy daughter,"
Haghag said.

Haghag was only a common person, but all the holy men
and women in God's house, relatives of God or people
touched by God, had to do what Haghag said. The nurse of
God's children was always a common person, chosen by
God Herself. Haghag had been chosen to be Omimo's nurse
when her own children were grown up, so when I first remember her she was quite old. She was always the same,
with strong hands and a soft voice, saying, "Maybe." She
liked to laugh and eat. We were in her heart, and she was in
mine. I thought I was her favorite, but when I told her so she
said, "After Didi." Didi is what the idiot called himself. I
asked her why he was deepest in her heart and she said, "Because he's foolish. And you because you're wise," she said,
laughing at me because I was jealous of Lord Idiot.

So now I said, "You fill my heart," and she, knowing it,
said hmph.

I think I was eight that year. Ruaway had been thirteen
when God the Father put his penis into her after killing her
father and mother in the war with her people. That made her
sacred, so she had to come live in God's house. If she had
conceived, the priests would have strangled her after she had
the baby, and the baby would have been nursed by a common woman for two years and then brought back to God's
house and trained to be a holy woman, a servant of God.
Most of the bodyservants were God's bastards. Such people
were holy, but had no title. Lords and ladies were God's relations, descendants of the ancestors of God. God's children

were called lord and lady too, except the two who were be-
trothed. We were just called Tazu and Ze until we became
God. My name is what the divine mother is called, the name
of the sacred plant that feeds the people of God. Tazu means
"great root," because when he was being born our father
drinking smoke in the childbirth rituals saw a big tree blown
over by a storm, and its roots held thousands of jewels in
their fingers.

When God saw things in the shrine or in sleep, with the
eyes in the back of their head, they told the dream priests.
The priests would ponder these sights and say whether the
oracle foretold what would happen or told what should be
done. But never had the priests seen the same things God
saw, together with God, until the birthday of the world that
made me fourteen years old and Tazu eleven.

Now, in these years, when the sun stands still over Mount
Kanaghadwa people still call it the birthday of the world and
count themselves a year older, but they no longer know and
do all the rituals and ceremonies, the dances and songs, the
blessings; and there is no feasting in the streets, now.

All my life used to be rituals, ceremonies, dances, songs,
blessings, lessons, feasts, and rules. I knew and I know now
on which day of God's year the first perfect ear of ze is to be
brought by an angel from the ancient field up by Wadana
where God set the first seed of the ze. I knew and know
whose hand is to thresh it, and whose hand is to grind the
grain, and whose lips are to taste the meal, at what hour, in
what room of the house of God, with what priests officiat-
ing. There were a thousand rules, but they only seem complicated when I write them here. We knew them and
followed them and only thought about them when we were
learning them or when they were broken.

I had slept all these years with Ruaway in my bed. She
was warm and comfortable. When she began to sleep with
me I stopped having bad sights at night as I used to do, seeing huge white clouds whirling in the dark, and toothed
mouths of animals, and strange faces that came and changed
themselves. When Kig and the other ill-natured holy people
saw Ruaway stay in my bedroom with me every night, they

dared not lay a finger or a breath on her. Nobody was allowed to touch me except my family and Haghag and the bodyservants, unless I told them to. And after I was ten, the punishment for touching me was death. All the rules had their uses.

The feast after the birthday of the world used to go on for four days and nights. All the storehouses were open and people could take what they needed. The servants of God served out food and beer in the streets and squares of the city of God and every town and village of God's country, and common people and holy people ate together. The lords and ladies and God's sons went down into the streets to join the feast; only God and I did not. God came out on the balcony of the house to hear the histories and see the dances, and I came with them. Singing and dancing priests entertained everyone in the Glittering Square, and drumming priests, and story priests, and history priests. Priests were common people, but what they did was holy.

But before the feast, there were many days of rituals, and on the day itself, as the sun stopped above the right shoulder of Kanaghadwa, God Himself danced the Dance that Turns, to bring the year back round.

He wore a gold belt and the gold sun mask, and danced in front of our house on the Glittering Square, which is paved with stones full of mica that flash and sparkle in the sunlight. We children were on the long south balcony to see God dance.

Just as the dance was ending a cloud came across the sun as it stood still over the right shoulder of the mountain, one cloud in the clear blue summer sky. Everybody looked up as the light dimmed. The glittering died out of the stones. All the people in the city made a sound, "Oh," drawing breath. God Himself did not look up, but his step faltered.

He made the last turns of the dance and went into the ash-house, where all the Goïz are in the walls, with the bowls where their food is burned in front of each of them, full of ashes.

There the dream priests were waiting for him, and God Herself had lighted the herbs to make the smoke to drink.

The oracle of the birthday was the most important one of the year. Everybody waited in the squares and streets and on the balconies for the priests to come out and tell what God Himself had seen over his shoulder and interpret it to guide us in the new year. After that the feasting would begin.

Usually it took till evening or night for the smoke to bring the seeing and for God to tell it to the priests and for them to interpret it and tell us. People were settling down to wait indoors or in shady places, for when the cloud had passed it became very hot. Tazu and Arzi and the idiot and I stayed out on the long balcony with Haghag and some of the lords and ladies, and Omimo, who had come back from the army for the birthday.

He was a grown man now, tall and strong. After the birthday he was going east to command the army making war on the Tegh and Chasi peoples. He had hardened the skin of his body the way soldiers did by rubbing it with stones and herbs until it was thick and tough as the leather of a ground-dragon, almost black, with a dull shine. He was handsome, but I was glad now that I was to marry Tazu not him. An ugly man looked out of his eyes.

He made us watch him cut his arm with his knife to show how the thick skin was cut deep yet did not bleed. He kept saying he was going to cut Tazu's arm to show how quickly Tazu would bleed. He boasted about being a general and slaughtering barbarians. He said things like, "I'll walk across the river on their corpses. I'll drive them into the jungles and burn the jungles down." He said the Tegh people were so stupid they called a flying lizard God. He said that they let their women fight in wars, which was such an evil thing that when he captured such women he would cut open their bellies and trample their wombs. I said nothing. I knew Ruaway's mother had been killed fighting beside her father. They had led a small army which God Himself had easily defeated. God made war on the barbarians not to kill them but to make them people of God, serving and sharing like all people in God's country. I knew no other good reason for war. Certainly Omimo's reasons were not good.

Since Ruaway slept with me she had learned to speak

well, and also I learned some words of the way she talked. One of them was techeg. Words like it are: companion, fights-beside-me, countrywoman or countryman, desired, lover, known-a-long-time; of all our words the one most like techeg is our word in-my-heart. Their name Tegh was the same word as techeg; it meant they were all in one another's heart. Ruaway and I were in each other's heart. We were techeg.

Ruaway and I were silent when Omimo said, "The Tegh are filthy insects. I'll crush them."

"Ogga! ogga! ogga!" the idiot said, imitating Omimo's boastful voice. I burst out laughing. In that moment, as I laughed at my brother, the doors of the ash house flew open wide and all the priests hurried out, not in procession with music, but in a crowd, wild, disordered, crying out aloud—

"The house burns and falls!"

"The world dies!"

"God is blind!"

There was a moment of terrible silence in the city and then people began to wail and call out in the streets and from the balconies.

God came out of the ash house, Herself first, leading Himself, who walked as if drunk and sun-dazzled, as people walk after drinking smoke. God came among the staggering, crying priests and silenced them. Then she said, "Hear what I have seen coming behind me, my people!"

In the silence he began speaking in a weak voice. We could not hear all his words, but she said them again in a clear voice after he said them: "God's house falls down to the ground burning, but is not consumed. It stands by the river. God is white as snow. God's face has one eye in the center. The great stone roads are broken. War is in the east and north. Famine is in the west and south. The world dies."

He put his face in his hands and wept aloud. She said to the priests, "Say what God has seen!"

They repeated the words God had said.

She said, "Go tell these words in the quarters of the city and to God's angels, and let the angels go out into all the country to tell the people what God has seen."

The priests put their foreheads to their thumbs and obeyed.

When Lord Idiot saw God weeping, he became so distressed and frightened that he pissed, making a pool on the balcony. Haghag, terribly upset, scolded and slapped him. He roared and sobbed. Omimo shouted that a foul woman who struck God's son should be put to death. Haghag fell on her face in Lord Idiot's pool of urine to beg mercy. I told her to get up and be forgiven. I said, "I am God's daughter and I forgive you," and I looked at Omimo with eyes that told him he could not speak. He did not speak.

When I think of that day, the day the world began dying, I think of the trembling old woman standing there sodden with urine, while the people down in the square looked up at us.

Lady Clouds sent Lord Idiot off with Haghag to be bathed, and some of the lords took Tazu and Arzi off to lead the feasting in the city streets. Arzi was crying and Tazu was keeping from crying. Omimo and I stayed among the holy people on the balcony, watching what happened down in Glittering Square. God had gone back into the ash house, and the angels had gathered to repeat together their message, which they would carry word for word, relay by relay, to every town and village and farm of God's country, running day and night on the great stone roads.

All that was as it should be; but the message the angels carried was not as it should be.

Sometimes when the smoke is thick and strong the priests also see things over their shoulder as God does. These are lesser oracles. But never before had they all seen the same thing God saw, speaking the same words God spoke.

And they had not interpreted or explained the words. There was no guidance in them. They brought no understanding, only fear.

But Omimo was excited: "War in the east and north," he said. "My war!" He looked at me, no longer sneering or sullen, but right at me, eye in eye, the way Ruaway looked at me. He smiled. "Maybe the idiots and crybabies will die," he said. "Maybe you and I will be God." He spoke low, standing close to me, so no one else heard. My heart gave a great leap. I said nothing.

Soon after that birthday, Omimo went back to lead the army on the eastern border.

All year long people waited for our house, God's house in the center of the city, to be struck by lightning, though not destroyed, since that is how the priests interpreted the oracle once they had time to talk and think about it. When the seasons went on and there was no lightning or fire, they said the oracle meant that the sun shining on the gold and copper roof-gutters was the unconsuming fire, and that if there was an earthquake the house would stand.

The words about God being white and having one eye they interpreted as meaning that God was the sun and was to be worshipped as the all-seeing giver of light and life. This had always been so.

There was war in the east, indeed. There had always been war in the east, where people coming out of the wilderness tried to steal our grain, and we conquered them and taught them how to grow it. General Lord Drowning sent angels back with news of his conquests all the way to the Fifth River.

There was no famine in the west. There had never been famine in God's country. God's children saw to it that crops were properly sown and grown and saved and shared. If the ze failed in the western lands, our carters pulled two-wheeled carts laden with grain on the great stone roads over the mountains from the central lands. If crops failed in the north, the carts went north from the Four Rivers land. From west to east carts came laden with smoked fish, from the Sunrise peninsula they came west with fruit and seaweed. The granaries and storehouses of God were always stocked and open to people in need. They had only to ask the administrators of the stores; what was needed was given. No one went hungry. Famine was a word that belonged to those we had brought into our land, people like the Tegh, the Chasi, the North Hills people. The hungry people, we called them.

The birthday of the world came again, and the most fearful words of the oracle—*the world dies*—were remembered. In public the priests rejoiced and comforted the common people, saying that God's mercy had spared the world. In our house there was little comfort. We all knew that God Himself was ill. He had hidden himself away more and more throughout the year, and many of the ceremonies took place without the divine presence, or only Herself was there. She seemed always quiet and untroubled. My lessons were mostly with her now, and with her I always felt that nothing had changed or could change and all would be well.

God danced the Dance that Turns as the sun stood still above the shoulder of the sacred mountain. He danced slowly, missing many steps. He went into the ash house. We waited, everybody waited, all over the city, all over the country. The sun went down behind Kanaghadwa. All the snow peaks of the mountains from north to south, Kayewa, burning Korosi, Aghet, Enni, Aziza, Kanaghadwa, burned gold, then fiery red, then purple. The light went up them and went out, leaving them white as ashes. The stars came out above them. Then at last the drums beat and the music sounded down in the Glittering Square, and torches made the pavement sparkle and gleam. The priests came out of the narrow doors of the ash house in order, in procession. They stopped. In the silence the oldest dream priest said in her thin, clear voice, "Nothing was seen over the shoulder of God."

Onto the silence ran a buzzing and whispering of people's voices, like little insects running over sand: That died out.

The priests turned and went back into the ash house in procession, in due order, in silence.

The ranks of angels waiting to carry the words of the oracle to the countryside stood still while their captains spoke in a group. Then the angels all moved away in groups by the five streets that start at the Glittering Square and lead to the five great stone roads that go out from the city across the lands. As always before, when the angels entered the streets they began to run, to carry God's word swiftly to the people. But they had no word to carry.

Tazu came to stand beside me on the balcony. He was twelve years old that day. I was fifteen.

He said, "Ze, may I touch you?"

I looked yes, and he put his hand in mine. That was comforting. Tazu was a serious, silent person. He tired easily, and often his head and eyes hurt so badly he could hardly see, but he did all the ceremonies and sacred acts faithfully, and studied with our teachers of history and geography and archery and dancing and writing, and with our mother studied the sacred knowledge, learning to be God. Some of our lessons he and I did together, helping each other. He was a kind brother and we were in each other's heart.

As he held my hand he said, "Ze, I think we'll be married soon."

I knew what his thoughts were. God our father had missed many steps of the dance that turns the world. He had seen nothing over his shoulder, looking into the time to come.

But what I thought in that moment was how strange it was that in the same place on the same day one year it was Omimo who said we should be married, and the next year it was Tazu.

"Maybe," I said. I held his hand tight, knowing he was frightened at being God. So was I. But there was no use being afraid. When the time came, we would be God.

If the time came. Maybe the sun had not stopped and turned back above the peak of Kanaghadwa. Maybe God had not turned the year.

Maybe there would be no more time—no time coming behind our backs, only what lay before us, only what we could see with mortal eyes. Only our own lives and nothing else.

That was so terrible a thought that my breath stopped and I shut my eyes, squeezing Tazu's thin hand, holding on to him, till I could steady my mind with the thought that there was still no use being afraid.

This year past, Lord Idiot's testicles had ripened at last, and he had begun trying to rape women. After he hurt a young holy girl and attacked others, God had him castrated. Since then he had been quiet again, though he often looked sad and lonely. Seeing Tazu and me holding hands, he seized Arzi's hand and stood beside him as Tazu and I were standing. "God, God!" he said, smiling with pride. But Arzi, who was nine, pulled his hand away and said, "You won't ever be God, you can't be, you're an idiot, you don't know anything!" Old Haghag scolded Arzi wearily and bitterly. Arzi did not cry, but Lord Idiot did, and Haghag had tears in her eyes.

The sun went north as in any year, as if God had danced the steps of the dance rightly. And on the dark day of the year, it turned back southward behind the peak of great Enni, as in any year. On that day, God Himself was dying, and Tazu and I were taken in to see him and be blessed. He lay all gone to bone in a smell of rot and sweet herbs burning. God my mother lifted his hand and put it on my head, then on Tazu's, while we knelt by the great bed of leather and bronze with our thumbs to our foreheads. She said the words of blessing. God my father said nothing, until he whispered, "Ze, Ze!" He was not calling to me. The name of God Herself is always Ze. He was calling to his sister and wife while he died.

Two nights later I woke in darkness. The deep drums were beating all through the house. I heard other drums begin to beat in the temples of worship and the squares farther away in the city, and then others yet farther away. In the countryside under the stars they would hear those drums and begin to beat their own drums, up in the hills, in the mountain passes and over the mountains to the western sea, across the fields eastward, across the four great rivers, from town to town clear to the wilderness. That same night, I thought, my brother Omimo in his camp under the North Hills would hear the drums saying God is dead.

A son and daughter of God, marrying, became God. This marriage could not take place till God's death, but always it took place within a few hours, so that the world would not be long bereft. I knew this from all we had been taught. It was ill fate that my mother delayed my marriage to Tazu. If we had been married at once, Omimo's claim would have been useless; not even his soldiers would have dared follow him. In her grief she was distraught. And she did not know or could not imagine the measure of Omimo's ambition, driving him to violence and sacrilege.

Informed by the angels of our father's illness, he had for days been marching swiftly westward with a small troop of loyal soldiers. When the drums beat, he heard them not in the far North Hills, but in the fortress on the hill called Ghari that stands north across the valley in sight of the city and the house of God.

The preparations for burning the body of the man who had been God were going forward; the ash priests saw to that. Preparations for our wedding should have been going forward at the same time, but our mother, who should have seen to them, did not come out of her room.

Her sister Lady Clouds and other lords and ladies of the household talked of the wedding hats and garlands, of the music priests who should come to play, of the festivals that should be arranged in the city and the villages. The marriage priest came anxiously to them, but they dared do nothing and he dared do nothing until my mother allowed them to act. Lady Clouds knocked at her door but she did not answer. They were so nervous and uneasy, waiting for her all day long, that I thought I would go mad staying with them. I went down into the garden court to walk.

I had never been farther outside the walls of our house than the balconies. I had never walked across the Glittering Square into the streets of the city. I had never seen a field or a river. I had never walked on dirt.

God's sons were carried in litters into the streets to the temples for rituals, and in summer after the birthday of the world they were always taken up into the mountains to Chimlu, where the world began, at the springs of the River of Origin. Every year when he came back from there, Tazu would tell me about Chimlu, how the mountains went up all around the ancient house there, and wild dragons flew from peak to peak. There God's sons hunted dragons and slept under the stars. But the daughter of God must keep the house.

The garden court was in my heart. It was where I could walk under the sky. It had five fountains of peaceful water, and flowering trees in great pots; plants of sacred ze grew against the sunniest wall in containers of copper and silver. All my life, when I had a time free of ceremonies and lessons, I went there. When I was little, I pretended the insects there were dragons and hunted them. Later I played throwbone with Ruaway, or sat and watched the water of the fountains well and fall, well and fall, till the stars came out in the sky above the walls.

This day as always, Ruaway came with me. Since I could not go anywhere alone but must have a companion, I had asked God Herself to make her my chief companion.

I sat down by the center fountain. Ruaway knew I wanted silence and went off to the corner under the fruit trees to wait. She could sleep anywhere at any time. I sat thinking how strange it would be to have Tazu always as my companion, day and night, instead of Ruaway. But I could not make my thoughts real.

The garden court had a door that opened on the street. Sometimes when the gardeners opened it to let each other in and out, I had looked out of it to see the world outside my house. The door was always locked on both sides, so that two people had to open it. As I sat by the fountain, I saw a man who I thought was a gardener cross the court and unbolt the door. Several men came in. One was my brother Omimo.

I think that door had been only his way to come secretly into the house. I think he had planned to kill Tazu and Arzi so that I would have to marry him. That he found me there in the garden as if waiting for him was the chance of that time, the fate that was on us.

"Ze!" he said as he came past the fountain where I sat. His voice was like my father's voice calling to my mother.

"Lord Drowning," I said, standing up. I was so bewildered that I said, "You're not here!" I saw that he had been wounded. His right eye was closed with a scar.

He stood still, staring at me from his one eye, and said nothing, getting over his own surprise. Then he laughed.

"No, sister," he said, and turning to his men gave them orders. There were five of them, I think, soldiers, with hardened skin all over their bodies. They wore angel's shoes on their feet, and belts around their waists and necks to support the sheaths for their penis and sword and daggers. Omimo looked like them, but with gold sheaths and the silver hat of a general. I did not understand what he said to the men. They came close to me, and Omimo came closer, so that I said, "Don't touch me," to warn them of their danger, for common men who touched me would be burned to death by the priests of the law, and even Omimo if he touched me without my permission would have to do penance and fast for a year. But he laughed again, and as I drew away, he took hold of my arm suddenly, putting his hand over my mouth. I bit down as hard as I could on his hand. He pulled it away and then slapped it again so hard on my mouth and nose that my head fell back and I could not breathe. I struggled and fought, but my eyes kept seeing blackness and flashes. I felt hard hands holding me, twisting my arms, pulling me up in the air, carrying me, and the hand on my mouth and nose tightened its grip till I could not breathe at all.

Ruaway had been drowsing under the trees, lying on the pavement among the big pots. They did not see her, but she saw them. She knew at once if they saw her they would kill her. She lay still. As soon as they had carried me out the gate into the street, she ran into the house to my mother's room and threw open the door. This was sacrilege, but, not knowing who in the household might be in sympathy with Omimo, she could trust only my mother.

"Lord Drowning has carried Ze off," she said. She told me later that my mother sat there silent and desolate in the dark room for so long that Ruaway thought she had not heard. She was about to speak again, when my mother stood up. Grief fell away from her. She said, "We cannot trust the army," her mind leaping at once to see what must be done, for she was one who had been God. "Bring Tazu here," she said to Ruaway.

Ruaway found Tazu among the holy people, called him to her with her eyes, and asked him to go to his mother at once. Then she went out of the house by the garden door that still stood unlocked and unwatched. She asked people in the Glittering Square if they had seen some soldiers with a drunken girl. Those who had seen us told her to take the northeast street. And so little time had passed that when she came out the northern gate of the city she saw Omimo and his men climbing the hill road toward Ghari, carrying me up to the old fort. She ran back to tell my mother this.

Consulting with Tazu and Lady Clouds and those people she most trusted, my mother sent for several old generals of the peace, whose soldiers served to keep order in the countryside, not in war on the frontiers. She asked for their obedience, which they promised her, for though she was not God she had been God, and was daughter and mother of God. And there was no one else to obey.

She talked next with the dream priests, deciding with them what messages the angels should carry to the people. There was no doubt that Omimo had carried me off to try to make himself God by marrying me. If my mother announced first, in the voices of the angels, that his act was not a marriage performed by the marriage priest, but was rape, then it might be the people would not believe he and I were God.

So the news went out on swift feet, all over the city and the countryside.

Omimo's army, now following him west as fast as they could march, were loyal to him. Some other soldiers joined him along the way. Most of the peacekeeping soldiers of the center land supported my mother. She named Tazu their general. He and she put up a brave and resolute front, but they had little true hope, for there was no God, nor could there be so long as Omimo had me in his power to rape or kill.

All this I learned later. What I saw and knew was this: I was in a low room without windows in the old fortress. The door was locked from outside. Nobody was with me and no guards were at the door, since nobody was in the fort but Omimo's soldiers. I waited there not knowing if it was day or night. I thought time had stopped, as I had feared it would. There was no light in the room, an old store-room under the pavement of the fortress. Creatures moved on the dirt floor. I walked on dirt then. I sat on dirt and lay on it.

The bolt of the door was shot. Torches flaring in the doorway dazzled me. Men came in and stuck a torch in the sconce on the wall. Omimo came through them to me. His penis stood upright and he came to me to rape me. I spat in his half-blind face and said, "If you touch me your penis will burn like that torch!" He showed his teeth as if he was laughing. He pushed me down and pushed my legs apart, but he was shaking, frightened of my scared being. He tried to push his penis into me with his hands but it had gone soft. He could not rape me. I said, "You can't, look, you can't rape me!"

His soldiers watched and heard all this. In his humiliation, Omimo pulled his sword from its gold sheath to kill me, but the soldiers held his hands, preventing him, saying, "Lord, Lord, don't kill her, she must be God with you!" Omimo shouted and fought them as I had fought him, and so they all went out, shouting and struggling with him. One of them seized the torch, and the door clashed behind them. After a little while I felt my way to the door and tried it, thinking they might have forgotten to bolt it, but it was bolted. I crawled back to the corner where I had been and lay on the dirt in the dark.

Truly we were all on the dirt in the dark. There was no God. God was the son and daughter of God joined in marriage by the marriage priest. There was no other. There was no other way to go. Omimo did not know what way to go, what to do. He could not marry me without the marriage priest's words. He thought by raping me he would be my husband, and maybe it would have been so: but he could not rape me. I made him impotent.

The only thing he saw to do was attack the city, take the house of God and its priests captive, and force the marriage priest to say the words that made God. He could not do this with the small force he had with him, so he waited for his army to come from the east.

Tazu and the generals and my mother gathered soldiers into the city from the center land. They did not try to attack Ghari. It was a strong fort, easy to defend, hard to attack, and they feared that if they besieged it, they would be caught between it and Omimo's great army coming from the east. So the soldiers that had come with him, about two hundred of them, garrisoned the fort. As the days passed, Omimo provided women for them. It was the policy of God to give village women extra grain or tools or crop-rows for going to fuck with the soldiers at army camps and stations. There were always women glad to oblige the soldiers and take the reward, and if they got pregnant of course they received more reward and support. Seeking to ease and placate his men, Omimo sent officers down to offer gifts to girls in the villages near Ghari. A group of girls agreed to come; for the common people understood very little of the situation, not believing that anyone could revolt against God. With these village women came Ruaway.

The women and girls ran about the fort, teasing and playing with the soldiers off duty. Ruaway found where I was by fate and courage, coming down into the dark passages under the pavement and trying the doors of the storerooms. I heard the bolt move in the lock. She said my name. I made some sound. "Come!" she said. I crawled to the door. She took my arm and helped me stand and walk. She shot the bolt shut again, and we felt our way down the black passage till we saw light flicker on stone steps. We came out into a torchlit courtyard full of girls and soldiers. Ruaway at once began to run through them, giggling and chattering nonsense, holding tight to my arm so that I ran with her. A couple of soldiers grabbed at us, but Ruaway dodged them, saying, "No, no, Tuki's for the Captain!" We ran on, and came to the side gate, and Ruaway said to the guards, "Oh, let us out, Captain, Captain, I have to take her back to her mother, she's vomiting sick with fever!" I was staggering and covered with dirt and filth from my prison. The guards laughed at me and said foul words about my foulness and opened the gate a crack to let us out. And we ran down the hill in the starlight.

To escape from a prison so easily, to run through locked doors, people have said, I must have been God indeed. But there was no God then, as there is none now. Long before God, and long after also, is the way things are, which we call chance, or luck, or fortune, or fate; but those are only names.

And there is courage. Ruaway freed me because I was in her heart.

As soon as we were out of sight of the guards at the gate we left the road, on which there were sentries, and cut across country to the city. It stood mightily on the great slope before us, its stone walls starlit. I had never seen it except from the windows and balconies of the house at the center of it.

I had never walked far, and though I was strong from the exercises I did as part of our lessons, my soles were as tender as my palms. Soon I was grunting and tears kept starting in my eyes from the shocks of pain from rocks and gravel underfoot. I found it harder and harder to breathe. I could not run. But Ruaway kept hold of my hand, and we went on.

We came to the north gate, locked and barred and heavily guarded by soldiers of the peace. Then Ruaway cried out, "Let God's daughter enter the city of God!"

I put back my hair and held myself up straight, though my lungs were full of knives, and said to the captain of the gate, "Lord Captain, take us to my mother Lady Ze in the house in the center of the world."

He was old General Rire's son, a man I knew, and he knew me. He stared at me once, then quickly thumbed his forehead, and roared out orders, and the gates opened. So we went in and walked the northeast street to my house, escorted by soldiers, and by more and more people shouting in joy. The drums began to beat, the high, fast beat of the festivals.

That night my mother held me in her arms, as she had not done since I was a suckling baby.

That night Tazu and I stood under the garland before the marriage priest and drank from the sacred cups and were married into God.

That night also Omimo, finding I was gone, ordered a death priest of the army to marry him to one of the village girls who came to fuck with the soldiers. Since nobody outside my house, except a few of his men, had ever seen me up close, any girl could pose as me. Most of his soldiers believed the girl was me. He proclaimed that he had married the daughter of the Dead God and that she and he were now God. As we sent out angels to tell of our marriage, so he sent runners to say that the marriage in the house of God was false, since his sister Ze had run away with him and married him at Ghari, and she and he were now the one true God. And he showed himself to the people wearing a gold hat, with white paint on his face, and his blinded eye, while the army priests cried out, "Behold! The oracle is fulfilled! God is white and has one eye!"

Some believed his priests and messengers. More believed ours. But all were distressed or frightened or made angry by hearing messengers proclaim two Gods at one time, so that instead of knowing the truth, they had to choose to believe.

Omimo's great army was now only four or five days' march away.

Angels came to us saying that a young general, Mesiwa, was bringing a thousand soldiers of the peace up from the rich coasts south of the city. He told the angels only that he came to fight for "the one true God." We feared that meant Omimo. For we added no words to our name, since the word itself means the only truth, or else it means nothing.

We were wise in our choice of generals, and decisive in acting on their advice. Rather than wait for the city to be besieged, we resolved to send a force to attack the eastern army before it reached Ghari, meeting it in the foothills above the River of Origin. We would have to fall back as their full strength came up, but we could strip the country as we did so, and bring the country people into the city. Meanwhile we sent carts to and from all the storehouses on the southern and western roads to fill the city's granaries. If the war did not end quickly, said the old generals, it would be won by those who could keep eating.

"Lord Drowning's army can feed themselves from the storehouses along the east and north roads," said my mother, who attended all our councils.

"Destroy the roads," Tazu said.

I heard my mother's breath catch, and remembered the oracle: The roads will be broken.

"That would take as long to do as it took to make them," said the oldest general, but the next oldest general said, "Break down the stone bridge at Almoghay." And so we ordered. Retreating from its delaying battle, our army tore down the great bridge that had stood a thousand years. Omimo's army had to go round nearly a hundred miles farther, through forests, to the ford at Domi, while our army and our carters brought the contents of the storehouses in to the city. Many country people followed them, seeking the protection of God, and so the city grew very full. Every grain of ze came with a mouth to eat it.

All this time Mesiwa, who might have come against the eastern army at Domi, waited in the passes with his thousand men. When we commanded him to come help punish sacrilege and restore peace, he sent our angel back with meaningless messages. It seemed certain that he was in league with Omimo. "Mesiwa the finger, Omimo the thumb," said the oldest general, pretending to crack a louse.

"God is not mocked," Tazu said to him, deadly fierce. The old general bowed his forehead down on his thumbs, abashed. But I was able to smile.

Tazu had hoped the country people would rise up in anger at the sacrilege and strike the Painted God down. But they were not soldiers and had never fought. They had always lived under the protection of the soldiers of peace and under our care. As if our doings now were like the whirlwind or the earthquake, they were paralyzed by them and could only watch and wait till they were over, hoping to survive. Only the people of our household, whose livelihood depended directly upon us and whose skills and knowledge were at our service, and the people of the city in whose heart we were, and the soldiers of the peace, would fight for us.

The country people had believed in us. Where no belief is, no God is. Where doubt is, foot falters and hand will not take hold.

The wars at the borders, the wars of conquest, had made our land too large. The people in the towns and villages knew no more who I was than I knew who they were. In the days of the origin, Babam Kerul and Bamam Ze came down from the mountain and walked the fields of the center lands beside the common people. The common people who laid the first stones of the great roads and the huge base stones of the old city wall had known the face of their God, seeing it daily.

After I spoke of this to our councils, Tazu and I went out into the streets, sometimes carried in litters, sometimes walking. We were surrounded by the priests and guards who honored our divinity, but we went among the people, meeting their eyes. They fell on their knees and put their foreheads to their thumbs, and many wept when they saw us. They called out from street to street, and little children cried out, "There's God!"

"You walk in their hearts," my mother said.

But Omimo's army had come to the River of Origin, and one day's march brought the vanguard to Ghari.

That evening we stood on the north balcony looking toward Ghari hill, which was swarming with men, as when a nest of insects swarms. To the west the light was dark red on the mountains in their winter snow. From Korosi a vast plume of smoke trailed, blood color.

"Look," Tazu said, pointing northwest. A light flared in the sky, like the sheet lightning of summer. "A falling star," he said, and I said, "An eruption."

In the dark of the night, angels came to us. "A great house burned and fell from the sky," one said, and the other said, "It burned but it stands, on the bank of the river."

"The words of God spoken on the birthday of the world," I said.

The angels knelt down hiding their faces.

What I saw then is not what I see now looking far off to the distant past; what I knew then is both less and more than I know now. I try to say what I saw and knew then.

That morning I saw coming down the great stone road to the northern gate a group of beings, two-legged and erect like people or lizards. They were the height of giant desert lizards, with monstrous limbs and feet, but without tails. They were white all over and hairless. Their heads had no mouth or nose and one huge single staring shining lidless eye.

They stopped outside the gate.

Not a man was to be seen on Ghari Hill. They were all in the fortress or hidden in the woods behind the hill.

We were standing up on the top of the northern gate, where a wall runs chest-high to protect the guards.

There was a little sound of frightened weeping on the roofs and balconies of the city, and people called out to us, "God! God, save us!"

Tazu and I had talked all night. We listened to what our mother and other wise people said, and then we sent them away to reach out our minds together, to look over our shoulder into the time that was coming. We saw the death and the birth of the world, that night. We saw all things changed.

The oracle had said that God was white and had one eye. This was what we saw now. The oracle had said that the world died. With it died our brief time of being God. This was what we had to do now: to kill the world. The world must die so that God may live. The house falls that it may stand. Those who have been God must make God welcome.

Tazu spoke welcome to God, while I ran down the spiral stairs inside the wall of the gate and unbolted the great bolts—the guards had to help me—and swung the door open. "Enter in!" I said to God, and put my forehead to my thumbs, kneeling.

They came in, hesitant, moving slowly, ponderously. Each one turned its huge eye from side to side, unblinking. Around the eye was a ring of silver that flashed in the sun. I saw myself in one of those eyes, a pupil in the eye of God.

Their snow-white skin was coarse and wrinkled, with bright tattoos on it. I was dismayed that God could be so ugly.

The guards had shrunk back against the walls. Tazu had come down to stand with me. One of them raised a box toward us. A noise came out of the box, as if some animal was shut in it.

Tazu spoke to them again, telling them that the oracle had foretold their coming, and that we who had been God welcomed God.

They stood there, and the box made more noises. I thought it sounded like Ruaway before she learned to talk right. Was the language of God no longer ours? Or was God an animal, as Ruaway's people believed? I thought they seemed more like the monstrous lizards of the desert that lived in the zoo of our house than they seemed like us.

One raised its thick arm and pointed at our house, down at the end of the street, taller than other houses, its copper gutters and goldleaf carvings shining in the bright winter sunlight.

"Come, Lord," I said, "come to your house." We led them to it and brought them inside.

When we came into the low, long, windowless audience room, one of them took off its head. Inside it was a head like ours, with two eyes, nose, mouth, ears. The others did the same.

Then, seeing their head was a mask, I saw that their white skin was like a shoe that they wore not just on the foot but all over their body. Inside this shoe they were like us, though the skin of their faces was the color of clay pots and looked very thin, and their hair was shiny and lay flat.

"Bring food and drink," I said to the children of God cowering outside the door, and they ran to bring trays of ze-cakes and dried fruit and winter beer. God came to the tables where the food was set. Some of them pretended to eat. One, watching what I did, touched the ze-cake to its forehead first, and then bit into it and chewed and swallowed. It spoke to the others, gre-gra, gre-gra.

This one was also the first to take off its body-shoe. Inside it other wrappings and coverings hid and protected most of its body, but this was understandable, because even the body skin was pale and terribly thin, soft as a baby's eyelid.

In the audience room, on the east wall over the double seat of God, hung the gold mask which God Himself wore to turn the sun back on its way. The one who had eaten the cake pointed at the mask. Then it looked at me—its own eyes were oval, large, and beautiful—and pointed up to where the sun was in the sky. I nodded my body. It pointed its finger here and there all about the mask, and then all about the ceiling.

"There must be more masks made, because God is now more than two," Tazu said.

I had thought the gesture might signify the stars, but I saw that Tazu's interpretation made more sense.

"We will have masks made," I told God, and then ordered the hat priest to go fetch the gold hats which God wore during ceremonies and festivals. There were many of these hats, some jewelled and ornate, others plain, all very ancient. The hat priest brought them in due order two by two until they were all set out on the great table of polished wood and bronze where the ceremonies of First Ze and Harvest were celebrated.

Tazu took off the gold hat he wore, and I took off mine. Tazu put his hat on the head of the one who had eaten the cake, and I chose a short one and reached up and put my hat on its head. Then, choosing ordinary-day hats, not those of the sacred occasions, we put a hat on each of the heads of God, while they stood and waited for us to do so.

Then we knelt bareheaded and put our foreheads against our thumbs.

God stood there. I was sure they did not know what to do. "God is grown, but new, like a baby," I said to Tazu. I was sure they did not understand what we said.

All at once the one I had put my hat on came to me and put its hands on my elbows to raise me up from kneeling. I pulled back at first, not being used to being touched; then I remembered I was no longer very sacred, and let God touch me. It talked and gestured. It gazed into my eyes. It took off the gold hat and tried to put it back on my head. At that I did shrink away, saying, "No, no!" It seemed blasphemy, to say No to God, but I knew better.

God talked among themselves then for a while, and Tazu and our mother and I were able to talk among ourselves. What we understood was this: the oracle had not been wrong, of course, but it had been subtle. God was not truly one-eyed nor blind, but did not know how to see. It was not God's skin that was white, but their mind that was blank and ignorant. They did not know how to talk, how to act, what to do. They did not know their people.

Yet how could Tazu and I, or our mother and our old teachers, teach them? The world had died and a new world was coming to be. Everything in it might be new. Everything might be different. So it was not God, but we, who did not know how to see, what to do, how to speak.

I felt this so strongly that I knelt again and prayed to God, "Teach us!"

They looked at me and talked to each other, brr-grr, gre-gra.

I sent our mother and the others to talk with our generals, for angels had come with reports about Omimo's army. Tazu was very tired from lack of sleep. We two sat down on the floor together and talked quietly. He was concerned about God's seat. "How can they all sit on it at once?" he said.

"They'll have more seats added," I said. "Or now two will sit on it, and then another two. They're all God, the way you and I were, so it doesn't matter."

"But none of them is a woman," Tazu said.

I looked at God more carefully and saw that he was right. This disturbed me slowly, but very deeply. How could God be only half human?

In my world, a marriage made God. In this world coming to be, what made God?

I thought of Omimo. White clay on his face and a false marriage had made him a false God, but many people believed he was truly God. Would the power of their belief make him God, while we gave our power to this new, ignorant God?

If Omimo found out how helpless they appeared to be, not knowing how to speak, not even knowing how to eat, he would fear their divinity even less than he had feared ours. He would attack. And would our soldiers fight for this God?

I saw clearly that they would not. I saw from the back of my head, with the eyes that see what is coming. I saw the misery that was coming to my people. I saw the world dead, but I did not see it being born. What world could be born of a God who was male? Men do not give birth.

Everything was wrong. It came very strongly into my mind that we should have our soldiers kill God now, while they were still new in the world and weak.

And then? If we killed God there would be no God. We

could pretend to be God again, the way Omimo pretended. But godhead is not pretense. Nor is it put on and off like a golden hat.

The world had died. That was fated and foretold. The fate of these strange men was to be God, and they would have to live their fate as we lived ours, finding out what it was to be as it came to be, unless they could see over their shoulders, which is one of the gifts of God.

I stood up again, taking Tazu's hand so that he stood beside me. "The city is yours," I said to them, "and the people are yours. The world is yours, and the war is yours. All praise and glory to you, our God!" And we knelt once more and bowed our foreheads deeply to our thumbs, and left them.

"Where are we going?" Tazu said. He was twelve years old and no longer God. There were tears in his eyes.

"To find Mother and Ruaway," I said, "and Arzi and Lord Idiot and Haghag, and any of our people who want to come with us." I had begun to say "our children," but we were no longer their mother and father.

"Come where?" Tazu said.

"To Chimlu."

"Up in the mountains? Run and hide? We should stay and fight Omimo."

"What for?" I said.

That was sixty years ago.

I have written this to tell how it was to live in the house of God before the world ended and began again. To tell it I have tried to write with the mind I had then. But neither then nor now do I fully understand the oracle which my father and all the priests saw and spoke. All of it came to pass. Yet we have no God, and no oracles to guide us.

None of the strange men lived a long life, but they all lived longer than Omimo.

We were on the long road up into the mountains when an angel caught up with us to tell us that Mesiwa had joined Omimo, and the two generals had brought their great army against the house of the strangers, which stood like a tower in the fields near Soze River, with a waste of burned earth around it. The strangers warned Omimo and his army clearly to withdraw, sending lightning out of the house over their heads that set distant trees afire. Omimo would not heed. He could prove he was God only by killing God. He commanded his army to rush at the tall house. He and Mesiwa and a hundred men around him were destroyed by a single bolt of lightning. They were burned to ash. His army fled in terror.

"They are God! They are God indeed!" Tazu said when he heard the angel tell us that. He spoke joyfully, for he was as unhappy in his doubt as I was. And for a while we could all believe in them, since they could wield the lightning. Many people called them God as long as they lived.

My belief is that they were not God in any sense of the word I understand, but were otherworldly, supernatural beings, who had great powers, but were weak and ignorant of our world, and soon sickened of it and died.

There were fourteen of them in all. Some of them lived more than ten years. These learned to speak as we do. One of them came up into the mountains to Chimlu, along with some of the pilgrims who still wanted to worship Tazu and me as God. Tazu and I and this man talked for many days, learning from each other. He told us that their house moved in the air, flying like a dragon-lizard, but its wings were broken. He told us that in the land they came from the sunlight is very weak, and it was our strong sunlight that made them sick. Though they covered their bodies with weavings, still their thin skins let the sunlight in, and they would all die soon. He told us they were sorry they had come. I said, "You had to come. God saw you coming. What use is it to be sorry?"

He agreed with me that they were not God. He said that God lived in the sky. That seemed to us a useless place for God to live. Tazu said they had indeed been God when they came, since they fulfilled the oracle and changed the world; but now, like us, they were common people.

Ruaway took a liking to this stranger, maybe because she had been a stranger, and when he was at Chimlu they slept together. She said he was like any man under his weavings and coverings. He told her he could not impregnate her, as his seed would not ripen in our earth. Indeed the strangers left no children.

This stranger told us his name, Bin-yi-zin. He came back up to Chimlu several times, and was the last of them to die. He left with Ruaway the dark crystals he wore before his eyes, which make things look larger and clearer for her, though to my eyes they make things dim. To me he gave his own record of his life, in a beautiful writing made of lines of little pictures, which I keep in the box with this writing I make.

When Tazu's testicles ripened we had to decide what to do, for brothers and sisters among the common people do not marry. We asked the priests and they advised us that our marriage being divine could not be unmade, and that though no longer God we were husband and wife. Since we were in each other's heart, this pleased us, and often we slept together. Twice I conceived, but the conceptions aborted, one very early and one in the fourth month, and I did not conceive again. This was a grief to us, and yet fortunate, for had we had children, the people might have tried to make them be God.

It takes a long time to learn to live without God, and some people never do. They would rather have a false God than none at all. All through the years, though seldom now, people would climb up to Chimlu to beg Tazu and me to come back down to the city and be God. And when it became clear that the strangers would not rule the country as God, either under the old rules or with new ones, men began to imitate Omimo, marrying ladies of our lineage and claiming to be a new God. They all found followers and they all made wars, fighting each other. None of them had Omimo's terrible courage, or the loyalty of a great army to a successful general. They have all come to wretched ends at the hands of angry, disappointed, wretched people.

For my people and my land have fared no better than I feared and saw over my shoulder on the night the world ended. The great stone roads are not maintained. In places they are already broken. Almoghay bridge was never rebuilt. The granaries and storehouses are empty and falling down. The old and sick must beg from neighbors, and a pregnant girl has only her mother to turn to, and an orphan has no one. There is famine in the west and south. We are the hungry people, now. The angels no longer weave the net of government, and one part of the land knows nothing of the others. They say barbarians have brought back the wilderness across the Fourth River, and ground dragons spawn in the fields of grain. Little generals and painted gods raise armies to waste lives and goods and spoil the sacred earth.

The evil time will not last forever. No time does. I died as God a long time ago. I have lived as a common woman a long time. Each year I see the sun turn back from the south behind great Kanaghadwa. Though God does not dance on the glittering pavement, yet I see the birthday of the world over the shoulder of my death.

Oracle

GREG EGAN

Greg Egan (www.netspace.net.au/~gregegan), who lives in Perth, West Australia, hit his stride in the early 1990s and became one of the most interesting new hard SF writers of the decade. He is internationally famous for his stories and novels. His name burst into international prominence in 1990 with several fine SF stories that focussed attention on his writing. His SF novels to date are Quarantine *(1992),* Permutation City *(1994),* Distress *(1995),* Diaspora *(1997), and* Teranesia *(1999); his short story collections are* Our Lady of Chernobyl *(1995),* Axiomatic *(1995), and* Luminous *(1999). As of 2000, he is the flagship hard SF writer of the younger generation.*

"Oracle," an alternate history hard SF tale that was published in Asimov's, *sets up a dramatic philosophical debate between figures who represent Alan Turing and C. S. Lewis. At issue is the existence of God, and reason versus the supernatural. In an interview first published in Spanish in* Gigamesh *magazine, Egan said, "There are people who think that if you ask the question 'Why is there something rather than nothing?' then the only meaningful answer is 'God.' I can understand why they feel that way, but I don't think that's really an answer at all . . . science is the only way we can hope to get the facts straight, about the world we're living in, and the consequences of our actions." This story is in the Gernsback and Campbell tradition, in which science is adequate to the task.*

1

On his eighteenth day in the tiger cage, Robert Stoney began to lose hope of emerging unscathed.

He'd woken a dozen times throughout the night with an overwhelming need to stretch his back and limbs, and none of the useful compromise positions he'd discovered in his first few days—the least-worst solutions to the geometrical problem of his confinement—had been able to dull his sense of panic. He'd been in far more pain in the second week, suffering cramps that felt as if the muscles of his legs were dying on the bone, but these new spasms had come from somewhere deeper, powered by a sense of urgency that revolved entirely around his own awareness of his situation.

That was what frightened him. Sometimes he could find ways to minimize his discomfort, sometimes he couldn't, but he'd been clinging to the thought that, in the end, all these fuckers could ever do was hurt him. That wasn't true, though. They could make him ache for freedom in the middle of the night, the way he might have ached with grief, or love. He'd always cherished the understanding that his self was a whole, his mind and body indivisible. But he'd failed to appreciate the corollary: through his body, they could touch every part of him. Change every part of him.

Morning brought a fresh torment: hay fever. The house was somewhere deep in the countryside, with nothing to be heard in the middle of the day but bird song. June had always been his worst month for hay fever, but in Manchester it had been tolerable. As he ate breakfast, mucus dripped from his face into the bowl of lukewarm oats they'd given him. He stanched the flow with the back of his hand, but suffered a moment of shuddering revulsion when he couldn't find a way to reposition himself to wipe his hand clean on his trousers. Soon he'd need to empty his bowels. They supplied him with a chamber pot whenever he asked, but they always waited two or three hours before removing it. The smell was bad enough, but the fact that it took up space in the cage was worse.

Toward the middle of the morning, Peter Quint came to see him. "How are we today, Prof?" Robert didn't reply. Since the day Quint had responded with a puzzled frown to the suggestion that he had an appropriate name for a spook, Robert had tried to make at least one fresh joke at the man's expense every time they met, a petty but satisfying indulgence. But now his mind was blank, and in retrospect the whole exercise seemed like an insane distraction, as bizarre and futile as scoring philosophical points against some predatory animal while it gnawed on his leg.

"Many happy returns," Quint said cheerfully.

Robert took care to betray no surprise. He'd never lost track of the days, but he'd stopped thinking in terms of the calendar date; it simply wasn't relevant. Back in the real world, to have forgotten his own birthday would have been considered a benign eccentricity. Here it would be taken as proof of his deterioration, and imminent surrender.

If he was cracking, he could at least choose the point of fissure. He spoke as calmly as he could, without looking up. "You know I almost qualified for the Olympic marathon, back in forty-eight? If I hadn't done my hip in just before the trials, I might have competed." He tried a self-deprecating laugh. "I suppose I was never really much of an athlete. But I'm only forty-six. I'm not ready for a wheelchair yet." The words did help: he could beg this way without breaking down completely, expressing an honest fear without revealing how much deeper the threat of damage went.

He continued, with a measured note of plaintiveness that

he hoped sounded like an appeal to fairness. "I just can't bear the thought of being crippled. All I'm asking is that you let me stand upright. Let me keep my health."

Quint was silent for a moment, then he replied with a tone of thoughtful sympathy. "It's unnatural, isn't it? Living like this: bent over, twisted, day after day. Living in an unnatural way is always going to harm you. I'm glad you can finally see that."

Robert was tired; it took several seconds for the meaning to sink in. *It was that crude, that obvious?* They'd locked him in this cage, for all this time, as a kind of ham-fisted *metaphor* for his crimes?

He almost burst out laughing, but he contained himself. "I don't suppose you know Franz Kafka?"

"Kafka?" Quint could never hide his voracity for names. "One of your Commie chums, is he?"

"I very much doubt that he was ever a Marxist."

Quint was disappointed, but prepared to make do with second best. "One of the other kind, then?"

Robert pretended to be pondering the question. "On balance, I suspect that's not too likely either."

"So why bring his name up?"

"I have a feeling he would have admired your methods, that's all. He was quite the connoisseur."

"Hmm." Quint sounded suspicious, but not entirely unflattered.

Robert had first set eyes on Quint in February of 1952. His house had been burgled the week before, and Arthur, a young man he'd been seeing since Christmas, had confessed to Robert that he'd given an acquaintance the address. Perhaps the two of them had planned to rob him, and Arthur had backed out at the last moment. In any case, Robert had gone to the police with an unlikely story about spotting the culprit in a pub, trying to sell an electric razor of the same make and model as the one taken from his house. No one could be charged on such flimsy evidence, so Robert had had no qualms about the consequences if Arthur had turned out to be lying. He'd simply hoped to prompt an investigation that might turn up something more tangible.

The following day, the CID had paid Robert a visit. The man he'd accused was known to the police, and fingerprints taken on the day of the burglary matched the prints they had on file. However, at the time Robert claimed to have seen him in the pub, he'd been in custody already on an entirely different charge.

The detectives had wanted to know why he'd lied. To spare himself the embarrassment, Robert had explained, of spelling out the true source of his information. Why was that embarrassing?

"I'm involved with the informant."

One detective, Mr Wills, had asked matter-of-factly, "What exactly does that entail, sir?" And Robert—in a burst of frankness, as if honesty itself was sure to be rewarded—had told him every detail. He'd known it was still technically illegal, of course. But then, so was playing football on Easter Sunday. It could hardly be treated as a serious crime, like burglary.

The police had strung him along for hours, gathering as much information as they could before disabusing him of this misconception. They hadn't charged him immediately; they'd needed a statement from Arthur first. But then Quint had materialized the next morning, and spelt out the choices very starkly. Three years in prison, with hard labor. Or Robert could resume his war-time work—for just one day a week, as a handsomely paid consultant to Quint's branch of the secret service—and the charges would quietly vanish.

At first, he'd told Quint to let the courts do their worst. He'd been angry enough to want to take a stand against the preposterous law, and whatever his feelings for Arthur, Quint had suggested—gloatingly, as if it strengthened his case—that the younger, working-class man would be treated far more leniently than Robert, having been led astray by someone whose duty was to set an example for the lower orders. Three years in prison was an unsettling prospect, but it would not have been the end of the world; the Mark I had changed the way he worked, but he could still function with nothing but a pencil and paper, if necessary. Even if they'd had him breaking rocks from dawn to dusk he probably would have been able to day-dream productively, and for all Quint's scaremongering he'd doubted it would come to that.

At some point, though, in the twenty-four hours Quint had given him to reach a decision, he'd lost his nerve. By granting the spooks their one day a week, he could avoid all the fuss and disruption of a trial. And though his work at the time—modeling embryological development—had been as challenging as anything he'd done in his life, he hadn't been immune to pangs of nostalgia for the old days, when the fate of whole fleets of battleships had rested on finding the most efficient way to extract logical contradictions from a bank of rotating wheels.

The trouble with giving in to extortion was, *it proved that you could be bought.* Never mind that the Russians could hardly have offered to intervene with the Manchester constabulary next time he needed to be rescued. Never mind that he would scarcely have cared if an enemy agent had threatened to send such comprehensive evidence to the newspapers that there'd be no prospect of his patrons saving him again. He'd lost any chance to proclaim that what he did in bed with another willing partner was not an issue of national security; by saying yes to Quint, he'd made it one. By choosing to be corrupted once, he'd brought the whole torrent of clichès and paranoia down upon his head: he was vulnerable to blackmail, an easy target for entrapment, perfidious by nature. He might as well have posed *in flagrante delicto* with Guy Burgess on the steps of the Kremlin.

It wouldn't have mattered if Quint and his masters had merely decided that they couldn't trust him. The problem was—some six years after recruiting him, with no reason to believe that he had ever breached security in any way— they'd convinced themselves that they could neither continue to employ him, nor safely leave him in peace, until they'd rid him of the trait they'd used to control him in the first place.

Robert went through the painful, complicated process of rearranging his body so he could look Quint in the eye. "You know, if it was legal there'd be nothing to worry about, would there? Why don't you devote some of your considerable Machiavellian talents to that end? Blackmail a few politicians. Set up a Royal Commission. It would only take you a couple of years. Then we could all get on with our real jobs."

Quint blinked at him, more startled than outraged. "You might as well say that we should legalize treason!"

Robert opened his mouth to reply, then decided not to waste his breath. Quint wasn't expressing a moral opinion. He simply meant that a world in which fewer people's lives were ruled by the constant fear of discovery was hardly one that a man in his profession would wish to hasten into existence.

When Robert was alone again, the time dragged. His hay fever worsened, until he was sneezing and gagging almost continuously; even with freedom of movement and an endless supply of the softest linen handkerchiefs, he would have been reduced to abject misery. Gradually, though, he grew more adept at dealing with the symptoms, delegating the task to some barely conscious part of himself. By the middle of the afternoon—covered in filth, eyes almost swollen shut—he finally managed to turn his mind back to his work.

For the past four years he'd been immersed in particle physics. He'd been following the field on and off since before the war, but the paper by Yang and Mills in '54, in which they'd generalized Maxwell's equations for electromagnetism to apply to the strong nuclear force, had jolted him into action.

After several false starts, he believed he'd discovered a useful way to cast gravity into the same form. In general relativity, if you carried a four-dimensional velocity vector around a loop that enclosed a curved region of spacetime, it came back rotated—a phenomenon highly reminiscent of the way more abstract vectors behaved in nuclear physics. In both cases, the rotations could be treated algebraically, and the traditional way to get a handle on this was to make use of a set of matrices of complex numbers whose relationships mimicked the algebra in question. Hermann Weyl had catalogued most of the possibilities back in the '20s and '30s.

In spacetime, there were six distinct ways you could rotate an object: you could turn it around any of three perpendicular axes in space, or you could boost its velocity in any of the same three directions. These two kinds of rotation were complementary, or "dual" to each other, with the ordinary rotations only affecting coordinates that were untouched by the corresponding boost, and *vice versa*. This meant that you could rotate something around, say, the *x*-axis, and speed it up in the same direction, without the two processes interfering.

When Robert had tried applying the Yang-Mills approach to gravity in the obvious way, he'd floundered. It was only when he'd shifted the algebra of rotations into a new, strangely skewed guise that the mathematics had begun to fall into place. Inspired by a trick that particle physicists used to construct fields with left- or right-handed spin, he'd combined every rotation with its own dual multiplied by *i*, the square root of minus one. The result was a set of rotations in four *complex* dimensions, rather than the four real ones of ordinary spacetime, but the relationships between them preserved the original algebra.

Demanding that these "self-dual" rotations satisfy Einstein's equations turned out to be equivalent to ordinary general relativity, but the process leading to a quantum-mechanical version of the theory became dramatically simpler. Robert still had no idea how to interpret this, but as a purely formal trick it worked spectacularly well—and when the mathematics fell into place like that, it had to mean *something*.

He spent several hours pondering old results, turning them over in his mind's eye, rechecking and reimagining everything in the hope of forging some new connection. Making no progress, but there'd always been days like that. It was a triumph merely to spend this much time doing what he would have done back in the real world—however mundane, or even frustrating, the same activity might have been in its original setting.

By evening, though, the victory began to seem hollow. He hadn't lost his wits entirely, but he was frozen, stunted. He might as well have whiled away the hours reciting the base-32 multiplication table in Baudot code, just to prove that he still remembered it.

As the room filled with shadows, his powers of concentration deserted him completely. His hay fever had abated, but he was too tired to think, and in too much pain to sleep. This wasn't Russia, they couldn't hold him forever; he simply had to wear them down with his patience. *But when, exactly, would they have to let him go?* And how much more patient could Quint be, with no pain, no terror, to erode his determination?

The moon rose, casting a patch of light on the far wall; hunched over, he couldn't see it directly, but it silvered the gray at his feet, and changed his whole sense of the space around him. The cavernous room mocking his confinement reminded him of nights he'd spent lying awake in the dormitory at Sherborne. A public school education did have one great advantage: however miserable you were afterward, you could always take comfort in the knowledge that life would never be quite as bad again.

"This room smells of mathematics! Go out and fetch a disinfectant spray!" That had been his form-master's idea of showing what a civilized man he was: contempt for that loathsome subject, the stuff of engineering and other low trades. And as for Robert's chemistry experiments, like the beautiful color-changing iodate reaction he'd learned from Chris's brother—.

Robert felt a familiar ache in the pit of his stomach. *Not now. I can't afford this now.* But the whole thing swept over him, unwanted, unbidden. He'd used to meet Chris in the library on Wednesdays; for months, that had been the only time they could spend together. Robert had been fifteen then, Chris a year older. If Chris had been plain, he still would have shone like a creature from another world. No one else in Sherborne had read Eddington on relativity, Hardy on mathematics. No one else's horizons stretched beyond rugby, sadism, and the dimly satisfying prospect of reading classics at Oxford then vanishing into the maw of the civil service.

They had never touched, never kissed. While half the school had been indulging in passionless sodomy—as a rather literal-minded substitute for the much too difficult task of imagining women—Robert had been too shy even to declare his feelings. Too shy, and too afraid that they might not be reciprocated. It hadn't mattered. To have a friend like Chris had been enough.

In December of 1929, they'd both sat the exams for Trinity College, Cambridge. Chris had won a scholarship; Robert hadn't. He'd reconciled himself to their separation, and prepared for one more year at Sherborne without the one person who'd made it bearable. Chris would be following happily in the footsteps of Newton; just thinking of that would be some consolation.

Chris never made it to Cambridge. In February, after six days in agony, he'd died of bovine tuberculosis.

Robert wept silently, angry with himself because he knew that half his wretchedness was just self-pity, exploiting his grief as a disguise. He had to stay honest; once every source of unhappiness in his life melted together and became indistinguishable, he'd be like a cowed animal, with no sense of the past or the future. Ready to do anything to get out of the cage.

If he hadn't yet reached that point, he was close. It would only take a few more nights like the last one. Drifting off in the hope of a few minutes' blankness, to find that sleep itself shone a colder light on everything. Drifting off, then waking with a sense of loss so extreme it was like suffocation.

A woman's voice spoke from the darkness in front of him. "Get off your knees!"

Robert wondered if he was hallucinating. He'd heard no one approach across the creaky floorboards.

The voice said nothing more. Robert rearranged his body so he could look up from the floor. There was a woman he'd never seen before, standing a few feet away.

She'd sounded angry, but as he studied her face in the moonlight through the slits of his swollen eyes, he realized that her anger was directed, not at him, but at his condition. She gazed at him with an expression of horror and outrage, as if she'd chanced upon him being held like this in some respectable neighbor's basement, rather than an MI6 facility. Maybe she was one of the staff employed in the upkeep of the house, but had no idea what went on here? Surely those people were vetted and supervised, though, and threatened with life imprisonment if they ever set foot outside their prescribed domains.

For one surreal moment, Robert wondered if Quint had sent her to seduce him. It would not have been the strangest thing they'd tried. But she radiated such fierce self assurance—such a sense of confidence that she could speak with the authority of her convictions, and expect to be heeded— that he knew she could never have been chosen for the role. No one in Her Majesty's government would consider self assurance an attractive quality in a woman.

He said, "Throw me the key, and I'll show you my Roger Bannister impression."

She shook her head. "You don't need a key. Those days are over."

Robert started with fright. *There were no bars between them.* But the cage couldn't have vanished before his eyes; she must have removed it while he'd been lost in his reverie. He'd gone through the whole painful exercise of turning to face her as if he were still confined, without even noticing. *Removed it how?*

He wiped his eyes, shivering at the dizzying prospect of freedom. "Who are you?" An agent for the Russians, sent to liberate him from his own side? She'd have to be a zealot, then, or strangely naive, to view his torture with such wide-eyed innocence.

She stepped forward, then reached down and took his hand. "Do you think you can walk?" Her grip was firm, and her skin was cool and dry. She was completely unafraid; she might have been a good Samaritan in a public street helping an old man to his feet after a fall—not an intruder helping a threat to national security break out of therapeutic detention, at the risk of being shot on sight.

"I'm not even sure I can stand." Robert steeled himself;

maybe this woman was a trained assassin, but it would be too much to presume that if he cried out in pain and brought guards rushing in, she could still extricate him without raising a sweat. "You haven't answered my question."

"My name's Helen." She smiled and hoisted him to his feet, looking at once like a compassionate child pulling open the jaws of a hunter's cruel trap, and a very powerful, very intelligent carnivore contemplating its own strength. "I've come to change everything."

Robert said, "Oh, good."

Robert found that he could hobble; it was painful and undignified, but at least he didn't have to be carried. Helen led him through the house; lights showed from some of the rooms, but there were no voices, no footsteps save their own, no signs of life at all. When they reached the tradesmen's entrance she unbolted the door, revealing a moonlit garden.

"Did you kill everyone?" he whispered. He'd made far too much noise to have come this far unmolested. Much as he had reason to despise his captors, mass murder on his behalf was a lot to take in.

Helen cringed. "What a revolting idea! It's hard to believe sometimes, how uncivilized you are."

"You mean the British?"

"All of you!"

"I must say, your accent's rather good."

"I watched a lot of cinema," she explained. "Mostly Ealing comedies. You never know how much that will help, though."

"Quite."

They crossed the garden, heading for a wooden gate in the hedge. Since murder was strictly for imperialists, Robert could only assume that she'd managed to drug everyone.

The gate was unlocked. Outside the grounds, a cobbled lane ran past the hedge, leading into forest. Robert was barefoot, but the stones weren't cold, and the slight unevenness of the path was welcome, restoring circulation to the soles of his feet.

As they walked, he took stock of his situation. He was out of captivity, thanks entirely to this woman. Sooner or later he was going to have to confront her agenda.

He said, "I'm not leaving the country."

Helen murmured assent, as if he'd passed a casual remark about the weather.

"And I'm not going to discuss my work with you."

"Fine."

Robert stopped and stared at her. She said, "Put your arm across my shoulders."

He complied; she was exactly the right height to support him comfortably. He said, "You're not a Soviet agent, are you?"

Helen was amused. "Is that really what you thought?"

"I'm not all that quick on my feet tonight."

"No." They began walking together. Helen said, "There's a train station about three kilometers away. You can get cleaned up, rest there until morning, and decide where you want to go."

"Won't the station be the first place they'll look?"

"They won't be looking anywhere for a while."

The moon was high above the trees. The two of them could not have made a more conspicuous couple: a sensibly dressed, quite striking young woman, supporting a filthy, ragged tramp. If a villager cycled past, the best they could hope for was being mistaken for an alcoholic father and his martyred daughter.

Martyred all right: she moved so efficiently, despite the burden, that any onlooker would assume she'd been doing this for years. Robert tried altering his gait slightly, subtly changing the timing of his steps to see if he could make her falter, but Helen adapted instantly. If she knew she was being tested, though, she kept it to herself.

Finally he said, "What did you do with the cage?"

"I time-reversed it."

Hairs stood up on the back of his neck. Even assuming that she could do such a thing, it wasn't at all clear to him how that could have stopped the bars from scattering light and interacting with his body. It should merely have turned electrons into positrons, and killed them both in a shower of gamma rays.

That conjuring trick wasn't his most pressing concern, though. "I can only think of three places you might have come from," he said.

Helen nodded, as if she'd put herself in his shoes and catalogued the possibilities. "Rule out one; the other two are both right."

She was not from an extrasolar planet. Even if her civilization possessed some means of viewing Ealing comedies from a distance of light years, she was far too sensitive to his specific human concerns.

She was from the future, but not his own.

She was from the future of another Everett branch.

He turned to her. "No paradoxes."

She smiled, deciphering his shorthand immediately. "That's right. It's physically impossible to travel into your own past, unless you've made exacting preparations to ensure compatible boundary conditions. That *can* be achieved, in a controlled laboratory setting—but in the field it would be like trying to balance ten thousand elephants in an inverted pyramid, while the bottom one rode a unicycle: excruciatingly difficult, and entirely pointless."

Robert was tongue-tied for several seconds, a horde of questions battling for access to his vocal chords. "But how do you travel into the past at all?"

"It will take a while to bring you up to speed completely, but if you want the short answer: you've already stumbled on one of the clues. I read your paper in *Physical Review,* and it's correct as far as it goes. Quantum gravity involves four complex dimensions, but the only classical solutions—the only geometries that remain in phase under slight perturbations—have curvature that's either *self-dual,* or *anti-self-dual.* Those are the only stationary points of the action, for the complete Lagrangian. And both solutions appear, from the inside, to contain only four real dimensions.

"It's meaningless to ask which sector we're in, but we might as well call it self-dual. In that case, the anti-self-dual solutions have an arrow of time running backward compared to ours."

"Why?" As he blurted out the question, Robert wondered if he sounded like an impatient child to her. But if she suddenly vanished back into thin air, he'd have far fewer regrets for making a fool of himself this way than if he'd maintained a façade of sophisticated nonchalance.

Helen said, "Ultimately, that's related to spin. And it's down to the mass of the neutrino that we can tunnel between sectors. But I'll need to draw you some diagrams and equations to explain it all properly."

Robert didn't press her for more; he had no choice but to trust that she wouldn't desert him. He staggered on in silence, a wonderful ache of anticipation building in his chest. If someone had put this situation to him hypothetically, he would have piously insisted that he'd prefer to toil on at his own pace. But despite the satisfaction it had given him on the few occasions when he'd made genuine discoveries himself, what mattered in the end was understanding as much as you could, however you could. Better to ransack the past and the future than go through life in a state of willful ignorance.

"You said you've come to change things?"

She nodded. "I can't predict the future here, of course, but there are pitfalls in my own past that I can help you avoid. In my twentieth century, people discovered things too slowly. Everything changed much too slowly. Between us, I think we can speed things up."

Robert was silent for a while, contemplating the magnitude of what she was proposing. Then he said, "It's a pity you didn't come sooner. In this branch, about twenty years ago—"

Helen cut him off. "I know. We had the same war. The same Holocaust, the same Soviet death toll. But we've yet to be able to avert that, anywhere. You can never do anything in just one history—even the most focused intervention happens across a broad 'ribbon' of strands. When we try to reach back to the '30s and '40s, the ribbon overlaps with its own past to such a degree that all the worst horrors are *faits accompli*. We can't shoot *any* version of Adolf Hitler, because we can't shrink the ribbon to the point where none of us would be shooting ourselves in the back. All we've ever managed are minor interventions, like sending projectiles back to the Blitz, saving a few lives by deflecting bombs."

"What, knocking them into the Thames?"

"No, that would have been too risky. We did some modeling, and the safest thing turned out to be diverting them onto big, empty buildings: Westminster Abbey, Saint Paul's Cathedral."

The station came into view ahead of them. Helen said, "What do you think? Do you want to head back to Manchester?"

Robert hadn't given the question much thought. Quint could track him down anywhere, but the more people he had around him, the less vulnerable he'd be. In his house in Wilmslow he'd be there for the taking.

"I still have rooms at Cambridge," he said tentatively.

"Good idea."

"What are your own plans?"

Helen turned to him. "I thought I'd stay with you." She smiled at the expression on his face. "Don't worry, I'll give you plenty of privacy. And if people want to make assumptions, let them. You already have a scandalous reputation; you might as well see it branch out in new directions."

Robert said wryly, "I'm afraid it doesn't quite work that way. They'd throw us out immediately."

Helen snorted. "They could try."

"You may have defeated MI6, but you haven't dealt with Cambridge porters." The reality of the situation washed over him anew at the thought of her in his study, writing out the equations for time travel on the blackboard. "*Why me?* I can appreciate that you'd want to make contact with someone who could understand how you came here—but why not Everett, or Yang, or Feynman? Compared to Feynman, I'm a dilettante."

Helen said, "Maybe. But you have an equally practical bent, and you'll learn fast enough."

There had to be more to it than that: thousands of people would have been capable of absorbing her lessons just as rapidly. "The physics you've hinted at—in your past, did I discover all that?"

"No. Your *Physical Review* paper helped me track you down here, but in my own history that was never published." There was a flicker of disquiet in her eyes, as if she had far greater disappointments in store on that subject.

Robert didn't care much either way; if anything, the less his alter ego had achieved, the less he'd be troubled by jealousy.

"Then what was it, that made you choose me?"

"You really haven't guessed?" Helen took his free hand and held the fingers to her face; it was a tender gesture, but much more like a daughter's than a lover's. "It's a warm night. No one's skin should be this cold."

Robert gazed into her dark eyes, as playful as any human's, as serious, as proud. Given the chance, perhaps any decent person would have plucked him from Quint's grasp. But only one kind would feel a special obligation, as if they were repaying an ancient debt.

He said, "You're a machine."

2

John Hamilton, Professor of Medieval and Renaissance English at Magdalene College, Cambridge, read the last letter in the morning's pile of fan mail with a growing sense of satisfaction.

The letter was from a young American, a twelve-year-old girl in Boston. It opened in the usual way, declaring how much pleasure his books had given her, before going on to list her favorite scenes and characters. As ever, Jack was delighted that the stories had touched someone deeply enough to prompt them to respond this way. But it was the final paragraph that was by far the most gratifying:

> However much other children might tease me, or grown-ups too when I'm older, I will NEVER, EVER stop believing in the Kingdom of Nescia. Sarah

stopped believing, and she was locked out of the Kingdom forever. At first that made me cry, and I couldn't sleep all night because I was afraid I might stop believing myself one day. But I understand now that it's good to be afraid, because it will help me keep people from changing my mind. And if you're not willing to believe in magic lands, of course you can't enter them. There's nothing even Belvedere himself can do to save you, then.

Jack refilled and lit his pipe, then reread the letter. This was his vindication: the proof that through his books he could touch a young mind, and plant the seed of faith in fertile ground. It made all the scorn of his jealous, stuck-up colleagues fade into insignificance. Children understood the power of stories, the reality of myth, the need to believe in something beyond the dismal gray farce of the material world.

It wasn't a truth that could be revealed the "adult" way: through scholarship, or reason. Least of all through philosophy, as Elizabeth Anscombe had shown him on that awful night at the Socratic Club. A devout Christian herself, Anscombe had nonetheless taken all the arguments against materialism from his popular book, *Signs and Wonders,* and trampled them into the ground. It had been an unfair match from the start: Anscombe was a professional philosopher, steeped in the work of everyone from Aquinas to Wittgenstein; Jack knew the history of ideas in medieval Europe intimately, but he'd lost interest in modern philosophy once it had been invaded by fashionable positivists. And *Signs and Wonders* had never been intended as a scholarly work; it had been good enough to pass muster with a sympathetic lay readership, but trying to defend his admittedly rough-and-ready mixture of common sense and useful shortcuts to faith against Anscombe's merciless analysis had made him feel like a country yokel stammering in front of a bishop.

Ten years later, he still burned with resentment at the humiliation she'd put him through, but he was grateful for the lesson she'd taught him. His earlier books, and his radio talks, had not been a complete waste of time—but the harpy's triumph had shown him just how pitiful human reason was when it came to the great questions. He'd begun working on the stories of Nescia years before, but it was only when the dust had settled on his most painful defeat that he'd finally recognized his true calling.

He removed his pipe, stood, and turned to face Oxford. "Kiss my arse, Elizabeth!" he growled happily, waving the letter at her. This was a wonderful omen. It was going to be a very good day.

There was a knock at the door of his study.

"Come."

It was his brother, William. Jack was puzzled—he hadn't even realized Willie was in town—but he nodded a greeting and motioned at the couch opposite his desk.

Willie sat, his face flushed from the stairs, frowning. After a moment he said, "This chap Stoney."

"Hmm?" Jack was only half listening as he sorted papers on his desk. He knew from long experience that Willie would take forever to get to the point.

"Did some kind of hush-hush work during the war, apparently."

"Who did?"

"Robert Stoney. Mathematician. Used to be up at Manchester, but he's a Fellow of Kings, and now he's back in Cambridge. Did some kind of secret war work. Same thing as Malcolm Muggeridge, apparently. No one's allowed to say what."

Jack looked up, amused. He'd heard rumors about Muggeridge, but they all revolved around the business of analyzing intercepted German radio messages. What conceivable use would a mathematician have been, for that? Sharpening pencils for the intelligence analysts, presumably.

"What about him, Willie?" Jack asked patiently.

Willie continued reluctantly, as if he was confessing to something mildly immoral. "I paid him a visit yesterday. Place called the Cavendish. Old army friend of mine has a brother who works there. Got the whole tour."

"I know the Cavendish. What's there to see?"

"He's doing things, Jack. *Impossible things.*"

"Impossible?"

"Looking inside people. Putting it on a screen, like a television."

Jack sighed. "Taking X-rays?"

Willie snapped back angrily, "I'm not a fool; I know what an X-ray looks like. This is different. You can see the blood flow. You can watch your heart beating. You can follow a sensation through the nerves from fingertip to brain. He says, soon he'll be able to watch a thought in motion."

"Nonsense." Jack scowled. "So he's invented some gadget, some fancy kind of X-ray machine. What are you so agitated about?"

Willie shook his head gravely. "There's more. That's just the tip of the iceberg. He's only been back in Cambridge a year, and already the place is overflowing with wonders." He used the word begrudgingly, as if he had no choice, but was afraid of conveying more approval than he intended.

Jack was beginning to feel a distinct sense of unease.

"What exactly is it you want me to do?" he asked.

Willie replied plainly, "Go and see for yourself. Go and see what he's up to."

The Cavendish Laboratory was a mid-Victorian building, designed to resemble something considerably older and grander. It housed the entire Department of Physics, complete with lecture theaters; the place was swarming with noisy undergraduates. Jack had had no trouble arranging a tour: he'd simply telephoned Stoney and expressed his curiosity, and no more substantial reason had been required.

Stoney had been allocated three adjoining rooms at the back of the building, and the "spin resonance imager" occupied most of the first. Jack obligingly placed his arm between the coils, then almost jerked it out in fright when the strange, transected view of his muscles and veins appeared on the picture tube. He wondered if it could be some kind of hoax, but he clenched his fist slowly and watched the image do the same, then made several unpredictable movements which it mimicked equally well.

"I can show you individual blood cells, if you like," Stoney offered cheerfully.

Jack shook his head; his current, unmagnified flaying was quite enough to take in.

Stoney hesitated, then added awkwardly, "You might want to talk to your doctor at some point. It's just that, your bone density's rather —" He pointed to a chart on the screen beside the image. "Well, it's quite a bit below the normal range."

Jack withdrew his arm. He'd already been diagnosed with osteoporosis, and he'd welcomed the news: it meant that he'd taken a small part of Joyce's illness—the weakness in her bones—into his own body. God was allowing him to suffer a little in her stead.

If Joyce were to step between these coils, what might that reveal? But there'd be nothing to add to her diagnosis. Besides, if he kept up his prayers, and kept up both their spirits, in time her remission would blossom from an uncertain reprieve into a fully-fledged cure.

He said, "How does this work?"

"In a strong magnetic field, some of the atomic nuclei and electrons in your body are free to align themselves in various ways with the field." Stoney must have seen Jack's eyes beginning to glaze over; he quickly changed tack. "Think of it as being like setting a whole lot of spinning tops whirling, as vigorously as possible, then listening carefully as they slow down and tip over. For the atoms in your body, that's enough to give some clues as to what kind of molecule, and what kind of tissue, they're in. The machine listens to atoms in different places by changing the way it combines all the signals from billions of tiny antennae. It's like a whispering gallery where we can play with the time that signals take to travel from different places, moving the focus back and forth through any part of any body, thousands of times a second."

Jack pondered this explanation. Though it sounded complicated, in principle it wasn't that much stranger than X-rays.

"The physics itself is old hat," Stoney continued, "but for imaging, you need a very strong magnetic field, and you need to make sense of all the data you've gathered. Nevill Mott made the superconducting alloys for the magnets. And I managed to persuade Rosalind Franklin from Birkbeck to collaborate with us, to help perfect the fabrication process for the computing circuits. We cross-link lots of little Y-shaped DNA fragments, then selectively coat them with metal; Rosalind worked out a way to use X-ray crystallography for quality control. We paid her back with a purpose-built computer that will let her solve hydrated protein structures in real time, once she gets her hands on a bright enough X-ray source." He held up a small, unprepossessing object, rimmed with protruding gold wires. "Each logic gate is roughly a hundred lightingstroms cubed, and we grow them in three-dimensional arrays. That's a million, million, million switches in the palm of my hand."

Jack didn't know how to respond to this claim. Even when he couldn't quite follow the man there was something mesmerizing about his ramblings, like a cross between William Blake and nursery talk.

"If computers don't excite you, we're doing all kinds of other things with DNA." Stoney ushered him into the next room, which was full of glassware, and seedlings in pots beneath strip lights. Two assistants seated at a bench were toiling over microscopes; another was dispensing fluids into test tubes with a device that looked like an overgrown eye-dropper.

"There are a dozen new species of rice, corn, and wheat here. They all have at least double the protein and mineral content of existing crops, and each one uses a different biochemical repertoire to protect itself against insects and fungi. Farmers have to get away from monocultures; it leaves them too vulnerable to disease, and too dependent on chemical pesticides."

Jack said, "You've bred these? All these new varieties, in a matter of months?"

"No, no! Instead of hunting down the heritable traits we needed in the wild, and struggling for years to produce cross-breeds bearing all of them, we designed every trait from scratch. Then we manufactured DNA that would make the tools the plants need, and inserted it into their germ cells."

Jack demanded angrily, "Who are you to say what a plant needs?"

Stoney shook his head innocently. "I took my advice from agricultural scientists, who took their advice from farmers. They know what pests and blights they're up against. Food crops are as artificial as Pekinese. Nature didn't hand them to us on a plate, and if they're not working as well as we need them to, nature isn't going to fix them for us."

Jack glowered at him, but said nothing. He was beginning to understand why Willie had sent him here. The man came across as an enthusiastic tinkerer, but there was a breath-taking arrogance lurking behind the boyish exterior.

Stoney explained a collaboration he'd brokered between scientists in Cairo, Bogotá, London and Calcutta, to develop vaccines for polio, smallpox, malaria, typhoid, yellow fever, tuberculosis, influenza and leprosy. Some were the first of their kind; others were intended as replacements for existing vaccines. "It's important that we create antigens without culturing the pathogens in animal cells that might themselves harbor viruses. The teams are all looking at variants on a simple, cheap technique that involves putting antigen genes into harmless bacteria that will double as delivery vehicles and adjuvants, then freeze-drying them into spores that can survive tropical heat without refrigeration."

Jack was slightly mollified; this all sounded highly admirable. What business Stoney had instructing doctors on vaccines was another question. Presumably his jargon made sense to them, but when exactly had this mathematician acquired the training to make even the most modest suggestions on the topic?

"You're having a remarkably productive year," he observed.

Stoney smiled. "The muse comes and goes for all of us.

But I'm really just the catalyst in most of this. I've been lucky enough to find some people—here in Cambridge, and further afield—who've been willing to chance their arm on some wild ideas. They've done the real work." He gestured toward the next room. "My own pet projects are through here."

The third room was full of electronic gadgets, wired up to picture tubes displaying both phosphorescent words and images resembling engineering blueprints come to life. In the middle of one bench, incongruously, sat a large cage containing several hamsters.

Stoney fiddled with one of the gadgets, and a face like a stylized drawing of a mask appeared on an adjacent screen. The mask looked around the room, then said, "Good morning, Robert. Good morning, Professor Hamilton."

Jack said, "You had someone record those words?"

The mask replied, "No, Robert showed me photographs of all the teaching staff at Cambridge. If I see anyone I know from the photographs, I greet them." The face was crudely rendered, but the hollow eyes seemed to meet Jack's. Stoney explained, "It has no idea what it's saying, of course. It's just an exercise in face and voice recognition."

Jack responded stiffly, "Of course."

Stoney motioned to Jack to approach and examine the hamster cage. He obliged him. There were two adult animals, presumably a breeding pair. Two pink young were suckling from the mother, who reclined in a bed of straw.

"Look closely," Stoney urged him. Jack peered into the nest, then cried out an obscenity and backed away.

One of the young was exactly what it seemed. The other was a machine, wrapped in ersatz skin, with a nozzle clamped to the warm teat.

"That's the most monstrous thing I've ever seen!" Jack's whole body was trembling. "What possible reason could you have to do that?"

Stoney laughed and made a reassuring gesture, as if his guest was a nervous child recoiling from a harmless toy. "It's not hurting her! And the point is to discover what it takes for the mother to accept it. To 'reproduce one's kind' means having some set of parameters as to what that is. Scent, and some aspects of appearance, are important cues in this case, but through trial and error I've also pinned down a set of behaviors that lets the simulacrum pass through every stage of the life cycle. An acceptable child, an acceptable sibling, an acceptable mate."

Jack stared at him, nauseated. "These animals fuck your machines?"

Stoney was apologetic. "Yes, but hamsters will fuck anything. I'll really have to shift to a more discerning species, in order to test that properly."

Jack struggled to regain his composure. "What on Earth possessed you, to do this?"

"In the long run," Stoney said mildly, "I believe this is something we're going to need to understand far better than we do at present. Now that we can map the structures of the brain in fine detail, and match its raw complexity with our computers, it's only a matter of a decade or so before we build machines that think.

"That in itself will be a vast endeavor, but I want to ensure that it's not stillborn from the start. There's not much point creating the most marvelous children in history, only to find that some awful mammalian instinct drives us to strangle them at birth."

Jack sat in his study drinking whisky. He'd telephoned Joyce after dinner, and they'd chatted for a while, but it wasn't the same as being with her. The weekends never came soon enough, and by Tuesday or Wednesday any sense of reassurance he'd gained from seeing her had slipped away entirely.

It was almost midnight now. After speaking to Joyce, he'd spent three more hours on the telephone, finding out what he could about Stoney. Milking his connections, such as they were; Jack had only been at Cambridge for five years, so he was still very much an outsider. Not that he'd ever been admitted into any inner circles back at Oxford: he'd always belonged to a small, quiet group of dissenters against the tide of fashion. Whatever else might be said about the Tiddly-winks, they'd never had their hands on the levers of academic power.

A year ago, while on sabbatical in Germany, Stoney had resigned suddenly from a position he'd held at Manchester for a decade. He'd returned to Cambridge, despite having no official posting to take up. He'd started collaborating informally with various people at the Cavendish, until the head of the place, Mott, had invented a job description for him, and given him a modest salary, the three rooms Jack had seen, and some students to assist him.

Stoney's colleagues were uniformly amazed by his spate of successful inventions. Though none of his gadgets were based on entirely new science, his skill at seeing straight to the heart of existing theories and plucking some practical consequence from them was unprecedented. Jack had expected some jealous back-stabbing, but no one seemed to have a bad word to say about Stoney. He was willing to turn his scientific Midas touch to the service of anyone who approached him, and it sounded to Jack as if every would-be skeptic or enemy had been bought off with some rewarding insight into their own field.

Stoney's personal life was rather murkier. Half of Jack's informants were convinced that the man was a confirmed pansy, but others spoke of a beautiful, mysterious woman named Helen, with whom he was plainly on intimate terms.

Jack emptied his glass and stared out across the courtyard. *Was it pride, to wonder if he might have received some kind of prophetic vision?* Fifteen years earlier, when he'd written *The Broken Planet,* he'd imagined that he'd merely been satirising the hubris of modern science. His portrait of the evil forces behind the sardonically named Laboratory Overseeing Various Experiments had been intended as a deadly serious metaphor, but he'd never expected to find himself wondering if real fallen angels were whispering secrets in the ears of a Cambridge don.

How many times, though, had he told his readers that the devil's greatest victory had been convincing the world that he did not exist? The devil was *not* a metaphor, a mere symbol of human weakness: he was a real, scheming presence, acting in time, acting in the world, as much as God Himself.

And hadn't Faustus's damnation been sealed by the most beautiful woman of all time: Helen of Troy?

Jack's skin crawled. He'd once written a humorous newspaper column called "Letters from a Demon," in which a Senior Tempter offered advice to a less experienced colleague on the best means to lead the faithful astray. Even that had been an exhausting, almost corrupting experience; adopting the necessary point of view, however whimsically, had made him feel that he was withering inside. The thought that a cross between the *Faustbuch* and *The Broken Planet* might be coming to life around him was too terrifying to contemplate. He was no hero out of his own fiction—not even a mild-mannered Cedric Duffy, let alone a modern Pendragon. And he did not believe that Merlin would rise from the woods to bring chaos to that hubristic Tower of Babel, the Cavendish Laboratory.

Nevertheless, if he was the only person in England who suspected Stoney's true source of inspiration, who else would act?

Jack poured himself another glass. There was nothing to be gained by procrastinating. He would not be able to rest until he knew what he was facing: a vain, foolish overgrown boy who was having a run of good luck—or a vain, foolish overgrown boy who had sold his soul and imperiled all humanity.

"A *Satanist?* You're accusing me of being a Satanist?"

Stoney tugged angrily at his dressing gown; he'd been in bed when Jack had pounded on the door. Given the hour, it had been remarkably civil of him to accept a visitor at all, and he appeared so genuinely affronted now that Jack was almost prepared to apologize and slink away. He said, "I had to ask you—"

"You have to be doubly foolish to be a Satanist," Stoney muttered.

"Doubly?"

"Not only do you need to believe all the nonsense of Christian theology, you then have to turn around and back the preordained, guaranteed-to-fail, absolutely futile *losing side.*" He held up his hand, as if he believed he'd anticipated the only possible objection to this remark, and wished to spare Jack the trouble of washing his breath by uttering it. "I *know,* some people claim it's all really about some pre-Christian deity: Mercury, or Pan—guff like that. But assuming that we're not talking about some complicated mislabelling of objects of worship, I really can't think of anything more insulting. You're comparing me to someone like *Huysmans,* who was basically just a very dim Catholic."

Stoney folded his arms and settled back on the couch, waiting for Jack's response.

Jack's head was thick from the whisky; he wasn't at all sure how to take this. It was the kind of smart-arsed undergraduate drivel he might have expected from any smug atheist—but then, short of a confession, exactly what kind of reply would have constituted evidence of guilt? *If you'd sold your soul to the devil, what lie would you tell in place of the truth?* Had he seriously believed that Stoney would claim to be a devout churchgoer, as if that were the best possible answer to put Jack off the scent?

He had to concentrate on things he'd seen with his own eyes, facts that could not be denied.

"You're plotting to overthrow nature, bending the world to the will of man."

Stoney sighed. "Not at all. More refined technology will help us tread more lightly. We have to cut back on pollution and pesticides as rapidly as possible. Or do you want to live in a world where all the animals are born as hermaphrodites, and half the Pacific islands disappear in storms?"

"Don't try telling me that you're some kind of guardian of the animal kingdom. You want to replace us all with machines!"

"Does every Zulu or Tibetan who gives birth to a child, and wants the best for it, threaten you in the same way?"

Jack bristled. "I'm not a racist. A Zulu or Tibetan has a *soul.*"

Stoney groaned and put his head in his hands. "It's half past one in the morning! Can't we have this debate some other time?"

Someone banged on the door. Stoney looked up, disbelieving. "What is this? Grand Central Station?"

He crossed to the door and opened it. A disheveled, unshaven man pushed his way into the room. "Quint? What a pleasant—"

The intruder grabbed Stoney and slammed him against the wall. Jack exhaled with surprise. Quint turned bloodshot eyes on him.

"Who the fuck are you?"

"John Hamilton. Who the fuck are you?"

"Never you mind. Just stay put." He jerked Stoney's arm up behind his back with one hand, while grinding his face into the wall with the other. "You're mine now, you piece of shit. No one's going to protect you this time."

Stoney addressed Jack through a mouth squashed against the masonry. "Dith ith Pether Quinth, my own perthonal thpook. I did make a Fauthtian bargain. But with thtrictly temporal—"

"Shut up!" Quint pulled a gun from his jacket and held it to Stoney's head.

Jack said, "Steady on."

"Just how far do your connections go?" Quint screamed. "I've had memos disappear, sources clam up—and now my superiors are treating *me* like some kind of traitor! Well, don't worry: when I'm through with you, I'll have the names of the entire network." He turned to address Jack again. "And don't *you* think you're going anywhere."

Stoney said, "Leave him out of dith. He'th at Magdalene. You mutht know by now: all the thpieth are at Trinity."

Jack was shaken by the sight of Quint waving his gun around, but the implications of this drama came as something of a relief. Stoney's ideas must have had their genesis in some secret war-time research project. He hadn't made a deal with the devil after all, but he'd broken the Official Secrets Act, and now he was paying the price.

Stoney flexed his body and knocked Quint backward.

Quint staggered, but didn't fall; he raised his arm menacingly, but there was no gun in his hand. Jack looked around to see where it had fallen, but he couldn't spot it anywhere. Stoney landed a kick squarely in Quint's testicles; barefoot, but Quint wailed with pain. A second kick sent him sprawling.

Stoney called out, "Luke? *Luke!* Would you come and give me a hand?"

A solidly built man with tattooed forearms emerged from Stoney's bedroom, yawning and tugging his braces into place. At the sight of Quint, he groaned. "Not again!"

Stoney said, "I'm sorry."

Luke shrugged stoically. The two of them managed to grab hold of Quint, then they dragged him struggling out the door. Jack waited a few seconds, then searched the floor for the gun. But it wasn't anywhere in sight, and it hadn't slid under the furniture; none of the crevices where it might have ended up were so dark that it would have been lost in shadow. It was not in the room at all.

Jack went to the window and watched the three men cross the courtyard, half expecting to witness an assassination. But Stoney and his lover merely lifted Quint into the air between them, and tossed him into a shallow, rather slimy-looking pond.

Jack spent the ensuing days in a state of turmoil. He wasn't ready to confide in anyone until he could frame his suspicions clearly, and the events in Stoney's rooms were difficult to interpret unambiguously. He couldn't state with absolute certainty that Quint's gun had vanished before his eyes. But surely the fact that Stoney was walking free proved that he was receiving supernatural protection? And Quint himself, confused and demoralised, had certainly had the appearance of a man who'd been demonically confounded at every turn.

If this was true, though, Stoney must have bought more with his soul than immunity from worldly authority. *The knowledge itself* had to be Satanic in origin, as the legend of Faustus described it. Tollers had been right, in his great essay "Mythopoesis": myths were remnants of man's pre-lapsarian capacity to apprehend, directly, the great truths of the world. Why else would they resonate in the imagination, and survive from generation to generation?

By Friday, a sense of urgency gripped him. He couldn't take his confusion back to Potter's Barn, back to Joyce and the boys. This had to be resolved, if only in his own mind, before he returned to his family.

With Wagner on the gramophone, he sat and meditated on the challenge he was facing. Stoney had to be thwarted, but how? Jack had always said that the Church of England—apparently so quaint and harmless, a Church of cake stalls and kindly spinsters—was like a fearsome army in the eyes of Satan. But even if his master was quaking in Hell, it would take more than a few stern words from a bicycling vicar to force Stoney to abandon his obscene plans.

But Stoney's intentions, in themselves, didn't matter. He'd been granted the power to dazzle and seduce, but not to force his will upon the populace. What mattered was how his plans were viewed by others. And the way to stop him was to open people's eyes to the true emptiness of his apparent cornucopia.

The more he thought and prayed about it, the more certain Jack became that he'd discerned the task required of him. No denunciation from the pulpits would suffice; people wouldn't turn down the fruits of Stoney's damnation on the mere say-so of the Church. Why would anyone reject such lustrous gifts, without a carefully reasoned argument?

Jack had been humiliated once, defeated once, trying to expose the barrenness of materialism. But might that not have been a form of preparation? He'd been badly mauled by Anscombe, but she'd made an infinitely gentler enemy than the one he now confronted. He had suffered from her taunts—but what was *suffering,* if not the chisel God used to shape his children into their true selves?

His role was clear, now. He would find Stoney's intellectual Achilles heel, and expose it to the world.

He would debate him.

3

Robert gazed at the blackboard for a full minute, then started laughing with delight. "That's so beautiful!"

"Isn't it?" Helen put down the chalk and joined him on the couch. "Any more symmetry, and nothing would happen: the universe would be full of crystalline blankness. Any less, and it would all be uncorrelated noise."

Over the months, in a series of tutorials, Helen had led him through a small part of the century of physics that had separated them at their first meeting, down to the purely algebraic structures that lay beneath spacetime and matter. Mathematics catalogued everything that was not self contradictory; within that vast inventory, physics was an island of structures rich enough to contain their own beholders.

Robert sat and mentally reviewed everything he'd learned, trying to apprehend as much as he could in a single image. As he did, a part of him waited fearfully for a sense of disappointment, a sense of anticlimax. *He might never see more deeply into the nature of the world. In this direction, at least, there was nothing more to be discovered.*

But anticlimax was impossible. To become jaded with *this* was impossible. However familiar he became with the algebra of the universe, it would never grow less marvelous.

Finally he asked, "Are there other islands?" Not merely other histories, sharing the same underlying basis, but other realities entirely.

"I suspect so," Helen replied. "People have mapped some possibilities. I don't know how that could ever be confirmed, though."

Robert shook his head, sated. "I won't even think about that. I need to come down to Earth for a while." He stretched his arms and leaned back, still grinning.

Helen said, "Where's Luke today? He usually shows up by now, to drag you out into the sunshine."

The question wiped the smile from Robert's face. "Apparently I make poor company. Being insufficiently fanatical about darts and football."

"He's left you?" Helen reached over and squeezed his hand sympathetically. A little mockingly, too.

Robert was annoyed; she never said anything, but he always felt that she was judging him. "You think I should grow up, don't you? Find someone more like myself. Some kind of *soulmate*." He'd meant the word to sound sardonic, but it emerged rather differently.

"It's your life," she said.

A year before, that would have been a laughable claim, but it was almost the truth now. There was a *de facto* moratorium on prosecutions, while the recently acquired genetic and neurological evidence was being assessed by a parliamentary subcommittee. Robert had helped plant the seeds of the campaign, but he'd played no real part in it; other people had taken up the cause. In a matter of months, it was possible that Quint's cage would be smashed, at least for everyone in Britain.

The prospect filled him with a kind of vertigo. He might have broken the laws at every opportunity, but they had still molded him. The cage might not have left him crippled, but he'd be lying to himself if he denied that he'd been stunted.

He said, "Is that what happened, in your past? I ended up in some lifelong partnership?" As he spoke the words, his mouth went dry, and he was suddenly afraid that the answer would be yes. *With Chris. The life he'd missed out on was a life of happiness with Chris.*

"No."

"Then what?" he pleaded. "What did I do? How did I live?" He caught himself, suddenly self-conscious, but added, "You can't blame me for being curious."

Helen said gently, "You don't want to know what you can't change. All of that is part of your own causal past now, as much as it is of mine."

"If it's part of my own history," Robert countered, "don't I deserve to know it? This man wasn't me, but he brought you to me."

Helen considered this. "You accept that he was someone else? Not someone whose actions you're responsible for?"

"Of course."

She said, "There was a trial, in 1952. For 'Gross Inde-
cency contrary to Section 11 of the Criminal Amendment
Act of 1885.' He wasn't imprisoned, but the court ordered
hormone treatments."

"*Hormone treatments?*" Robert laughed. "What—testosterone, to make him more of a man?"

"No, estrogen. Which in men reduces the sex drive. There
are side-effects, of course. Gynecomorphism, among other
things."

Robert felt physically sick. *They'd chemically castrated
him, with drugs that had made him sprout breasts.* Of all the
bizarre abuse to which he'd been subjected, nothing had
been as horrifying as that.

Helen continued, "The treatment lasted six months, and
the effects were all temporary. But two years later, he took
his own life. It was never clear exactly why."

Robert absorbed this in silence. He didn't want to know
anything more.

After a while, he said, "How do you bear it? Knowing that
in some branch or other, every possible form of humiliation
is being inflicted on someone?"

Helen said, "I don't *bear* it. I change it. That's why I'm
here."

Robert bowed his head. "I know. And I'm grateful that
our histories collided. But how many histories don't?" He
struggled to find an example, though it was almost too
painful to contemplate; since their first conversation, it was a
topic he'd deliberately pushed to the back of his mind.
"There's not just an unchangeable Auschwitz in each of our
pasts, there are an astronomical number of others—along
with an astronomical number of things that are even worse."

Helen said bluntly, "That's not true."

"What?" Robert looked up at her, startled.

She walked to the blackboard and erased it. "Auschwitz
has happened, for both of us, and no one I'm aware of has
ever prevented it—but that doesn't mean that *nobody* stops
it, anywhere." She began sketching a network of fine lines

on the blackboard. "You and I are having this conversation in countless microhistories—sequences of events where various different things happen with subatomic particles throughout the universe—but that's irrelevant to us, we can't tell those strands apart, so we might as well treat them all as one history." She pressed the chalk down hard to make a thick streak that covered everything she'd drawn. "The quantum decoherence people call this 'coarse graining.' Summing over all these indistinguishable details is what gives rise to classical physics in the first place.

"Now, 'the two of us' would have first met in many perceivably different coarse-grained histories—and furthermore, you've since diverged by making different choices, and experiencing different external possibilities, after those events." She sketched two intersecting ribbons of coarse-grained histories, and then showed each history diverging further.

"World War II and the Holocaust certainly happened in both of *our* pasts—but that's no proof that the total is so vast that it might as well be infinite. Remember, what stops us successfully intervening is the fact that we're reaching back to a point where some of the parallel interventions start to bite their own tail. So when we fail, it can't be counted twice: it's just confirming what we already know."

Robert protested, "But what about all the versions of '30s Europe that don't happen to lie in either your past or mine? Just because we have no direct evidence for a Holocaust in those branches, that hardly makes it unlikely."

Helen said, "Not unlikely *per se,* without intervention. But not fixed in stone either. We'll keep trying, refining the technology, until we can reach branches where there's no overlap with our own past in the '30s. And there must be other, separate ribbons of intervention that happen in histories we can never even know about."

Robert was elated. He'd imagined himself clinging to a rock of improbable good fortune in an infinite sea of suffering—struggling to pretend, for the sake of his own sanity, that the rock was all there was. But what lay around him was not inevitably worse; it was merely unknown. In time, he might even play a part in ensuring that every last tragedy was *not* repeated across billions of worlds.

He reexamined the diagram. "Hang on. Intervention doesn't end divergence, though, does it? You reached *us,* a year ago, but in at least some of the histories spreading out from that moment, won't we still have suffered all kinds of disasters, and reacted in all kinds of self-defeating ways?"

"Yes," Helen conceded, "but fewer than you might think. If you merely listed every sequence of events that superficially appeared to have a non-zero probability, you'd end up with a staggering catalog of absurdist tragedies. But when you calculate everything more carefully, and take account of Planck-scale effects, it turns out to be nowhere near as bad. There are *no* coarse-grained histories where boulders assemble themselves out of dust and rain from the sky, or everyone in London or Madras goes mad and slaughters their children. Most macroscopic systems end up being quite robust—people included. Across histories, the range of natural disasters, human stupidity, and sheer bad luck isn't overwhelmingly greater than the range you're aware of from this history alone."

Robert laughed. "And that's not bad enough?"

"Oh, it is. But that's the best thing about the form I've taken."

"I'm sorry?"

Helen tipped her head and regarded him with an expression of disappointment. "You know, you're still not as quick on your feet as I'd expected."

Robert's face burned, but then he realized what he'd missed, and his resentment vanished.

"*You don't diverge?* Your hardware is designed to end the process? Your environment, your surroundings, will still split you into different histories—but on a coarse-grained level, you don't contribute to the process yourself?"

"That's right."

Robert was speechless. Even after a year, she could still toss him a hand grenade like this.

Helen said, "I can't help living in many worlds; that's beyond my control. But I do know that I'm one person. Faced with a choice that puts me on a knife-edge, I know I won't split and take every path."

Robert hugged himself, suddenly cold. "Like I do. Like I have. Like all of us poor creatures of flesh."

Helen came and sat beside him. "Even that's not irrevocable. Once you've taken this form—if that's what you choose—you can meet your other selves, reverse some of the scatter. Give some a chance to undo what they've done."

This time, Robert grasped her meaning at once. "Gather myself together? Make myself whole?"

Helen shrugged. "If it's what you want. If you see it that way."

He stared back at her, disoriented. Touching the bedrock of physics was one thing, but this possibility was too much to take in.

Someone knocked on the study door. The two of them exchanged wary glances, but it wasn't Quint, back for more punishment. It was a porter bearing a telegram.

When the man had left, Robert opened the envelope.

"Bad news?" Helen asked.

He shook his head. "Not a death in the family, if that's what you meant. It's from John Hamilton. He's challenging me to a debate. On the topic 'Can A Machine Think?' "

"What, at some university function?"

"No. On the BBC. Four weeks from tomorrow." He looked up. "Do you think I should do it?"

"Radio or television?"

Robert reread the message. "Television."

Helen smiled. "Definitely. I'll give you some tips."

"On the subject?"

"No! That would be cheating." She eyed him appraisingly. "You can start by throwing out your electric razor. Get rid of the permanent five o'clock shadow."

Robert was hurt. "Some people find that quite attractive."

Helen replied firmly, "Trust me on this."

The BBC sent a car to take Robert down to London. Helen sat beside him in the back seat.

"Are you nervous?" she asked.

"Nothing that an hour of throwing up won't cure."

Hamilton had suggested a live broadcast, "to keep things interesting," and the producer had agreed. Robert had never been on television; he'd taken part in a couple of radio discussions on the future of computing, back when the Mark I had first come into use, but even those had been taped.

Hamilton's choice of topic had surprised him at first, but in retrospect it seemed quite shrewd. A debate on the proposition that "Modern Science is the Devil's Work" would have brought howls of laughter from all but the most pious viewers, whereas the purely metaphorical claim that "Modern Science is a Faustian Pact" would have had the entire audience nodding sagely in agreement, while carrying no implications whatsoever. If you weren't going to take the whole dire fairy tale literally, everything was "a Faustian Pact" in some sufficiently watered-down sense: everything had a potential downside, and this was as pointless to assert as it was easy to demonstrate.

Robert had met considerable incredulity, though, when he'd explained to journalists where his own research was leading. To date, the press had treated him as a kind of eccentric British Edison, churning out inventions of indisputable utility, and no one seemed to find it at all surprising or alarming that he was also, frankly, a bit of a loon. But Hamilton would have a chance to exploit, and reshape, that perception. If Robert insisted on defending his goal of creating machine intelligence, not as an amusing hobby that might have been chosen by a public relations firm to make him appear endearingly daft, but as both the ultimate vindication of materialist science and the logical endpoint of most of his life's work, Hamilton could use a victory tonight to cast doubt on everything Robert had done, and everything he symbolized. By asking, not at all rhetorically, "Where will this all end?", he was inviting Robert to step forward and hang himself with the answer.

The traffic was heavy for a Sunday evening, and they arrived at the Shepherd's Bush studios with only fifteen minutes until the broadcast. Hamilton had been collected by a separate car, from his family home near Oxford. As they crossed the studio Robert spotted him, conversing intensely with a dark-haired young man.

He whispered to Helen, "Do you know who that is, with Hamilton?"

She followed his gaze, then smiled cryptically. Robert said, "What? Do you recognize him from somewhere?"

"Yes, but I'll tell you later."

As the make-up woman applied powder, Helen ran through her long list of rules again. "Don't stare into the camera, or you'll look like you're peddling soap powder. But don't avert your eyes. You don't want to look shifty."

The make-up woman whispered to Robert, "Everyone's an expert."

"Annoying, isn't it?" he confided.

Michael Polanyi, an academic philosopher who was well-known to the public after presenting a series of radio talks, had agreed to moderate the debate. Polanyi popped into the make-up room, accompanied by the producer; they chatted with Robert for a couple of minutes, setting him at ease and reminding him of the procedure they'd be following.

They'd only just left him when the floor manager appeared. "We need you in the studio now, please, Professor." Robert followed her, and Helen pursued him part of the way. "Breathe slowly and deeply," she urged him.

"As if you'd know," he snapped.

Robert shook hands with Hamilton then took his seat on one side of the podium. Hamilton's young adviser had retreated into the shadows; Robert glanced back to see Helen watching from a similar position. It was like a duel: they both had seconds. The floor manager pointed out the studio monitor, and as Robert watched it was switched between the feeds from two cameras: a wide shot of the whole set, and a closer view of the podium, including the small blackboard on a stand beside it. He'd once asked Helen whether television had progressed to far greater levels of sophistication in her branch of the future, once the pioneering days were left behind, but the question had left her uncharacteristically tongue-tied.

The floor manager retreated behind the cameras, called

for silence, then counted down from ten, mouthing the final numbers.

The broadcast began with an introduction from Polanyi: concise, witty, and non-partisan. Then Hamilton stepped up to the podium. Robert watched him directly while the wide-angle view was being transmitted, so as not to appear rude or distracted. He only turned to the monitor when he was no longer visible himself.

"Can a machine think?" Hamilton began. "My intuition tells me: *no.* My heart tells me: *no.* I'm sure that most of you feel the same way. But that's not enough, is it? In this day and age, we aren't allowed to rely on our hearts for anything. We need something scientific. We need some kind of proof.

"Some years ago, I took part in a debate at Oxford University. The issue then was not whether machines might behave like people, but whether people themselves might *be* mere machines. Materialists, you see, claim that we are all just a collection of purposeless atoms, colliding at random. Everything we do, everything we feel, everything we say, comes down to some sequence of events that might as well be the spinning of cogs, or the opening and closing of electrical relays.

"To me, this was self-evidently false. What point could there be, I argued, in even conversing with a materialist? By his own admission, the words that came out of his mouth would be the result of nothing but a mindless, mechanical process! By his own theory, he could have no reason to think that those words would be the truth! Only believers in a transcendent human soul could claim any interest in the truth."

Hamilton nodded slowly, a penitent's gesture. "I was wrong, and I was put in my place. This might be self-evident to *me,* and it might be self-evident to *you,* but it's certainly not what philosophers call an 'analytical truth': it's not actually a nonsense, a contradiction in terms, to believe that we are mere machines. There might, there just *might,* be some reason why the words that emerge from a materialist's mouth are truthful, despite their origins lying entirely in unthinking matter.

"There might." Hamilton smiled wistfully. "I had to concede that possibility, because I only had my instinct, my gut feeling, to tell me otherwise.

"But the reason I only had my instinct to guide me was because I'd failed to learn of an event that had taken place many years before. A discovery made in 1930, by an Austrian mathematician named Kurt Gödel."

Robert felt a shiver of excitement run down his spine. He'd been afraid that the whole contest would degenerate into theology, with Hamilton invoking Aquinas all night—or Aristotle, at best. But it looked as if his mysterious adviser had dragged him into the twentieth century, and they were going to have a chance to debate the real issues after all.

"What is it that we *know* Professor Stoney's computers can do, and do well?" Hamilton continued. "Arithmetic! In a fraction of a second, they can add up a million numbers. Once we've told them, very precisely, what calculations to perform, they'll complete them in the blink of an eye—even if those calculations would take you or me a lifetime.

"But do these machines *understand* what it is they're doing? Professor Stoney says, 'Not yet. Not right now. Give them time. Rome wasn't built in a day.'" Hamilton nodded thoughtfully. "Perhaps that's fair. His computers are only a few years old. They're just babies. Why should they understand anything, so soon?

"But let's stop and think about this a bit more carefully. A computer, as it stands today, is simply a machine that does arithmetic, and Professor Stoney isn't proposing that they're going to sprout new kinds of brains all on their own. Nor is he proposing *giving* them anything really new. He can already let them look at the world with television cameras, turning the pictures into a stream of numbers describing the brightness of different points on the screen on which the computer can then perform *arithmetic*. He can already let them speak to us with a special kind of loudspeaker, to which the computer feeds a stream of numbers to describe how loud the sound should be, a stream of numbers produced by more *arithmetic*.

"So the world can come into the computer, as numbers,

and words can emerge, as numbers too. All Professor Stoney hopes to add to his computers is a 'clever' way to do the arithmetic that takes the first set of numbers and churns out the second. It's that 'clever arithmetic,' he tells us, that will make these machines think."

Hamilton folded his arms and paused for a moment. "What are we to make of this? Can *doing arithmetic,* and nothing more, be enough to let a machine *understand* anything? My instinct certainly tells me no, but who am I that you should trust my instinct?

"So, let's narrow down the question of understanding, and to be scrupulously fair, let's put it in the most favorable light possible for Professor Stoney. If there's one thing a computer *ought* to be able to understand—as well as us, if not better—it's arithmetic itself. If a computer could think at all, it would surely be able to grasp the nature of its own best talent.

"The question, then, comes down to this: can you *describe* all of arithmetic, *using* nothing but arithmetic? Thirty years ago—long before Professor Stoney and his computers came along—Professor Gödel asked himself exactly that question.

"Now, you might be wondering how anyone could even *begin* to describe the rules of arithmetic, using nothing but arithmetic itself." Hamilton turned to the blackboard, picked up the chalk, and wrote two lines:

$$\text{If } x + z = y + z$$
$$\text{then } x = y$$

"This is an important rule, but it's written in symbols, not numbers, because it has to be true for *every* number, every x, y and z. But Professor Gödel had a clever idea: why not use a code, like spies use, where every symbol is assigned a number?" Hamilton wrote:

The code for "a" is 1.
The code for "b" is 2.

"And so on. You can have a code for every letter of the alphabet, and for all the other symbols needed for arithmetic: plus signs, equals signs, that kind of thing. Telegrams are sent this way every day, with a code called the Baudot code, so there's really nothing strange or sinister about it.

"All the rules of arithmetic that we learned at school can be written with a carefully chosen set of symbols, which can then be translated into numbers. Every question as to what does or does not *follow from* those rules can then be seen anew, as a question about numbers. If *this* line follows from *this* one." Hamilton indicated the two lines of the cancellation rule, "we can see it in the relationship between their code numbers. We can judge each inference, and declare it valid or not, purely by doing arithmetic.

"So, given *any* proposition at all about arithmetic—such as the claim that 'there are infinitely many prime numbers'—we can restate the notion that we have a proof for that claim in terms of code numbers. If the code number for our claim is x, we can say 'There is a number p, ending with the code number x, that passes our test for being the code number of a valid proof.' "

Hamilton took a visible breath.

"In 1930, Professor Gödel used this scheme to do something rather ingenious." He wrote on the blackboard:

There DOES NOT EXIST a number p meeting the following condition: p is the code number of a valid proof of this claim.

"Here is a claim about arithmetic, about numbers. It has to be either true or false. So let's start by supposing that it happens to be true. Then there *is no* number p that is the code number for a proof of this claim. So this is a true statement about arithmetic, but it can't be proved merely by *doing* arithmetic!"

Hamilton smiled. "If you don't catch on immediately, don't worry; when I first heard this argument from a young friend of mine, it took a while for the meaning to sink in. But remember: the only hope a computer has for understanding *anything* is by doing arithmetic, and we've just found a statement that *cannot* be proved with mere arithmetic.

"Is this statement really true, though? We mustn't jump to conclusions, we mustn't damn the machines too hastily. Suppose this claim is false! Since it claims there is no number p that is the code number of its own proof, to be false there would have to be such a number, after all. And that number would encode the 'proof' of an acknowledged falsehood!"

Hamilton spread his arms triumphantly. "You and I, like every schoolboy, know that you can't prove a falsehood from sound premises and if the premises of arithmetic aren't sound, what is? So *we* know, as a matter of certainty, that this statement is true.

"Professor Gödel was the first to see this, but with a little help and perseverance, any educated person can follow in his footsteps. *A machine could never do that.* We might divulge to a machine our own knowledge of this fact, offering it as something to be taken on trust, but the machine could neither stumble on this truth for itself, nor truly comprehend it when we offered it as a gift.

"You and I *understand* arithmetic, in a way that no electronic calculator ever will. What hope has a machine, then, of moving beyond its own most favorable milieu and comprehending any wider truth?

"None at all, ladies and gentlemen. Though this detour into mathematics might have seemed arcane to you, it has served a very down-to-Earth purpose. It has proved—beyond refutation by even the most ardent materialist or the most pedantic philosopher—what we common folk knew all along: no machine will ever think."

Hamilton took his seat. For a moment, Robert was simply exhilarated; coached or not, Hamilton had grasped the essential features of the incompleteness proof, and presented them to a lay audience. What might have been a night of shadow-boxing—with no blows connecting, and nothing for the audience to judge but two solo performances in separate arenas—had turned into a genuine clash of ideas.

As Polanyi introduced him and he walked to the podium, Robert realized that his usual shyness and self-consciousness had evaporated. He was filled with an altogether different kind of tension: he sensed more acutely than ever what was at stake.

When he reached the podium, he adopted the posture of someone about to begin a prepared speech, but then he caught himself, as if he'd forgotten something. "Bear with me for a moment." He walked around to the far side of the blackboard and quickly wrote a few words on it, upside-down. Then he resumed his place.

"Can a machine think? Professor Hamilton would like us to believe that he's settled the issue once and for all, by coming up with a statement that *we* know is true, but a particular machine—programmed to explore the theorems of arithmetic in a certain rigid way—would never be able to produce. Well, we all have our limitations." He flipped the blackboard over to reveal what he'd written on the opposite side:

> If Robert Stoney speaks these words, he will NOT be telling the truth.

He waited a few beats, then continued.

"What I'd like to explore, though, is not so much a question of limitations, as of opportunities. How exactly is it that we've all ended up with this mysterious ability to know that Gödel's statement is true? Where does this advantage, this great insight, come from? From our souls? From some immaterial entity that no machine could ever possess? Is that the only possible source, the only conceivable explanation? Or might it come from something a little less ethereal?

"As Professor Hamilton explained, we believe Gödel's statement is true because we trust the rules of arithmetic not to lead us into contradictions and falsehoods. But where does that trust come from? How does it arise?"

Robert turned the blackboard back to Hamilton's side, and pointed to the cancellation rule. "If x plus z equals y plus z, then x equals y. Why is this so *reasonable?* We might not learn to put it quite like this until we're in our teens, but if you showed a young child two boxes—without revealing their contents—added an equal number of shells, or stones, or pieces of fruit to both, and then let the child look inside to see that each box now contained the same number of items, it wouldn't take any formal education for the child to understand that the two boxes must have held the same number of things to begin with.

"The child knows, we all know, how a certain kind of object behaves. Our lives are steeped in direct experience of whole numbers: whole numbers of coins, stamps, pebbles, birds, cats, sheep, buses. If I tried to persuade a six-year-old that I could put three stones in a box, remove one of them, and be left with four, he'd simply laugh at me. Why? It's not merely that he's sure to have taken one thing away from three to get two, on many prior occasions. Even a child understands that some things that appear reliable will eventually fail: a toy that works perfectly, day after day, for a month or a year, can still break. But not arithmetic, not taking one from three. He can't even picture *that* failing. Once you've lived in the world, once you've seen how it works, the failure of arithmetic becomes unimaginable.

"Professor Hamilton suggests that this is down to our souls. But what would he say about a child reared in a world of water and mist, never in the company of more than one person at a time, never taught to count on his fingers and toes. I doubt that such a child would possess the same certainty that you and I have, as to the impossibility of arithmetic ever leading him astray. To banish whole numbers entirely from his world would require very strange surroundings, and a level of deprivation amounting to cruelty, but would that be enough to rob a child of his *soul?*

"A computer, programmed to pursue arithmetic as Professor Hamilton has described, is subject to far more deprivation than that child. If I'd been raised with my hands and feet tied, my head in a sack, and someone shouting orders at me, I doubt that I'd have much grasp of reality—and I'd still be better prepared for the task than such a computer. It's a great mercy that a machine treated that way wouldn't be able to think: if it could, the shackles we'd placed upon it would be criminally oppressive.

"But that's hardly the fault of the computer, or a revelation of some irreparable flaw in its nature. If we want to judge the potential of our machines with any degree of honesty, we have to play fair with them, not saddle them with restrictions that we'd never dream of imposing on ourselves. There really is no point comparing an eagle with a spanner, or a gazelle with a washing machine: it's our jets that fly and our cars that run, albeit in quite different ways than any animal.

"*Thought* is sure to be far harder to achieve than those other skills, and to do so we might need to mimic the natural world far more closely. But I believe that once a machine is endowed with facilities resembling the inborn tools for learning that we all have as our birthright, and is set free to learn the way a child learns, through experience, observation, trial and error, hunches and failures—instead of being handed a list of instructions that it has no choice but to obey—we will finally be in a position to compare like with like.

"When that happens, and we can meet and talk and argue with these machines—about arithmetic, or any other topic—there'll be no need to take the word of Professor Gödel; or Professor Hamilton, or myself, for anything. We'll invite them down to the local pub, and interrogate them in person. And if we play fair with them, we'll use the same experience and judgment we use with any friend, or guest, or stranger, to decide for ourselves whether or not they can think."

The BBC put on a lavish assortment of wine and cheese in a small room off the studio. Robert ended up in a heated argument with Polanyi, who revealed himself to be firmly on the negative side, while Helen flirted shamelessly with Hamilton's young friend, who turned out to have a Ph.D. in algebraic geometry from Cambridge; he must have completed the degree just before Robert had come back from Manchester. After exchanging some polite formalities with Hamilton, Robert kept his distance, sensing that any further contact would not be welcome.

An hour later, though, after getting lost in the maze of corridors on his way back from the toilets, Robert came across Hamilton sitting alone in the studio, weeping.

He almost backed away in silence, but Hamilton looked up and saw him. With their eyes locked, it was impossible to retreat.

Robert said, "It's your wife?" He'd heard that she'd been seriously ill, but the gossip had included a miraculous recovery. Some friend of the family had lain hands on her a year ago, and she'd gone into remission.

Hamilton said, "She's dying."

Robert approached and sat beside him. "From what?"

"Breast cancer. It's spread throughout her body. Into her bones, into her lungs, into her liver." He sobbed again, a helpless spasm, then caught himself angrily. "*Suffering is the chisel God uses to shape us.* What kind of idiot comes up with a line like that?"

Robert said, "I'll talk to a friend of mine, an oncologist at Guy's Hospital. He's doing a trial of a new genetic treatment."

Hamilton stared at him. "One of your *miracle cures?*"

"No, no. I mean, only very indirectly."

Hamilton said angrily, "She won't take your poison."

Robert almost snapped back: *She won't? Or you won't let her?* But it was an unfair question. In some marriages, the lines blurred. It was not for him to judge the way the two of them faced this together.

"They go away in order to be with us in a new way, even closer than before." Hamilton spoke the words like a defiant incantation, a declaration of faith that would ward off temptation, whether or not he entirely believed it.

Robert was silent for a while, then he said, "I lost someone close to me, when I was a boy. And I thought the same thing. I thought he was still with me, for a long time afterward. Guiding me. Encouraging me." It was hard to get the words out; he hadn't spoken about this to anyone for almost thirty years. "I dreamed up a whole theory to explain it, in which 'souls' used quantum uncertainty to control the body during life, and communicate with the living after death, without breaking any laws of physics. The kind of thing every science-minded seventeen-year-old probably stumbles on, and takes seriously for a couple of weeks, before realizing how nonsensical it is. But I had a good reason not to see the flaws, so I clung to it for almost two years. Because I missed him so much, it took me that long to understand what I was doing, how I was deceiving myself."

Hamilton said pointedly, "If you'd not tried to explain it, you might never have lost him. He might still be with you now."

Robert thought about this. "I'm glad he's not, though. It wouldn't be fair on either of us."

Hamilton shuddered. "Then you can't have loved him very much, can you?" He put his head in his arms. "Just fuck off, now, will you."

Robert said, "What exactly would it take, to prove to you that I'm not in league with the devil?"

Hamilton turned red eyes on him and announced triumphantly, "Nothing will do that! I saw what happened to Quint's gun!"

Robert sighed. "That was a conjuring trick. Stage magic, not black magic."

"Oh yes? Show me how it's done, then. Teach me how to do it, so I can impress my friends."

"It's rather technical. It would take all night."

Hamilton laughed humourlessly. "You can't deceive me. I saw through you from the start."

"Do you think X-rays are Satanic? Penicillin?"

"Don't treat me like a fool. There's no comparison."

"*Why not?* Everything I've helped develop is part of the same continuum. I've read some of your writing on medieval culture, and you're always berating modern commentators for presenting it as unsophisticated. No one really thought the Earth was flat. No one really treated every novelty as witchcraft. So why view any of my work any differently than a fourteenth-century man would view twentieth-century medicine?"

Hamilton replied, "If a fourteenth-century man was suddenly faced with twentieth-century medicine, don't you think he'd be entitled to wonder how it had been revealed to his contemporaries?"

Robert shifted uneasily on his chair. Helen hadn't sworn him to secrecy, but he'd agreed with her view: it was better to wait, to spread the knowledge that would ground an understanding of what had happened, before revealing any details of the contact between branches.

But this man's wife was dying, needlessly. And Robert was tired of keeping secrets. Some wars required it, but others were better won with honesty.

He said, "I know you hate H.G. Wells. But what if he was right, about one little thing?"

Robert told him everything, glossing over the technicalities but leaving out nothing substantial. Hamilton listened without interrupting, gripped by a kind of unwilling fascination. His expression shifted from hostile to incredulous, but there were also hints of begrudging amazement, as if he could at least appreciate some of the beauty and complexity of the picture Robert was painting.

But when Robert had finished, Hamilton said merely, "You're a grand liar, Stoney. But what else should I expect, from the King of Lies?"

Robert was in a somber mood on the drive back to Cambridge. The encounter with Hamilton had depressed him, and the question of who'd swayed the nation in the debate seemed remote and abstract in comparison.

Helen had taken a house in the suburbs, rather than inviting scandal by cohabiting with him, though her frequent visits to his rooms seemed to have had almost the same effect. Robert walked her to the door.

"I think it went well, don't you?" she said.

"I suppose so."

"I'm leaving tonight," she added casually. "This is goodbye."

"What?" Robert was staggered. "Everything's still up in the air! I still need you!"

She shook her head. "You have all the tools you need, all the clues. And plenty of local allies. There's nothing truly urgent I could tell you, now, that you couldn't find out just as quickly on your own."

Robert pleaded with her, but her mind was made up. The driver beeped the horn; Robert gestured to him impatiently.

"You know, my breath's frosting visibly," he said, "and you're producing nothing. You really ought to be more careful."

She laughed. "It's a bit late to worry about that."

"Where will you go? Back home? Or off to twist another branch?"

"Another branch. But there's something I'm planning to do on the way."

"What's that?"

"Do you remember once, you wrote about an Oracle? A machine that could solve the halting problem?"

"Of course." Given a device that could tell you in advance whether a given computer program would halt, or go on running forever, you'd be able to prove or disprove any theorem whatsoever about the integers: the Goldbach conjecture, Fermat's Last Theorem, anything. You'd simply show this "Oracle" a program that would loop through all the integers, testing every possible set of values and only halting if it came to a set that violated the conjecture. You'd never need to run the program itself; the Oracle's verdict on whether or not it halted would be enough.

Such a device might or might not be possible, but Robert had proved more than twenty years before that no ordinary computer, however ingeniously programmed, would suffice. If program H could always tell you in a finite time whether or not program X would halt, you could tack on a small addition to H to create program Z, which perversely and deliberately went into an infinite loop whenever it examined a program that halted. If Z examined itself, it would either halt eventually, or run forever. But either possibility contradicted the alleged powers of program H: if Z actually ran forever, it would be because H had claimed that it wouldn't, and *vice versa*. Program H could not exist.

"Time travel," Helen said, "gives me a chance to become an Oracle. There's a way to exploit the inability to change your own past, a way to squeeze an infinite number of time-like paths—none of them closed, but some of them arbitrarily near to it—into a finite physical system. Once you do that, you can solve the halting problem."

"How?" Robert's mind was racing. "And once you've done that what about higher cardinalities? An Oracle for Oracles, able to test conjectures about the real numbers?"

Helen smiled enigmatically. "The first problem should only take you forty or fifty years to solve. As for the rest," she pulled away from him, moving into the darkness of the hallway, "what makes you think I know the answer myself?" She blew him a kiss, then vanished from sight.

Robert took a step toward her, but the hallway was empty.

He walked back to the car, sad and exalted, his heart pounding.

The driver asked wearily, "Where to now, sir?"

Robert said, "Further up, and further in."

4

The night after the funeral, Jack paced the house until three a.m. When would it be bearable? *When?* She'd shown more strength and courage, dying, than he felt within himself right now. But she'd share it with him, in the weeks to come. She'd share it with them all.

In bed, in the darkness, he tried to sense her presence around him. But it was forced, it was premature. It was one thing to have faith that she was watching over him, but quite another to expect to be spared every trace of grief, every trace of pain.

He waited for sleep. He needed to get some rest before dawn, or how would he face her children in the morning?

Gradually, he became aware of someone standing in the darkness at the foot of the bed. As he examined and reexamined the shadows, he formed a clear image of the apparition's face.

It was his own. Younger, happier, surer of himself.

Jack sat up. "What do you want?"

"I want you to come with me." The figure approached; Jack recoiled, and it halted.

"Come with you, where?" Jack demanded.

"To a place where she's waiting."

Jack shook his head. "No. I don't believe you. She said she'd come for me herself, when it was time. She said she'd guide me."

"She didn't understand, then," the apparition insisted gently. "She didn't know I could fetch you myself. Do you think I'd send her in my place? Do you think I'd shirk the task?"

Jack searched the smiling, supplicatory face. "Who are you?" *His own soul, in Heaven, remade?* Was this a gift God offered everyone? To meet, before death, the very thing you would become—if you so chose? So that even this would be an act of free will?

The apparition said, "Stoney persuaded me to let his friend treat Joyce. We lived on, together. More than a century has passed. And now we want you to join us."

Jack choked with horror. "No! This is a trick! *You're the Devil!*"

The thing replied mildly, "There is no Devil. And no God, either. Just people. But I promise you: people with the powers of gods are kinder than any god we ever imagined."

Jack covered his face. "Leave me be." He whispered fervent prayers, and waited. It was a test, a moment of vulnerability, but God wouldn't leave him naked like this, face-to-face with the Enemy, for longer than he could endure.

He uncovered his face. The thing was still with him.

It said, "Do you remember, when your faith came to you? The sense of a shield around you melting away, like armor you'd worn to keep God at bay?"

"Yes." Jack acknowledged the truth defiantly; he wasn't frightened that this abomination could see into his past, into his heart.

"That took strength: to admit that you needed God. But it takes the same kind of strength, again, to understand that *some needs can never be met.* I can't promise you Heaven. We have no disease, we have no war, we have no poverty.

But we have to find our own love, our own goodness. There is no final word of comfort. We only have each other."

Jack didn't reply; this blasphemous fantasy wasn't even worth challenging. He said, "I know you're lying. Do you really imagine that I'd leave the boys alone here?"

"They'd go back to America, back to their father. How many years do you think you'd have with them, if you stay? They've already lost their mother. It would be easier for them now, a single clean break."

Jack shouted angrily, "Get out of my house!"

The thing came closer, and sat on the bed. It put a hand on his shoulder. Jack sobbed, "Help me!" But he didn't know whose aid he was invoking any more.

"Do you remember the scene in *The Seat of Oak?* When the Harpy traps everyone in her cave underground, and tries to convince them that there is no Nescia? Only this drab underworld is real, she tells them. Everything else they think they've seen was just make believe." Jack's own young face smiled nostalgically. "And we had dear old Shrugweight reply: he didn't think much of this so-called 'real world' of hers. And even if she was right, since four little children could make up a better world, he'd rather go on pretending that their imaginary one was real.

"But we had it all upside down! The real world is richer, and stranger, and more beautiful than anything ever imagined. Milton, Dante, John the Divine are the ones who trapped you in a drab, gray underworld. That's where you are now. But if you give me your hand, I can pull you out."

Jack's chest was bursting. *He couldn't lose his faith. He'd kept it through worse than this. He'd kept it through every torture and indignity God had inflicted on his wife's frail body. No one could take it from him now.* He crooned to himself, "In my time of trouble, He will find me."

The cool hand tightened its grip on his shoulder. "You can be with her, now. Just say the word, and you will become a part of me. I will take you inside me, and you will see through my eyes, and we will travel back to the world where she still lives."

Jack wept openly. "Leave me in peace! Just leave me to mourn her!"

The thing nodded sadly. "If that's what you want."

"I do! *Go!*"

"When I'm sure."

Suddenly, Jack thought back to the long rant Stoney had delivered in the studio. Every choice went every way, Stoney had claimed. No decision could ever be final.

"Now I know you're lying!" he shouted triumphantly. "If you believed everything Stoney told you, how could my choice ever mean a thing? I would always say yes to you, and I would always say no! It would all be the same!"

The apparition replied solemnly, "While I'm here with you, touching you, *you can't be divided.* Your choice will count."

Jack wiped his eyes, and gazed into its face. It seemed to believe every word it was speaking. What if this truly was his metaphysical twin, speaking as honestly as he could, and not merely the Devil in a mask? Perhaps there was a grain of truth in Stoney's awful vision; perhaps this was another version of himself, a living person who honestly believed that the two of them shared a history.

Then it was a visitor sent by God, to humble him. To teach him compassion toward Stoney. To show Jack that he too, with a little less faith, and a little more pride, might have been damned forever.

Jack stretched out a hand and touched the face of this poor lost soul. *There, but for the grace of God, go I.*

He said, "I've made my choice. Now leave me."

Author's note: Where the lives of the fictional characters of this story parallel those of real historical figures, I've drawn on biographies by Andrew Hodges and A.N. Wilson. The self-dual formulation of general relativity was discovered by Abhay Ashtekar in 1986, and has since led to ground-breaking developments in quantum gravity, but the implications drawn from it here are fanciful.

To Cuddle Amy

NANCY KRESS

Nancy Kress is one of the major SF writers of the last two decades, well-known for her complex medical SF stories and for her biological and evolutionary extrapolations in such classics as Beggars in Spain *(1993),* Beggars and Choosers *(1994), and* Beggars Ride *(1996). In recent years, she has written two science thrillers,* Oaths and Miracles *(1995) and* Stinger *(1998), the SF novel* Maximum Light *(1998), and last year published* Probability Moon *(2000), the first book in a trilogy of hard SF novels set against the background of a war between humanity and an alien race. In 1998 she married SF writer Charles Sheffield. Her stories are rich in texture and in the details of the inner life of character and have been collected in* Trinity and Other Stories *(1985),* The Aliens of Earth *(1993), and* Beakers Dozen *(1998). She teaches regularly at summer writing workshops such as Clarion, and during the year at the Bethesda Writing Center in Bethesda, Maryland. She is the "Fiction" columnist for* Writers Digest.*

"To Cuddle Amy" is a tiny SF horror story with a sit-com tone. It appeared in Asimov's. *It is an interesting contrast to Michael Flynn's story, "Built Upon the Sands of Time." There were a number of stories published last year about the anxieties of parents and children in the coming era of genetic engineering that is creeping up on us, but none better than this one.*

Campbell entered the living room to find his wife in tears. "Allison! What's wrong?"

She sprang up from the sofa and raged at him. "What do you think is wrong, Paul? What's *ever* wrong? Amy! Only this time she's gone too far.

"*This* time, she . . . she . . . the police just left. . . ." She broke down into sobs.

Campbell had had a lot of experience dealing with his wife. They'd been married almost forty years. Pushing down his own alarm, he took Allison in his arms and sat on the sofa, cradling her as if she were a child. Which, in some ways, she still was. Allison had always been high strung, finely tuned. Sensitive. He was the strong one. "Tell me, sweetie. Tell me what happened."

"I . . . she . . ."

"The police. You said the police just left. What did Amy do now?"

"Van . . . vandalism. She and those awful friends of hers . . . the Hitchens boy, that slut Kristy Arnold . . . they . . ."

"They *what*? Come on, honey, you'll feel better if you tell me."

"They were throwing rocks at cars from the overpass! Throwing rocks!"

Campbell considered. It could be far worse. Still . . . something didn't add up here. "Allison—why did the cops leave? Are they going to arrest Amy?"

"No. They said they"—more sobbing—"couldn't be sure it was her. Not enough evidence. But they suspected it was, and wanted us to know . . . oh, Paul, I don't think I can take much more!"

"I know, honey. I know. Shhh, don't cry."

"She just throws away everything we do for her!"

"Shhhhhh," Campbell said, but Allison went on crying. Campbell gazed over her heaving shoulder at the wall, covered with framed photos of Amy. Amy at six months, asleep on a pink blanket in a field of daisies. Amy at two, waving her moo-cow, a toddler so adorable that people had stopped Allison in the street to admire her. Amy at seven in a ballet tutu. Amy at twelve, riding her horse. Amy at sixteen in a prom dress, caught in a rare smile.

Amy, fourteen, came through the front door.

Allison didn't give her daughter a chance to attack first. "So there you are! You just missed the cops, Amy, telling us what you've done *this* time, and it's the *last straw,* do you hear me, young lady? We forgave you the awful school grades! We forgave you the rudeness and ingratitude and sullen self-centeredness! We even forgave you the shop-lifting, God help us! But this is over the line! Throwing rocks at cars! Someone could have been killed—how much more do you expect us to *take* from you? Answer me!"

Amy said angrily, "I didn't do it!"

"You're lying! The cops said—"

"Allison, wait," Campbell said. "Amy, the cops said you were a suspect."

"Well, I didn't do it! Kristy and Jed did, but I went home! And I don't care if you believe me or not, you bitch!"

Allison gasped. Amy stormed through the living room, a lanky mass of fury in deliberately torn clothes, pins through her lip and eyebrow, purple lipstick smeared. She raced upstairs and slammed her bedroom door.

"Paul . . . oh, Paul . . . did you *hear* what she called me? Her *mother?*" Allison collapsed against him again, her slim body shaking so hard that Campbell's arms tightened to steady her.

But he felt shaky, too. This couldn't go on. The sullen

rudeness, the fights, the breaking the law . . . their lives were being reduced to rubble by a fourteen-year-old.

"Paul . . ." Allison sobbed, "do you remember how she *used* to be? Oh, God, the day she was born . . . remember? I was so happy I thought I'd die. And then how she was as a little girl, climbing on our laps for a cuddle . . . oh, Paul, I want my little girl back!"

"I know. I know, dearest."

"Don't *you?*"

He did. He wanted back the Amy who was so sweet, so biddable. Who thought he was the best daddy in the world. The feel of that light little body in his arms, the sweet baby smell at the back of her neck. . . .

He said slowly, "She's fourteen now. Legal age."

Immediately, Allison stopped sobbing. She stood still against him. Finally she said, "It isn't as if she'd be without resources. The Hitchenses might take her in. Or somebody. And anyway, there are lots more like her out there." Allison's lower lip stuck out. "Might even do her good to learn how good she had it here with us!"

Campbell closed his eyes. "But we wouldn't know."

"You're damn right we wouldn't know! She doesn't want any part of *us,* then I don't want any part of *her!*" Again, Allison leaned against him. "But it isn't that, Paul. You know it isn't. I just want my little girl back again! I want to cuddle my lost little girl! Oh, I'd give anything to cuddle Amy again! Don't you want that, too?"

Campbell did. And the present situation really wasn't fair to Allison, who'd never been strong. Allison's health was being affected. She shouldn't have to be broken by this spiteful stranger who'd developed in their midst in the last year. Allison had rights, too.

His wife continued to sob against his chest, but softly now. Campbell felt strong, in control. He could make it all right for his wife, for himself. For everybody.

He said, "There are three embryos left."

Three of six. Three frozen vials in the fertility clinic, all from the same in-vitro fertilization, stored as standard procedure against a failure to carry to term. Or other need.

Three more versions of the same embryo, the product of forced division before the first implantation. Standard procedure, yes, all over the country.

"I'll throw her out tonight," he told Allison, "and call the clinic in the morning."

Steppenpferd

BRIAN W. ALDISS

Brian W. Aldiss, The Encyclopedia of Science Fiction *says, is "one of the SF field's two or three most prolific authors of substance, and perhaps its most exploratory." In 2000, Aldiss was given the Grand Master award of the Science Fiction Writers of America. The influence of his works is deep and widespread in SF. His* Billion Year Spree, *in which Aldiss proposed Mary Shelley as the progenitor of SF, is one of the most influential works of criticism ever published about SF. He burst into prominence in the late 1950s, and has never ceased to push the boundaries of SF since. Over five decades, he has published more than 300 stories and a number of fine novels—high points include the classics* Hothouse, Frankenstein Unbound, *and the* Helliconia Trilogy— *but he has written very few in recent years. In the last couple of years, Aldiss has published his autobiography (*The Twinkling of an Eye*) and a book of autobiographical postscript (*When the Feast is Finished—*about the recent death of his wife, Margaret).*

"Steppenpferd" (which contains perhaps a wordplay on Thomas Mann's title, Steppenwolf*) is set on a distant planet in the distant future, where pieces of Earth (in this case, a fragment of 19th century Scandinavia) have been reconstructed by aliens and things are not as they seem. It was published in* Fantasy & Science Fiction.

From a cosmological perspective, the sun was a solitary, isolated on the fringes of its galaxy. The supergiant belonged in spectral class K5. Seen more closely, it appeared as a dull smoky globe, a candle about to gutter out, the smoke consisting of myriads of particles dancing in the solar magnetism.

Despite its size, it was a cold thing, registering no more than 3,600°K. All about its girth, stretching far out along the plane of the ecliptic, a series of artificial spheres moved in attendance. Each of these spheres contained captive solar systems.

The species which brought the globes here over vast distances called themselves the Pentivanashenii, a word that eons ago had meant "those who once grazed." This species had cannibalized their own planets and gone forth into the great matrix of space, returning to their home star only to deliver their prizes into orbit.

Father Erik Predjin walked out of the dormitory into the early light. In a short while, the monastery bell would toll and his twelve monks and as many novices would rise and go into the chapel for First Devotions. Until then, the little world of the island was his. Or rather, God's.

The low damp cold came through the birches at him. Father Predjin shivered inside his habit. He relished the bite of dawn. With slow steps, he skirted the stack of adzed timbers designated for the re-roofing, the piled stones with their numbers painted on which would eventually form part of the rebuilt apse. Ever and again, he looked up at the fabric of the old building to which, with God's guidance and his own will, he was restoring spiritual life.

The monastery was still in poor condition. Some of its foundations dated from the reign of Olav the Peaceful in the eleventh century. The main fabric was of later date, built when the Slav Wends had sought refuge on the island.

What Father Predjin most admired was the southern facade. The arched doorway was flanked by blind arcading with deeply stepped molded columns. These were weather-worn but intact.

"Here," Father Predjin often told the so-called tourists, "you may imagine the early monks trying to recreate the face of God in stone. He is grand, ready to allow entrance to all who come to him, but sometimes blind to our miseries. And by now perhaps the Almighty is worn down by the uncertain Earthly weather."

The tourists shuffled at this remark. Some looked upward, upward, where, hazily beyond the blue sky, the sweep of metal sphere could be seen.

The father felt some small extra contentment this morning. He made no attempt to account for it. Happiness was simply something that occurred in a well-regulated life. Of course, it was autumn, and he always liked autumn. Something about early autumn, when the leaves began to flee before a northern breeze and the days shortened, gave an extra edge to existence. One was more aware of the great spirit which informed the natural world.

A cock crowed, celebrating the morning's freshness.

He turned his broad back on the ochre-painted building and walked down toward the shore by the paved path he had helped the brothers build. Here, he made his way along by the edge of the water. This meeting of the two elements of land and water was celebrated by a cascade of stones and pebbles. They had been shed from the flanks of retreating glaciers. Those mighty grindstones had polished them so that they lay glistening in the morning light, displaying, for those who cared to look, a variety of colors and origins. No less than the monastery, they were proof for the faithful of a guiding hand.

A dead fish lay silvery among the cobbles, the slight lap of the waves of the lake giving it a slight lifelike movement. Even in death, it had beauty.

Walking steadily, the father approached a small jetty. An old wooden pier extended a few meters into Lake Mannsjo, dripping water into its dark reflection. To this pier workers would come and, later, another boat with extra-galactic tourists. Directly across the water, no more than a kilometer away, was the mainland and the small town of Mannjer, from which the boats would arrive. A gray slice of pollution spread in a wedge from above the town, cutting across the black inverted image of mountains.

The father studied the mountains and the roofs of the town. How cunningly they resembled the real thing which once had been. He crossed himself. At least this little island had been preserved, for what reason he could not determine. Perhaps the day would come when all returned to normal—if he persevered in prayer.

On the water margin of the island lay old oil drums and remains of military equipment. The island had, until five years ago, been commandeered by the military for their own purposes. Father Predjin had erased most of the reminders of that occupation, the graffiti in the chapel, the bullet holes in the walls, the shattered trees. He was slow to permit these last military remains to be cleared. Something told him the old rusty landing craft should remain where it was, half sunk in the waters of the lake. Now that it had ceased to function, it was not out of harmony with its surroundings. Besides, no harm was done in reminding both brothers and the alien visitors of past follies—and the present uncertain nature of the world. Of the world and, he added to himself, of the whole solar system, now encased in that enormous sphere and transported. . . . He knew not where.

Somewhere far beyond the galaxy. But not beyond the reach of God?

He breathed deeply, pleased by the lap-lap-lap of the waters of the lake. He could look west from his little island—the Lord's and his—to what had been Norway and a distant railway line. He could look east to the mountains of what had been Sweden. Lake Mannsjo lay across the border between the two countries. Indeed, the imaginary line of the border, as projected by rulers plied in Oslo and Stockholm ministerial offices, cut across the Isle of Mannsjo and, indeed, right through the old monastery itself. Hence its long occupation by the military, when territorial opinions had differed and the two Scandinavian countries had been at loggerheads.

Why had they quarreled? Why had they not imagined . . . well . . . the unimaginable?

He knew the skimpy silver birches growing among the stones on the shore, knew one from the next: was amused to think of some as Norwegian, some as Swedish. He touched them as he went by. The mist-moistened papery bark was pleasing to his hand.

Now that the military had left, the only invaders of Mannsjo were those tourists. Father Predjin had to pretend to encourage their visits. A small boat brought them over, a boat which left Mannjer on the mainland promptly every summer morning, five days a week, and permitted the beings two hours ashore. In that time, the tourists were free to wander or pretend to worship. And the novices, selling them food and drink and crucifixes, made a little money to help with the restoration fund.

The father watched the boat coming across the water and the grotesque horse-like beings slowly taking on human shape and affecting human clothing.

August was fading from the calendar. Soon there would be no more tourists. Mannsjo was less than five degrees south of the Arctic Circle. No tourists came in the long dark winter. They copied everything that had once been, including behavior.

"I shall not miss them," said the father, under his breath,

looking toward the distant shore. "We shall work through the winter as if nothing has happened." He recognized that he would miss women visitors especially. Although he had taken the vow of chastity many years previously, God still permitted him to rejoice at the sight of young women, their flowing hair, their figures, their long legs, the sound of their voices. Not one of the order—not even pretty young novice Sankal—could match the qualities of women. Antelope qualities. But of course an illusion; in reality there were seven black ungainly limbs behind every deceiving pair of neat legs.

The beings entered his mind. He knew it. Sometimes he sensed them there, like mice behind the paneling of his room.

He turned his face toward the east, closing his eyes to drink in the light. His countenance was lean and tanned. It was the face of a serious man who liked to laugh. His eyes were generally a gray-blue, and the scrutiny he turned on his fellow men was enquiring but friendly: perhaps more enquiring than open: like shelves of books in a library, whose spines promise much but reveal little of their contents. It had been said by those with whom Father Predjin had negotiated for the purchase of the island that he confided in no one, probably not even his God.

His black hair, as yet no more than flecked by gray, was cut in pudding basin fashion. He was clean-shaven. About his lips played a sort of genial determination; his general demeanor also suggested determination. In his unself-conscious way, Erik Predjin did not realize how greatly his good looks had eased his way through life, rendering that determination less frequently exercised than would otherwise have been the case.

He thought of a woman's face he had once known, asking himself, Why were not men happier? Had not men and women been set on Earth to make one another happy? Was it because humanity had failed in some dramatic way that this extraordinary swarm of beings had descended, to wipe out almost everything once regarded as permanent?

How is it that the world was so full of sin that it was necessary to destroy it? Now those who sequestered themselves on Mannsjo would continue to do Him reverence. Attempt in their frailty to do Him reverence. To save the world and restore it to what once it was, and make it whole and happy again. "Without sin."

Cobbles crunched under his sandals. Hugging his body against the cold, he turned away from the water, up another path which climbed round a giant boulder. Here in a sheltered dell, hens clucked. Here were gardens where the Order grew vegetables—potatoes especially—and herbs, and kept bees. All barely enough to sustain the company, but the Almighty approved of frugality. As the father walked among them, casting an expert gaze over the crops, the monastery bell started to toll. Without quickening his pace, he went on, under the apple trees, to his newly repaired church.

He said aloud as he went, clasping his hands together, "Thank you, O Lord, for another of your wonderful days through which we may live. And bless my fellow workers, that they also may taste your joy."

After the morning prayers came breakfast. Homemade bread, fish fresh from the lake, well water. Enough to fill the belly.

Shortly after ten in the morning, Father Predjin and two of the brothers went down to the quay to meet the morning boat bringing the workers from Mannjer. The workers were voluntary labor. They appeared to include not only Scandinavians but men, mainly young, from other parts of Europe, together with a Japanese who had come to visit Mannsjo as a tourist two years ago and had stayed. While he was awaiting novitiate status, he lodged in Mannjer with a crippled woman.

Oh, they all had their stories. But he had seen them from his window, when they thought no one was looking, revert into that lumpish shape with those great trailing hands, seven-fingered, gray in color.

This was the father's secret: since he knew that these be-ings were asymmetrical, and not symmetrical, or nearly so, as were human beings, he understood that God had turned his countenance from them. In consequence, they were evil.

The monks welcomed the fake workers and blessed them. They were then directed to the tasks of the day. Few needed much instruction. Plasterers, carpenters, and stone masons carried on as previously.

Should I allow such alien and god-hating beings to par-ticipate in the construction of God's edifice? Will He curse us all for permitting this error?

Now a little urgency was added to the workers' usual businesslike manner; winter was coming. Over the drum of the main dome an almost flat tiled roof was being installed, closing it against the elements. There was no money at pres-ent for a copper-clad dome it was hoped for, provided funds were forthcoming.

When the father had seen that all were employed, he re-turned to the main building and climbed a twisting stair to his office on the third floor.

It was a narrow room, lit by two round windows and fur-nished with little more than an old worm-eaten desk and a couple of rickety chairs. A Crucifix hung on the white-washed wall behind the desk.

One of the novices came up to talk to Father Predjin about the question of heating in the winter. The problem arose every year at this time. As usual it remained unresolved.

Immediately next came Sankal. He must have been wait-ing on the stairs outside the door.

His Father gestured to him to take a seat, but the young man preferred to stand.

Sankal stood twisting his hands about his rough-woven habit, shy as ever but with the air of a young man who has something important to say and looks only for an opening.

"You wish to leave the order?" Father Predjin said, laugh-ing to show he was joking and merely offering the chance for a response.

Julius Sankal was a pale and pretty youth with down on

his upper lip. Like many of the other novices in Mannsjo, he had been given refuge by Predjin because the rest of the globe was disappearing.

In those days, Predjin had stood by his church and looked up at the night sky, to see the stars disappear as the sphere encased them bit by bit. And, as surely, the world was disappearing, bit by bit, to be replaced by a cheap replica—perhaps a replica without mass, to facilitate transport. Such things could only be speculated upon, with a burdened sense of one's ignorance and fear.

Sankal had arrived at Mannjer in the snow. And later had stolen a boat in order to cross to the island, to throw himself on the mercy of the ruinous monastery, and of its master. Now he had the job of baking the monastery's bread.

"Perhaps it is necessary I leave," the youth said. He stood with downcast eyes. Father Predjin waited, hands resting, lightly clasped, on the scarred top of his desk. "You see . . . I cannot explain. I am come to a wrong belief, father. Very much have I prayed, but I am come to a wrong belief."

"As you are aware, Julius, you are permitted to hold any one of a number of religious beliefs here. The first important thing is to believe in a God, until you come to see the true God. Thus we light a tiny light in a world utterly lost and full of darkness. If you leave you go into a damned world of illusion."

The sound of hammering echoed from above them. New beams were going into the roof of the apse.

The noise almost drowned Sankal's response, which came quietly but firmly.

"Father, I am shy person, you know it. Yet am I at maturity. Always have many inward thoughts. Now those thoughts move like a stream to this wrong belief." He hung his head.

Predjin stood, so that he dominated the youth. His expression was grave and sympathetic. "Look at me, son, and do not be ashamed. All our lives are filled with such hammering as we hear now. It is the sound of an enormous material world breaking in on us. We must not heed it. This wrong belief must make you miserable."

"Father, I have respects for your theology. But maybe what is wrong belief is right for me. No, I mean . . . Is hard to say it. To arrive at a clear belief—it's good, is it?—even if the belief is wrong. Then maybe is not wrong after all. Is instead good."

With the merest hint of impatience, Father Predjin said, "I don't understand your reasoning, Julius. Can we not pull out this wrong belief from your mind, like a rotten tooth?"

Sankal looked up at his mentor defiantly. He showed clenched fists, white-knuckled above the desk.

"My belief is that this island has not been maked—*made* by God. It also is an illusion, made by God's terrible Adversary."

"That's nothing more than non-belief."

It came out defiantly: "No, no. I believe the Evil Ones made our place where we live. Our goodness itself is an illusion. I have proof it is so."

Thinking deeply before he replied, Father Predjin said, "Let us suppose for an instant that we are living on an island made by these frightful beings who now possess the solar system, so that all is illusion. But yet Goodness is not an illusion. Goodness is never an illusion, wherever found. Evil is the illusion . . ."

Even as he spoke, he imagined he saw something furtive and evil in the eyes of the youth standing before him.

Father Predjin studied Sankal carefully before asking, "And have you come suddenly to your conclusion?"

"Yes. No. I realize I have always felt like this way. I just did not know it. I've always been running, have I? Only coming here—well, you gave me time for thinking. I realize the world is evil, and it gets worse. Because the Devil rules it. We always spoke of the devil in our family. Well, now he has come in this horse-like shape to overwhelm us."

"What is this proof you speak of?"

Sankal jumped up, to face the father angrily. "It's in me, in the scars on my mind and on my body since I am a boy. The Devil does not have to knock to come in. He is inside already."

After a pause, the father sat down again, and crossed himself. He said, "You must be very unhappy to believe such a thing. That is not belief as we understand it, but sickness. Sit down, Julius, and let me tell you something. For if you seriously believe what you say, then you must leave us. Your home will be in the world of illusion."

"I know that." The youth looked defiant, but seated himself on the rickety chair. The hammering above continued.

"I was just discussing with someone how we were going to keep warm in the coming winter," the father said, conversationally. "When first I arrived on the island with two companions, we managed somehow to survive the long winter. This building was then in a terrible condition, with half the roof missing. We had no electricity and could not have afforded it had it been available.

"We burnt logs, which we chopped from fallen trees. Mannsjo was then more wooded than now it is. We lived virtually in two rooms on the ground floor. We lived off fish and little else. Occasionally, the kind people of Mannjer would skate across the ice to bring us warm clothes, bread, and aquavit. Otherwise, we prayed and we worked and we fasted.

"Those were happy days. God was with us. He rejoices in scarcity.

"As the years have passed, we have become more sophisticated. At first we made do with candles. Then with oil lamps and oil heaters. We are now reconnected to the electricity supply from Mannjer. Somehow it still works. Now we have to prepare for a longer darker winter, the winter of Unbelief."

"I do not understand what you hope for," Sankal said. "This little piece of the past is lost somewhere outside the galaxy, where God—where your God has never been heard of."

"They hear of him now." The priest spoke very firmly. "The so-called tourists hear of him. The so-called workers labor on his behalf. As long as the evil does not enter into us, we do the Lord's work, wherever in the universe we happen to be."

Sankal gave a shrug. He looked over one shoulder. "The

Devil can get to you, because he owns all—every things in the world he made."

"You will make yourself ill believing that. Such beliefs were once held by the Cathars and Bogomils. They perished. What I am trying to tell you is that it is easy to mistake the danger we are in—the more than mortal danger—for the work of the Devil. There is no Devil. There is merely a desertion of God, which in itself is extremely painful in many spiritual ways. You are missing God's peace."

From under his brows, Sankal shot Predjin a look of mischievous hatred. "I certainly am! So I wish to leave."

The hammering above them ceased. They heard the footsteps of the workers overhead.

Father Predjin cleared his throat. "Julius, there is evil in men, in all of us, yes."

Sankal's shouted interruption: "And in the horse-devils who did such a thing in the world!"

The priest flinched but continued. "We must regard what has happened to be part of God's strategy of free will. We can still choose between good and evil. We have the gift of life, however hard that life may be, and in it we must choose. If you go from here, you cannot come back."

They looked at each other across the wormy old desk. Outside, beyond the round windows, a watery sun had risen from behind the eastern mountains.

"I want you to stay and help us in the struggle, Julius," the father said. "For your sake. We can get another baker. Another soul is a different matter."

Again Sankal gave a cunning look askance.

"Are you afraid my hideous belief will spread among the other people in the monastery?"

"Oh yes," said Father Predjin. "Yes, I am. Leprosy is contagious."

When the youth had left, almost before his footsteps had faded from the winding wooden stair, Father Predjin hitched up his cassock and planted his knees on the worn boards of the floor. He clasped his hands together. He bowed his head. Now there was no sound, the workmen having finished their hammering, except for a tiny flutter such as a heart might make; a butterfly flew against a window pane, unable to comprehend what held it back from freedom.

The father repeated a prayer mantra until his consciousness stilled and sank away into the depths of a greater mind. His lips ceased to move. Gradually, the scripts appeared, curling, uncurling, twisting about themselves in a three dimensional Sanskrit. There was about this lettering a sense of benediction, as if the messages they conveyed were ones of good will; but in no way could the messages be interpreted, unless they were themselves the message, saying that life is a gift and an obligation, but containing a further meaning which must remain forever elusive.

The scripts were in a color, as they writhed and elaborated themselves, like gold, and often appeared indistinct against a sandy background.

With cerebral activity almost dormant, there was no way in which intelligence could be focused on any kind of interpretation. Nor could a finite judgment be arrived at. Labyrinthine changes taking place continually would have defied such attempts. For the scripts turned on themselves like snakes, now forming a kind of *tugra* upon the vellum of neural vacancy. Ascenders rose upward, creating panels across which tails wavered back and forth, creating within them polychrome branches or tuft-like abstractions from twigs of amaranth.

The elaboration continued. Color increased. Large loops created a complex motorway of lettering and filled themselves with two contrasting arrangements of superimposed spiral scrolls in lapis blue with carmine accents. The entanglement spread, orderly in its growth and replication.

Now the entire design, which seemed to stretch infinitely, was either receding or pressing closer, transforming into a musical noise. That noise became more random, more like the flutter of wings against glass. As the scripts faded, as consciousness became a slowly inflowing tide, the fluttering took on a more sinister tone.

Soon—intolerably soon—breaking the mood of transcendent calm—the fluttering was a thundering of inscrutable nature. It was like a sound of hooves, as though a large animal was attempting clumsily to mount impossible stairs. Blundering—but brutishly set upon success.

Father Predjin came to himself. Time had passed. Cloud obscured the sky in the pupil-less eye of the round window. The butterfly lay exhausted on the sill. Still the infernal noise continued. It was as if a stallion was endeavoring to climb the wooden twisting stair from below.

He rose to his feet. "Sankal?" he asked, in a whisper.

The father ran to the door and set his back against it, clenching the skin of his cheeks back in terror, exposing his two rows of teeth.

Sweat burst like tears from his brow.

"Save me, sweet heavenly Father, save me, damn you! I'm all you've got!"

Still the great beast came on, the full power of Pentivanashenii behind it.

Sheena 5

STEPHEN BAXTER

Stephen Baxter (www.sam.math.ethz.ch/%7Epkeller/Baxter-Page.html) is now one of the big names in hard SF, the author of a number of highly regarded novels (he has won the Philip K. Dick Award, the John W. Campbell Memorial Award, the British SF Association Award, and others for his novels) and many short stories. He published four books in 2000, including a collaboration with Arthur C. Clarke, The Light of Other Days; Longtusk *(Mammoth, book two);* Reality Dust; *and* Space: Manifold 2 *(to be titled* Manifold: Space *in the US); and won the Philip K. Dick Award for his collection* Vacuum Diagrams *(1999). In the mid and late 1990s he produced nearly ten short stories a year in fantasy, SF, and horror venues, and in 2000 he did it again. He appeared in most of the major magazines, sometimes twice, and there were several of his stories in contention for a place in this book. No wonder his collections are so good.*

"Sheena 5" was published in Analog, *which like its companion magazine* Asimov's *had a particularly strong year in 2000. Baxter exploited this same setting and characters in a short piece in* Nature. *This story is good old-fashioned hard SF adventure, with a sympathetic (though non-human) heroic central character and vistas of wonder in space and in the future.*

Sheena didn't mean it to happen. Of course not; she knew the requirements of the mission as well as anyone, as well as Dan himself. She had her duty to NASA. She understood that.

But it felt so *right*.

It came after the kill.

The night was over. The sun, a fat ball of light, was already glimmering above the water's surface.

The squid emerged from the grasses and corals where they had been feeding. Shoals formed in small groups and clusters, eventually combining into a community a hundred strong.

Court me. Court me.

See my weapons!

I am strong and fierce.

Stay away! Stay away! She is mine! . . .

It was the ancient cephalopod language, a language of complex skin patterns, body posture, texture, words of sex and danger and food; and Sheena shoaled and sang with joy.

. . . But there was a shadow on the water.

The sentinels immediately adopted concealment or bluff postures, blaring lies at the approaching predator.

Sheena knew that there would be no true predators here. The shadow could only be a watching NASA machine.

The dark shape lingered close, just as a true barracuda would before diving into the shoal, seeking to break it up.

A strong male broke free. He spread his eight arms, raised

his two long tentacles, and his green binocular eyes fixed on
the fake barracuda. Confusing patterns of light and shade
pulsed across his hide. *Look at me. I am large and fierce. I
can kill you.* Slowly, cautiously, the male drifted towards the
barracuda, coming to within a mantle-length.

At the last moment the barracuda turned, sluggishly.

But it was too late.

The male's two long tentacles whipped out, and their
clublike pads of suckers pounded against the barracuda hide,
sticking there. Then the male wrapped his eight strong arms
around the barracuda's body, his pattern changing to an ex-
ultant uniform darkening. And he stabbed at the barracuda's
skin with his beak, seeking meat.

And meat there was, what looked like fish fragments to
Sheena, booty planted there by Dan.

The squid descended, lashing their tentacles around the
stricken prey. Sheena joined in, cool water surging through
her mantle, relishing the primordial power of this kill despite its artifice.

. . . That was when it happened.

As she clambered stiffly down through the airlock into the
habitat, the smell of air freshener overwhelmed Maura
Delia.

"Ms. Delia, welcome to Oceanlab," Dan Ystebo said. Ystebo, marine biologist, was fat, breathy, intense, thirtyish,
with Coke bottle glasses and a mop of unlikely red hair, a
typical geek scientist type.

Maura found a seat before a bank of controls. The seat
was just a canvas frame, much repaired with duct tape. The
working area of this hab was a small, cramped sphere, its
walls encrusted with equipment. A sonar beacon pinged
softly, like a pulse.

The sense of confinement, the feel of the weight of water
above her head, was overwhelming.

She leaned forward, peering into small windows. Sunlight
shafted through empty gray water. She saw a school of squid
jetting through the water in complex patterns.

"Which one is Sheena 5?"

Dan pointed to a softscreen pasted over a scuffed hull section.

The streamlined, torpedo-shaped body was a rich burnt-orange, mottled black. Winglike fins rippled elegantly alongside the body.

The Space Squid, Maura thought. The only mollusk on NASA's payroll.

"*Sepioteuthis sepioidea,*" Dan said. "The Caribbean reef squid. About as long as your arm. Squid, all cephalopods in fact, belong to the phylum Mollusca. But in the squid the mollusk foot has evolved into the funnel, here, leading into the mantle, and the arms and tentacles here. The mantle cavity contains the viscera and gills. Sheena can use the water passing through her mantle cavity for jet propulsion—"

"How do you know that's her?"

Dan pointed again. "See the swelling between the eyes, around the oesophagus?"

"That's her enhanced brain?"

"A squid's neural layout isn't like ours. Sheena has two nerve cords running like rail tracks the length of her body, studded with pairs of ganglia. The forward ganglia pair is expanded into a mass of lobes. We gen-enged Sheena and her grandmothers to—"

"To make a smart squid."

"Ms. Della, squid are smart anyway. They evolved—a long time ago, during the Jurassic—in competition with the fish. They have senses based on light, scent, taste, touch, sound—including infrasound—gravity, acceleration, perhaps even an electric sense. Sheena can control her skin patterns consciously. She can make bands, bars, circles, annuli, dots. She can even animate the display."

"And these patterns are signals?"

"Not just the skin patterns: skin texture, body posture. There may be electric or sonic components too; we can't be sure."

"And what do they use this marvelous signaling for?"

"We aren't sure. They don't hunt cooperatively. And they live only a couple of years, mating only once or twice." Dan scratched his beard. "But we've been able to isolate a number of primal linguistic components which combine in a primitive grammar. Even in unenhanced squid. But the language seems to be closed. It's about nothing but food, sex, and danger. It's like the dance of the bee."

"Unlike human languages."

"Yes. So we opened up Sheena's language for her. In the process we were able to prove that the areas of the brain responsible for learning are the vertical and superior frontal lobes that lie above the oesophagus."

"How did you prove that?"

Dan blinked. "By cutting away parts of squid brains."

Maura sighed. What great PR if that got broadcast.

They studied Sheena. Two forward-looking eyes, blue-green rimmed with orange, peered briefly into the camera.

Alien eyes. Intelligent.

Do we have the right to do this, to meddle with the destiny of other sentient creatures, to further our own goals—when we don't even understand, as Ystebo admits, what the squid use their speech for? What it is they talk about?

How does it *feel,* to be Sheena?

And could Sheena possibly understand that humans are planning to have her fly a rocket ship to an asteroid?

He came for her: the killer male, one tentacle torn on some loose fragment of metal.

She knew this was wrong. And yet it was irresistible.

She felt a skin pattern flush over her body, a pied mottling, speckled with white spots. *Court me.*

He swam closer. She could see his far side was a bright uniform silver, a message to the other males: *Keep away. She is mine!* As he rolled, the colors tracked around his body, and she could see the tiny muscles working the pigment sacs on his hide.

And already he was holding out his hectocotylus towards her, the modified arm bearing the clutch of spermatophores at its tip.

Mission, Sheena. Mission. Bootstrap! Mission! NASA! Dan!

But then the animal within her rose, urgent. She opened her mantle to the male.

His hectocotylus reached for her, striking swiftly, and lodged the needle-like spermatophore among the roots of *her arms.*

Then he withdrew. Already it was over.

. . . And yet it was not. She could choose whether or not to embrace the spermatophore and place it in her seminal receptacle.

She knew she must not.

All around her, the squid's songs pulsed with life. Ancient songs that reached back to a time before humans, before whales, *before even the fish.*

Her life was short: lasting one summer, two at most, a handful of matings. But the songs of light and dance made every squid aware she was part of a continuum that stretched back to those ancient seas; and that her own brief, vibrant life was as insignificant, yet as vital, as a single silver scale on the hide of a fish.

Sheena, with her human-built mind, was the first of all cephalopods to be able to understand this. And yet every squid knew it, on some level that transcended the mind.

But Sheena was no longer part of that continuum.

Even as the male receded, she felt overwhelmed with sadness, loneliness, isolation. Resentment.

She closed her arms over the spermatophore, and drew it inside her.

"I have to go to bat for you on the Hill Monday," Maura said to Dan. "I have to put my reputation on the line to save this project. You're sure, absolutely sure, this is going to work?"

"Absolutely," Dan said. He spoke with a *calm conviction* that made her want to believe him. "Look, the squid are adapted to a zero-gravity environment—unlike us. And Sheena can hunt in three dimensions; she will be able to navigate. If you were going to evolve a creature equipped for space travel, it would be a cephalopod. And she's much cheaper than any robotic equivalent. . . ."

"But," Maura said heavily, "we don't have any plans to bring her back."

He shrugged. "Even if we had the capability, she's too short-lived. We have plans to deal with the ethical contingencies."

"That's bullshit."

Dan looked uncomfortable. But he said, "We hope the public will accept the arrival of the asteroid in Earth orbit as a memorial to her. A just price. And Senator, every moment of her life, from the moment she was hatched, Sheena has been oriented to the goal. It's what she lives for. The mission."

Somberly Maura watched the squid, Sheena, as she flipped and jetted in formation with her fellows.

We have to do this, she thought. I have to force the funding through, on Monday.

If Sheena succeeded she would deliver, in five years or so, a near-Earth asteroid rich in organics and other volatiles to Earth orbit. Enough to bootstrap, at last, an expansion off the planet. Enough, perhaps, to save mankind.

And, if the gloomier State Department reports about the state of the world were at all accurate, it might be the last chance anybody would get.

But Sheena wouldn't live to see it.

The squid shoal collapsed to a tight school and jetted away, rushing out of sight.

Sheena 5 glided at the heart of the ship, where the water that passed through her mantle, over her gills, was warmest, richest. The core machinery, the assemblage of devices that maintained life here, was a black mass before her, lights winking over its surface.

She found it hard to rest without the shoal, the mating and learning and endless dances of daylight.

Restless, she swam away from the machinery cluster. As she rose, the water flowing through her mantle cooled, the rich oxygen thinning. She sensed the subtle sounds of living things: the smooth rush of fish, the bubbling murmur of the krill on which they browsed, and the hiss of the diatoms and algae which fed them. In Sheena's spacecraft, matter and energy flowed in great loops, sustained by sunlight, regulated by its central machinery as if by a beating heart.

She reached the wall of the ship. It was translucent. If she pushed at it, it pushed back. Grass algae grew on the wall, their long filaments dangling and wafting in the currents.

Beyond the membrane shone a milky, blurred sun—with, near it, a smaller crescent. That, she knew, was the Earth, all its great oceans reduced to a droplet. This craft was scooting around the sun after Earth like a fish swimming after its school.

She let the lazy, whalelike roll of the ship carry her away from the glare of the sun, and she peered into the darkness, where she could see the stars.

She had been trained to recognize many of the stars. She used this knowledge to determine her position in space far more accurately than even Dan could have, from far-off Earth.

But to Sheena the stars were more than navigation beacons. Sheena's eyes had a hundred times the number of receptors of human eyes, and she could see a hundred times as many stars.

To Sheena the Universe was crowded with stars, vibrant and alive. The Galaxy was a reef of stars beckoning her to come jet along its length.

But there was only Sheena here to see it. Her sense of loss grew inexorably.

So, swimming in starlight, Sheena cradled her unhatched young, impatiently jetting clouds of ink in the rough shape of a male with bright, mindless eyes.

Maura Della was involved in all this because—in the year 2030, as the planet's resources dwindled—Earth had become a bear pit.

Take water, for instance.

Humanity was using more than all the fresh water that fell on the planet. Unbelievable. So, all over Asia and elsewhere, water wars were flaring up, and at least one nuke had been lobbed, between India and Pakistan.

America's primary international problem was the small, many sided war that was flaring in Antarctica, now that the last continent had been "opened up" to a feeding frenzy of resource-hungry nations—a conflict that constantly threatened to spill out to wider arenas.

And so on.

In Maura's view, all humanity's significant problems came from the world's closure, the lack of a frontier.

Maura Della had grown up believing in the importance of the frontier. Frontiers were the forcing ground for democracy and inventiveness. In a closed world, science was strangled by patent laws and other protective measures, and technological innovation was restricted to decadent entertainment systems and the machinery of war. It was a vicious circle, of course; only smartness could get humanity out of this trap of closure, but smartness was the very thing that had no opportunity to grow.

America, specifically, was going to hell in a handbasket. Long dwarfed economically by China, now threatened militarily, America had retreated, become risk-averse. The rich cowered inside vast armored enclaves; the poor lost themselves in VR fantasy worlds; American soldiers flew over the Antarctic battle zones in armored copters, while the Chinese swarmed over the icebound land they had taken.

And, such were the hangovers from America's dominant days, the US remained the most hated nation on Earth.

The irony was, there were all the resources you could wish for, floating around in the sky: the asteroids, the moons of Jupiter and Saturn, free power from the sun. People had known about this for decades. But after seventy years of spaceflight nobody had come up with a way to get into Earth orbit that was cheap and reliable enough to make those sky mines an economic proposition.

But now this NASA back-room wacko, Dan Ystebo from JPL, had come up with a way to break through the bottleneck, a Space Squid that could divert one of those flying mountains.

Maura didn't care what his own motives were; she only cared how she could use his proposals to achieve her own goals.

So when Dan invited her to JPL for the rendezvous, she accepted immediately.

* * *

Maura looked around Dan Ystebo's JPL cubicle with distaste, at the old coffee cups and fast-food wrappers amid the technical manuals and rolled-up softscreens. Dan seemed vaguely embarrassed, self-conscious; he folded his arms over his chest.

One softscreen, draped across a partition, showed a blue-green, rippling spacecraft approaching an asteroid. The asteroid was misshapen and almost black, the craters and cracks of its dusty surface picked out by unvarying sunlight.

"Tell me what I'm getting for my money here, Dan."

He waved his plump hand. "Near-Earth asteroid 2018JW, called Reinmuth. A ball of rock and ice half a mile across. It's a C type." Dan was excited, his voice clipped and wavering, a thin sweat on his brow as he tried to express himself. "Maura, it's just as we hoped. A billion tons of water, silicates, metals, and complex organics—aminos, nitrogen bases. Even Mars isn't as rich as this, pound for pound . . ."

Dan Ystebo was out of his time, Maura thought. He would surely have preferred to work here in the 1960s and '70s, when science was king, and the great probes were being planned, at outrageous expense: Viking, Voyager, Galileo. But that wasn't possible now.

JPL, initiated as a military research lab, had been taken back by the Army in 2016.

It hadn't been possible to kill off JPL's NASA heritage immediately, not while the old Voyagers still bleeped away forlornly on the rim of the Solar System, sending back data about the sun's heliopause and other such useless mysteries.

And Dan Ystebo was making the best of it, in this military installation, with his Nazi-doctored Space Squid. He would probably, Maura realized, have gen-enged her and stuck her in a box if it got him a mission to run.

She said, "Before somebody asks me, tell me again why we have to bring this thing to Earth orbit."

"Reinmuth's orbit is close to Earth's. But that means it doesn't line up for low-energy missions very often; the orbits are like two clocks running slightly adrift of each other.

The NEOs were never as easy to reach as the space junkie types like to believe. We'd have to wait all of forty years before we could repeat Sheena's trajectory."

"Or bring Sheena home."

". . . Yes. But that's irrelevant anyhow."

Irrelevant. He doesn't understand, she thought. This had been the hardest point of the whole damn mission to sell, to the House and the public. If we are seen to have killed her for no purpose, we're all finished.

. . . And now the moment of rendezvous was here.

The firefly spark tracked across the blackened surface. The gentle impact came unspectacularly, with a silent turning of digits from negative to positive.

There was a small splash of gray dust.

And then she could see it, a green fragment of Earth embedded in the hide of the asteroid.

Beneath the translucent floor Sheena could see a grainy, gray-black ground. Dan told her it was a substance older than the oceans of Earth. And, through the curving walls of the ship, she was able to see this world's jagged horizon, barely tens of yards away.

Her world. She pulsed with pride, her chromatophores prickling.

And she knew, at last, she was ready.

Sheena laid her eggs.

They were cased in jelly sacs, hundreds of them in each tube. There was no spawning ground here, of course. So she draped the egg sacs over the knot of machinery at the heart of her miniature ocean, which had now anchored itself to the surface of Reinmuth.

Fish came to nose at the eggs. She watched until she was sure that the fish were repelled by the jelly that coated the eggs, which was its purpose.

All this was out of sight of Dan's cameras. She did not tell him what she had done. She could not leave her water habitat; yet she was able to explore.

Small firefly robots set off from the habitat, picking their way carefully over the surface of the asteroid. Each robot was laden with miniature instruments, as exquisite as coral, all beyond her understanding.

But the fireflies were under her control. She used the waldo, the glovelike device into which she could slip her long arms and so control the delicate motions of each firefly.

. . . Soon the babies were being hatched: popping out of their dissolving eggs one by one, wriggling away, alert, active, questioning. With gentle jets of water, she coaxed them towards sea grass.

Meanwhile, she had work to do.

Sheena sent the fireflies to converge at one pole of Reinmuth. There, patiently, piece by piece, she had them assemble a small chemical factory, pipes and tanks and pumps, and a single flaring nozzle which pointed to the sky. Precious solar panels, spread over the dusty ground, provided power.

The factory began its work. Borers drew up surface regolith and the rock and ice which lay deeper within. Chemical separation processes filtered out methane ice and stored it, while other processes took water, ice, melted it and passed it through electrical cells to separate it into its components, oxygen and hydrogen.

This whole process seemed remarkable to Sheena. To take rock and ice, and to transform it into other substances! But Dan told her that this was old, robust technology, practiced by NASA and other humans for many times even his long lifetime.

Mining asteroids was easy. You just had to get there and do it.

Meanwhile the young were growing explosively quickly, converting half of all the food they ate to body mass. She watched the males fighting: I am large and fierce. Look at my weapons. Look at me!

Most of the young were dumb. Four were smart.

She was growing old now, and tired easily. Nevertheless she taught the smart ones how to hunt. She taught them about the reef, the many creatures that lived and died there.

And she taught them language, the abstract signs Dan had given her. Soon their mantles rippled with questions. *Who? Why? Where? What? How?*

She did not always have answers. But she showed them the machinery that kept them alive, and taught them about the stars and sun, and the nature of the world and universe, and about humans.

At last the structure at the pole was ready for its test.

Under Sheena's control, simple valves clicked open. Gaseous methane and oxygen rushed together and burned in a stout chamber. Through robot eyes Sheena could see combustion products emerge, ice crystals that caught the sunlight, receding in perfectly straight lines. It was a fire fountain, quite beautiful.

And Sheena could feel the soft thrust of the rocket, the huge waves that pulsed slowly through the hab's water.

The methane rocket, fixed at the axis of the asteroid's spin, would push Reinmuth gradually out of its orbit and send it to intercept Earth.

Dan told her there was much celebration, within NASA. He did not say so, but Sheena understood that this was mainly because she had finished her task before dying.

Now, she was no longer needed. Not by the humans, anyway.

The young ones seemed to understand, very quickly, that Sheena and all her young would soon exhaust the resources of this one habitat. Already there had been a number of problems with the tightly closed environment loops: unpredictable crashes and blooms in the phytoplankton population.

The young were very smart. Soon they were able to think in ways that were beyond Sheena herself.

For instance, they said, perhaps they should not simply repair this fabric shell, but extend it. Perhaps, said the young, they should even make new domes and fill them with water.

Sheena, trained only to complete her primary mission, found this a very strange thought.

But there weren't enough fish, never enough krill. The waters were stale and crowded.

This was clearly unacceptable.

So the smart young hunted down their dumb siblings, one by one, and consumed their passive bodies, until only these four, and Sheena, were left.

When the storm broke, Dan Ystebo was in his cubicle in the science rooms at JPL, in the middle of an online conference on results from Reinmuth.

Maura Della stood over him, glaring.

He touched the softscreen to close down the link. "Senator—"

"You asshole, Ystebo. How long have you known?"

He sighed. "Not long. A couple of weeks."

"Did you know she was pregnant before the launch?"

"No. I swear it. If I'd known I'd have scrubbed the mission."

"Don't you get it, Ystebo? We'd got to the point where the bleeding-heart public would have accepted Sheena's death. But this has changed everything . . ."

It's over, he thought, listening to her anger and frustration.

She visibly tried to calm down. "The thing is, Dan, we can't have that asteroid showing up in orbit with a cargo of sentient squid corpses. People would think it was monstrous." She blinked. "In fact, so would I."

He closed his eyes. "I don't suppose it's any use pointing out how stupid it is to stop now. We spent the money already. We have the installation on Reinmuth. It's working; all we have to do is wait for rendezvous. We achieved the goal, the bootstrap."

"It doesn't matter," she said gently, regretfully. "People are—not rational, Dan."

"And the future, the greater goal—"

"We're still engaged in a race between opportunity and catastrophe. We have to start again. Find some other way."

"This was the only chance. We just lost the race."

"I pray not," she said heavily. "Look—do it with decency. Let Sheena die in comfort. Then turn off the rockets."

"And the babies?"

"We can't save those either way, can we?" she said coolly.

"I just hope they forgive us."

"I doubt that," Dan said.

The water which trickled through her mantle was cloudy and stank of decay. She drifted, aching arms limp, dreaming of a male with bright, mindless eyes.

But the young wouldn't let her alone.

Danger near. You die we die. They were flashing the fast, subtle signals employed by a shoal sentinel, warning of the approach of a predator.

There was no predator here, of course, save death itself.

She tried to explain it to them. Yes, they would all die—but in a great cause, so that Earth, NASA, the ocean, could live. It was a magnificent vision, worthy of the sacrifice of their lives.

Wasn't it?

But they knew nothing of Dan, of NASA, of Earth.

No. You die we die.

They were like her. But in some ways they were more like their father. Bright. Primal.

Dan Ystebo cleared his desk, ready to go work for a gen-eng biorecovery company in equatorial Africa. All he was hanging around JPL for was to watch Sheena die, and the bio-signs in the telemetry indicated that wouldn't be so long now.

Then the Deep Space Network radio telescopes would be turned away from the asteroid for the last time, and whatever followed would unfold in the dark and cold, unheard, and to hell with it.

. . . Here was a new image in his softscreen. A squid, flashing signs at him: *Look at me. Dan. Look at me. Dan. Dan. Dan.*

He couldn't believe it. "Sheena?"

He had to wait the long seconds while his single word, translated to flashing signs, was transmitted across space.

Sheena 6.

". . . Oh." One of the young.

Dying. Water. Water dying. Fish. Squid. Danger near. Why.

She's talking about the habitat biosphere, he realized. She wants me to tell her how to repair the biosphere. "That's not possible."

Not. Those immense black eyes. *Not. Not. Not.* The squid flashed through a blizzard of body patterns, bars and stripes pulsing over her hide, her head dipping, her arms raised. *I am large and fierce. I am parrotfish, seagrass, rock, coral, sand. I am no squid, no squid, no squid.*

He had given Sheena 5 no sign for "liar," but this squid, across millions of miles, bombarding him with lies, was doing its best.

But he was telling the truth.

Wasn't he? How the hell could you extend the fixed-duration closed-loop life support system in that ball of water to support more squid, to last much longer, even indefinitely?

. . . But it needn't stay closed-loop, he realized. The Bootstrap hab was sitting on an asteroid full of raw materials. That had been the point of the mission in the first place.

His brain started to tick at the challenge.

It would be a hell of an effort, though. And for what? His NASA pay was going to run out any day, and the soldier boys who had taken back JPL, and wanted to run nothing out of here but low-Earth-orbit milsat missions, would kick his sorry ass out of here sooner than that.

To tell the truth he was looking forward to moving to Africa. He'd live in comfort, in the Brazzaville dome, far from the arenas of the global conflict likely to come; and the work there would be all for the good, as far as he was concerned. None of the ethical ambiguities of Bootstrap.

So why are you hesitating, Ystebo? Are you growing a conscience, at last?

"I'll help you," he said. "What can they do, fire me?"

That wasn't translated.

The squid turned away from the camera.

Dan started to place calls.

Sheena 6 was the smartest of the young.

It was no privilege. There was much work.

She learned to use the glovelike systems that made the firefly robots clamber over the asteroid ground. The mining equipment was adapted to seek out essentials for the phytoplankton, nitrates and phosphates.

Even in the hab itself there was much to do. Dan showed her how to keep the water pure, by pumping it through charcoal filters. But the charcoal had to be replaced by asteroid material, burned in sun fire. And so on.

With time, the hab was stabilized. As long as the machines survived, so would the hab's cargo of life.

But it was too small. It had been built to sustain one squid.

So the firefly robots took apart the rocket plant at the pole and began to assemble new engines, new flows of material, sheets of asteroid-material plastic.

Soon there were four habs, linked by tunnels, one for each of Sheena's young, the smart survivors. The krill and diatoms bred happily. The greater volume required more power, so Sheena extended the sprawling solar cell arrays.

The new habs looked like living things themselves, spawning and breeding.

But already another cephalopod generation was coming: sacs of eggs clung to asteroid rock, in all the habs.

It wouldn't stop, Sheena 6 saw, more generations of young and more habs, until the asteroid was full, used up. What then? Would they turn on each other at last?

But Sheena 6 was already aging. Such questions could wait for another generation.

In the midst of this activity, Sheena 5 grew weaker. Her young gathered around her.

Look at me, she said. *Court me. Love me.*

Last confused words, picked out in blurred signs on a mottled carapace, stiff attempts at posture by muscles leached of strength.

Sheena 6 hovered close to her mother. What had those darkening eyes seen? Was it really true that Sheena 5 had been hatched in an ocean without limits, an ocean where hundreds—thousands, millions—of squid hunted and fought, bred and died?

Sheena 5 drifted, purposeless, and the soft gravity of Reinmuth started to drag her down for the last time.

Sheena's young fell on her, their beaks tearing into her cooling, sour flesh.

Dan Ystebo met Maura Della once more, five years later.

He met her at the entrance to the Houston ecodome, on a sweltering August day. Dan's project in Africa had collapsed when ecoterrorists bombed the Brazzaville dome—two Americans were killed—and he'd come back to Houston, his birthplace.

He took her to his home, on the south side of downtown. It was a modern house, an armored box with fully-equipped closed life-support.

He gave her a beer.

When she took off her resp mask he was shocked; she was wasted, and her face was pitted like the surface of the Moon.

He said, "An eco-weapon? Another WASP plague from the Chinese?"

"No." She forced a hideous smile. "Not the war, as it happens. Just a closed-ecology crash, a prion plague." She drank her beer, and produced some hardcopy photographs. "Have you seen this?"

He squinted. A blurred green sphere. A NASA reference on the back showed these were Hubble II images. "I didn't know Hubble II was still operating."

"It doesn't do science. We use it to watch the Chinese Moon base. But some smart guy in the State Department thought we should keep an eye on—that."

She passed him a pack of printouts. These proved to be results from spectrography and other remote sensors. If he was to believe what he saw, he was looking at a ball of water, floating in space, within which chlorophyll reactions were proceeding.

"My God," he said. "They survived. How the hell?"

"You showed them," she said heavily.

"But I didn't expect this. It looks as if they transformed the whole damn asteroid."

"That's not all. We have evidence they've travelled to some of the other rocks out there. Methane rockets, maybe."

"I guess they forgot about us."

"I doubt it. Look at this."

It was a Doppler analysis of Reinmuth, the primary asteroid. It was moving. Fuzzily, he tried to interpret the numbers. "I can't do orbital mechanics in my head. Where is this thing headed?"

"Take a guess."

There was a silence.

He said, "Why are you here?"

"We're going to send them a message. We'll use English, Chinese, and the sign system you devised with Sheena. We want your permission to put your name on it."

"Do I get to approve the contents?"

"No."

"What will you say?"

"We'll be asking for forgiveness. For the way we treated Sheena."

"Do you think that will work?"

"No," she said. "They're predators, like us. Only smarter. What would we do?"

"But we have to try."

She began to collect up her material. "Yes," she said. "We have to try."

As the water world approached, swimming out of the dark, Sheena 46 prowled through the heart of transformed Reinmuth.

On every hierarchical level mindshoals formed, merged, fragmented, combining restlessly, shimmers of group consciousness that pulsed through the million-strong cephalopod community, as sunlight glimmers on water. But the great shoals had abandoned their songdreams of Earth, of the deep past, and sang instead of the huge, deep future which lay ahead.

Sheena 46 was practical.

There was much to do, the demands of expansion endless: more, colony packets to send to the ice balls around the outer planets, for instance, more studies of the greater ice worlds that seemed to orbit far from the central heat.

Nevertheless, she was intrigued. Was it possible this was Earth, of legend? The home of Dan, of NASA?

If it were so, it seemed to Sheena that it must be terribly confining to be a human, to be trapped in the skinny layer of air that clung to the Earth.

But where the squid came from scarcely mattered. Where they were going was the thing.

Reinmuth entered orbit around the water world.

The great hierarchies of mind collapsed as the cephalopods gave themselves over to a joyous riot of celebration, of talk and love and war and hunting: *Court me. Court me. See my weapons! I am strong and fierce. Stay away! Stay away! She is mine! . . .*

Things had gone to hell with startling, dismaying speed. People died, all over the planet, in conflicts and resource crashes nobody even kept track of any more—even before the first major nuclear exchanges.

But at least Dan got to see near-Earth object Reinmuth enter Earth orbit.

It was as if his old Project Bootstrap goals had at last been fulfilled. But he knew that the great artifact up there, like a shimmering green, translucent Moon, had nothing to do with him.

At first it was a peaceful presence, up there in the orange, smoggy sky. Even beautiful. Its hide flickered with squid signs, visible from the ground, some of which Dan even recognized, dimly.

He knew what they were doing. They were calling to their cousins who might still inhabit the oceans below.

Dan knew they would fail. There were almost certainly no squid left in Earth's oceans: they had been wiped out for food, or starved or poisoned by the various plankton crashes, the red tides.

The old nations that had made up the USA briefly put aside their economic and ethnic and religious and nationalistic squabbles, and tried to respond to this threat from space.

They tried to talk to it again. And then they opened one of the old silos and shot a nuke-tipped missile at it, by God.

But the nuke passed straight through the watery sphere, without leaving a scratch.

It scarcely mattered anyway. He had sources which told him the signature of the squid had been seen throughout the asteroid belt, and on the ice moons, Europa and Ganymede and Triton, and even in the Oort Cloud, the comets at the rim of the system.

Their spread was exponential, explosive.

It was ironic, he thought. We sent the squid out there to bootstrap us into an expansion into space. Now it looks as if they're doing it for themselves.

But they always were better adapted for space than we were. As if they had evolved that way. As if they were waiting for us to come along, to lift them off the planet, to give them their break.

As if that was our only purpose.

Dan wondered if they remembered his name.

The first translucent ships began to descend, returning to Earth's empty oceans.

The Fire Eggs

DARRELL SCHWEITZER

Darrell Schweitzer is the co-editor of Weird Tales *and a writer whose principal reputation has been as a fantasy and horror writer, editor, critic, and poet. He has been a familiar figure at SF conventions since the early 1970s as a dealer and a huckster of his own (mainly small press) books. His nonfiction includes books on Lord Dunsany and H.P. Lovecraft, a number of nonfiction anthologies (*Discovering Classic Horror Fiction, *etc.),* On Writing Science Fiction: The Editors Strike Back *(with George Scithers and John M. Ford) and numerous interviews. A recent volume of his critical and other essays is* Windows Of The Imagination *(1998). His reviews have appeared widely and he currently has a review column in* Aboriginal SF. *He is the author of three published fantasy novels,* The White Isle, The Shattered Goddess, *and* The Mask Of The Sorcerer. *He has published more than 250 stories; some of his stories are collected in the following volumes:* We Are All Legends, Tom O'Bedlam's Night Out, Transients, Refugees From An Imaginary Country, Nightscapes, Necromancies And Netherworlds *(in collaboration with Jason Van Hollander) and* The Great World And The Small.*

"The Fire Eggs" was published in Interzone. *Floating Alien "Eggs" that appeared all over the world one day in 2004 are in our midst and have been for 35 years as this story takes place. Schweitzer does an excellent job of sketching the societal reactions to the appearance of the objects. The story is perceptive as extrapolation, and insightful into human nature.*

Uncle Rob's voice was breaking up, either from emotion or a bad transmission or a combination of both. I tapped the enhancer key and he came through a little better.

"It's your Aunt Louise. She's worse."

"She's already dying," I said without thinking, and just barely stopped myself before blurting out, *so how could she be any worse?* Even over the phone, at that distance, I knew I had caused my uncle pain. "I'm sorry, I—"

How hideously selfish we can be at such moments.

But the moment passed. Rob was beyond grief, I think, into some sort of acceptance of the fact that his Louise was doing to die soon of one of those new and untreatable cancer-like diseases that were going around.

Then he told me.

"She's talking to the Fire Eggs, Glenn."

"Jesus—" to use a slightly obsolete expression. Of course lots of people had talked to the luminous, two-and-a-half metre high ovoids since they first appeared all over the world in the course of half an hour on January 23rd, 2004, anchoring themselves in the air precisely 1.3 metres above the ground. Sure, lots of people claimed the Eggs *answered back* by some means which evaded all recording devices but was an article of faith among believers. More than one religion had started that way. There were dozens of bestselling books from the revelations. Countless millions had merely surrendered to the inexplicable and were comforted.

But not Louise. She and Rob were *both* too supremely rational for that, even Louise, who liked to tweak his pride by pretending to believe in astrology or psychic healing. It was just a game with her. Or had been.

Uncle Rob had once told me that he regarded true mental decay, meaning organic senility, as the worst of all possible fates. "If I get like that, shoot me," he said, and he wasn't joking.

And now Louise was talking to the Fire Eggs.

She'd once compared them to lava lamps, from the way they glow in the night, the darker colours rising and swirling and flowing within the almost translucent skin to no discernible purpose. She was old enough to remember lava lamps. She explained to me what they were and what they were for, which was, in essence, nothing. Purely aesthetic objects.

But I am ahead of myself. The first theory to explain the presence of Fire Eggs was that they were bombs, the initial barrage in an invasion from space.

I *am* old enough to remember that. I was almost six in 2004, the night of the Arrival, when the things popped into existence with muted thunderclaps (though some reported a crackling sound). There was panic then, the roadways clogged with carloads of people trying to flee somewhere where there weren't any Fire Eggs, all devolving into one huge, continent-wide traffic jam when it became clear that there *was* no such place.

My own family never got that far. My father bundled us all into the car, backed out of the garage with a roar, and then made the discovery shared by so many others that first night, that a Fire Egg could not be removed from where it had situated itself by any human agency. We crashed into the one which blocked our driveway. I remember the trunk of the car flying open, my mother screaming, my father screaming back.

Later, I saw that the rear of the car was crumpled like a soda can.

That night, we all sat up bleary-eyed in front of the television, slowly concluding that the world's governments and scientists were just as helpless as we were.

We also learned that it had been worse elsewhere. Innumerable traffic accidents. In the London underground, a train hit one of the things in the tunnel just north of Charing Cross. The first car disintegrated, the second accordioned, and almost a hundred people were killed.

Another one, on a runway in South Africa, had destroyed an airliner, which "fortunately" was empty at the time, but for the crew, who died.

My father made a noise of disgust and shut off the TV.

I remember that we prayed together that night, something we didn't often do. I think my parents, like a lot of people just then, were waiting for, expecting imminent death.

But nothing happened. Days, weeks, months passed. Life settled down, nervously. If the Fire Eggs are bombs, they're still ticking away, silently, 35 years later.

So I dropped down from orbit, invoking the compassionate leave clause in my contract in ways I never would have gotten away with if I were not tenured, and as I drove from the airport I did something very few members of my generation have ever bothered to do and certainly none of my students would ever have tried.

I counted the Fire Eggs, the ones hovering above lawns, others in abandoned stretches of roadway off to my right or left. There was a larger accumulation near the city limits, which might have made some sort of sense, but then they were so thick in an empty field that they reminded me of a herd of sheep mindlessly grazing on the gently sloping hillside.

But I couldn't count them any more than anybody really knew how many had been served by that fast-food restaurant, the one with the Golden Eggs; but of course those were man-made imitations, since, as was apparent from innumerable tests, not to mention attempts to adorn them with graffiti or redecorate them as conceptual art, nothing of terrestrial origin would adhere to a Fire Egg. Indeed, you really couldn't touch them. There was some kind of electrical barrier which made the surface totally frictionless.

I gave up counting somewhere in the low thousands. Of

course there were no such easy answers, though numerologists and even serious mathematicians had done their best.

The next theory was that Fire Eggs were alien probes. All the religions were based on that one, The Church of Somebody Watching. This was not wholly without merit, or even benefit. There had been no wars since the Fire Eggs arrived. Maybe they'd put mankind on good behaviour.

Uncle Rob's house looked pretty much as it always had, the towering tulip-poplars along the driveway now leafless and waiting for winter, the house's split-level "ranch" design a leftover from the previous century, even a decorative "mailbox" out front, for all nobody had actually received mail that way in years; and of course the Fire Eggs on the front lawn, arranged by random chance into a neat semi-circle. We'd named them once, years after they'd arrived, when few people were afraid of them any more and Fire Eggs had become just part of the landscape and Uncle Rob's last book, *What To Name Your Fire Egg*, had enjoyed a modest success. We called ours Eenie, Meenie, Moe, and Shemp.

They glowed as they always did in the evening twilight, completely unchanged. The one on the far right was Shemp.

And there was Uncle Rob in the driveway, who was very much changed, not merely showing his years, but worn out, defeated. Here was a man who had been a world-famous celebrity before his retirement, the ebullient apostle of rationality to the world, his generation's successor to Carl Sagan, and he had four utterly defiant enigmas practically on his doorstep and Louise was dying and she'd started talking to them.

"I'm glad you could come," was all he said. He insisted on taking my bag, a leftover courtesy from a time long ago, when there were no Fire Eggs.

My students could never remember such a time. Many couldn't even imagine it. A landscape without Fire Eggs wasn't real to them. Art gallery attendance dropped off, first from disinterest, then from security problems as every now and then someone tried to "improve" various famous canvases by painting Fire Eggs onto them. It was a compulsion for a while in the 2020s, a kind of mania, which spawned several cults of its own.

Then came the fads, the t-shirts with the Mona Lisa Fire Egg, *Starry Night* with Fire Eggs hovering somewhat unrealistically up in the sky, *The Last Supper* with a Fire Egg on either side of Christ.

I've even seen a redigitalized version of *Casablanca*, still in black and white to satisfy the purists, but with the occasional Fire Egg added to the background in some of the scenes.

I did my graduate thesis on the retro-impact of Fire Eggs on the arts. You know, Hamlet addressing his famous soliloquy to an Egg.

Uncle Rob, Aunt Louise, and I had a very uncomfortable dinner together. It was a shock that she came downstairs to see me at all. I had envisioned her bedridden, with tubes and drips, surrounded by monitors. I *knew* they'd sent her home to die, so I was shocked, not just mildly surprised, when she descended the stairs in her bathrobe and slippers. She flashed me her patented mischievous smile and a wink, and sashayed down, swinging her hips and bathrobe belt in time like a showgirl.

Then she stumbled and I could see the pain on her face. Uncle Rob and I caught her by either arm and cased her into a chair.

"Take it easy," he whispered. "Just take it easy. Glenn is here. You'll be all right."

"I can see for myself that he's here and you don't really believe I will be all right. Stop lying."

"Louise, please—"

She was still able to eat a little, or at least go through the motions for my benefit. We three went through the motions of a nice friendly meal, doting uncle and aunt and favourite nephew, the Fire Eggs on the lawn glowing through the curtains of the front picture window like Christmas lights glimpsed through snow.

"How was your conference, Glenn?" Louise said.

"I, ah . . . had to leave early. I missed most of it."

"Oh."

"And what's . . . with you?"

One of the other things I investigated in the course of becoming one of the leading academic experts on Fire Eggs was what I labelled the Nuke Rumour. During the period in which the world's governments had assigned their top scientists the task of Finding Out What Those Things Are At All Costs, after the attempts to probe, scan, drill through, transmit into, or otherwise penetrate the Eggs had failed, so the story goes, somebody somewhere—always in a nasty, remote place where They Have No Respect For Human Life—set off a nuclear device under a Fire Egg. It made a huge crater, destroyed much of the countryside, killed thousands directly and thousands more from the subsequent radiation, but the *Egg* was utterly unperturbed. The world held its breath, waiting for retaliation.

And nothing happened.

As I first heard the story, it happened in China, but a colleague at Beijing University I knew on the Worldnet assured me no, it was in India. In India they said it was in the Pan-Arabic Union and the Arabs said it was the Russians and the Russians said the French; and I was able to follow the story all the way back to Wyoming, where people were sure the blast had wiped out some luckless desert town and the CIA had covered the whole thing up.

"I think the aliens are trying to exterminate us with boredom," some late-night comedian quipped. "I mean, who the hell *cares* any more?"

"I've been having dreams," Louise said.

"*Please*—" Rob whispered.

She reached over and patted his hand. "Now you hush. This is what you called the boy all the way down from his conference to listen to, so he might as well hear it. You can't fool me, Robert. You never could."

"Just . . . dreams?" I said.

"You know the kind where you know you're dreaming, and

you say to yourself, *this isn't right*, but you go on dreaming anyway? It was like that. I fell asleep in front of the TV and woke up inside my dream, and it was *The Smothers Brothers* on the screen, and I was a girl again. Then somebody turned it off and the room filled up with my friends from school—and I knew a lot of them had to be dead by now, so they couldn't be here—but they were all young too, and dressed in bell-bottoms and beads, and barefoot with their toenails painted, the whole works. You know, like hippies, which is what we pretended to be. Somebody put on a Jefferson Airplane record and it was going on about sister lovers and how in time there'd be others. And there were Fire Eggs with us, there in my own living room—here, in *this* house, not where my parents lived when I was a girl—one Egg for each of us, and they seemed to radiate warmth and love. Fred Hemmings, Fat Freddie we called him, tried to get his Egg to take a toke of pot, and it seemed *so* funny that I was still laughing when I woke up, and you know, *there were ashes on the rug!*"

Aunt Louise laughed softly, and for a while seemed lost in a world of her own, and Rob and I exchanged wordless glances which said, *I don't get it* and *You wouldn't want to, believe me.*

"It was just a dream, Aunt Louise. I'm glad it made you happy."

"I didn't use to have dreams like that."

"Maybe now—"

"Yes, maybe now it's time. I can hear my dreams now."

"Hear them?"

She sat for a time, oblivious to us both, and she seemed to be listening to her dreams from long ago, which had Fire Eggs in them.

As always, nothing happened. The four Fire Eggs glowed softly on the lawn and the world was still.

Uncle Rob took me aside into the kitchen.

"If this weren't so awful, I suppose you'd find it academically interesting."

"Is there anything I can actually *do?* Why exactly did you ask me to come here?"

"She's going away, Glenn."

"Don't mince words. She's dying. You know that. I know that. *She* knows that. It is not news. If there is anything I can do to provide comfort, Uncle Rob, or otherwise help you cope, please tell me. Right now I feel about as useless as an ornamental mailbox."

"Or a Fire Egg, doing nothing."

"Maybe they're *supposed* to do nothing. For 35 years, they've just sat there. We've waited for them to speak, to open up, to explode, to vanish and leave gifts behind, to *hatch*, for Christ's sake. But they will not hatch, which may be the whole point."

"Always you change the subject, Glenn. I suppose it is helpful to have a questing mind, but you are changing the subject."

"Not entirely. Please. Hear me out. Maybe they're like the plastic sunken ships and mermaids and stuff we put into the fishbowl. They're decorations, and make little sense to the goldfish. Most of the goldfish, after a while, just keep on swimming, but maybe a few, the sensitive ones, respond in some way. That's what the objects are for. That's why they're passive. They're waiting for just the right people to respond."

Uncle Rob began to cry. He held onto my shoulder. I was afraid he was going to fall over. I just stood there, wondering exactly what I'd said wrong, but he explained soon enough. "You're talking crap, Glenn. You know it. You're an educated man. Before I retired, I was the world's top science guru. We're goddamn *experts*, both of us. Our job is to know. When we're up against something we *can't* know, it just tears us down. We've both been sceptics. We've both published articles debunking all the crazy stories and rumours about the Fire Eggs. You were the one who pointed out that the stories of people being taken inside were just a continuation of the UFO mythology of the last century. We kept ourselves clean of mysticism. We were *rational*. Now this. Louise wants me to believe that as she approaches the threshold of death she can hear things from the beyond, and the beyond is inside those Fire Eggs, as if whoever sent them is building a gateway to Heaven—"

"I thought it was a stairway."

"What?"

"One of her old songs."

"Can't we at least retain a little *dignity?* That's what you're here for, Glenn. I want you to help her retain a little dignity."

The presence of Fire Eggs actually stimulated the moribund space programs of the world, a bit cautiously at first, as if everybody were afraid that They would swoop down and crush us if we started pressing out into the universe. This was called the Tripwire Theory, the Fire Eggs as alarm device, ready to start screaming if the goldfish tried to climb out of the bowl. But, as always, nothing happened. The Eggs remained inert. No pattern was ever detected in their subtle, shifting interior light. There was no interference as robots, then live astronauts, then a combination of the two proved definitively that there were no Fire Eggs on the Moon or on Mercury, or Venus, or Mars, or on the rocky or ice satellites of the gas planets. The results from Pluto, I understand, are still being evaluated, but meanwhile the first interstellar probes have been launched, and some people began to look out into the universe again for an answer, rather into their own navels. They began to regard the Fire Egg problem as one which could be solved.

The optimists said that was the whole purpose of the Fire Eggs being here in the first place.

I looked back into the dining room.

"She's gone."

"Another damn thing after another I have to put up with," said Uncle Rob, opening a closet, getting out a coat, handing me mine. "She wanders sometimes. But she never goes very far."

I put on my coat. "In her condition? Should she be out at all?"

"No. But her mind is sick too, not just her body."

I didn't ask any more. There was no sense making him review the endless futilities, the grinding, subtle agonies he'd gone through as each and every medical option had been exhausted. She couldn't be put in an institution. There was no money for that. All his was gone. The various plans had long since run out of coverage. Besides, the legalistic wisdom went, what actual harm was there in an old lady wandering around the neighbourhood talking to the Fire Eggs? Which is a bureaucratic euphemism for *nobody gives a shit*.

"Come on," I said, nudging Uncle Rob toward the door. "I'll help you find her."

If they'd appeared precisely in the year 2000, things would have been really crazy, but in any case the Fire Eggs rekindled millennialist fears. Clergymen denounced them as tools or emissaries of Satan and searched the scriptures, particularly *Revelations*, to come up with a variety of imaginative answers. There had been a time when Uncle Rob and I had enjoyed deflating this sort of thing. "The Beast of the Apocalypse does not lay eggs," I had concluded an article, and Rob had used that line on his TV show and gotten a lot of applause.

But the Spiritualists took over anyway. Fire Eggs were Chariots of the Dead, they told us, come to carry us into the next life. They were also alive, like angels. They knew our innermost secrets. They could speak to us through mediums, or in dreams.

Rob and I found Louise on the front lawn, sitting crosslegged on the icy ground in her bathrobe, gazing up at the Fire Eggs. It was almost winter. The night air was clear, sharp.

"Come on." She patted the ground beside her. "There's plenty of room."

"Louise, please go back inside," Rob said.

"Tush! No, you sit. You have to see this."

"Let me at least get you a coat."

"No, you sit."

Rob and I sat.

"Just look at them for a while," she said, meaning the Fire Eggs. "I think that it's important there's one for each of us."

"But there are four, Aunt Louise."

She smiled and laughed and punched me lightly on the shoulder and said, "Well isn't that lovely? There's room for one more. Ask your wife to join us, Glenn."

"I'm not married, Aunt Louise."

She pretended to frown, then smiled again. "Don't worry. You will be."

"Did . . . *they* tell you that?"

She ignored me. To both of us she said, "I want you to just sit here with me and look and listen. Aren't they *beautiful?*"

I regarded Eenie, Meenie, Moe, and Shemp, and they looked as they always had. I suppose in other circumstances they could indeed have seemed beautiful, but just now they were not.

I started to say something, but then Louise put her dry, bony hand over my mouth and whispered, "Quiet! They're singing! Can't you hear it? Isn't it heavenly?"

I only heard the faint whine and whoosh of a police skimmer drifting along the block behind us. Otherwise the night was still.

Uncle Rob began sobbing.

"I can't stand any more of this," he said, and got up and went toward the door. "Can't we have a little dignity?"

I hauled Louise to her feet and said, "You've got to come inside, *now.*"

But she looked up at me with such a hurt expression that I let go of her. She wobbled. I caught hold of her. "Yes," she said, "let me have a little dignity." I think she was completely lucid at that moment. I think she knew exactly what she was doing. She sat down again.

I turned to Uncle Rob. "You go on in. We'll stay out here a while longer."

So we sat in the cold, autumn air, in front of the Fire Eggs, like couch potatoes in front of a four-panel TV. No, that's not right. It doesn't describe what Louise did at all. She listened raptly, *rapturously*, to voices I could not hear, to something which, perhaps, only dying people *can* hear as they slide out of this life. She turned from one Fire Egg to the next, to the next, as if all of them were conversing together. She reached out to touch them, hesitantly, like one of the apes in the ancient flatvideo classic, *2001: A Space Odyssey*, but of course she could not touch them, and her fingers slid away as if her hand couldn't quite locate the points of space where the Fire Eggs were.

At times she answered back, and sang something, as if accompanying old voices, but I think it was some rock-and-roll song from her psychedelic childhood, not an ethereal hymn from the Hereafter.

Or maybe the Hereafter just likes Jefferson Airplane. Or the Fire Eggs do.

I would like to be able to say that I achieved some epiphany myself, that I saw the Fire Eggs in a new way, as if the scales had fallen from my eyes and I saw truly for the first time. I would like to say that I heard something, that I received some revelation.

But I only watched the pale reds and oranges drifting within the creamy, luminous white. I only saw the Fire Eggs, as every human being on Earth sees Fire Eggs every day of his or her life.

I only heard the police skimmer slide around the block. Maybe one of the cops was staring at us through the darkened windows. Maybe not. The skimmer didn't stop.

And I looked up and saw the autumn stars, as inscrutable as the Fire Eggs, never twinkling, almost as if I were looking at them from space.

Louise died during the night. She started drooling blood, but she looked content where she was, and it wouldn't have made any difference anyway, which may be a euphemism for something too painful to put into words.

I just stayed there with her. After a while, her breathing had a gurgling sound to it, and she leaned over into my lap. I could see by the light of the Fire Eggs that she was bleeding from the bowels and the whole back of her bathrobe was stained dark. But she didn't want to leave. She had what I suppose someone else might have called a beatific expression on her face. She reached up toward the Fire Eggs once more, groping in the air.

And then I rocked her to sleep, by the light of the unblinking stars and of the Fire Eggs.

Somehow I fell asleep too. At dawn, Uncle Rob shook me awake. I got up stiffly, but I'd been dressed warmly enough that I was all right.

He couldn't bring himself to say anything, but the look in his eyes told me everything.

I didn't have to ask. I didn't have to search. Aunt Louise was gone, bloody bathrobe and all.

Of course any number of disappearances and murders had been attributed to the Fire Eggs in the past, as had so much else. "The Fire Egg ate my homework" was an old joke. "The Fire Egg ate Aunt Louise" didn't go over well with the authorities, so there *was* an investigation, which concluded, for lack of any real evidence, that, despite what the two of us claimed, Louise had wandered off in the night and died of exposure or her disease, and finding her body would only be a matter of time.

"I'll tell you what the fucking things are," said Uncle Rob. "They're pest-disposal units. They're roach motels. They're here to kill us, then to clean the place out to make room for somebody else. Maybe the poison tastes good to the roach and it dies happy, but does it make any difference?"

"I don't know, Uncle. I really don't."

The night before I was to leave, he went out on the lawn and lay down underneath one of the Fire Eggs and blew his brains out with a pistol. I heard the shot. I saw him lying there.

I just waited. I wanted to see what would happen. But I fell asleep again, or somehow failed to perceive the passing of time, and when I came to myself again, he was gone. The pistol was left behind.

It was Aunt Louise who first named them Fire Eggs. Not everybody knows that. Uncle Rob used the term on his television show, and it caught on. He gave her credit, over and over again, but no one listened and the whole world believes he was the one who coined it.

That's what his obituaries said, too.

I think that we're wrong to wait for something to happen. I think it's been happening all along.

The New Horla

ROBERT SHECKLEY

Robert Sheckley first came to prominence in the 1950s as one of the leading writers in Galaxy, *became a novelist in the 1960s, and still (but too infrequently) produces fiction today that is thought-provoking, memorable, and stylish. His reputation is based primarily on the quality of his quirky, subversive, satirical short fiction, a body of work admired by everyone from Kingsley Amis and J. G. Ballard to Harlan Ellison. As an ironic investigator of questions of identity and of the nature of reality, he is a peer of Philip K. Dick and Kurt Vonnegut. In a recent interview on the web (www.fantascienza.net/sfpeople/robert.sheckley) this exchange took place:*

> Delos: Why is there something, instead of there being nothing?
> Sheckley: There isn't something. There's only nothing masquerading as something and looking very like Gerard Depardieu. That, by the way, is the real meaning of cyberspace.

This story, from Fantasy & Science Fiction, *where he published several stories in 2000, is an hommage to the great 19th Century French writer, Guy de Maupassant. Maupassant wrote the classic story "The Horla," arguably an early proto-SF story, about an horrific invisible being, not long before Maupassant himself went mad. Here, a young man alone in a ski lodge meets an invisible alien/supernatural being but is more worried by mundane matters of business.*

"How deep it is, this mystery of the Invisible. We cannot plump its depths with our wretched senses, with our eyes, which are incapable of perceiving things that are too small, things that are too big, things too far away, the inhabitants of a star—or the inhabitants of a drop of water . . . And our ears deceive us, because they convey to us vibrations in the air in the form of sounds—they are like fairies performing this miracle of changing movement into sound, and through this transformation they give birth to music, turning into melody the silent rhythms of nature . . . And what of our sense of smell, inferior to that possessed by a dog . . . and our sense of taste, which can scarcely detect the age of a wine!

"Ah! If only we had other sense-organs to work other miracles for us, who can tell how many other things we should discover in the world around us?"

—"Le Horla," Guy de Maupassant

The train ride from Concord up into the White Mountains was spectacular. The snows were deep, with the tops of the trees poking through like stubble on a dead man's cheek. We topped the range and came at last into Mountain Station. Here I got off, with my skis, my backpack, and my ski boots.

There was no one around to greet me. The little station house was empty, though not locked. I went inside and got on my ski boots, put my shoes into my backpack, came out and strapped on my skis. Although I had told Edwin I'd ski down to his chalet without any difficulty, now that I was actually there the idea seemed less than brilliant. It was late in the day, after four P.M., and the sun was already lost in the white sky. We'd been held up almost an hour at Manchester, and hadn't made up the time across New England. I took the sketch map from an inner pocket, smoothed it out, oriented myself, went over the way I'd go once again.

It had all seemed perfectly straightforward when I'd arranged with Edwin to use his family's ski chalet for a few days. We had been roommates at Dartmouth and had remained friends afterward. He had often offered me the use of the chalet. This holiday I took him up on it.

Originally, I had meant to drive there, and Edwin had carefully laid out the route. But as it turned out, my car was back in the shop with miscellaneous electrical problems. With Edwin's help, I had worked out a different route. I would take the train to Mountain Station, New Hampshire, and then ski down to the lodge.

Edwin had been more than a little dubious. "Are you quite sure? I don't really recommend it."

"It's perfectly straightforward on the map," I told him. The chalet was only a thousand or so feet below Mountain Station, which stood at the top of Standish Pass in the White Mountains. It was a short run and there were no obstructions.

"You've made the run yourself, or so you told me."

"Well, yes," Edwin said, "I have, but I'm acquainted with the area. For a first time . . ."

"From what you've described, there's nothing to it. Out of the station I face just west of north, with the spire of Stanley Church in sight just to my left, and it's a straight run down to the dogleg. Then I go left around the construction site and the chalet—white with green trim—is in sight."

"It's just never a good idea, skiing in the mountains alone," Edwin said.

"I'll take it easy," I assured him. "I'll snowplow all the way down." If only I had taken my own light-hearted promise seriously!

Orienting myself wasn't difficult. Just to the left of the small station house was a storage shed, painted black. Edwin had told me to use this as my takeoff point. I stood there in front of it for a moment, poised on my skis, checking out the slope. It was steep, but not too steep, a perfect white blanket untouched by any other skiers' marks. There was a dark clump of trees to the right, about a hundred yards down, and beyond that, just out of sight from here, was the construction site I needed to ski around. I checked my bindings, adjusted my pack, pulled down my goggles, and took off.

It was a beautiful day for a run. The sky was white, and there was an accumulation of dark clouds to the east, a promise of weather making up over toward the Atlantic Coast. My skis slid smoothly on the surface, not going too rapidly over the somewhat wet snow, then picking up speed as the incline steepened. I leaned into it, enjoying that exhilaration that the first run of the season brings. It was an easy slope and I was in perfect balance going down it.

After a few minutes I caught sight of the obstruction. It was a mound of building materials, covered in last night's fresh snow, with here and there a gleam of green canvas where the wind had blown away the cover. I was over too far to my right, and now I bent into a sharp turn that would take me below the building materials. The thrill of leaning into that first turn of the season caused me to cut it a little fine. I straightened out to give the mounded materials a sufficient berth, then crouched to build up speed. Perhaps I wasn't paying sufficient attention to the terrain. But there was really nothing to see, since the fresh snow covered everything.

I knew I was in trouble when my skis started chattering on a series of long, slick, rounded objects just beneath the snow. They were like a corduroy road surface, only much higher.

Later I learned that I had crossed a pile of plastic pipes that had been unloaded only two or three days ago, and had been concealed by last night's snow. They had been set down at the lower edge of the construction, and I was going right over them.

All would still have been well if I hadn't been tucked into my turn. I went across those pipes at an angle. All I knew at the time was that I was crossing a hard, bumpy, unstable surface and my skis were sliding out from under me. The pipes were concealed under an inch or so of fresh snow, and they were frosty and slick. But they hadn't been on the ground long enough to freeze to the ground, so they slid out from under me and I fell hard, my skis kicking into the air, and I was tumbling over them until at last I came to rest beyond the pipes, in soft snow.

It took me a while to pull myself together. It's important not to underestimate the shock of a sudden unexpected fall. For a while I felt as though the mountain had exploded under me. I was numb from head to toe, and it was not unpleasant. But I knew, somewhere in the back of my mind, that when this numbness wore off, I was likely to find myself in a sorry state. It had really been quite a fall.

While I was still numb and feeling no pain, I determined to get to the chalet. It was only a few hundred yards away, down the slope. I tried to get to my feet, and found that my right leg would not support me. I got halfway up and fell. Checking, I found that my right foot was twisted at an odd angle. I also noted various rips in my twill ski pants, and a slow welling of blood from what I took to be a wound in my shoulder, just above the shoulder blade, where the backpack hadn't protected me.

I was not at all cold. Nor was I in much pain. But I knew I was not in a good way, and that I needed to get to shelter as soon as possible. Above all, I had to get my ski boots off before the swelling started.

My first thought was to carry my skis and poles with me and limp down the slope to the chalet, whose roof I could make out at the edge of the fall line. This proved impossible. I was unable to stand up. Nor did I have my skis, as I had first imagined. They were somewhere back up on the slope. All I had was one pole, and my knapsack was still strapped to my back.

I hobbled and crawled downhill toward the chalet, through snow that became increasingly deep as I descended. I felt all right when I began, but soon began to experience a deep fatigue. The day had grown very dark, and heavy clouds were boiling up over Mount Adams. My left ankle was beginning to ache abominably. And I noticed that I was leaving quite a trail of blood behind me. I couldn't tell where on my person it came from—I was beginning to hurt in half a dozen places—and this seemed no time to stop and examine myself. I didn't even have a first aid kit in my knapsack.

The forerunners of the storm arrived just as I got to the chalet, on my feet now, or rather, on one foot, with the other raised, supporting myself by my remaining ski pole. Overhead were long dark streaky clouds, what the old Scandinavians called the storm's maidens—those long, thin wild clouds that come out in advance of the main body of wind, snow, and rain. The wind was whipping around my head when I got to the chalet's front door and searched for the key under the log pile to the left. Edwin had been as good as his word. The key was right where he'd said it would be, under a bit of seasoned oak, and I got the door open and dragged myself inside.

It was a modern small ski chalet, bright birch and cedar. An A-frame with two guest rooms, a good-sized living room, bathroom and kitchen in the rear. I got my boots off and turned the power switch near the door. Even though it gave a satisfying click, it brought no power. Edwin had promised to have the electricity turned on by the time I got there, but apparently he had forgotten, or hadn't succeeded.

I was in better luck with the propane. The chalet ran on its own tank. I made sure the pilot was on, found the valve and turned it, and soon had the living room heaters going nicely. Then and only then did I feel secure enough to look to myself.

There was no telephone. I had known that beforehand.

I wanted to get out of my ski clothes: My elasticized twill pants didn't want to stretch over my swollen ankle, and I decided not to press the issue. I could keep my pants on for a while. My clothing was torn up enough to make it no difficulty to find where I had been abraded.

The cuts and scrapes on my sides and legs were painful but not serious, not even especially disabling. It was my ankle that was the problem, that and a puncture wound beneath my right shoulder blade, made by a tree branch, perhaps. Touching it gently, I found it was as big as the small end of a pool cue, and it was oozing blood. Not in a great stream, but steadily.

For a long time I just lay on the living room carpet in the growing gleam of the early evening. I may have dozed for a little while. It was almost dark when I determined to pull myself together.

Negotiating the living room made it seem a very big place indeed. I was quite weak. I had the feeling that I had injured myself worse than I'd first thought. That deep gouge in my back wouldn't stop bleeding. Finally I gave all my attention to trying to do something about it.

I made a pad with a small pillow and bound it in place on my back with a sheet I found in one of the drawers under the picture window. That slowed the blood loss some, but it didn't stop it. Blood continued to leak out of me and whenever I moved the pillow slipped off. I began to wonder how many pints of blood I could lose without passing out or going into shock. No matter what I did, the pillow wouldn't stay in place. I couldn't seem to get enough pressure on it, and finally discarded it.

The heaters soon took the chill off the chalet. I found two candles in the kitchen and brought them out to the living room. I put them in an ashtray and lighted them. By this small dancing light, I saw the shadows of evening gathering swiftly as the storm struck. There commenced a rattle of windows like the devil's own tattoo. That's the way my thoughts were trending. I was wounded and depressed and wallowing in my own feeling of stupidity, my embarrassment over this stupid accident with the pipes. It made me feel incompetent. And I was worried about the wound in my back. The flow of blood was slow, but it was steady. How much could I lose before I was in trouble?

The wind began gusting up and driving tree branches against the windows. Those trees should have been cut back. I was sure it was only a matter of time before a branch broke through. There seemed nothing I could do about it. There were wooden shutters, but I'd have to go outside to get at them, and I doubted my present ability to do that. I just lay there on the floor beside the couch, and felt the hollowness in my stomach, because I hadn't eaten anything since breakfast early that morning in Hanfield Station. I lay there and waited to see if the window would hold.

It held, as it turned out. But something strange happened. There was a sharp crack and something came through the picture window. It didn't shatter it. It bored through it like a rifle bullet. But it was bigger than a rifle bullet, to judge by the starred hole it left behind. And unlike a rifle bullet, it didn't spend itself in the room. Like some sort of living thing, it buzzed and danced around the room.

I just cowered there on the floor watching it darting around and thinking to myself, "Well, this really is too much." I mean, not only had I been hurt, now I was being forced to take part in some sort of weird, perhaps supernatural matter. For what else could this thing be?

"Stop that," I told it irritably as it buzzed around my head. But if the thing, whatever it was, heard, it showed no signs of it. I don't know what it had been when it came through the window, but now it was a sphere about the size of a baseball, and sparkling with many colors. It was spinning furiously and darting around the room like a large angry hornet. It dodged around and slammed into a wall, and changed shape, going all misshapen for a moment, before popping out again into a sphere. I couldn't decide whether something was really happening or if I was having an hallucination. I was rooting for the hallucination, because the supernatural or the supernormal or whatever it was was exactly what I didn't want.

Does this seem over-emphatic to you? Consider my position. I am twenty-seven years old. A junior stockbroker in a well-known Boston company. I'm doing very well, thank you, through a combination of intelligence, steady nerve, rational assessment of the factors involved, and self-discipline. By self-discipline, I mean that I didn't spend much time asking myself why I was doing the work I was doing. I sensed that asking that could open up a nasty can of worms. Spiritually, stockbroker might be hard to justify. But I figured I'd get around to that later; in my fifties, maybe, when I'd retire rich and move with Janie to some warmer climate.

I guess I haven't mentioned Janie yet. Janie Sommers. We're engaged. I'm head over heels in love. Not just with Janie, though she's extremely lovable, but with what Janie and I were planning to do with our lives.

It was going to be a good life, a rich life, filled with shiny cars and a swimming pool and a big house filled with excellent art objects. Janie's stipend from *Vogue* wouldn't bring that about. But her inheritance when she turned twenty-five would. Together, we could have everything we wanted. That may sound crass. But how could I not calculate our joint incomes, with a view to making life better for Janie as well as for me?

I really don't want to get into all this. But I thought I should explain why I was so dead set against visionary experience. It would commit me to something I wanted no part in. To giving up the delightful, worldly life I had planned and turning to disseminating the "truth" as I had conceived it.

Once I admitted to visionary experience, I knew I was a goner. I could hear myself bending my friends' ears: "Let me tell you what happened to me one strange night in New Hampshire. . . ."

I wanted none of that.

And yet, the logic of visionary experience demands that you spread it around. Tell the world about it. But that was the last thing in the world I wanted to do as I watched the glowing, spinning sphere dance around the room against all the laws of gravity and common sense, and I heard myself saying, "I don't want to be the subject of a National Public Radio hour on strange unexplained experiences, I want to do something I'm good at, stockbrokering, make a lot of money, live well."

The sphere took one more brush against the wall, dislodging Edwin's high school graduation certificate, and then it split in two, its halves fluttering to the floor. Something came out of it. Something small and smoky that grew in size and then solidified for a moment into a small body and staring face—staring at me—and then this thing, whatever it was, faded and became invisible and I had my hands full to control the seizures I was considering falling into. ("Yes, I saw it with my own eyes! It was not of this world!")

I resisted the impulse of the true believer and looked at the shell the thing had come in. It drooped, it melted, and then it was gone, leaving behind only a trace of moisture on the rug.

I looked around the room. I saw the storm pouncing against the picture windows. Blown snow slanting past in hypnotic lines, accompanied by the wavering mutter of the wind. Inside the room, there was a profound darkness contrasting with the glaring white rectangle of the picture window. Although the room was in darkness, a few objects in it—the top of a ladder chair, the head of a plaster statue of some classical deity—were still bathed in light. A Rembrandt effect. And the creature or whatever it was that came out of the sphere was nowhere to be seen. But that didn't mean that it was gone.

"You look for it in the kitchen," I told Janie. "I'll keep on checking here."

No, Janie wasn't there. But in some weird way, she was. I can't explain it. I can only report to you how it seemed to me at the time.

I checked the room again. Looking for the creature from the sphere. Looking for her. Funny how I'd already decided it was a she. Funny how I could sense her presence still in the room, watching me.

Something watching me. The moment stretched out. . . .

And dissolved in my sudden annoyance. I don't want her looking at me! How dare this invisible thing look at me?

What else was she intending?

My mind had taken a curious turn. From judging an event as an hallucination to rejudging it as something real. And now I was really worried.

It had been so much more comfortable when I'd thought it was an hallucination. But I'd had to give up that comforting thought. Trying to force myself to believe I was hallucinating felt like a bad idea. It would make my judgments unreliable. It's madness to consider yourself unreliable. In a situation like that, who are you going to rely on?

I summed up what I thought I knew. I had the distinct feeling that the storm had plucked something invisible out of the air and hurled it through my picture window. The thing it had thrown was let's say a sort of very small spaceship. Inside the living room, the little ship had buzzed around like a deranged being. No doubt it was no longer working right. Finally it fell apart, and something came out.

That was as far as my thought took me at the time. I just knew that something uncanny was in the same room with me, watching me, and I had no idea what that invisible thing intended with me.

Since I had nothing to go on but my suppositions, I decided to give them free rein.

It seemed to me that this being had blundered into this room by accident, and now couldn't find her way out. I remembered the way the sphere had darted back and forth and bumped into walls. I'd seen a robin do the same thing, trapped in an attic window that Janie had opened to air out, and dashed itself to death before we could shoo it out the window which it couldn't find.

I suspected it was going to attack me.

With a shudder I turned defensive. My hands were raised in boxer's position. My head slowly turned from one side of the room to another. Although I knew I could not see her, yet I thought I could sense her. And, with a little luck, do something about it before she did me a mischief.

It was an eerie time for me as I sat propped up against the couch, my ankle throbbing, the hole in my back oozing blood, the wind rattling the windows and the darkness engulfing everything as night came on. I couldn't see the thing and therefore I saw it everywhere. It was the odd humpbacked shape on the mantel, the suspicious shadow on the rug, the triangle of greater darkness that peered out of closets and cubbyholes.

I caught a glimpse of it for a moment, then lost sight of it in the darkening living room. And then I felt something at my back, near my wound, felt something wet and sticky on my skin, I turned, and saw it. It was glued to my back. It seemed to be sucking my blood. I screamed and swatted at it, and it darted away and lost itself in a corner of the room.

Janie came out of the kitchen then. "Where is it?" I pointed. She went at it with a pillow, flailing, shouting, "Leave him alone, damn you!" And she caught the thing one solid whack as it darted around, sending it crashing to the floor. And then she was pounding at it with the pillow, and I had gotten off the couch and was stomping it with my good foot. I think we were both shouting then, or maybe screaming. Or maybe it was just me, because of course Janie wasn't really there.

I guess I went a little off my head at that point. I started imagining Janie was there, and I was talking to her, telling her about this discovery I'd made, this Horla. Because that was what I was certain it was—a Horla, the uncanny creature described by Guy de Maupassant.

Janie was saying, "Look, Ed. None of this is happening. I want a normal life. We can have it all. The best. The summer house in Connecticut, the apartment in Manhattan, the beach bungalow in Mustique. You're making money and I've got money coming to me. We can do this: But honey, we can't put any supernatural stuff in this. You can't go around telling people you had this visitation from another world. Who's going to buy stocks from you if you do that? We don't want to be unreliable. People who've had visions are unreliable. Fanatical. You can't tell what they'll do. And our life is based on knowing very well what we can and will do. And what we will not do. Talking about our mystic experiences is one thing we won't do."

I've often thought about asking Janie if she was there that night. If she remembers any of it. If she can say anything at all that might account for what I saw, or thought I saw. But of course, that's getting into pretty weird stuff, and Janie and I don't do that. The Horla is one of a number of things we don't talk about.

Janie is so pretty. And she makes such good sense. And I

was in such agony as I sat there, listening to her. Because this thing had happened, the more she talked, the surer of it I became. I sensed that to repudiate it, pretend it never happened—well, that would be a pretty crass thing to do. If I did that, it would be difficult to live with myself.

On the other hand, Janie was right. If you go around talking about your other-worldly experiences, you never again have quite the same relationship with people. You're a zealot, a fanatic, a crazy, someone most right-thinking people try to avoid. You're seeing visions, and that's weird. You're telling everyone, I've found something more important than what you've staked your life to get. I've got news from the other side!

People don't like you when you talk like that.

I didn't want to be driven by the force of an experience I'd never bargained for, didn't want now that I had it, wanted to get rid of it.

"Whatever it was, we don't owe it anything," Janie said. "We've killed it. Let's just never mention it again."

I nodded.

She looked at me very seriously. "It's agreed, then."

I nodded again. And we never talked about it again.

Except that I'm writing about it now. Janie doesn't know. Won't know until I publish it. And then?

I don't know. But I have to write this.

You see, I figured out, after a very long time, just what the creature was up to.

She was sealing off that puncture wound in my back. What else was that sticky stuff she sprayed on me but some way of stopping the wound? Even the doctor, when I finally got to see one the next day, asked me about it.

The Horla had just finished sealing my wound when Janie got her with the pillow.

Not that I'm blaming Janie.

I figure we killed that thing together. Or maybe I did it alone. Because I sure wanted to, even if I didn't actually do it. But I think I did.

We weren't ready for the Horla, and for what it might bring.

Anyway, Janie wasn't really there, so I must have killed the Horla myself. But in another way, Janie did it.

I'm not going to change anything now. It's impossible to get the weird stuff that happens to you down all neat and straight. But I figured I needed to tell the story. In case the Horla's family—lover—friends—she must have had some-one—never learned what happened to her, blown off course by a sudden storm, trapped in a weird room, pursued by a big creature—or maybe the ghost of a big creature—whom she was trying to help and who wanted only to kill her. And finally did.

The Horla gave up her life for me. If she has any friends, family, or lovers out there, if there's any way my words can get to them, I thought they'd be proud of her.

Well, that's the only experience I can call genuinely weird in a rather ordinary life. A story I've never told. Especially that last part about Janie swatting it with a pillow. Because, of course, I did that. Janie wasn't there.

As for Janie and me, we're as well as can be expected.

Madame Bovary, *C'est Moi*

DAN SIMMONS

Dan Simmons (www.erinyes.org/simmons) was born in Peoria, Illinois, and lives in Longmont, Colorado, where he was for years an elementary school teacher. His first novel, Song of Kali *(1985), won the World Fantasy Award. It was followed by* Phases of Gravity *(1989), an excellent mainstream novel about an astronaut,* Carrion Comfort *(1989), a huge and ambitious horror novel, and The Hyperion Cantos—*Hyperion *(1989), an equally large and ambitious SF novel that won the Hugo Award, and its companion (the two are really one large work),* The Fall of Hyperion *(1990). By 1991 he was famous and successful in both the horror and SF genres. He has since gone on to write SF, horror, and mainstream novels and stories for the last decade, and has maintained both his ambition and versatility. Most notable in SF are* Endymion *(1996) and* The Rise of Endymion *(1997), another pair of novels. Even though his attention has been spread among genres for the last decade, his place in SF is central to the fiction of the 1990s and beyond. Two forthcoming SF novels have been announced,* Ilium *and* Olympos.

Simmons's fiction is filled with literary allusions (just look at the titles, above). This little story, another piece from Nature, *is no exception. It is a showpiece for Simmons's wit, giving an SF rationalization for the real existence of the literary universes of fiction.*

2052 AD: the current migration of millions of people to novel universes by quantum teleportation (QT) was a shock even to the system's inventor, Jian-Wei Martini. "I don't know why it took me by surprise," said Dr Martini in a 2043 interview. "I had the basic idea for QT when I read an ancient *New Yorker* story by Woody Allen, but the potential was all there in Schrödinger's classic wave equation." Dr Martini has since QT'd to Madame Bovary's universe and is currently living in Flaubert's Paris as Monsieur Leon.

The quantum-mechanical entanglement effect had been analysed (in Einstein's sceptical term) as "spooky action at a distance" since 1935, but it was not until 1998 that a research group at the University of Innsbrück demonstrated actual quantum teleportation of a photon—or more precisely, the complete quantum state of that photon.

These initial quantum-state teleportations avoided violating Heisenberg's principle and Einstein's speed-of-light restrictions because teleported photons carried no information, even about their own quantum state. However, by producing entangled pairs of photons and teleporting one of the pair while transmitting the Bell-state analysis of the second photon through subluminal channels, the recipient of the teleported photon-data had a one-in-four chance of guessing its quantum state and then utilizing the quantum bits of teleported data.

All of this would have amounted to very little except for remarkable advances in human-consciousness research. Re-

searchers at the University of Kiev interested in improving
memory function used quantum computers to analyse biochemical cascades in human synapses. In 2025, they discovered that the human mind—as opposed to the brain—was
neither like a computer nor a chemical memory machine,
but exactly like a quantum-state holistic standing wavefront.

The human brain, it turned out, collapsed probability
functions of this standing wavefront of consciousness in the
same way that an interferometer determined the quantum
state of a photon or any other wavefront phenomenon. Using
terabytes of qubit quantum data and applying relativistic
Coulomb field transforms to these mind-consciousness
holographic wavefunctions, it was quickly discovered that
human consciousness could be quantum-teleported to points
in space-time where entangled-pair wavefronts already existed.

And where were these places? Nothing as complex as an
entangled consciousness-wavefront existed elsewhere in our
continuum. QT researchers soon realized that they were
teleporting human consciousness—or, rather, the complete
quantum state of these consciousnesses—to alternate universes that had, in turn, come into being through the focus of
pre-existing holographic wavefronts: in other words, complete alternate universes created by the sheer force of human
imagination. These singularities of genius act as Bell-state
analyser/editors on the quantum-foam of reality, simultane-
ously interpreting one universe while creating a new one.

It seems that poets, playwrights and novelists already understood this. "The imagination may be compared to
Adam's dream," wrote John Keats: "he awoke and found it
truth."

The QT charting of "fiction universes" began immediately, but even before a hundred alternate universes were
confirmed, the QT migration from our Earth began.

Meanwhile, the "agon"—the imperative to rank the rela-
tive importance of creative works—now had a scientific tool
at its disposal. The long literary debate as to which works
belonged in the so-called "Western Canon" was settled by
QT exploration. For example, 21 of Shakespeare's 38 plays

generated complete alternate universes, as complex and expansive as our own, each capable of supporting a human population from a few thousand (*Measure for Measure*) to many billions (*King Lear*), despite the fact that each play may have had a cast of a score or fewer players when it was performed. More than a million people have migrated to Elsinore, whereas fewer than 5,000—mostly clinically depressed Scandinavians—have seen fit to re establish themselves in Lear's universe.

Flaubert, it turned out, generated two complete universes—the so called "Madame Bovary's World" and that of *Sentimental Education*—whereas Alice Walker, it seems, to the frustration of American academics, had created none.

The alternate universe of Dante's *Inferno* has received more than 385,000 emigrants (mostly from Southern California), but his Paradiso Planet shows only 649 transplants. The current count of those who have QT'd to Huckleberry Finn's "River World" is 3,622,406, and more than a million have been transported to each of Charles Dicken's five extant universes.

It is true that more than 60 million people volunteered to QT to D. H. Lawrence's "Lady Chatterley's World," but—sadly—no such discrete universe has been found. Some have made do with the universe of *Sons and Lovers*. Recent QT stampedes to the worlds of Jane Austen, Robert Louis Stevenson and the effectively infinite number of universes created by Jorge Luis Borges may reflect current social trends.

It remains to be seen whether QT technology will solve the current global population crisis or if it will remain an option of the rich, bored and educated. It also remains to be seen whether any universes will be found—beyond the paltry handful already discovered—that owe their origins to 21st-century imaginations.

"That which is creative must create itself," said John Keats. And perhaps more pointedly, from William Blake—"I must create a system or be enslaved by another man's."

Which brings us to the central question of this new quantum reality. None of the millions of ancillary characters living in Madame Bovary's universe (except for the QT emigrés) know that they are characters in a work of fiction. Nor do they know that Madame Bovary is the main character.

So who wrote our universe? And who are the central characters?

Grandma's Jumpman

ROBERT REED

Robert Reed was born and raised and lives in Nebraska. He published nearly a dozen SF and fantasy stories in 2000, of which six or more were worthy of consideration for this book, an amazing and continuing explosion of SF writing. His first story collection, The Dragons of Springplace *(1999), fine as it is, skims only a bit of the cream from his works. And he writes a novel every year or two as well (his first,* The Leeshore, *appeared in 1987; his ninth is* Marrow, *2000, a distant future large scale story that seems to be a break-through in his career). He has been publishing SF since 1986, but has reached his present level of achievement only in the mid-1990s. Given his level of achievement, he is one of the most underappreciated writers in contemporary SF.*

"Grandma's Jumpman" appeared in Century *(edited by Robert J. K. Killheffer and Jenna Felice), the literate quar-terly of speculative fiction that was reborn at the end of 1999, adding Bryan Cholfin, formerly of* Crank!, *to its staff, and got out three issues in 2000. Although only a minority of the fiction in* Century *is SF, it is still very important as a model of the well-produced and well-edited semi-prozine in the field. This story uses SF, in the manner Ray Bradbury did in the 1950s. It is set in a rural area (that might be Ne-braska) years after a war on Earth against humanoid aliens and is about love, loss of innocence, and combating the prej-udices fostered by propaganda during any war in the gener-ation after.*

Someone's wasting fireworks—that's what I'm thinking.

I'm out by the road, just playing, and I hear all these pops and bangs coming from the west. It's the middle of the day, bright and hot, and what's the point in shooting fireworks now? Someone sure is stupid, I'm thinking. Then comes this big old *whump* that I feel through the hard ground. I drop all my soldiers and climb out of the ditch, looking west, watching a black cloud lifting. That's over by the old prison camp, isn't it? I'm trying to guess what's happening, and that's when he tries sneaking up on me. But I hear him first. I turn around fast and catch him staring at me. Grandma's ugly old jumpie.

His name is Sam. At least that's what it is now, and he's not a bad sort. For being what he is.

"Did I startle you, Timmy?" he asks. "I'm sorry if I caught you unaware."

"You didn't," I tell him.

He says, "Good."

"I'm watching the fireworks," I tell him.

"Fireworks?" He gives the black cloud a look, then says, "I think you're mistaken." His voice is made inside a box sewn into his neck, and the words come out soft and slow. Sam doesn't sound human, but he doesn't sound not-human either. If you know what I mean. He's been here for thirty years, and that's a long time to practice talking. He's one of the prisoners—a genuine war criminal—but he lives up here in his own little house. He helps Grandma with the farm, and after so long people almost seem to trust him.

I don't trust him. I watch him as he watches the black cloud, both of us thinking that maybe it's not fireworks.

"Something's happening," Sam says. He's not big, not even for a jumpie. And he's old, fat gray hairs showing in the red ones, his long face and forearms halfway to white. "They're probably detonating old ammunition. That's all." He waits a moment, then tells me, "Perhaps you should stay near the house, for the time being."

"You can't boss me," I warn him. I won't let him boss me.

"You're right," he says. "It's not my place." Then he says, "Do it for your grandmother, please. You know how she worries."

There comes a second *whump*, followed by two more.

And Sam forgets about me. His big eyes stare at the new clouds, then he shakes his tongue and starts for Grandma's house. He doesn't say another word, walking slowly in the earth's high gravity, his long bare feet doing the jumpie shuffle.

And I go back to my soldiers. There are more pops and bangs, and I use them with my pretend sounds. Then it's quiet, and I'm thinking it was nothing. It was just like Sam said, someone blowing off old bombs. I put my soldiers down and climb up to the yard, sitting under the big pine tree. I'm thinking about the old prison camp. Grandma's driven me past it, a bunch of times. It's still got wire fences and guard towers, but almost nobody's there. That's what Grandma says. Just some ordinary human crooks stashed there by the county. All the important Chonk-*squeal-squeal-oonkkk*—what jumpies call themselves—died long ago or were shipped home. Except for Sam, that is. He's the last one left, and even he's got a death certificate with his hairy face on it. "He died of heatstroke," Grandma told me, driving us past the camp. "And the cumulative effects of gravity, too."

The black clouds have vanished. Blown away. Whatever happened, it's done, and I can't hear anything but the wind.

I start to rip up pine cones, wishing for something to do. I'm bored, like always. I'm sick of being bored, wishing I could be anywhere else, doing anything even halfway fun.

And that's when I hear the truck coming, grinding its gears on the hill. A big green Guard truck rolls past. Its back end is stuffed full of soldiers, rifles pointed at the sky. I'm watching them. Unlike my plastic soldiers, their faces aren't worn smooth. Noses and cheeks are sharp. Their eyes are spooked. Nobody waves when I wave, and they barely notice me. Then the truck is past and a cloud of white, white dust rolls over Grandma's lawn, and I'm looking west, wishing I could ride on that truck.

Wishing hard and tasting the rough dust against my teeth.

My folks got called up for Guard duty in June, for their usual six weeks. But this time it was summer and school was out, there was nobody to watch me. That's why they put me on the new Bullet train, shipping me off to the farm.

Grandma came to get me at the station. She's a big woman with gray hair and a couple million wrinkles, and she's strong from all her hard work. Bags that I could barely lift got thrown into the back end of her pickup. Then she slapped the dirt off her jeans and climbed behind the wheel, driving fast all the way home. She doesn't drive like a grandmother, I can tell you. And I don't know any other old woman who strings fences and drives tractors and calls shit, shit. Mom says that she's the most successful lady farmer in the state. I wonder about that lady part. Her only help is an old jumpie that she borrowed from the prison camp. He was an officer on one of their big rocket bombers. "He's called Sam," Mom told me before I left home, standing over me while she spoke. "Be nice to Sam. He's a very nice sentient entity."

"He's a war criminal," I told her. "The bastard bombed our cities!"

Mom just stared at me, shaking her head. She does that a lot. Then she said, "Don't cause me grief, Timmy. Please?"

"I hate the bastards," I told her. "They came to kill us, Mom."

"A long time ago," she said, "and the war is over." Then she told me, "Please. I don't want my mother thinking you're some brutal little boy."

"I'm not so little," I said.

She didn't say anything.

Then I asked, "Does that jumpie really live with Grandma?"

"Sam is called a jumpman, and he has his own house, Timmy." She made a windy sound, shaking her finger at my nose. "Since I was a little girl, and don't forget it."

I don't forget much. Riding to Grandma's farm, watching the other farms slide past, I remembered everything I'd ever learned about the war. How the jumpies came into the solar system in giant starships dressed up like ordinary comets. How they launched a surprise attack, trying to take out our defenses in a day. Later, they said they were being nothing but reasonable. Once our offensive weapons were removed, they would have become our best friends, colonizing only our cold places. They said. But they didn't get the chance since they didn't cripple us in the first day, or, for that matter, in the next thousand days.

It was the biggest war ever, and it could have been bigger. But the jumpies wanted to live on Earth, which meant they didn't like nuking us too often. And in the end, when things turned our way, we had the tools to blow away every last one of their starships. But instead of finishing them for good, we made peace. We ended up with a damned sister-kissing draw.

"What isn't won, isn't done," I've heard people say.

That's why we can't relax. The jumpies—jumpmen, sorry—are still out there, mostly hanging around Mars, battering it with fresh comets, trying to make that world livable for them. We can't let them get their own world. That's what I think. What I want to be someday is a general leading the attack, winning everything for all time. Finally.

That's what I was thinking, smiling as Grandma pulled up in front of her house. "We're here," she announced. I climbed out, taking a good look at my first farm. Then I saw the jumpie coming out of the barn, doing little hops instead of walking, and I realized that I'd never seen one before. Not in person. Not moving free and easy, I can tell you. But what really startled me was what he was wearing, which was overalls cut and resewn to fit his body, and how he showed me a big bright almost-human smile.

Jumpies have different muscles in their faces. Showing his thick yellow teeth must have been work. Like all of them, he was red—thick red fur; blood-red skin; black-red eyes. His tall ears turned toward me. Somehow the smile got bigger. Then his almost-human voice said, "And you must be Timmy. It's a great pleasure to meet you at last."

I felt cold and scared inside.

"I've heard fine things about you," he told me, shaking my hand with his rough two-thumbed hand. "Your grandmother comes home from Christmas with such stories. How you've grown, and what a wonderful young man you are."

He didn't sound like the jumpies on TV. I tried picturing him and Grandma talking about me. Standing together in the barn, I imagined. Shoveling shit and gossiping.

"He's rather quiet," Sam told Grandma. "Somehow I expected him to make a commotion."

"No, he's just frightened." She laughed when she said it, then laughed harder when I said:

"I'm not scared. Ever!"

Sam's smile changed. He tugged on the white whiskers that grew from his heavy bottom jaw. Then he said, "I've got chores to do." *Chores.* He sounded as if he'd been born here, and that bothered me more than anything. "I hope you enjoy yourself, Timmy. Bye now." Nothing was what I had pictured, and I was glad to see him turn and shuffle off, his tail dragging in the brown dirt.

Grandma took me upstairs to a sunny and hot little bedroom. She told me to unpack and showed me where to put my things. "You can go where you want," she said, "but close every gate behind you and stay off the machinery."

I knew the rules. Mom had told them to me, maybe a thousand times.

Grandma left, but I didn't unpack. I was feeling curious. I decided to go out exploring, first thing.

Grandma's bedroom was at the end of the hall—a big dark place with the shades down and the heat thick just the same. I took a couple steps inside, looking at the old-person stuff on the walls and on top of the dressers. Brown pictures were in silver frames, and there were some fancy doo-dads.

Three out of four pictures showed my mom, one from back when she was my age. I found only one shot of Grandpa, and it was set behind the others. As if he was hiding back there, almost.

Compared to upstairs, it was practically cool at ground level. I turned on the little TV in the living room. There wasn't any cable attached, and no dish outside. There was just one local channel, and it was mostly static and snow. What was I going to do for six whole weeks?

I wandered through the smelly kitchen, then outside. Tractors and a fancy combine were parked in the yard. The combine had big metal arms in front for sweeping and plucking at the crops, and on top, a big glass cab and foam-padded seat. I climbed up and sat with my hands on the wheel. Maybe Grandma would teach me to drive, I was thinking. If I asked real nice. Rocking the wheel back and forth, I made engine sounds, thinking how much fun it would be to mow through a field of corn.

Sam's cottage was behind the other buildings. I found it eventually—a tiny white wood building—and walking up onto its groaning porch, I peered into the dusty windows.

Mom had told me the story a million times. Grandpa died when she was little. It was at the end of the war, but the fighting didn't kill him. His tractor rolled over him, by accident. Mom barely remembered him. What she remembered were the tough times afterwards. Two billion people had died. Life had fallen back a hundred years, or more. Grandma had to farm with old tractors and her own hands. Help was scarce and stupid, the best men still in the military. Finally Grandma said enough was enough, and she marched down to the prison camp and gave its warden ten chickens and her problems. Was there a prisoner who could be loaned to her? Just once in a while? She needed someone who knew machinery, someone who could keep a murderous old tractor in the field. Was there any jumpie worth trusting? And that's how Sam came to Grandma, on loan from the United States government.

"He was brought up every morning for a year," Mom told me. "By armed guard. But that was silly, said your grandma.

She took Sam permanently and took responsibility, letting him live in the cottage. Hot in summer, but in the winter, just right for a jumpman."

Jumpies come from a cold place. A place that was getting even colder—too cold for life, they like to claim—which was why they moved here to live.

Mom would always laugh, telling how Grandma promised that Sam wouldn't escape, that if he tried she would hunt him down by herself. "And the warden, knowing her, said that she was better than a ten-foot wall of electrified razor-wire." That's the part that always made her laugh the hardest, shaking her head and looking off into the distance. "And now it's been what? Thirty years. Sam likes it so well there that he's never left. Even when the treaties were signed, when he could have gone home, he didn't. He won't ever."

"Why not?" I always asked.

And here Mom always said something different. Sam was too accustomed to our heat, or he liked Grandma's peach cobbler too much. Always a new reason why, and I got the feeling that none of those reasons were entirely true.

I was staring into the cottage's dirty windows, seeing nothing, and Sam sneaked up behind me, saying, "Can I help you, Timmy?"

I jerked around. He wasn't smiling, but he didn't seem angry either. At least none of his red fur was standing on end. He asked if he had startled me. I told him no. I was thinking about leading the attack on his people. I almost told him what I was thinking. But instead he told me, "I doubt if you can see anything through that grime, Timmy. For that I apologize."

I wished he wouldn't say my name so much.

Despite everything, I stood my ground. This was my first day on the farm, and I'd be damned if he was going to spook me.

"You're remarkably quiet, I think." He laughed and reached into a pocket on his overalls.

I watched his hand.

He brought out a single key, saying, "Let's go inside and look. Would you like that, Timmy?"

"Inside?" I muttered.

"Because you're feeling curious. You want to see where I live." He came past me, smelling of hay and something else. Something sweet. He fought with the lock for a minute, then the door swung open. Every window was closed, and the air inside was staler than it was hot, and it was plenty hot. The cottage was just one room with a bed at the back and some curling photographs stuck on the plaster wall. Sam was behind me, starting to pant. I went to take a look at the photos, long red faces smiling at me in that goofy jumpie way; and he said, "My family. From long ago." His voice sounded more like I expected it to be, high-pitched and sloppy. Talking past his panting tongue, he asked, "Do you see me, Timmy?"

I wasn't sure.

With a long black nail, he pointed at a photo, at a little jumpie with adults on one side of him, a giant crab or spider on the other.

"What's that?" I asked.

"A pet. It's called a *such-and-such*." I couldn't understand what he was saying. "There's nothing like it on Earth. I know it doesn't look it, but a *such-and-such* is almost as smart as a pig."

The kid in the photo did sort of look like him. Sort of. I swallowed and asked, "What's your real name?"

"Sam."

"I don't mean that one." Why was he being this way?

"My birth-name was *such-and-such*." He said it twice, slower the second time. But it never sounded like real words.

"Did Grandma pick Sam?"

"No, that was me. It's a very American name."

There was another photo of him as a boy. A really strange one. He was standing beside a dead jumpie, the carcass propped up with poles and wire, its body dried out and both of its eyes gone.

"A famous ancestor of mine," he told me. Then a moment

later, with a different voice, he said, "I know you don't approve of me, Timmy."

I blinked and looked at him.

"I know what you're taught in school."

"You're a war criminal," I said. Point blank.

"Am I?"

"You bombed our cities."

"I was a navigator on an attack craft, yes. But we never
dropped our bombs, if that makes any difference to you. It
was my first mission, and we were intercepted before we
reached our target. A purely military target." He tried another human smile. "One of your brave pilots shot me down
before I could harm a soul."

But war criminals are war criminals, I was thinking. You
can't just be a little one.

Walking around the cottage, I ended up at the nightstand.
Its wind-up clock wasn't running. I pulled a couple fingers
through the dust that covered everything. And I was thinking
something, that something working on my insides.

"Who am I?"

I looked at him, wondering what he meant.

"Names matter," he told me. "To my species, a name is essential. It's the peg on which an individual hangs his worth."

I watched the spit dripping off his red tongue.

"Long ago," he told me, "I made peace with my circumstances. I knew I would never return home. I had died in that
crash, and I was reborn. And that's why I claimed my good
American name."

I started slipping toward the door.

"In many ways, I am lucky. My particular tribe, my
race . . . we came from the warmest part of our home world.
By our standards, I'm quite tolerant of heat . . ."

Tolerant or not, he looked like hell.

"I never expected the exchange of prisoners. That's not a
Chonk-*squeal-squeal*-oonkkkk thing to do." He was looking
out the grimy windows, talking quietly. "When the exchange
was looming, your grandmother was kind enough to use her
influence, and a death certificate went home in my stead.
'*Such-and-such* died while working in the field,' it read. 'Out

of ignorance, the body was buried where it fell, his master unaware of his species's customary mummification rite.' "

I felt sorry for him, sort of. He wasn't what I'd expected, and I tried not to listen, trying not to feel anything at all.

"This is my home, Timmy." He meant the cottage, only he didn't mean it. "You're welcome to visit me any time. All right?"

I didn't answer. I shuffled outdoors, the air feeling a hundred degrees cooler. But Sam stayed inside, opening windows and dusting with his sleeves and thumbs. When I stepped off the groaning porch, he said, "Good-bye."

I might have muttered, "Bye."

I'm not sure.

I went back to Grandma's house, aiming for my room but ending up in hers. I knew something—a huge secret—only I didn't know it. I couldn't find the words. I kept staring at that darkened room, trying to think. Finally I walked over to the big bed, bending down. And sure enough, I could smell hay and that sweet something that I'd smelled on Sam. And I had a big weight on my chest, making me gasp, the force of it trying to steal my breath away.

We're eating supper in the kitchen. It's still day, still hot, but it's been hours since the explosions down at the prison camp. Grandma and Sam aren't talking about the camp or the soldiers in the truck. I can practically hear them not talking about those things. Instead they're making noise about a neighbor lady who broke her hip, and how many pheasants they've seen in the fields, and the chances that the local school can win State two years running. That's what they're saying. A lot of nothing. And then we hear someone at the front door, knocking fast and loud.

I beat Grandma to the door, but not by much. A man waits, tall and tired. "John?" says Grandma. "What are you doing here?" A dusty bike is propped against the porch rail. "Come in here. Would you like supper? We're just having a bite—"

"No. Rose," he says. "I can't. I'm going places."

She doesn't say anything, watching him.

Sam shuffles into the room. He's the one who asks, "What happened this afternoon, John? It seemed to involve the camp."

"It did," says the tall man. "Oh, it did."

"An accident?" Grandma asks. "Was it some kind of fire?"

"No, it was a fight." The man shakes his head, talking in a careful voice and not looking at anyone. "This isn't to be told, okay? But I thought you should hear it. I was walking in my pasture north of the camp when the fight started—"

"Who was fighting?" asks Grandma.

"Soldiers. Special commandos, I guess they were." He shrugs his shoulders. "They went through the old wire, then broke into the barracks. They were after the prisoners."

I say, "But there aren't any."

The man halfway glances at me. "Drunks," he says. "Speeders. One wife beater. Remember Lester Potts . . . ?" He pauses, shaking his head. "Anyway, a deputy spotted the soldiers. Shot one of them. Then the rest took cover in the east barracks—"

"Oh, shit," says Grandma.

"—and I heard the shooting. I got my deer rifle and went down to help. We had them surrounded. The Guard was rushing us help. You know the Wicker boys? The ones that drag race on the highway every weekend? Well, the sheriff freed them and gave them guns, and they were plugging the east end. Which is the direction the bastards decided to go. They set off the old stockpile for a diversion . . . that's the explosions you heard . . . and things just plain went to hell!"

Grandma puts her fists on her hips, halfway looking at Sam. She has a tough face when she wants, blue eyes bright and strong. "When you say 'commandos,' do you mean human soldiers? Or not?"

"They were human, all right."

He says it quietly, as if it's a bad thing.

"At least it's not jumpies," I tell him. And everyone.

Nobody seems to hear me.

"What happened to these commandos?" Grandma asks.

"Some died," John says. "I'm sure of that much."

Nobody talked for a long moment. Then I said, "But at least it's not jumpies. It's not jumpies!"

Sam touched me, just for an instant. "But Timmy, why would humans be interested in the old camp?"

How should I know?

"On the other hand, jumpmen would be interested. They might send human agents." He's talking to everyone, including himself. "After all, humans can move at will here."

"But where would they get people like that?" I ask, not having a clue.

It was Grandma who says, "Think."

But I can't see it.

"Think of me," says Sam. "I stayed behind willingly. Didn't I? And doesn't it make sense that some of the human prisoners might have preferred life in space?"

That's stupid idea, but I don't get a chance to say so.

Instead, Grandma says to John, "But these commandos are all dead now. That's what you've come to tell us, right?"

Sam asks, "How many were there?"

"Three or four," says the tall man. "Or five, maybe."

"How many are dead?" Grandma wants to know.

"We've found three bodies. So far." His eyes were seeing things. "The other bodies might be in the barracks. The Guard will search through the mess in the morning, when the ammo cools down enough."

Sam says, "I'm sure everything's being taken care of."

Nobody else talks.

Sam comes up beside Grandma and touches her arm, lightly. Both John and me watch him. Then he says, "What if one of them escapes? He saw no one but human prisoners. No one, and everything's fine."

Grandma's jaw is working, her teeth grinding.

Sam asks John, "How bad was it? Were any of us hurt?"

Us?

"A deputy," says John. "And one of the Wicker boys. They were killed."

Sam shakes his head. He looks small and soft next to Grandma.

"And the other brother is missing. We haven't found his

body, or he ran off. Hopefully that's all. He got scared and ran."

I would never run off in battle. Never.

John rocks back and forth, saying. "I've got to go, folks. I'm trying to warn people, and we're not supposed to talk about this on the phone." He walks onto the porch. Grandma and Sam thank him for coming, and he tells us, "Now you people take care." Then he straddles his bike and pumps the pedals, working his way through the soft dust. He's moving like a bike rider in a dream, at half-speed. Something about him real frantic, but real slow, too.

The three of us watch the news at ten. The sun is down and the heat is finally starting to seep out of the house. Grandma is sitting on the sofa, like always. Sam is squatting against a wall, against a cushion, not close to her but not far away either. And I'm on the floor, legs crossed. I'm squinting through the snow on the little screen. The news doesn't mention anything about commandos or explosions. It's going to be hot tomorrow, I hear. And for the rest of the week, too. Then they go to a commercial, selling headache pills with a pounding hammer.

A helicopter passes overhead. *Thump-thump-thump.*

When it's gone, Sam says, "Rose," and I realize how nobody else says her name with that voice. It's not a jumpie voice, or a human's. It's just Sam's. Then he tells her, "I know what it is. It's the new Chonk-*squeal-squeal*-oonkkkk council. They hear rumors about people like me, and they're looking for an issue to pull all the tribes together."

"Politics," she says. A low, tight voice.

"Exactly." He gives me a little wink, nodding to himself. "I bet that's it."

Now the sports comes on, the baseball scores too fuzzy to read.

"From now on," he says, "I'll stay on the farm. No more visits to the neighbors. No more working by the road."

Grandma says, "Perhaps that's best."

Then Sam takes a deep breath and says, "Timmy? Do me

a big favor. Go to my house and get those old pictures. Bring them to me, please."

I do it. I go out the front door and around, past the barn and the fancy combine—everything huge and dangerous-looking in the darkness—and I slip into the cottage, working fast. The photos feel slick and odd, made of something besides ordinary paper. Keeping quiet, I come back the same way. I hear Grandma saying, "I'm not giving you up." She sounds angry and strong and certain. "Nobody's taking you anywhere. Do you hear me?"

I'm up on the porch, and she stops talking.

I come inside.

Sam has pulled his cushion up beside Grandma, rearing back against the sofa with his long feet beneath the coffee table. "That's the boy," he says, taking the photos. He doesn't look at them. Pulling a long match from his chest pocket, he strikes it and sets them on fire in a candle bowl. All of them. I watch for the dead jumpie and the boy, only Sam's put them facedown. It's just the slick non-paper burning. And he tells Grandma, "Nothing will happen. They found nothing, and they're dead."

Grandma says, "All right," and nods. Once.

Then the fire is out, and he tells me, "Go dump this, please."

I'm out on the porch, throwing ashes off the rail, and Grandma says, "You didn't need to do that. Why did you think you needed to?"

"To end any doubts," he says.

"Whose doubts?"

"Not mine," he says. Then he says, "This is my home, Rose."

Rose. Just the way he says it makes me shiver.

I grab the rail with both hands, watching the sky. Mars is the pink star in the east. Before too many more years, it'll turn white with clouds. Sam's told me. His people are flinging comets down at it, sometimes two a day, trying to make it livable. And for a moment, without warning I feel jealous of the humans that might be up there, imagining them throwing those comets, having that much fun every day.

"I've been here my entire life," says Sam, "and I won't leave you."

"You're damned right you won't," says Grandma. Then she adds something too soft for me to hear, despite all my trying.

We go to bed, and I fall asleep for five hours, or maybe five minutes. Then I'm awake, flat on my back and completely awake. Why am I? There comes a sound from downstairs. A bang, and then a thud. Then more thuds. I sit up in bed, my heart pounding. People are coming upstairs. Suddenly my bedroom door flies open, and some guy in jeans and a torn shirt stands in front of me. He's got a funny look on his face, tired and sad. He keeps his empty hands at his sides, very still, asking me, "Where is he?" with a tiny voice. "The prisoner . . . where is he . . . ?"

I don't say a word.

Someone else says, "Who is it? Who's there?"

"A boy," says the guy.

"More!"

He moves back, and a commando fills the doorway. He is huge, both tall and thick, wearing nothing except for battle armor and an ammunition belt. He's holding a big gun as if it's a toy. It's a mean looking thing with a curled clip filled with rocket-jacketed bullets, and he's pointing the barrel straight at me.

"Where is the prisoner?" he says to me.

I can't talk.

"Tell me. Now."

I have no voice or breath, my heart beating behind my eyes.

The commando's face is huge and wild, big eyes shining at me. He looks maybe twenty-five. He seems ready for anything. When Grandma's door comes open, he wheels around. And then the guy with him—the missing Wicker brother, I guess—suddenly bolts. I hear him on the stairs, half-stumbling, and the commando—the human traitor— aims fast and fires. My bedroom is lit up by the flashes. I see myself sitting in my bed, sheets pulled up around me. Then the firing stops, and I smell rocket exhaust hanging in the air. I can feel how nobody moves. Nobody is running down the stairs. And now the commando looks at Grandma while pointing the smoking barrel straight at my head.

"You're holding an illegal prisoner of war," he says. "Tell me where to find the navigator, or I'll execute this child."

"Don't hurt the boy," says Grandma. Her voice is dry and tough and angry. "Sam is out back. But he doesn't want to go with you, you bastard!"

The commando smiles, telling us, "Thank you." The gun drops, and he adds, "I don't want to fight old women and boys. So if you promise to stay here, I'll leave you here. Safe."

I want to believe him.

"Get the hell out of my house!" Grandma screams. "I'm warning you! Get out!"

She scares me, talking that way.

But the traitor doesn't notice us anymore. Stepping back, he melts into the darkness. I hear him on the stairs, then running through the kitchen. And Grandma picks up the phone in her room, saying, "Dead," and then, "Shit," as she slams it down again.

I stand, creeping out into the hallway.

Grandma's wearing a long white nightgown, and she's half-running. "Come with me," she whispers. "Now."

A dead body lies on the stairs. He scares me. I've never seen anyone dead, and all of a sudden I'm tiptoeing through his blood, the stairs warm and sticky under my bare feet.

"How could that man know about Sam?" I ask.

"That boy must have told him." She kneels and looks at me, then says, "Run. Cross the road and hide in the corn. Whatever happens, stay hidden."

The dead boy was a traitor for telling. I never would have told. Never.

"Go on now! Go!"

I run out the front door, out across the dusty yard. I get as far as the pine tree, stopping there to breathe. That's when I hear Sam and the commando talking. Fighting, they are. They're beside the barn, and Sam is saying, "What did you do to her?" He's caught up in one of the big man's arms, trying not to be carried. The commando tells him to be quiet. "I haven't hurt anyone," the bastard lies. Then he says something in jumpie, a jumpie-built box implanted in his neck letting him squeak and squeal like a native. And Sam turns still and quiet, letting himself be carried, the commando taking him to the pickup and throwing him inside, then climbing in after him, and with both hands he tries to hot wire the engine.

A big engine starts up.

It's too loud and deep to belong to the pickup. The air seems to throb. The commando's gun is beside him, then it isn't. Sam has a good hold on it, I realize, and suddenly the two men are fighting for it. I can see them when the combine's headlights come on. And the big machine lurches and starts to charge.

Everything's happening fast and crazy.

The commando wrestles his gun free, then turns and fires out the window. Sam slips out the passenger door, bouncing faster than I ever thought possible, trying to reach the barn. The commando starts chasing him, but not fast enough. A scared old jumpie can cover ground even on Earth, at least for a few feet. In he goes, and the big barn door starts pulling shut, and the commando reaches it too late, pulling at it with his free hand while he turns and fires at the charging combine.

Glass breaks.

Headlights die.

I can just see Grandma behind the steering wheel, crouched down low. The mechanical arms are turning and turning. Her target tries to run but he picks the wrong direction. There's a utility shed beside the barn, and he gets caught in the corner, shoots twice, then throws the gun and turns and leaps higher than seems possible or right. He's lived all his life with jumpies, I realize. He's too young to have been taken prisoner during the war. Trying to be a jumpie has given his legs extra bounce, which isn't enough. Because instead of leaping over the spinning arms, he falls into them, his body flung back into the barn's wooden wall just as the combine strikes home with a big sharp *crunch*.

I hear him scream, maybe.

Or maybe it's me.

Then the scream is done, and Grandma turns off the engine and climbs down. Sam comes hopping out of the barn. Both of them are wearing nightclothes. They hold each other and squeeze, saying nothing. And I walk past them, making for the barn. I'm curious to see what happened to that poor stupid man.

Only Sam sees me first and says, "No, Timmy. Come back here, please."

I turn and look at them. Then I walk over to them. I'm not scared or anything. That's what I'll say if they ask. But all of the sudden I'm sort of glad to be stopped.

I won't admit it, but I am.

Soldiers come in their helicopters and trucks, then pick up and leave again taking the bodies with them. The officer in charge warns us that nothing happened here. Everything needs to stay secret. He shakes my hand then Grandma's. And, after a pause, Sam's. And he tells my grandmother that she can expect a confidential commendation. Then as he climbs into his helicopter, he tells us, "Our enemies underestimate us. They don't appreciate the gift of our ordinary citizens." Or something like that. I can barely hear him as the helicopter starts revving its engines.

By then it's morning, and time for breakfast.

It's just the three of us, and Grandma makes pancakes and sausage. I drown everything under thin syrup. Eating is more wonderful than I could ever have guessed. I keep feeling happy and lucky, glad about everything. Grandma's wearing a bright country dress, and Sam's already in his overalls. Nobody says much until Sam finishes his cakes, puts his fork down and announces, "Once I can make the arrangements, I'll contact my old family. Just to tell them that I am well and happy."

He says it, but I don't believe it.

Neither does Grandma. She says, "You can't be serious. What in hell will that accomplish?"

"How many others are there like me?" he asks. "Dozens?

Hundreds? But as long as we're secrets, we're dangerous. Not just to us, but to our adopted families. Our adopted species."

Grandma stares through him, saying nothing.

"I want to show my people that it's possible to coexist with humans. At peace." He smiles like a human, and like a jumpie, his ears lying down flat. "Until last night, I didn't know that I was important. But since I am, I need to do the right thing."

And after that, nobody says much of anything.

Done with dishes, we drift outside. Sam studies the barn and combine, talking about what needs to be fixed first. I'm pushing at the splintered wood, looking at the dark red smear but never touching it. Then Grandma says something to Sam. I can't hear what. And she comes to me and says, "Would you do me a favor, Timmy? Go play with your soldiers out by the road. Stay there until I say otherwise. Would you do that for your old grandmother?"

I ask, "Why?" and suddenly wish I hadn't.

She gives me a look, level and strong.

Then Sam calls to her. "Rose," he says, taking little hops over toward the cottage.

"Play by the road," she repeats. "Now."

I start walking.

"And don't tell anyone," she warns me, her hard old face looking into me. I don't have any secrets. Not with her, I don't.

"Yes, ma'am," I say.

She follows Sam.

I go to the ditch and find my soldiers buried in the dust, and I play with them without liking it. They're just toys, I'm thinking. And the plastic jumpies don't even look real. But all of the sudden I get an idea. It just sort of comes to me. And I get up on my feet and climb out of the ditch, walking until I've got the cottage in sight. Just one peek, I'm thinking. Just that. Only my feet stop moving all at once, and I get cold inside. And then I turn around and start running back toward the ditch, running faster than I've ever run in my life.

After last night—after what I saw Grandma do last night—there's no way I'm leaving my little ditch.

I hunker down with my soldiers, and I stare at their worn-out faces.

Only one face in this ditch is scared, I tell myself.

Only one face doesn't belong to an idiot. That's what I'm thinking right now.

Bordeaux Mixture

CHARLES DEXTER WARD

According to the Nature *Web site (www.nature.com/nsu/pro-files/profiles.html), "Henry Gee's birth was accompanied by eldritch psychical phenomena and several outbreaks of random happiness, but things have quietened down a lot since then. Henry has a B.Sc. in zoology and genetics from the University of Leeds, and a Ph.D. in Zoology from the University of Cambridge. Having set up the Nature News Service he now devotes most of his time as a senior biology editor specializing in integrative and comparative biology and evolution. He is the author of* Before the Backbone: Views on the Origin of the Vertebrates *(Chapman and Hall, 1996);* In Search of Deep Time: Beyond the Fossil Record to a New History of Life *(Free Press 1999/Fourth Estate 2000); and innumerable popular science articles." During 2000, the distinguished science journal* Nature *generously allowed him to commission and edit a weekly series of SF 800-word short fictions entitled "Futures." Many SF luminaries contributed, including Arthur C. Clarke, Greg Bear, Frederik Pohl, Michael Moorcock, Ted Chiang and Bruce Sterling (and see Brin, Ford, Simmons, Slonczewski, Spinrad).*

"Bordeaux Mixture" was one that Gee wrote himself, under the Lovecraftian pseudonym Charles Dexter Ward. It is a piece of deadpan scientific humor with a submerged literary reference to the metaphysical poetry of Andrew Marvell that HPL himself might have enjoyed.

I'm spraying my tomatoes with bordeaux mixture and it feels great. My wife says I do the tomatoes a disservice, dousing them with Bergerac, when our pension could easily spare Clydebank Cabernet. But the tomatoes love it. No sooner do I get to their row with the sprayer, than their desiccated leaves flush with green; their blooms perk up; their ripening fruits blush with a richer glow. They love me, my tomatoes, and I love them back. Today is special—it's 2090, and my tomatoes and I are celebrating the safe passage of our life-giving Sun through yet another total eclipse.

Anyway, while I'm up there schmoozing, I think how far we've come in just one lifetime. Once upon a time, tomatoes were monotonous plants that took a lot of looking after; constant watering and spraying against greenfly and rot. Today's GM tomatoes are as different from the crop of my youth as the einkorn and emmer they harvested in the Fertile Crescent with obsidian sickles.

I've got rows of them—tomatoes, that is—all the latest kinds: juicy blue ones as big as canteloupes; fluorescent orange fruits the size of pinheads but as hot as habañeros; long thin ones like cucumbers; tetrahedral ones; ones with edible roots; ones that grow like trees which I harvest like apples. And they look after themselves, pretty much; they farm their own mycorrhizae, nurse their own symbionts, kill off the weeds with endogenous antibiotics, and suck what little water they need out of the air. No, I only spray my tomatoes with bordeaux mixture because they enjoy it. They want me to, and, willingly, I oblige.

These days, the word "tomato" seems almost redundant, as everything else in the garden has undergone much the same kind of transformation. If every plant can be made into anything you want, and made to taste like any other crop, it rather breaks down the barriers. If you have lettuces that look like onions and taste like lemon meringue pie, who cares about horizontal gene transfer?

You'd think that this uncertainty about what's what in the garden would worry me, given that I've always seen myself as something of a tomato connoisseur and never knew my onions. What if I found myself growing an aubergine by mistake, an aubergine that looks like a tomato? But the fact is I don't care: the tomatoes themselves see to that. It gives me such a thrill to see them practically whoop with solanaceous pleasure as they see me advancing up the garden; such a feeling of contentment as I can hardly describe.

It hardly seems possible that, less than a century ago, people objected so violently to genetic modification, when subsequent history shows it to have been such a wonderful innovation. How silly it all now seems: all those people who trashed test crops seem, in retrospect, like those weavers who broke up power looms. But then, I was doing some of the modification, so perhaps I'm biased.

Now I'm long since retired, and the company I was working for back in 2007—when everything changed—has gone the way of Microsoft and Tharsis Telomerase, I can tell all. In 2007, GM was so unpopular with the public that bioscience companies had to fund research and development almost in secret. Progress advanced in giant steps, but all behind the scenes. Unknown to the public, there were plants that did everything except talk back; plants that created their own self-sufficient ecospheres. A few were dropped on the martian South Pole. There were no announcements, no press releases. I hear that a few small stands of martian maize still thrive.

Then a few of us at the lab hit on an idea. We transfected maize with genes for human pheromones. With our corporate heads, we thought that this would do wonders for brand loyalty. The thing is, human pheromones influence behaviour subconsciously. To tell people what we were doing would defeat the object, wouldn't it? Late one night we planted a stand of GM maize in California (I forget exactly where) and within weeks there were activists pounding the door of the Capitol in Sacramento demanding GM crops. Success breeds success—we got the same encouraging results with courgettes in Chihuahua, tomatoes in Thailand and greengages in Glasgow.

But that was long ago, and anyway, when I'm up here with the tomatoes, all that matters is the continuous present, when I am surrounded by the rapturous cacophony of my gorgeous plants—all mine—the plant I love and that love me so much in return, filling the green ether with triumphant shout of radiant joy.

The Dryad's Wedding

ROBERT CHARLES WILSON

Robert Charles Wilson lives in Toronto, Ontario, and is one of the leading Canadian SF writers. His first SF novel, The Hidden Place, *appeared in 1986 and his seventh,* Mysterium *(1994), won a Philip K. Dick Award. His big breakthrough novel however was* Darwinia *(1998).* Bios *(1999) is his most recent novel and he published his first collection,* The Perseids, *all SF stories set in Toronto, in 2000. In an interview a couple of years ago, he said: "I've been reading some of the British and Australian hard SF—Stephen Baxter, Greg Egan. I tend to like the hard SF, because it seems to me disciplined in a certain way. We can do all kinds of things in SF, but these guys keep us honest. . . . I admire that kind of disciplined work. In some ways it's the heart of the field. We need it there, even if that's not what interests us at the time—even if we're exploring over here, writing more humanist SF, more poetic SF, we need that solid core of hard SF" (from* Challenging Destiny *#7). It seems to me this gives a good idea of Wilson's stance as a writer of SF.*

"The Dryad's Wedding" is a prequel to Wilson's novel, Bios, *and is a tale of strange adventures on an alien planet in the distant future. It was published in the paperback anthology* Star Colonies, *edited by Ed Gorman, Martin A. Greenberg, and John Helfers. Its lush setting and moody concentration on the inner life of the central character remind me of the fiction of Brian Aldiss, perhaps his* Hothouse *series.*

Chaia Martine was nineteen years old. In seven days she would marry the man she had been married to once before, in another life. And she suspected that something was terribly wrong with her.

Not the familiar something. She was actually thirty-five years old, not nineteen. She felt nineteen because nineteen years ago her skull had been fractured by a falling tree in a fierce summer storm. She had lain in the flooded Copper River for almost an hour before her rescuers reached her, and had lost so much dura mater and brain tissue that her memories could not be saved. The Humantown clinic had salvaged her body, but not her mind. She had had to wear diapers and learn to walk and talk all over again, as nano-bacters built her a new cerebral hemisphere from fetal stem cells out of the colony's medical reserves. She had almost died and had been born a second time—awkwardly, painfully. Yes, certainly, *that* was wrong with her. (And problem enough for one person, Chaia thought.)

But that didn't explain why she sometimes heard the voice of the forest calling her name. And it didn't explain, above all else, the way the spiders had assembled themselves into the shape of a man.

The spider incident happened in a glade uphill from the Copper River. The Copper was a gentle river now, herds of epidonts grazing peacefully at the grasses and faux-lilies that grew along the banks. Chaia loved the look of it, at least at the end of a placid Isian summer. (She was inevitably nervous, frightened on some fundamental physiological level, whenever mountain rains made the river run fast and white.) This glade was one of Chaia's private places, a place she came to be alone, away from the crowds and confusing expectations of Humantown, away from the hovering mystery of her once-and-future husband Gray McInnes. Standing, she could watch the river unfold like a perfect blue ribbon into the western prairies.

For the most part she was enclosed here, wrapped in green shade. Chaia was not now and never had been afraid of the Isian forest. Guardian remensors, small as sandflies, flew a twenty-meter perimeter around her wherever she went. They would warn her if any dangerous animal—a triraptor or a digger—came too close; they would sting and bite the creature if it attempted to stalk her.

There were Isian insects in the glade, a great many of them, but Chaia wasn't troubled by insects. Her skin exuded pheromones that repelled the most dangerous species. If one should somehow chance to bite, her enhanced immune system would quickly neutralize the poison. In fact, she had grown familiar with the insect population of the glade, some species of which she had studied in her bios and taxonomy classes. She often spent a lazy afternoon here doing nothing more than watching the bugs: the black noonbugs, like tiny pompous cartoon men, rolling balls of sticky fungal spores; or the diogenes flies, with their pollen sacs like miniature Victorian lanterns.

The spiders were less obvious but no less plentiful. They were called "spiders" because they resembled a namesake Terrestrial insect Chaia had never seen (or could not remember seeing, though she had once, in her lost life, lived on Earth). They looked like button-sized, rust-red marbles equipped with a radial mass of legs. The spiders were harvesters, cutting leaves and taking the fragments back to their ground nests, which rose like ankle-high pyramids from the forest floor.

She was not ordinarily aware of the spiders—they passed through the fallen leaves and green reeds as lightly as idle thoughts—but today they were numerous and active, as if vying for her attention. Chaia sat on a fallen log and watched, fascinated, as they marched among the damp thread-mosses, gathering in pale clumps and clinging together.

This was unusual behavior, and Chaia supposed it must reflect some event of great significance in the spider universe, a mass mating or the founding of a new colony. She lifted her feet so that she would not inadvertently disturb the complex protocols of the creatures.

A breeze from the west rattled the long brella leaves above her head. Chaia was due back at Humantown for the evening meal (and a wedding rehearsal at the Universalist chapel), but that was still two hours away. Her afternoon was her own, and she meant to spend it doing absolutely nothing useful or productive. She watched the spiders gather in the glade, watched them idly at first but then with increasing attention, until it became obvious that what was happening here was not, perhaps, wholly natural.

Still, the feverish activity of the insects fascinated her. Spiders poured into the glade from several directions and several nests at once, parade lines of them. They avoided Chaia systematically but gathered before her in lacy sheets, stacked one atop another until the combined mass of their pale bodies took on a smoked-glass color and they rose in a seething mound to half her own height.

Carefully—disquieted but not yet terrified—Chaia stood and took a step backward. The spider-mass moved in response, shifting its borders until it became (and now Chaia's fear began to intensify) a nearly human shape. The spiders had made a man. Well, not a man, exactly, but a human form, neither male nor female, really just the suggestion of a torso, arms, a head. The head was the most detailed part of the spider-sculpture. Its eyes were a shadowed roundness, its nose a pale protruberance.

Chaia was about to flee the glade when the spider-thing opened its uncertain mouth and spoke.

The voice was very faint, as if the massed insects had enclosed a volume of air in a kind of leaky lung, expelling moist breezes through vocal cords made of insect parts or dried reeds. Or perhaps only Chaia heard the voice; she thought this was possible. But the spider-thing spoke, and the awful thing about this was, Chaia recognized its voice.

She hadn't heard it for a long time. But she had heard it often when she was younger, in the woods, in her dreams. She called it the voice of the forest because it had no real name, and she never spoke of it because she knew, somehow, she mustn't.

"Chaia," the spider-thing whispered.

It knew her name. It had always known her name. It had called her name from wind-tossed trees, from the rippling flow of the Copper River. She sensed an uneasiness in the voice, an anxiety, an unfulfilled need.

"Chaia," the spider-thing said. (The voice of the forest said.)

That was all. That was enough.

Then the man-shaped mass began to lose its form, to collapse into a collection of mere insects, thousands of them flowing like water at her feet, and she thought she heard the voice say, "No, not like this, not this." Chaia tried to answer it, to say *something*, because surely a sound of her own would disperse the hallucination (it *must* be a hallucination) and jolt the forest back to reality. But her throat was as dry and breathless as a sealed room. Her courage collapsed; she turned and ran downhill until she found the trail to Humantown, a cloud of guardian remensors following her like agitated gnats; ran all the way back with the forest singing in her ears, certain that something was wrong with her, that some part of her was deeply and permanently broken . . . and how could she bring herself to marry Gray McInnes, how could she even have contemplated it, when she was probably not even sane?

Humantown had been established half a century ago, deep in the arboreal hinterland of the Great Western Continent. It was the first truly successful human settlement on Isis. But it was not, strictly speaking, the first.

There had been human beings on Isis more than a century earlier. That had been when the great Trusts ruled the Earth, when the outer solar system had been a checkerboard of independent republics (Mars, the asteroids, the Uranian moons, and the Kuiper kibbutzim), when a single interstellar launch had consumed a significant fraction of the system's gross economic product. People had come to Isis because Isis was one of the few biologically active worlds within practical reach, and because it seemed so invitingly Earthlike in its size, mass, climate, and atmosphere.

The problem: Isis was toxic.

It was, in fact, deadly. Its biosphere had evolved far before the Earth's, and without the periodic massive diebacks that punctuated Terrestrial evolution. The Isian ecology was deeply complex, driven by predation and parasitism. The Isian equivalents of viruses, bacteria, and prions made short work of any unprotected Terrestrial organic matter. From an Isian point of view, human beings were nothing more than an ambulatory buffet of choice long-chain proteins waiting passively to be devoured.

The first settlers—scientists living in the sterile cores of multilayered biohazard facilities—had underestimated the virility of the Isian bios. They had died. All of them, including thousands in the Isian orbital station, when their defenses were breached. Lovely as she was, Isis was also a murderess.

Humanity had not returned to the planet for a hundred years, by which time the oligarchy of the Trusts had collapsed and a gentler regime controlled the Earth.

And still, no unprotected human being could survive more than a few minutes in the Isian bios. But protection had grown more subtle, less intrusive. Chaia, for instance, possessed immune system prostheses clustered in genned sacs around her abdominal aorta; countless genetic fixes had hardened her cellular barriers against Isian invasion as well. With periodic upgrades, she could live here indefinitely.

She felt as if she had lived here all her life. She was not a true Isian, like the babies born in Humantown, because she had lived another life on Earth; but that life was lost to her. All she remembered was Isis. She knew the forests and uplands around Humantown intimately because they were her cradle and her home. She knew the wildlife. She knew the town itself, almost too well. And she knew the people.

She knew there was no one she could talk to about the spiders.

Humantown had grown up above an S-curve in the Copper River, a ploughed terrace dotted with simple Turing-fabricated structures. It was fenced to keep dangerous wild animals away, but the fence recognized Chaia and opened to admit her (chiming "Welcome, Chaia Martine!" from a hidden sonodot). Chaia suppressed her anxiety as she walked down dusty Main Street. She passed the hardware shelter, where Gray McInnes wrote Turing protocols for the assembly robots; she was obscurely relieved not to see him there. She passed the health center where she had spent her first five years under the care of her trauma-mother Lizabeth Chopra and a half-dozen surrogate fathers in the form of therapists and doctors. She passed the Universalist Chapel, where all the religious people except Orthodox Jews and Reform Mormons gathered once a week to worship . . . then she turned back, rang the rectory bell, and told Clergyman Gooding to cancel tonight's rehearsal. She wasn't feeling well, she said. No, nothing serious. A headache. She just needed to lie down.

Then she walked up Main Street, past Reyes Avenue where her own small private shelter stood, and down a back lane through a stand of cultivated brella trees where children played with brightly-colored mentor robots, and then—surprising herself—through the fence and out into the wildwood once more.

Dusk was slow on Isis. Sunsets lingered. The forest grew shadows as Chaia walked. She would be missed at the evening meal at the town kitchen, but perhaps Rector Gooding would make excuses for her.

That would not prevent Gray McInnes (wonderful, patient, enduring Gray) from seeking her out. And she wouldn't be at home, but she didn't think Gray would be terribly surprised at that. Chaia often went walking late in the woods and had even spent some nights there. After all, she had her remensors to protect her; the Humantown computers could pinpoint her location if some need arose. Would Gray follow her into the woods? No, she thought, not likely. He understood her periodic need to be alone. He understood all her quirks. If Gray had a fault, it was this relentless understanding. It suggested he still thought of her as a kind of invalid, as if she were the original Chaia Martine he had married back on Earth, only suffering from a long-term amnesia.

But she was not that Chaia Martine. She was only the sum of what she had been on Isis. Plus a few random delusions.

She followed an old path up the foothills above the human settlement and the river. She had no destination in mind, at least not consciously; but she walked for more than an hour, and when she awoke to herself she saw lights in the distance. Glaring portable flarelights, much brighter than the setting sun. This was a remote research site, an abandoned digger complex where the planetary ecologist Werner Eastman had excavated a nest of ancient tunnels.

She came out of the woods into a blizzard of light and sound.

Most of the heavy work here had been done by construction and mining robots. The huge yellow machines still roamed the site, sectioning the earth with a delicacy that belied their great size and noise. They sorted what they found, excreting chipped flint and knapping stones into neat mesh trays.

Werner and his two apprentices should have been finished for the night, but they seemed absorbed in their work, huddling in a polyplex shelter over some choice discovery. Chaia simply stood at the edge of the excavation, peering down the steeply terraced border into a layer of resected tunnels like limestone wormtracks. A cooling breeze tangled her long hair.

Werner must have noticed her at some point. She looked up from her thoughts and he was there, gazing at her with a gentle concern. "Hello, Chaia. Come to watch?"

"Not really. Just . . . walking."

"Late for that, isn't it? You'll be missing dinner."

"I felt restless."

She liked Werner Eastman. He was an old Isis hand, dedicated to his work. A tall man, graying at the temples after at least two juvenation cycles. He was older than Humantown itself, though still young by Terrestrial standards. He had been one of her surrogate fathers.

They had drifted apart in recent years. Werner disapproved of her marriage to Gray McInnes. He felt that Gray was taking advantage of her, exploiting the fact of his prior marriage to that other Chaia Martine, the one who had died in the Copper River. Gray wanted everything to slide back in time to the way it had been before, Werner insisted. And that was maybe true, Chaia thought. But she couldn't forget or ignore Gray's many kindnesses. And Gray, after all, had been the only courtier in her brief new life. The only one not repelled or at least dismayed by her strangeness, her awkward in-betweenness.

But Werner meant no harm. His concern had always touched her, even when she considered it misplaced. She said, "You're working late, too."

"Yes. Well, we found something quite interesting in the lower excavations. Care to have a look?"

She agreed, but only to be polite. What could be interesting, except to a specialist, about these old digger tunnels? She had seen diggers often enough—live ones, clutching crude spears in their manipulating arms. They were occasionally dangerous, but nothing about them inspired her curiosity. They were not truly sentient, though they manufactured simple levers and blades. In fact they were emotionally affectless, bland as turtles. She couldn't imagine befriending a digger, even the way she might befriend an ordinary animal. They had no true speech. They lived in tunnels lined with hardened excreta, and their diet consisted of rotting carrion and a few roots and vegetables. If food was scarce, they would devour their own young.

Werner took her to the shelter where the day's discoveries were laid out on a table. Here were the usual simple flint tools, the kind Werner had been cataloguing since Chaia was young. But a few other items, too. The ones he had called "interesting." Bits of corroded metal. (Diggers weren't met-alworkers.) This one, for instance, clotted with clay, looked like the kind of firefly lamp every colonist carried in his pouch. Here, a sort of buckle. Chipped fragments of glass.

"Humans made these," Chaia said, an odd uneasiness haunting her.

"Yes. But they're old. They date from the first Isian settle-ment, almost two hundred years ago."

"What are they doing in these old digger tunnels?"

"That's the interesting question, isn't it? But we also found this."

Werner reached into a specimen box and withdrew some-thing already washed free of its embedding mud and clay, something smooth and white.

A jawbone.

A human jawbone.

"My God," Chaia breathed.

Werner began to explain what the jawbone represented . . . something about the first research colonists who had occu-pied the modern site of Humantown, and how one of them must have ventured into the digger colony when it was still active, or had been carried there, or . . .

But Chaia didn't really hear him.

The jawbone—dead, motionless on the table—spoke to her.

Werner went on talking. Werner couldn't hear.

But Chaia heard it quite plainly.

"Chaia," the jawbone said.

And Chaia fainted.

There is a phenomenon in the universe called, loosely, "sentience." It occurs in quasi-homeostatic systems of a cer-tain complexity. Human beings are an example of such a system. Certain of their machines are also sentient. Else-where in the known universe, sentience is elusive.

Chaia, dreaming, remembered this much from her bios textbooks.

She dreamed of herself, of her brain regrown from fetal

stem cells. Sentience requires communication. Nerve cells talk to nerve cells. They talk electrically; they talk chemically. Her fresh, new neurons had exfoliated into a mind.

"Mind," the textbooks said, was what happened in the gaps between the neurons. Signals were exchanged or inhibited. But the space between neurons is essentially empty. "Mind" was a hollowness where patterns bloomed and died.

Like flowers growing between the stars.

What were the places that mind could live? In a human nervous system. In the countless virtual gates of a quantum computer. And—and—

But the dream-thought drifted away, a pattern that had blossomed and withered before she could grasp it.

She woke to find Gray McInnes at her bedside, frowning.

She said, idiotically, "Am I sick?"

(Because of course she was sick; that was why she heard voices. . . .)

But Gray shook his head reassuringly. "Overtired, or so the therapist tells me. I guess you've been under a lot of stress. The wedding plans and all. What were you doing out in the wildwood?"

His expression was open and guileless, but she heard an accusation. "Just walking. Thinking."

He smiled. "The nervous bride?"

"Maybe some of that."

She turned her head. She was home, in her own shelter. They hadn't put her in the clinic, which was a good sign. Through the bedroom window she could see a patch of sky, clouds racing out of the west. When those clouds broke against the flanks of the Copper Mountains there would surely be rain. Summer was over.

Gray brushed a strand of hair away from her eyes. His hand was gentle. He smelled warm and solid. He was a big man, robust, stocky in the way that distinguished Earth-born colonists from their Martian or Kuiper-born colleagues. Chaia always felt tiny next to him.

He said, "The doctor gave you something. You'll probably want to sleep some more."

Chaia wondered whether it was Gray she loved or just his

constant presence—the reassurance of him, like a favorite chair or a familiar blanket. She dreaded hurting him.

But how could she go through with the wedding, when she was probably not even sane? How much longer could she pass among people and pretend to be normal? They would notice, soon enough; Gray would notice first, was perhaps even now in that first awful stage of discovery, the warmth of him hiding a kernel of repugnance. . . .

"Close your eyes," he said, smoothing her forehead.

Cloud shadows stole across the room.

He stayed with her that night.

Humantown's particle-pair communications link with Earth had lately downloaded a series of fresh entertainments, and Gray picked one to watch while Chaia dimmed the ambient light. The videostory was called *The American's Daughter* and was set in the wild years of the twentieth century, when there were hundreds of quasi-independent Terrestrial nation-states and not even the moon had been settled. Gray, a history buff, pointed out some factual errors the producers had missed or ignored—the robotic servant that carried messages between the President's daughter and the penniless alchemy student was almost certainly an anachronism, for instance.

The story was placed in North America, with most of the conventional settings of an *histoire americain:* huge concrete buildings, pavement streets crowded with beggars and bankers, a cathedral, a "factory," a carnival. The story ended with a reunion, supposedly in New York City, but Chaia thought the buildings looked like the old city of Brussels, gently morphed to more closely resemble a twentieth-century city.

Gray turned to her curiously when she remarked on it. "What do you know about Brussels?"

"Well, I—" She was suddenly puzzled. "I guess I must have seen pictures."

Brussels.

A place on Earth.

But it had seemed so familiar. She just . . . well, *recognized* it.

Remembered it.

When had she seen Brussels? Can you remember a place you've never been? Or was this another neurological tic, like seeing spiders turn into people, like hearing jawbones talk?

Chaia's mood darkened. Gray stayed with her, and she was grateful for his company. But when they went to bed she turned her back to him, nestled against his big body in a way that meant she was ready to sleep. Only sleep. Or try to sleep.

Soon he was snoring. Chaia, restless, opened her eyes and watched the pebble-sized moon dart across the sky beyond the window. She thought of "lunacy," an old English word that had figured in *The American's Daughter*. After "Luna," the Earth's moon, linked in ancient mythology to madness, strangeness, the uncertainties of great distances and time.

Isis was a stepping stone to the stars.

Star travel was not a simple business even today. Interstellar launches were more efficient than the original Higgs translations of two hundred years ago, but they still consumed enormous resources—in the energy and materials necessary to produce the exotic-matter Higgs lenses; and in sheer real estate, each launch requiring the conversion to its nascent energy of an entire small asteroid or Kuiper body. And all of that would take you no farther than the nearest thousand stars.

But from Isis, a living world at the periphery of the human diaspora, a thousand new stars became (at least theoretically) accessible. Isis didn't have the industrial base to support even a single outward-bound Higgs launch, not yet, but the time would come. Already self-reproducing Turing factories had colonized the icy fringes of the Isian system, building planetary interferometers to scout likely stars. Already, remensors and industrial robots had begun digging into selected cometary bodies, hollowing them out for the Higgs launches that would happen, if all went well, in fifty or a hundred years. Chaia herself might well live another hundred or two hundred years; she might see some of these great public works come to fruition.

In the meantime the daily work of Humantown went on: tending robots, harvesting food and medicinals from the wilderness, writing and revising Turing protocols, making sense of the strange Isian bios. And the simple work of living. Making love, making babies; growing up, even dying.

Getting married.

In the morning she went to the Universalist chapel with Gray for a brief rehearsal: essentially a walk up the aisle, a feigned exchange of yubiwa (finger rings made of gold mined from the mountains by robots), the pronunciation of the banns. Weddings were a Terrestrial custom; relations among Martians and Kuiper folk were more fluid, less formal. Not that a Universalist ceremony was exactly formal. Universalism was not even really a religion in the old sense. Its only dogma was a prescribed humility in the face of the mysteries of the natural world, the unfathomables of ultimate beginning and ultimate end. Its icon was a black circle: the abyss, the primordial singularity; the infinitely receding spacetime of a black hole.

Chaia walked listlessly through the rehearsal. She noticed, but could not bring herself to care, when Gray exchanged glances with Rector Gooding, their expressions reflecting—what? Disappointment? Doubt? Had she been too restrained, too distant? Maybe it would be better if Gray came to doubt her sincerity. Then maybe he could set aside the quest that had consumed him for almost twenty years: to recreate and remarry the woman he had married once on Earth, the other Chaia Martine, her old shadow-self.

After the rehearsal she pled fatigue and left Gray at the chapel. She would go home and rest, she said. A lie. Instead she went to see Werner Eastman, determined to confront the mystery of her madness before she married Gray McInnes and perhaps widowed him again, a fate he hardly deserved.

"How much do you know about the first Isian colonists?" Werner asked, sipping coffee from a shiny blue mug.

He wasn't at the tunnel excavation today. He was in his laboratory in the medical-biological complex, a large space strewn with Isian bones and fossils, insects killed and mounted on card stock, loose terminal scrolls with cladistic charts sketched onto them. There was another human skull section on the table in front of him. Chaia carefully avoided looking at it, lest it call her name.

"Not much," she said. "Just what you learn in school. They weren't hardened against the bios. They died."

"More or less correct. Did you know one of the original research stations was located just west of here? The ruins were cleared for farmland thirty years ago—the old hands wanted to preserve it as a historical site, but we were out-voted. We saved what we could from the antique data-storage systems, however, anything that hadn't been hopelessly corrupted by weather and time."

"Do you know who *that* is?" Chaia asked, meaning the skull fragment that lingered in her peripheral vision like a warning sign.

"I think so," Werner said. He sounded pleased with himself at this bit of detective work—he had obviously been ransacking the archives. "I think what we have here are the remains of a young Terrestrial woman named Zoe Fisher."

Chaia didn't recognize the name, though perhaps she had heard it once long ago—it seemed familiar in that faraway fashion.

"Zoe Fisher," Werner continued, "was out in the wild-wood testing new isolation and immune-enhancement technologies when the research station lost its perimeters and went hot. She missed the evacuation. She was abandoned on Isis, captured by the local diggers and carried into their warren, where she died and was presumably devoured."

The diggers didn't like fresh meat. They preferred their victuals predigested by decay enzymes. Ghastly, Chaia thought. She imagined, far too vividly, that early explorer, Zoe Fisher, lost in the woods with no hope of rescue, the toxic bios slowly but certainly eroding her defenses.

(Had it been raining back then? It was raining today: gently, on Humantown, and fiercely, far up the foothills of the Copper Mountains. The first explorers had never even felt the touch of Isian rain on their skin. Without their barriers of steel and latex and smartgels they had been horribly vulnerable; a single drop of rain contained enough Isian disease vectors to kill one of them literally within minutes.)

She thought of Zoe Fisher, lost in the rain, dragged unwilling into the deep and foul complexities of the digger tunnels. The picture was almost too vivid in her mind, too painfully close.

"An awful way to die," Chaia said.

"She was delirious at the end. In a way, almost happy."

Delirious, Chaia thought. Like me. "How do you know that?"

"She was in sporadic radio contact with another colonist. Some fragments of her dialogue were stored to local cyberspace and recovered when we archived the ruins. Zoe Fisher thought the bios of the planet had somehow entered her mind—that is, she believed she was talking to Isis itself. And not just Isis. All the living worlds of the galaxy, linked by some kind of shadowy quantum connection on the cellular level."

Chaia was startled.

The bios, she thought. The voice of the forest. Had the voice of the forest spoken to Zoe Fisher, down there in the darkness of the digger middens?

She said carefully, "Could there be any truth to that?"

Werner smiled. "I doubt it. We have some evidence that DNA-based life spread through the galaxy in a slow panspermia—at least that's the prevailing theory. But as far as we know, the only objects that can communicate at greater than relativistic speed are highly-engineered particle-pair links. Certainly not microscopic unicells."

She had dreamed, had she not, of the way a mind grows out of the chemically-charged spaces between neurons? Well, how *else* might a mind grow? In the bios of a planet? In the stew of virtual particles seething in the vacuum between the stars?

"But it's possible," she whispered, "isn't it?"

"Well, no, probably not. Zoe Fisher wasn't a biologist or a physicist, and she wasn't exactly presenting a scientific thesis. But she *was* an orphan, and she talked about Earth as an 'orphan planet,' cut off somewhere from the galactic bios.

Essentially, she was talking about herself. She imagined she'd found the family she'd never had, even if it was a family of inconceivably vast intelligences."

But that's glib, Chaia thought. *That's not the whole story. It can't be.*

Nor was any of this the reason she had come to see Werner Eastman. He sat patiently, sharing the room with her, waiting for her to speak. The silence grew weighty until at last she confessed: "I'm worried about Gray. What I might be doing to him."

Werner's expression softened. He became a kind of father again, and she felt unbearably young and unbearably lonely next to him. "Chaia," he said. "Maybe you should be worried about yourself."

"No . . . it's Gray." She pictured Gray the way she had seen him last night, curled in bed, vulnerable for all his husky size. "He lost me once. . . ."

"Chaia, that's not true. I know Gray sees it that way. The Chaia Martine you used to be . . . the woman who almost died in the river . . . Gray loved her deeply. He's never abandoned the hope that some part of her would resurface in you. But that's simply not going to happen. You're what that Chaia Martine might have been, if she had been born and raised on Isis. That's all, and it ought to be enough. If he loved you on that basis, I would bless the marriage. But what moves Gray is a combination of loss and guilt. He misses his wife, and he blames himself because he couldn't save her from the river. He thinks he should have been out there with her in that awful storm, tying down beacon pylons. Well, he can't go back and rescue her. So he's doing the next best thing. He's marrying the woman he will always think of, on some level, as Chaia's ghost."

"No one has ever been nicer to me than Gray."

"And he'll go on being nice to you, year after year, and concealing his disappointment, year after year. And you deserve better than that."

Maybe. But Werner had failed to grasp the subtlety, the nuance of her relationship with Gray. *I am not a diagram,* she thought. *I'm not one of your cladistic charts.*

"I think my memory's coming back," she said, surprising herself.

"Pardon me?"

"My memory of Earth. Of being that other Chaia Martine."

Gray shook his head sadly. "It can't happen, Chaia. It's even less plausible than the idea of talking planets."

"I saw Brussels in a videostory last night. And I recognized it. Not, you know, from a photograph or a book. I *knew* I'd been there. I had walked those streets."

"Brussels? On Earth?"

It sounded ridiculous—another delusion—but she blushed and nodded.

"Chaia, that couldn't be a genuine memory."

"Why not?"

"I was one of your therapists, remember? You ought to read your own file more closely. Chaia Martine was born and lived in Brisbane. She was educated in the Emigre Academy in Near Earth Orbit from the age of ten, then traveled to the Kuper Belt for pre-Isian training. She couldn't have seen Brussels because she was never there."

An Isian day is slightly longer than the Terrestrial day. The circadian rhythms of the colonists had been adjusted to suit. Still, something in the ancient human biology took notice of the discrepancy. Afternoons were long; nights could be endless.

Chaia went to bed alone, far later than she had planned. Her head was throbbing. A thousand half-formed ideas flickered through her mind. She fell asleep almost inadvertently, between one fevered notion and the next.

A rattle of thunder woke her deep in the belly of the night.

Storms came hard out of the west this time of year, rolling over the basinlands toward the spine of the continent. Wind whispered around the facets of her personal shelter.

You ought to read your own file more closely, Werner had said. But she never had, had she? She had explicitly avoided learning very much about the Chaia Martine who had once inhabited this body, the Terrestrial woman who had married

Gray McInnes once long ago . . . not because she was incurious but because that woman was dead, and it was better, her therapists had insisted, not to disturb her ghost, not to confuse the issue of her own fragile identity.

But perhaps some ghosts needed disturbing.

Sleepless, Chaia took her personal scroll into her lap and addressed the Humantown archives.

She had been trained in archival management and it was simple enough for her to scroll into the medical and personnel records and root out Chaia Martine's detailed *curriculum vitae*. Chaia Martine—*that* Chaia Martine—had been groomed from birth for Isis duty. Biologically, she was the daughter of a Catalonian peasant couple who bartered a half-dozen viable embryos to the State Service in exchange for tax relief. She had been decanted in Brisbane and educated under the Colonial Necessities Act; her specialty had been agricultural genning and management, a skill lost to her now. She had met and married the young Gray McInnes at the orbital Emigre Academy.

And she had never been to Brussels.

Could there have been an unscheduled or unrecorded vacation? Well, perhaps so; but she doubted it. The State Service kept excellent records, especially in the case of a duty ward like Chaia Martine. If Chaia Martine had seen Brussels without registering the journey in her daily records, it represented a triumph of intrigue.

But Chaia Martine was nobody's rebel. She gave every evidence of being happy in her work. The prospect of traveling to Isis had apparently pleased her enormously. As had her marriage to Gray McInnes.

Then had come the Higgs translation, her first year on the planet, the terrible storm, her stupid heroism, lashing beacon pylons against the wind when the robots were disabled, and inevitably suffering for it—dying for it, essentially, when her skull was split and (according to the medical record) "large portions of the left and right parietal and occipital lobes were completely obliterated, with attendant massive blood loss and the penetration of untreated river water through the pontine and lumbar cisterns."

They could have let her body die, but enough of Chaia Martine remained intact that triage protocols dictated a cerebral rebuild. And thus the new Chaia Martine was born. With Gray McInnes, no doubt, weeping at her bedside.

Gray had avoided her assiduously for the first twelve years of her new life, because she had been, neurologically, a child—maturing in her adult body more rapidly than any normal child, but a child nevertheless. But he had remained loyal to her.

A loyalty born of guilt and grief, if Werner Eastman was to be believed.

But Gray loves me, Chaia thought. She had seen it a thousand times, in the way he looked at her, the way he held her. A love complete and forgiving and therefore terrible in its weight.

She scrolled deeper into the archives now, searching the name Zoe Fisher.

Zoe, the doomed colonist who had died in the digger warrens. Yes, here was Zoe, the records fragmentary, rescued from decaying atomic memory abandoned for years or pieced together from Terrestrial records equally incomplete. But enough to sense the shape of Zoe Fisher, a clonal baby raised in the hothouse politics of twenty-second-century Earth, young, fragile, terribly naive. Zoe Fisher, born into a Devices and Personnel crèche in North America; lost for a time in the brothels of Tehran; educated in Paris, Madrid, Brussels—

Brussels.

Fat drops of rain pelted her face. Chaia hardly noticed them. The rain was bad, but the rain would inevitably get worse. A ridge of low pressure was flowing from the west, moisture from the equatorial oceans breaking against the Copper Mountains like a vast, slow wave.

She walked as if in a trance and found herself once more in the wildwood.

Had she been dreaming? Walking in her sleep? She was alone in the forest, well before dawn in the rainy dark. The darkness was nearly absolute; even with her corneal enhancements she could see only the scrim of foliage around her, and a glint that must have been the Copper River far down a slope of rock and slipgrass.

It was dangerous to be out at night in this weather. The rain and wind made it impossible for her insect-sized guardian remensors to follow her. She could not even say where she was or how she had come here, except that it looked like, now that she thought of it, the glade, her private glade where she came to be alone—the glade where she had seen the spiders take a human shape.

The spiders.

Chaia heard a rustly movement behind her.

She turned, knowing what she must expect to see.

She was not afraid this time; or if she was, the fear was submerged in a thousand other incomprehensible feelings. She turned and saw the looming bulk of something as large as herself. It glistened in the rain that rushed from the forest canopy leaf-by-leaf, reflecting the firefly lamps she wore on her clothing. Its darkness was a deep amber darkness, and it smelled earthy and familiar.

She understood, now, that this was not something the spiders had done. The spiders were simply a vehicle. They were moved by something else, something vastly larger, something which had taken Zoe Fisher to its incomprehensible breast a hundred years ago and had recreated her now for some dire and essential purpose.

The creature spoke.

And Chaia Martine, at last, was ready to listen.

Gray McInnes found her in the glade a little before dawn, shivering and semiconscious; he carried her back through the wind-tossed forest to Humantown, to the infirmary, where she was dressed in warm hospital whites and put to bed with graduated doses of some gentle anxiolytic drug.

Chaia slept long and hard, oblivious to the wild wind beating at the shelters of Humantown.

She was aware, periodically, of the doctors at her bedside, of Gray (from time to time) or Werner Eastman, and once she thought she saw her therapy-mother Lizabeth Chopra, though nowadays Lizabeth worked in the orbital station a hundred miles above the Isian equator, so this must have been a dream.

She dreamed constantly and copiously. She dreamed about the ten million worlds of the Galactic Bios.

Zoe had explained all this to her in the glade above the Copper River.

Before the Earth was born, simple unicellular life had swept across the galaxy in a slow but inexorable panspermia. It was life doing what life always did, adapting to diverse environments, hot and frozen worlds, the icy rings of stars or their torrid inner planets. And all of this life carried within it something Zoe called a "resonance," a connection that linked every cell to every sibling cell in the way coherent subatomic particles linked Isis to Earth.

Life was pervasive, and life was a medium (immense, invisible) in which, in time, minds grew. Minds like flowers in a sunny meadow, static but ethereally beautiful.

Chaia was awake when the doctor (it was Dr. Plemyanikov, she saw, who wore a beard and sang tenor at the weekly Universalist services) told her he would be taking a sample of her cerebrospinal fluid for analysis.

She felt the needle in her neck just as the robotic anasthistat eased her back into dreamtime.

You have to warn them, Zoe Fisher insisted.

The walls of the clinic rattled with rain.

When she woke again, she found that the drugs, or something, had enhanced her sense of hearing. She could hear the rain battering the clinic with renewed intensity. She could hear the blood pulsing through her body. She could hear a cart rattling down the corridor outside her room. And she could hear Dr. Plemyanikov in the corridor with Werner Eastman, discussing her case.

—*The contamination must have taken place during her initial injuries*, Plemyanikov said, *almost twenty years ago.* . . .

She opened her eyes sleepily and saw that Gray McInnes was with her, occupying a chair at her bedside. He smiled when he found her looking at him. "The doctors tell me you've been sick."

—Some microorganism we didn't manage to flush out of her body after she was rescued from the river all those years ago, something almost unimaginably subtle and elusive. Lying dormant, or worse, riding on her neurological rebuild, feeding on it. A miracle it didn't kill her. . . .

The minds that grew on and between the living worlds of the galaxy were sentient, but it was not a human sentience— it was nothing like a human sentience. Human sentience was a novelty, an accident. Once the minds of the Bios understood this, understood that mind could grow *inside the bodies of animals*, they regretted the deaths Isis had imposed on her first colonists and had attempted some small restitution by absorbing the mind of Zoe Fisher.

Gray McInnes took Chaia's hand and smiled. "You should have told me you were having problems."

—Once we localized and identified the infectious agent, it was simple enough to engineer a cure. . . .

Zoe Fisher had lived inside the Isian bios for more than a century, without body or location, preserved as a ghost, or a specimen, or an ambassador, or a pet—or some combination of all these things. She had even learned to control the local bios a little, in ways that never would have occurred to its native minds. The spiders, for instance, that had spoken to Chaia, or the delicately manipulated unicells that had invaded Chaia's broken skull and had made her meeting with Zoe possible.

"Chaia, there's nothing to be afraid of. Because the doctors say they can cure—"

—cure the dementia—

The meeting was important, because humanity needed to know that it was expanding into territory already occupied by minds hugely strange and not necessarily benign, minds diffuse and achingly beautiful but so different from human minds that their motives and desires could not always be predicted. The history of the future would be the history of the interaction between mankind and the Bios, between orphaned humanity and its ancient progenitors.

Gray said, "I couldn't sleep because of the storm. Too

many bad memories, I guess. So I headed for the robotics bay to get a little work done. I saw the light in your shelter, but when I knocked and no one answered . . ."

—*In fact*, Plemyanikov said, *we've already administered a vaccine*. . . .

It was all alive with voices: the spaces between the stars, the spaces between any two living cells. The things that live there are the Lords of the Bios, Zoe had said, but they're invisible to human beings, and you have to tell people, Chaia, tell people about the Bios, *warn* people. . . .

"So I had the Humantown computer locate you, and I knew there was something wrong because you were out in the woods in a storm—God knows why—"

—*She was rapidly approaching a crisis, and if Gray McInnes hadn't brought her out of the rain*—

"But this time," Gray said, unable to conceal his pleasure, the gratification that welled out of him like fast white river water, "this time I wasn't too late."

—*Fortunately the vaccine is already doing its work*—

And something lurched inside Chaia, the voices fading now, even Zoe's strange and urgent voice, the voice of the forest, growing dim and oddly distant, and the word *cure* hung in her consciousness like a bright unpleasant light, and she struggled against the watery pressure of the sedatives and tried to tell Gray what was wrong, why they *mustn't* cure her, but all she could manage was "No, not like this, not this," before the tide of drugs took her and she slept again.

The storm broke during the night. By morning the winds had gentled. The air was cool, and the clouds were rag-ends and afterthoughts in the blue Isian sky.

It had been postponed a month while Chaia recovered, but in the end the wedding was a simple and pretty ceremony.

The vaccine had flushed the infection from her body. Her hallucinations were as distant now as bad dreams, fading memories, feverish delusions, and she knew who she was: she was Chaia Martine, nothing more, and she was marrying the man who loved her.

She walked up the aisle with Gray McInnes—good and loyal Gray, who had finally saved her from the river. Rector Gooding stood beneath the black circle that was the symbol of the Mysteries and said the binding words. Then Gray took the golden yubiwa from a filigreed box, and he placed one ring on her finger and she placed one on his, and they kissed.

She was fully recovered, the doctors had told her. She was sane now. The delusions were finished, and she recognized them as symptoms of her lingering illness, refractions of half-learned history, a peculiarly Isian madness that had ridden into her brain when she was opened to the planet like a broken egg.

She left the church with Gray at her side, flower petals strewn at her feet, and she thought nothing of the spider that had nested at the side of the rectory, or the sound of the wind in the brella trees, or the white clouds that moved through the clearing sky like the letters of an unknown language.

Built Upon the
Sands of Time

MICHAEL F. FLYNN

Michael Flynn's first story appeared in Analog *in 1984, and, according to the* Encyclopedia of Science Fiction, *he "soon became identified as one of the most sophisticated and stylistically acute 1980s Analog regulars." A statistician by profession, in his fiction Flynn is interested in technology and the people who work with it. So he's a perfect match for the traditional image of the hard SF writer, except that his interest in characterization goes deeper than most. His first novel was* In the Country of the Blind *(1990), now revised and reissued in hardcover in 2001; his second novel was* Fallen Angels *(1991) in collaboration with Larry Niven and Jerry Pournelle. His third,* The Nanotech Chronicles *(1991), is a series of linked stories. His major work of the 1990s began with* Firestar *(1996),* Rogue Star *(1998),* Lodestar *(2000) and* Falling Star *(2001), four volumes in an ongoing future history, done in a very Heinleinesque manner. Many of his best stories, including the excellent novella "Melodies of the Heart," are collected in* The Forest of Time and Other Stories *(1997).*

"Built Upon the Sands of Time" is Flynn the Analog *writer doing a bar story about scientists and ordinary people. It is notable for its characterization, humor, scientific twist, and also as a contrast to the Nancy Kress story "To Cuddle Amy." There were a number of excellent SF stories about parents and parenting this year and this is also one of the best of that strain.*

A wise man once said that we can never step in the same river twice. A very wise man, indeed; because by that he did not mean we should refrain from bathing, as some half-wits at the Irish Pub have suggested, but that times change and the same circumstances are never fully repeated. You are not the same person you were yesterday; nor am I.

But perhaps that old Greek was not half so wise as he thought. Perhaps you cannot step into the same river even once; and you may not be the same person yesterday as you were yesterday.

Friday nights at the Irish Pub are busier than a husband whose wife has come home early. When The O Neil and myself arrived, the neighborhood crowd was there bending elbows with the University folks from down the street and making, as they like to say, a joyful noise. It was so busy, in fact, that Hennesey, O Daugherty's partner, had joined him behind the bar and even so they were barely keeping ahead of the orders. There were another dozen or so boyos in the back room, watching the progress of the pool table and providing encouragement or not to the players, as the case might be. The O Neil placed his challenge by laying a quarter down on the rail and promised to call me in for a game as soon as he won the table. Then he set himself to study the opposition. Seeing as how the quarters were lined up on the rail like so many communion children, I knew it would be a long, sad time before I held a cue in my hand, so I took myself back out to the bar.

O Daugherty Himself was a wise man, for he had saved a stool for my sitting and, more quickly than I could order it, had placed a pint of Guinness before me. O Daugherty is a man who knows his manners; and his customers, as well. After a polite nod to the man on my right, whom I did not know, I occupied myself with the foamy stout.

Hennesey was a contrast to his partner. Where O Daugherty was short, dark, and barrel-chested, Hennesey was tall, fair, and dour, one of the "red-haired race" from the North of Ireland. His long, thick, drooping face seemed always on the verge of tears, though never quite crossing over into the real thing. His shoulders were stooped because, tall as he was, he had to bend over to communicate with the common ruck. He gave me a smile, which for him consisted of raising the corners of his mouth from the vicinity of his chin to a nearly horizontal position. I hoisted my own mug in reply.

But no sooner had I taken the first, bitter sip than I heard Doc Mooney, on the far side of the oval bar, complain. In itself, this was no unusual thing, since complaint is the blood and spit of the man. But the nature of his complaint was more than a little out of the ordinary.

"Which of ye spalpeens," he cried, "has taken my jaw-bone?"

Danny Mulloney, sitting two stools to his left, looked at him. "Why, no one, you omadhaun, seeing as how you're still flapping it."

Doc gave him the squint-eye. "It's not my own jawbone I'm speaking of, ye lout; as you would know if you applied what little thought you have to it; but the jawbone we keep at the medical school for purposes of demonstration. I had put it in my pocket when I left for the day."

"Ah," said Danny with a sad shake of his head, "and I would hate to be your wife, then, after turning out your pockets for the laundering. Sure, a pathologist should never take his work home with him."

There was a ripple of laughter at our end of the bar. I confess that I smiled, myself, though it is my constant purpose never to encourage the wit of Danny Mulloney.

Doc turned a shade darker and tapped the bar top with a

stiff finger. "I had set it right there, and now it is gone. Someone has taken it."

"You weren't thinking of leaving it as a tip, Doc?" I asked, getting into the spirit of the thing.

Doc gave me a look of betrayal. *Et tu, Mickey?* But Himself spoke up, a twinkle in his eye. "It would depend, I'm thinking, on how many teeth were yet in the jaw. Placed under my pillow, it might draw a tidy sum from the wee folk."

Hennesey only shook his head at the blathering of mortals. "Now, who would wish to steal such a thing?" he asked, *contrabasso.*

"Samson," Danny suggested, "were there any Philistines about?" Danny being of a religious frame of mind, a Biblical example came most naturally to him.

Doc, who knows a little of Scripture himself, leaned past the poor man who sat between him and Danny and consequently had to listen to the argument with both his ears, and said sweetly, "Nor is it your own jawbone we're speaking of."

"There is too much foam," said the man sitting between them.

Both Danny and Doc pulled away, puzzled at the nonce of the sequitur. Himself reared up. "Too much foam, d'you say? Why, I give honest measure; and the man who says I do not is a liar."

The man blinked several times. "What? Oh." He glanced at the sturdy glass mug before him. "Oh, no, I did not mean your fine beer. I was responding to this gentleman's question concerning his jawbone. I meant the quantum foam."

Hennesey scratched his jaw. "The quantum foam, is it? And that would be an Australian beer?"

"No. I mean the timelessness that came 'before' the Big Bang. We call it the quantum foam."

O Daugherty drew a fresh mug and set it down with a flourish before the man. "Sure and it is worth the price of a good pint to hear what connection there might be between the Big Bang and Doc Mooney's jawbone."

Doc protested again, "It's not *my* jawbone," but no one paid him any heed.

"Well," said the man, "not to the jawbone, but to the *disappearance* of the jawbone." He seemed hesitant and a little sad. For a moment, he managed to make even Hennesey look cheerful. Then he sighed and picked up the mug. "It's like this," he said.

"My name is Owen fitzHugh. I am a physicist at the University, but my hobby has always been the oddities of the Universe. Quirks, as well as quarks, as a colleague of mine has remarked . . .

"One of these quirks is what I call 'phantom recollections' and 'causeless objects.' Non-Thomistic events, if you must have a fine philosophical name for it. Have you ever looked in vain, as your friend here, for an object you clearly recall having placed in a certain spot? Or, conversely, found small objects for which you cannot account? Or recalled telephone numbers or appointments that turned out not to exist?"

"I had a key on my key chain, once," said Maura Lafferty, "that I did not recognize and that fit no lock that I own. I still have no idea where it came from."

"I had a date one time with Bridey Lynch," said Danny, "but when I called on her, she had no recollection of it."

Doc made an evil grin. "Why, there is no mystery at all in that."

FitzHugh nodded. "They are usually small objects or bits of information, these anomalies of mine. Usually, when we notice them at all, we ascribe them to a faulty recollection; but I'm a natural contrarian. I wondered: What if it is the Universe, and not ourselves, that sometimes forgets."

Danny and Doc flanked the poor man with a bookend of skeptical looks. Danny, I was sure, believed in God's Infallible Memory; while Doc reasoned from the predictability of Natural Law. Still their thoughts had come to rest in the same place. Himself shifted his apron and cocked his head in interest. "Now what might that mean?"

"History is contingent," said fitzHugh.

Himself nodded. "Aye, so it is." But Danny scratched his head. "If it is, I've never caught it." Doc leaned past the unfortunate physicist once more.

"He said 'contingent,' not 'contagious.' "

FitzHugh looked at Danny. "I should have said that history is a chain of cause-and-effect," he said. "One event leads to others, and then to still others. Often, great events hinge on small occurrences."

Wilson Cartwright, a history professor at the University, spoke up from the booth behind fitzHugh. "That's gospel truth. In 1862, a Confederate courier lost a copy of Lee's troop dispositions. Two Union foragers found them and McClellan managed—barely—to win the battle of Antietam, which gave Lincoln the opportunity to issue the Emancipation Proclamation. And when the news of the Proclamation reached England, the cabinet reversed its decision to intervene on the Confederate side. In consequence of which . . ." He lifted his drink in salute to the bar. ". . . my great-grandpappy became a free man."

Hennesey nodded. "Da met me Ma in the same way. Another small chance—though the outcome was not so momentous as war and freedom. He was on the run—. This was during the Troubles, when the Big Fella and the Long Fella had their row—bad cess to 'em both—and Da, he found himself in on the wrong side. O Daugherty, you know what I'm speakin' of, and enough has been said about that. Da took himself to the Waterford hills and, finding himself at a crossroads, tossed a coin. The shilling sent him to Ballinahinch, where me ol' Gran was keeping a pub in those days and Ma waited tables. Now Da was not the man to pass a pub without a drop of the creature, so he stopped and . . ." The man's long, doughy face turned a deep red. ". . . here I am. Had the shilling read tails, he was a dead man, for his enemies were waiting down the other road. As it was, what with one thing and another . . ." And he pointed with his drooping chin to the photograph on the wall opposite, where a far younger Hennesey and O Daugherty stood side by side in black-and-white, stern-faced splendor, arms crossed and legs akimbo before the newly opened Irish Pub.

Doc Mooney raised his pint. "I have always thought you an unlikely man, Hennesey."

"But that's just the point," fitzHugh said. "*Everything* is unlikely . . . and therefore fragile."

" 'Fragile,' " said Himself. "A curious word."

"Fragile," said fitzHugh with an affirmative nod. "Because the slightest bump and. . . . You see, the quantum foam is subject to sudden, spontaneous disturbances. These create 'probability waves' in the continuum that propagate down the time stream creating a new past. The old past is obliterated. As it was in the beginning, is not, and never more shall be."

Himself scowled a bit at the altered quotation, but Danny Mulloney brightened, which is always a bad sign. "Do you mean to say," he said. "Do you mean to say that all those dinosaur fossils and such might have been put in the ground only a few thousand years ago?"

FitzHugh blinked and looked thoughtful. "Certainly, it's *conceivable*," he said slowly. "Yes. Suppose that evolution originally followed a different course—perhaps those strange Burgess Shale creatures I've read of won out over our own familiar phyla, and after a time strange *things* stalked the Earth of sixty million years ago—things that never held the promise of man. Then, a bubble bursts in the foam and a probability wave ripples down the timeline—and now dinosaurs leave their bones in the mud instead of things with no names. So, yes, in one sense, this new past could have been laid down a few thousand years ago; but in another sense, once it had been laid down, it had *always* been there."

Danny pursed his lips, for I do not think he had envisioned a *different* evolution when he raised his question. Meanwhile, a ripple of wisely nodding heads showed the incomprehension propagating around the oval bar. FitzHugh noticed and said, "Perhaps a sketch will clear it up." He seized a napkin and immediately began to doodle on it. Sitting as I was on the far side, I could not see what he sketched and Hennesey, noting my frustration, waved me inside the Sacred Oval. "Here," he said, handing me a bar apron. " 'Tis a busy night and we can use the help." Then he set off to the front end of the bar to tend to the raging thirst there.

Tying the apron, I stepped across in time to hear fitzHugh say, "This was the continuum in its original state." I glanced at the napkin and saw he had written:

$$A \rightarrow \quad B \rightarrow \quad C$$

"Then, a quantum disturbance alters event A to event A*. A stray chronon—a quantum of time—emitted from the foam, strikes like a billiard ball." He turned to Dr. Cartwright, who had left his booth to stand behind him. "Perhaps your Confederate courier, Wilson, doesn't drop his packet." He held up the napkin again.

$$A^* \quad B \rightarrow \quad C \rightarrow \quad D$$

The big historian looked thoughtful, and nodded. Maura Lafferty, who had also joined the little group at the back end of the bar, leaned over the man's shoulder. "Why did you add the 'D'?"

"Oh, time doesn't stop just because there is a bit of re-decorating going on," fitzHugh said. "The present is . . . call it the 'bow wave' of the Big Bang, plowing through *formlessness* and leaving *time* in its wake. But behind it is coming the 'bow wave' of the *new* version, altering all the original consequences of A. When the wave front reaches B, event B 'unhappens.' Something else—call it G—happens instead."

$$A^* \overset{\rightarrow}{} \quad \cancel{B}^{G} \quad C \rightarrow \quad D \rightarrow \quad E$$

"Why G?" Danny asked, frowning over the sketch. "Why not call it B?"

"It doesn't matter what he calls it, ye spalpeen," said Doc Mooney.

FitzHugh grimaced. "Actually, it does. I don't want to imply that B happens *differently*—because it might not happen at all."

Cartwright bobbed his head. "That's right. If McClellan hadn't intercepted Lee's orders, it wouldn't have changed the outcome of Antietam. There wouldn't have *been* a battle at Antietam. McClellan only attacked there because he had Lee's orders. Without them, there would have been a different battle at some other time and place."

I scratched my head. "So why didn't you alter C, D and E?"

"Because the wave front hasn't 'caught up' to them yet." He busied himself at the napkin. "Here, this is then next quantum of time, the next parasecond."

$$A^* \rightarrow \quad B^{G} \rightarrow \quad C^{H} \rightarrow \quad D^{I} \quad E \rightarrow \quad F$$

"You'll notice that the original causal chain is still propagating itself, and event E has led to event F. But the revision is catching up. Change waves move faster than one second per second—just as water moves faster down a channel already dug than it does across virgin ground—but you really need two different kinds of time to talk about it intelligently. Eventually, the change wave reaches the present, merges into the original Big Bang wave, and the revision is complete." He held the napkin up one last time.

$$A^* \rightarrow \quad B^{G} \rightarrow \quad C^{H} \rightarrow \quad D^{I} \rightarrow \quad E^{J} \rightarrow \quad F^{K} \rightarrow \quad L$$

"Even our memories are reconfigured," he said. "The right ripple and . . . who knows? We might be sitting here discussing Lee's victory."

"*You* might be," said Cartwright dryly.

Doc Mooney rubbed his chin and frowned. "I see a problem," he said. He spoke with a chuckle, as if he suspected his leg of being pulled. "If our memories are reconfigured, how could we possibly know the past was ever different?"

The shadow passed over fitzHugh's face once more. "Normally . . . we wouldn't."

Doc Mooney slapped his forehead. "Now, I am an old fool. I had *started* to put the jawbone into my jacket pocket, then I laid it back on my desk." Defiance flashed. "And it has been sitting back there in the lab, all along," he insisted.

FitzHugh nodded with solemn fish-eyes. "Yes. Though perhaps not 'all along.' If at the very moment you laid the jawbone on the bar, a change wave 'caught up' with the present, you would have for a bare instant two conflicting memories. A fragment of the original memory can survive and you sit here at 'L' remembering a bit of 'F,' instead of 'K.' The French have a word for it . . ." He snapped his fingers, searching for the word.

"*Merde?*" suggested Doc innocently.

"*Déjà vu?*" said Maura.

FitzHugh shook his head. "No. *Déjà vu* is when the change wave does not affect your own personal history, so instead of a fossil memory, you have an instant of remembering the same thing twice." He looked at each of us, and it seemed to me that his eyes held immeasurable loneliness in them. "That's why these phantom memories almost always involve trivia." He shrugged, looked off at the corner. "Only an idle fancy. Who can say?"

Himself lifted fitzHugh's now-empty mug and cradled it in his hands. He gave the physicist an intent look. "*Almost* always," he said, with a suggestive pause at the end.

FitzHugh shook his head and gestured at the mug. "Another, please."

"Perhaps," said Himself, "it would be better if you let it pour out instead of in."

("What's he mean?" Danny asked. "Wisht," said Doc.)

Someone put "The Reconciliation Reel" on the juke box and fitzHugh winced as the wild skirling of whistles and fiddles filled the room. Some of the old neighborhood shouted Hoo! and began to clap their hands. "You'll think I'm a fool. Deluded."

Himself shrugged. "Does it matter if we do?"

"Sure," said Doc Mooney, "we all think that Danny here is a deluded fool; but that doesn't stop me from buying him a beer now and then."

Danny, who could be quick on the uptake when the stakes were high, held his mug out to me and said, "You heard him."

Sure, it is not often that Doc is hoist by his own petard, but he had the good grace to accept it cheerfully. While I filled Danny's mug, fitzHugh looked on some inner place in his soul.

"You see," fitzHugh said finally, "the brain stores memories both holographically and associatively. Because the memory is a hologram, one may recapture the entirety from a surviving fragment; and because they are 'filed' associatively, one recovered memory may lead to others. These shards of overwritten memories lie embedded in our minds like junk genes in our DNA, an explanation perhaps for stories of 'past lives'; for false memory syndrome; or for inexplicable fugues or personality changes or . . . Or. . . ." He paused again and shuddered. "Ah, God, what have I done?"

"Something," O Daugherty suggested, "that needs a hearing."

"From the likes of you?"

Himself took no offense. "From the likes of us," he agreed, "or the likes of Father McDevitt."

FitzHugh bowed his head. There had been fear in his eye, and sorrow, and despair. I wondered what odd confession we were about to hear, and ourselves with no power to bind or loose. Maura placed a hand on his arm. "Go on," she urged. Cartwright rumbled something encouraging and Danny had God's grace to keep his mouth shut.

Finally, fitzHugh drew a shuddering breath and blew it out through pursed lips. "A man cannot be responsible for something that never happened, can he?"

Himself shrugged. "Responsibility is a rare thing in any case: a bastard child, often denied."

"It started with a dream," fitzHugh said.

"Such things often do. And end there, too."

"I'm not married," fitzHugh said. "I never have been. There have been women from time to time, and we get along well enough; but there was never one to settle down with. Always it was too early to wed; until it became too late."

"It's never too late," O Daugherty said, "when the right one comes along."

FitzHugh's smile was faint. "That's the very problem, you see. It may be that she did, once. But . . ." Melancholy closed his face again and he inhaled a long, slow breath. "I live alone in a house in the middle of the block over by Thirteenth Street. It's a little large for my needs and the neighborhood is not the best, but the price was right and I enjoy the puttering. There is a parlor, a dining room and kitchen, plus two bedrooms, one of which I use as an office. From the kitchen, a stairway leads to a rough, unfinished basement.

"Recently, I began to have a recurring dream. It always starts the same way. I walk through my kitchen to the back stairwell and go down, not to my own basement, but to another house entirely, where I walk past empty bedrooms, then a kitchen with dishes piled in the sink and a greasy patina to the stove, coming at last to a parlor containing comfortable, out-of-style furniture. There are large windows on two of the walls and, in the corner, a front door. The whole of it has such an air of dust and neglect and familiarity and long abandonment that I often find myself reduced inexplicably to tears when I awake."

"It was your subconscious," said Doc, "playing with that unfinished basement."

FitzHugh gave a brief shake of the head. "I thought that, too; at first. Only . . . Well, the first few dreams, that was all. Just a silent walk through an empty house accompanied by a feeling of loss, as if I had had these disused rooms all along, but had forgotten about them. Once, I reached the front door before waking up, and stepped outside. An ordinary-looking neighborhood, but no place I've ever seen. The house sat on a slight rise on a corner lot. Not much traffic. If I had to guess, I would say a residential neighborhood in a medium-big city, but somewhere off the major thoroughfares. I travel a great deal, going to conferences and such, but I have never identified that city."

He looked deeply into his ale while the rest of us waited. "The dream had a curious air to it. It felt like a memory more than a dream. Maybe it was the dirty dishes in the sink, or the out-of-date furniture in the parlor." Another quirky smile. "If a dream-world, why so drab and ordinary a one?"

I left the group to answer an urgent call at the front end of the bar, where a shortage of brew threatened several collegians with imminent dehydration. When I returned to the discussion, fitzHugh was answering some question of Doc Mooney's.

". . . so the more I thought about it and puzzled over it, the more real it grew in my mind. I remembered things I never actually saw in the dream. It seemed to me that the sink ought to have separate hot and cold water faucets. And that upstairs there would be an office and a sewing room and another bedroom. So you see, the details had the *texture* of memory. How could I remember those things unless they were real?"

Doc pulled the squint-eye like he always does. I think he still suspected some elaborate joke at his expense. "Imagination can be as detailed as memory. Your dream left blanks and you began to fill them in."

FitzHugh nodded. "That's an answer I yearn for. If only I could embrace it."

"What happened next?" Himself prompted. "There must be more to it than you've told to account for such a melancholy."

The physicist drew a deep breath. "One evening, reading at home, I became acutely aware of the silence. Now I am a man that likes his solitude and his peace and quiet; but just for a moment the silence seemed *wrong,* and I wondered, *What's he up to?*"

"Who?" asked Danny. "What was *who* up to?"

FitzHugh shook his head. "I didn't know, then. But I glanced at the ceiling as I wondered, even though there is nothing up there but a crawlspace and storage. And then I heard a woman's voice."

"A woman, was it?" said Himself. "And saying what?"

"I don't know. I couldn't make out the words, only the tone of voice. I knew that I had been addressed, and inexplicably my heart both soared and sank. I can't explain it any other way. It was as if I had been yearning for that voice and dreading it, all at once.

"Well," he continued, "associative memory means that one recovered memory can lead to others; and having found a fragment of one hologram, other fragments began to surface in my mind. I had only to close my eyes and imagine the phantom house. With each return, it became more real, and the conviction grew that I *had* lived there at one time, and not alone. Voices—there were two of them—grew more distinct. Often angry, but not always. Once, I'm embarrassed to say, whispering a sexual invitation. And then, one day, I saw her."

He lifted his mug to his lips, but it hovered there without him drinking as he gazed into the dark, reflective surface. "I was puttering in the parlor, sanding down some woodwork in order to stain it. It was the sort of mechanical task that allows the mind to wander. And so mine did, until it seemed to me that I was in the kitchen of my 'secret house,' drying dishes with a towel. A tall, straw-haired woman was standing beside me washing them in the sink. She had the nagging near-familiarity of a once-met stranger. Perhaps I had seen her at a party in college and I never got up the nerve to walk over and introduce myself—only maybe, once, I did. I knew she was angry because she would *shove* the dishes into my hands in that silent-aggressive way that women sometimes use. She bore the harried look of someone once very beautiful but for whom beauty had lately become a chore. No makeup. Hair cropped in the simplest, most 'practical' style. Perhaps she blamed the me-that-was. Later, I remembered cutting remarks. She could have been this, or she could have married that. I don't know why she kept slipping such hurts into our conversation . . ." He smiled ruefully. "But this first time, she turned to me and said very distinctly, 'You have no ambition.'

"I was so startled that I snapped out of my daydream, and there I was, back in my own parlor." He grimaced, ran a finger up and down the condensate on the outside of his glass. "Alone."

"It's only natural," said Doc Mooney, "that a man living alone might grow wistful and imagine a married life he never had."

FitzHugh laughed without humor. "Then why imagine such an unpleasant one?"

"Because you need to feel that you made the right choice."

"You're a psychiatrist, then, and not a pathologist?" The tones were sarcastic and Doc flushed red. FitzHugh fell into a brown study, and fixed his eyes on the far wall. The rest of us, supposing the story had come to an unsatisfying conclusion, went about our own affairs: O Daugherty and myself to filling glasses and the others to emptying them, which division of labor made for an efficient process. Once or twice, I glanced at fitzHugh, noted his unfocused eyes, and wondered on what inner landscape he gazed. There were tears in the rims of his eyes. When he lifted his glass to me and signalled, I gave Himself a look and he gave me the high sign, so I switched fitzHugh's drink to a non-alcoholic beer. I don't think the man ever noticed.

"I had a son," he told me when I handed him the freshened glass. No one spoke. Doc, from wounded pride; Danny, because of a firm headshake I gave him.

"A son, was it?" said Himself. "Sure, that's a comfort to a man."

FitzHugh made a face. "Lenny was anything but a comfort. Sullen, secretive. Seldom home, even for meals. Lisa blamed me for that, too."

"He was a teenager, then."

FitzHugh started and a rueful smile curled his lips. "Yes. He was. Is that normal behavior for that age? For the sake of other parents, I hope not. I've remembered flashes of him mouthing off, and once or twice I've even heard echoes of the foul words he used. I've another memory of a policeman standing in the front door holding Lenny by the arm and lecturing me." He sighed. "Sometimes I wished we had never met, Lisa and I; and that I had married someone else and had different children; that, well . . . that everything had turned out better than it had."

"Then it was good fortune," I said, "that some bubble in the foam erased it."

FitzHugh was a big man; not muscular exactly, but not frail-looking, either. Yet, he gave me a desolate look and laid his head on his arms and began to weep. O Daugherty and myself traded glances and Wilson Cartwright said, "I know where he lives. I'll drive him home." FitzHugh raised his head.

"Sometimes, I remember other things. Huddled over a

kitchen table with Lisa, planning a future full of hope. A young boy bursting with laughter showing me a horse he had modeled out of clay. A camping trip in the Appalachians. Holding hands in a movie theater. Fleeting moments of simple pleasures. The joy had all leaked out, but once upon a time . . . Once upon a time, there had been joy."

A wretched tale, for who among us has not known friend or family in a like situation? Sure, the wine may turn to vinegar in the bottle. And yet, who can forget how sweet it once tasted?

Himself nodded as he wiped a glass clean. "Are you ready to tell us now?"

FitzHugh grunted, as if struck. His eyes darted about our little group and found me. "It was no chance bubble," he said, shaking his head sadly.

That startled me. "Then, what—?"

"I don't know what sort of research my dream-self was doing. I recall enough tantalizing bits to realize it was down a different avenue than I've explored. But I do remember one especially vivid dream. I had built a chronon projector."

Doc Mooney snorted, but Himself only nodded, as if he had expected it. Maura Lafferty wrinkled up her forehead and asked, "What's a chronon projector?"

Frustration laced the physicist's voice. "I'm not sure. A device to excite time quanta, I think. Into the past, of course. There's nothing but formlessness futureward of the bow wave. Perhaps I had some notion of sending messages to warn of tornados or disasters. I don't know. The projector was only a prototype, capable only of emitting a single chronon to a single locus. Enough to create a ripple in the pond; not enough to encode a message." He upended his mug and drained it and set it down hard on the bar top. "Call it a 'cue stick,' if you wish. Something to send a billiard ball into the packed chronons of yesterday and start random ricochets of cause and effect.

"Yesterday, I had no classes to teach, so I stayed home to paint my dining room. I was thinking about mutable time; and I had my hand raised, so." And he held his right hand just before his face. "There must have been some congruence of my train of thought and my posture, because in that instant I was standing in a lab before some great machine and my hand was gripping a switch, and I remember . . . Lisa and I had had an argument over Lenny, and I remember . . . I remember thinking that if I projected the chronon to the locus when Lisa and I met—to that time and place—I could create a ripple in the Dirac Sea, a disturbance in the probabilities and . . . It would all never have happened. None of it. The heartache, the bitching, the sullen anger—" He fell silent.

Himself prompted him. "And . . . ?"

"And I awoke in a strange house, silent and alone." He looked a long way off, seeing what, I do not know. Himself laid a hand on his arm.

"Wisht. What you had, you lost well before you threw the switch."

FitzHugh grabbed O Daugherty's hand and held it tight. "But, don't you see? I lost all the hope, too. The memories of all the joy that went before; of a bright-eyed five-year-old whose smile could light the room. Of the possibility that Lisa and I might have worked it through." He and O Daugherty exchanged a long, mutual look. "I owed her that, didn't I? I owed it to her to try to solve our problems and not abolish them as things that never were."

"Sure," said Himself, "the bad comes mingled with the good; and if you excise the first, you lose the other as well."

"There's one thing I hold on to," fitzHugh said.

"And what's that?"

"That Lisa—whoever she is, from whichever college mixer or classroom where we never met—that in this revision, she's had a better life than the one I gave her. I hold that hope tight as a shield against my crime."

"Crime?" said Danny. "What crime was that?"

FitzHugh wiped his eyes with the sleeve of his jacket. "Lenny. He was never born. He'll never have a chance to grow out of his rebellion and become a better person. Lisa is out there somewhere. Lisa has . . . possibilities. But there is no Lenny. There never was that bright-eyed five-year-old. There never will be. When I disturbed the time-stream, I wiped him out. I obliterated his life: all the hopes and fears and hates and joys . . . All the *possibilities* that were him. How is that so different from murder?"

The silence grew long.

Then fitzHugh pushed himself away from the bar and stood a little uneasily. Alarmed, Professor Cartwright took him by the elbow to steady him. FitzHugh looked at the rest of us. "But it all never happened, right? There oughtn't be any guilt over something that never happened."

It was Danny who spoke—hesitantly, and with more kindness than I had looked for. "Could you not build another of those chronon projectors and aim it back and correct what you did . . . ?" But he trailed off at the end, as if he already suspected what the answer must be.

FitzHugh turned haunted eyes on him. "No. History is contingent. There's no chance that a random disturbance to the revision would recreate the original. You may break the pack on a pool table with a well-aimed shot. You cannot bring the balls back together with another." Cartwright guided him to the door, and the rest of us watched in silence.

"The poor man," said Maura, when he had gone.

O Daugherty rapped hard on the maple counter top, as if testing its solidity. "So fragile," he said, almost to himself. "Who knows if another time wave might be roaring down on us even now, a vast tsunami to wash all of us away?"

The O Neil returned from the back room with a glower on his face. "Ireland will get the Six Counties back before I get that pool table," he said. "Let's go on back to the house, Mickey."

"I'll catch you later," I told him. "It's a busy night and Himself can use the help as much as I can use the cash."

The O Neil shook his head. "O Daugherty, you need to take on a partner, and that's a fact."

Himself shrugged and served him a parting glass of black Guinness. "Someday, maybe," he said. Me, I glanced over at the photograph on the wall, where O Daugherty stood, arms crossed and legs akimbo, before his newly opened pub; and it seemed to me, though I don't know why, that the picture was all out of kilter, as if something large were missing.

Seventy-Two Letters

TED CHIANG

Ted Chiang is a technical writer who occasionally writes short SF that is then usually nominated for, or the winner of, awards. He is a private person whose short bio goes like this: "Ted Chiang was born in Port Jefferson, New York, and currently lives in Bellevue, Washington. Of his nonfiction, written in his capacity as a technical writer, perhaps the most popular is the C++ Tutorial packaged with certain versions of Microsoft's C++ compiler. He reads some comics, enjoys going to the movies, and watches television more than is good for him." He has published four previous SF stories, all of which are distinctive and highly accomplished.

"Seventy-Two Letters" is another piece (see the Bell, page 85) that was published in Vanishing Acts, *edited by Ellen Datlow. Although it is only tangentially related to the theme of the anthology, it is certainly one of the best stories in a strong book. It is in that small category of alternate science alternate history fiction pioneered a few years ago by Richard Garfinkle (in his novel* Celestial Matters). *The story takes place in an alternate 19th Century. In this case, as critic Mark Kelly notes, various medieval scientific theories such as the doctrine of preformation, which supposed that fetuses existed fully formed inside the sperm or eggs of their parents, are real. In a year of excellent novellas, none was better than this.*

When he was a child, Robert's favorite toy was a simple one, a clay doll that could do nothing but walk forward. While his parents entertained their guests in the garden outside, discussing Victoria's ascension to the throne or the Chartist reforms, Robert would follow the doll as it marched down the corridors of the family home, turning it around corners or back where it came from. The doll didn't obey commands or exhibit any sense at all; if it met a wall, the diminutive clay figure would keep marching until it gradually mashed its arms and legs into misshapen flippers. Sometimes Robert would let it do that, strictly for his own amusement. Once the doll's limbs were thoroughly distorted, he'd pick the toy up and pull the name out, stopping its motion in mid-stride. Then he'd knead the body back into a smooth lump, flatten it out into a plank, and cut out a different figure: a body with one leg crooked, or longer than the other. He would stick the name back into it, and the doll would promptly topple over and push itself around in a little circle.

It wasn't the sculpting that Robert enjoyed; it was mapping out the limits of the name. He liked to see how much variation he could impart to the body before the name could no longer animate it. To save time with the sculpting, he rarely added decorative details; he refined the bodies only as was needed to test the name.

Another of his dolls walked on four legs. The body was a nice one, a finely detailed porcelain horse, but Robert was more interested in experimenting with its name. This name obeyed commands to start and stop and knew enough to avoid obstacles, and Robert tried inserting it into bodies of his own making. But this name had more exacting body requirements, and he was never able to form a clay body it could animate. He formed the legs separately and then attached them to the body, but he wasn't able to blend the seams smooth enough; the name didn't recognize the body as a single continuous piece.

He scrutinized the names themselves, looking for some simple substitutions that might distinguish two-leggedness from four-leggedness, or make the body obey simple commands. But the names looked entirely different; on each scrap of parchment were inscribed seventy-two tiny Hebrew letters, arranged in twelve rows of six, and so far as he could tell, the order of the letters was utterly random.

Robert Stratton and his fourth form classmates sat quietly as Master Trevelyan paced between the rows of desks.

"Langdale, what is the doctrine of names?"

"All things are reflections of God, and, um, all—"

"Spare us your bumbling. Thorburn, can *you* tell us the doctrine of names?"

"As all things are reflections of God, so are all names reflections of the divine name."

"And what is an object's true name?"

"That name which reflects the divine name in the same manner as the object reflects God."

"And what is the action of a true name?"

"To endow its object with a reflection of divine power."

"Correct. Halliwell, what is the doctrine of signatures?"

The natural philosophy lesson continued until noon, but because it was a Saturday, there was no instruction for the rest of the day. Master Trevelyan dismissed the class, and the boys of Cheltenham school dispersed.

After stopping at the dormitory, Robert met his friend Lionel at the border of school grounds. "So the wait's over? Today's the day?" Robert asked.

"I said it was, didn't I?"

"Let's go, then." The pair set off to walk the mile and a half to Lionel's home.

During his first year at Cheltenham, Robert had known Lionel hardly at all; Lionel was one of the day-boys, and Robert, like all the boarders, regarded them with suspicion. Then, purely by chance, Robert ran into him while on holiday, during a visit to the British Museum. Robert loved the museum: the frail mummies and immense sarcophagi; the stuffed platypus and pickled mermaid; the wall bristling with elephant tusks and moose antlers and unicorn horns. That particular day he was at the display of elemental sprites: He was reading the card explaining the salamander's absence when he suddenly recognized Lionel, standing right next to him, peering at the undine in its jar. Conversation revealed their shared interest in the sciences, and the two became fast friends.

As they walked down the road, they kicked a large pebble back and forth between them. Lionel gave the pebble a kick, and laughed as it skittered between Robert's ankles. "I couldn't wait to get out of there," he said. "I think one more doctrine would have been more than I could bear."

"Why do they even bother calling it natural philosophy?" said Robert. "Just admit it's another theology lesson and be done with it." The two of them had recently purchased *A Boy's Guide to Nomenclature*, which informed them that nomenclators no longer spoke in terms of God or the divine name. Instead, current thinking held that there was a lexical universe as well as a physical one, and bringing an object together with a compatible name caused the latent potentialities of both to be realized. Nor was there a single "true name" for a given object: Depending on its precise shape, a body might be compatible with several names, known as its ["euonyms,"] and conversely a simple name might tolerate significant variations in body shape, as his childhood marching doll had demonstrated.

When they reached Lionel's home, they promised the cook they would be in for dinner shortly and headed to the garden out back. Lionel had converted a tool shed in his family's garden into a laboratory, which he used to conduct experiments. Normally Robert came by on a regular basis, but recently Lionel had been working on an experiment that he was keeping secret. Only now was he ready to show Robert his results. Lionel had Robert wait outside while he entered first, and then let him enter.

A long shelf ran along every wall of the shed, crowded with racks of vials, stoppered bottles of green glass, and assorted rocks and mineral specimens. A table decorated with stains and scorch marks dominated the cramped space, and it supported the apparatus for Lionel's latest experiment: a cucurbit clamped in a stand so that its bottom rested in a basin full of water, which in turn sat on a tripod above a lit oil lamp. A mercury thermometer was also fixed in the basin.

"Take a look," said Lionel.

Robert leaned over to inspect the cucurbit's contents. At first it appeared to be nothing more than foam, a dollop of suds that might have dripped off a pint of stout. But as he looked closer, he realized that what he thought were bubbles were actually the interstices of a glistening latticework. The froth consisted of *homunculi*: tiny seminal foetuses. Their bodies were transparent individually, but collectively their bulbous heads and strand-like limbs adhered to form a pale, dense foam.

"So you wanked off into a jar and kept the spunk warm?" he asked, and Lionel shoved him. Robert laughed and raised his hands in a placating gesture. "No, honestly, it's a wonder. How'd you do it?"

Mollified, Lionel said, "It's a real balancing act. You have to keep the temperature just right, of course, but if you want them to grow, you also have to keep just the right mix of nutrients. Too thin a mix, and they starve. Too rich, and they get over-lively and start fighting with each other."

"You're having me on."

"It's the truth; look it up if you don't believe me. Battles amongst sperm are what cause monstrosities to be born. If an injured foetus is the one that makes it to the egg, the baby that's born is deformed."

"I thought that was because of a fright the mother had

when she was carrying." Robert could just make out the miniscule squirmings of the individual foetuses. He realized that the froth was ever so slowly roiling as a result of their collective motions.

"That's only for some kinds, like ones that are all hairy or covered in blotches. Babies that don't have arms or legs, or have misshapen ones, they're the ones that got caught in a fight back when they were sperm. That's why you can't provide too rich a broth, especially if they haven't any place to go: They get in a frenzy. You can lose all of them pretty quick that way."

"How long can you keep them growing?"

"Probably not much longer," said Lionel. "It's hard to keep them alive if they haven't reached an egg. I read about one in France that was grown till it was the size of a fist, and they had the best equipment available. I just wanted was to see if I could do it at all."

Robert stared at the foam, remembering the doctrine of preformation that Master Trevelyan had drilled into them: All living things had been created at the same time, long ago, and births today were merely enlargements of the previously imperceptible. Although they appeared newly created, these *homunculi* were countless years old; for all of human history they had lain nested within generations of their ancestors, waiting for their turn to be born.

In fact, it wasn't just them who had waited; he himself must have done the same thing prior to his birth. If his father were to do this experiment, the tiny figures Robert saw would be his unborn brothers and sisters. He knew they were insensible until reaching an egg, but he wondered what thoughts they'd have if they weren't. He imagined the sensation of his body, every bone and organ soft and clear as gelatin, sticking to those of myriad identical siblings. What would it be like, looking through transparent eyelids, realizing the mountain in the distance was actually a person, recognizing it as his brother? What if he knew he'd become as massive and solid as that colossus, if only he could reach an egg? It was no wonder they fought.

*   *   *

Robert Stratton went on to read nomenclature at Cambridge's Trinity College. There he studied kabbalistic texts written centuries before, when nomenclators were still called *ba'alei shem* and automata were called *golem*, texts that laid the foundation for the science of names: the *Sefer Yezirah*, Eleazar of Worms' *Sodei Razayya*, Abulafia's *Hayyei ha-Olam ha-Ba*. Then he studied the alchemical treaties that placed the techniques of alphabetic manipulation in a broader philosophical and mathematical context: Llull's *Ars Magna*, Agrippa's *De Occulta Philosophia*, Dee's *Monas Hieroglyphica*.

He learned that every name was a combination of several epithets, each designating a specific trait or capability. Epithets were generated by compiling all the words that described the desired trait: cognates and etymons, from languages both living and extinct. By selectively substituting and permuting letters, one could distill from those words their common essence, which was the epithet for that trait. In certain instances, epithets could be used as the bases for triangulation, allowing one to derive epithets for traits undescribed in any language. The entire process relied on intuition as much as formulae; the ability to choose the best letter permutations was an unteachable skill.

He studied the modern techniques of nominal integration and factorization, the former being the means by which a set of epithets—pithy and evocative—were commingled into the seemingly random string of letters that made up a name, the latter by which a name was decomposed into its constituent epithets. Not every method of integration had a matching factorization technique: A powerful name might be refactored to yield a set of epithets different from those used to generate it, and those epithets were often useful for that reason. Some names resisted refactorization, and nomenclators strove to develop new techniques to penetrate their secrets.

Nomenclature was undergoing something of a revolution during this time. There had long been two classes of names: those for animating a body, and those functioning as amulets. Health amulets were worn as protection from injury or illness, while others rendered a house resistant to fire or a ship less likely to founder at sea. Of late, however, the distinction between these categories of names was becoming blurred, with exciting results.

The nascent science of thermodynamics, which established the interconvertibility of heat and work, had recently explained how automata gained their motive power by absorbing heat from their surroundings. Using this improved understanding of heat, a *Namenmeister* in Berlin had developed a new class of amulet that caused a body to absorb heat from one location and release it in another. Refrigeration employing such amulets was simpler and more efficient than that based on the evaporation of a volatile fluid, and had immense commercial application. Amulets were likewise facilitating the improvement of automata: An Edinburgh nomenclator's research into the amulets that prevented objects from becoming lost had led him to patent a household automaton able to return objects to their proper places.

Upon graduation, Stratton took up residence in London and secured a position as a nomenclator at Coade Manufactory, one of the leading makers of automata in England.

Stratton's most recent automaton, cast from plaster of paris, followed a few paces behind him as he entered the factory building. It was an immense brick structure with skylights for its roof; half of the building was devoted to casting metal, the other half to ceramics. In either section, a meandering path connected the various rooms, each one housing the next step in transforming raw materials into finished automata. Stratton and his automaton entered the ceramics portion.

They walked past a row of low vats in which the clay was mixed. Different vats contained different grades of clay, ranging from common red clay to fine white kaolin, resembling enormous mugs abrim with liquid chocolate or heavy cream; only the strong mineral smell broke the illusion. The paddles stirring the clay were connected by gears to a drive shaft, mounted just beneath the skylights, that ran the length of the room. At the end of the room stood an automatous engine: a castiron giant that cranked the drive wheel tirelessly. Walking past, Stratton could detect a faint coolness in the air as the engine drew heat from its surroundings.

The next room held the molds for casting. Chalky white shells bearing the inverted contours of various automata were stacked along the walls. In the central portion of the room, apron-clad journeymen sculptors worked singly and in pairs, tending the cocoons from which automata were hatched.

The sculptor nearest him was assembling the mold for a putter, a broad-headed quadruped employed in the mines for pushing trolleys of ore. The young man looked up from his work. "Were you looking for someone, sir?" he asked.

"I'm to meet Master Willoughby here," replied Stratton.

"Pardon, I didn't realize. I'm sure he'll be here shortly." The journeyman returned to his task. Harold Willoughby was a Master Sculptor First-Degree; Stratton was consulting him on the design of a reusable mold for casting his automaton. While he waited, Stratton strolled idly amongst the molds. His automaton stood motionless, ready for its next command.

Willoughby entered from the door to the metalworks, his face flushed from the heat of the foundry. "My apologies for being late, Mr. Stratton," he said. "We've been working toward a large bronze for some weeks now, and today was the pour. You don't want to leave the lads alone at a time like that."

"I understand completely," replied Stratton.

Wasting no time, Willoughby strode over to the new automaton. "Is this what you've had Moore doing all these months?" Moore was the journeyman assisting Stratton on his project.

Stratton nodded. "The boy does good work." Following Stratton's requests, Moore had fashioned countless bodies, all variations on a single basic theme, by applying modeling clay to an armature, and then used them to create plaster casts on which Stratton could test his names.

Willoughby inspected the body. "Some nice detail; looks straightforward enough—hold on now." He pointed to the automaton's hands: Rather than the traditional paddle or mitten design, with fingers suggested by grooves in the surface, these were fully formed, each one having a thumb and four distinct and separate fingers. "You don't mean to tell me those are functional?"

"That's correct."

Willoughby's skepticism was plain. "Show me."

Stratton addressed the automaton. "Flex your fingers." The automaton extended both hands, flexed and straightened each pair of fingers in turn, and then returned its arms to its sides.

"I congratulate you, Mr. Stratton," said the sculptor. He squatted to examine the automaton's fingers more closely. "The fingers need to be bent at each joint for the name to take?"

"That's right. Can you design a piece mold for such a form?"

Willoughby clicked his tongue several times. "That'll be a tricky bit of business," he said. "We might have to use a waste mold for each casting. Even with a piece mold, these'd be very expensive for ceramic."

"I think they will be worth the expense. Permit me to demonstrate." Stratton addressed to the automaton. "Cast a body; use that mold over there."

The automaton trudged over to a nearby wall and picked up the pieces of the mold Stratton had indicated: It was the mold for a small porcelain messenger. Several journeymen stopped what they were doing to watch the automaton carry the pieces over to a work area. There it fitted the various sections together and bound them tightly with twine. The sculptors' wonderment was apparent as they watched the automaton's fingers work, looping and threading the loose ends of the twine into a knot. Then the automaton stood the assembled mold upright and headed off to get a pitcher of clay slip.

"That's enough," said Willoughby. The automaton stopped its work and resumed its original standing posture. Examining the mold, Willoughby asked, "Did you train it yourself?"

"I did. I hope to have Moore train it in metal casting."

"Do you have names that can learn other tasks?"

"Not as yet. However, there's every reason to believe that an entire class of similar names exists, one for every sort of skill needing manual dexterity."

"Indeed?" Willoughby noticed the other sculptors watching, and called out, "If you've nothing to do, there's plenty I can assign to you." The journeymen promptly resumed their work, and Willoughby turned back to Stratton. "Let us go to your office to speak about this further."

"Very well." Stratton had the automaton follow the two of them back to the frontmost of the complex of connected buildings that was Coade Manufactory. They first entered Stratton's studio, which was situated behind his office proper. Once inside, Stratton addressed the sculptor. "Do you have an objection to my automaton?"

Willoughby looked over a pair of clay hands mounted on a work-table. On the wall behind the table were pinned a series of schematic drawings showing hands in a variety of positions. "You've done an admirable job of emulating the human hand. I am concerned, however, that the first skill in which you trained your new automation is sculpture."

"If you're worried that I am trying to replace sculptors, you needn't be. That is absolutely not my goal."

"I'm relieved to hear it," said Willoughby. "Why did you choose sculpture, then?"

"It is the first step of a rather indirect path. My ultimate goal is to allow automatous engines to be manufactured inexpensively enough so that most families could purchase one."

Willoughby's confusion was apparent. "How, pray tell, would a family make use of an engine?"

"To drive a powered loom, for example."

"What are you going on about?"

"Have you ever seen children who are employed at a textile mill? They are worked to exhaustion; their lungs are clogged with cotton dust; they are so sickly that you can hardly conceive of their reaching adulthood. Cheap cloth is bought at the price of our workers' health; weavers were far better off when textile production was a cottage industry."

"Powered looms were what took weavers out of cottages. How could they put them back in?"

Stratton had not spoken of this before, and welcomed the opportunity to explain. "The cost of automatous engines has always been high, and so we have mills in which scores of looms are driven by an immense coal-heated Goliath. But an automaton like mine could cast engines very cheaply. If a small automatous engine, suitable for driving a few machines, becomes affordable to a weaver and his family, then they can produce cloth from their home as they did once before. People could earn a decent income without being subjected to the conditions of the factory."

"You forget the cost of the loom itself," said Willoughby gently, as if humoring him. "Powered looms are considerably more expensive than the hand looms of old."

"My automata could also assist in the production of cast-iron parts, which would reduce the price of powered looms and other machines. This is no panacea, I know, but I am nonetheless convinced that inexpensive engines offer the chance of a better life for the individual craftsman."

"Your desire for reform does you credit. Let me suggest, however, that there are simpler cures for the social ills you cite: a reduction in working hours, or the improvement of conditions. You do not need to disrupt our entire system of manufacturing."

"I think what I propose is more accurately described as a restoration than a disruption."

Now Willoughby became exasperated. "This talk of returning to a family economy is all well and good, but what would happen to sculptors? Your intentions notwithstanding, these automata of yours would put sculptors out of work. These are men who have undergone years of apprenticeship and training. How would they feed their families?"

Stratton was unprepared for the sharpness in his tone. "You overestimate my skills as a nomenclator," he said, trying to make light. The sculptor remained dour. He continued. "The learning capabilities of these automata are extremely limited. They can manipulate molds, but they could never design them; the real craft of sculpture can be performed only by sculptors. Before our meeting, you had just finished directing several journeymen in the pouring of a large bronze; automata could never work together in such a coordinated fashion. They will perform only rote tasks."

"What kind of sculptors would we produce if they spend their apprenticeship watching automata do their jobs for them? I will not have a venerable profession reduced to a performance by marionettes."

"That is not what would happen," said Stratton, becoming exasperated himself now. "But examine what you yourself are saying: The status that you wish your profession to retain is precisely that which weavers have been made to forfeit. I believe these automata can help restore dignity to other professions, and without great cost to yours."

Willoughby seemed not to hear him. "The very notion that automata would make automata! Not only is the suggestion insulting, it seems ripe for calamity. What of that ballad, the one where the broomsticks carry water buckets and run amuck?"

"You mean 'Der Zauberlehrling'?" said Stratton. "The comparison is absurd. These automata are so far removed from being in a position to reproduce themselves without human participation that I scarcely know where to begin listing the objections. A dancing bear would sooner perform in the London Ballet."

"If you'd care to develop an automaton that can dance the ballet, I would fully support such an enterprise. However, you cannot continue with these dexterous automata."

"Pardon me, sir, but I am not bound by your decisions."

"You'll find it difficult to work without sculptors' cooperation. I shall recall Moore and forbid all the other journeymen from assisting you in any way with this project."

Stratton was momentarily taken aback. "Your reaction is completely unwarranted."

"I think it entirely appropriate."

"In that case, I will work with sculptors at another manufactory."

Willoughby frowned. "I will speak with the head of the

Brotherhood of Sculptors, and recommend that he forbid all of our members from casting your automata."

Stratton could feel his blood rising. "I will not be bullied," he said. "Do what you will, but you cannot prevent me from pursuing this."

"I think our discussion is at an end." Willoughby strode to the door. "Good day to you, Mr. Stratton."

"Good day to you," replied Stratton heatedly.

It was the following day, and Stratton was taking his midday stroll through the district of Lambeth, where Coade Manufactory was located. After a few blocks he stopped at a local market; sometimes among the baskets of writhing eels and blankets spread with cheap watches were automatous dolls, and Stratton retained his boyhood fondness for seeing the latest designs. Today he noticed a new pair of boxing dolls, painted to look like an explorer and a savage. As he looked them over, he could hear nostrum peddlers competing for the attention of a passerby with a runny nose.

"I see your health amulet failed you, sir," said one man whose table was arrayed with small square tins. "Your remedy lies in the curative powers of magnetism, concentrated in Doctor Sedgewick's Polarising Tablets!"

"Nonsense!" retorted an old woman. "What you need is tincture of mandrake, tried and true!" She held out a vial of clear liquid. "The dog wasn't cold yet when this extract was prepared! There's nothing more potent."

Seeing no other new dolls, Stratton left the market and walked on, his thoughts returning to what Willoughby had said yesterday. Without the cooperation of the sculptors' trade-union, he'd have to resort to hiring independent sculptors. He hadn't worked with such individuals before, and some investigation would be required: ostensibly they cast bodies only for use with public-domain names, but for certain individuals these activities disguised patent infringement and piracy, and any association with them could permanently blacken his reputation.

"Mr. Stratton."

Stratton looked up. A small, wiry man, plainly dressed, stood before him. "Yes; do I know you, sir?"

"No, sir. My name is Davies. I'm in the employ of Lord Fieldhurst." He handed Stratton a card bearing the Fieldhurst crest.

Edward Maitland, third earl of Fieldhurst and a noted zoologist and comparative anatomist, was President of the Royal Society. Stratton had heard him speak during sessions of the Royal Society, but they had never been introduced. "What can I do for you?"

"Lord Fieldhurst would like to speak with you, at your earliest convenience, regarding your recent work."

Stratton wondered how the earl had learned of his work. "Why did you not call on me at my office?"

"Lord Fieldhurst prefers privacy in this matter." Stratton raised his eyebrows, but Davies didn't explain further. "Are you available this evening?"

It was an unusual invitation, but an honor nonetheless. "Certainly. Please inform Lord Fieldhurst that I would be delighted."

"A carriage will be outside your building at eight tonight." Davies touched his hat and was off.

At the promised hour, Davies arrived with the carriage. It was a luxurious vehicle, with an interior of lacquered mahogany and polished brass and brushed velvet. The tractor that drew it was an expensive one as well, a steed cast of bronze and needing no driver for familiar destinations.

Davies politely declined to answer any questions while they rode. He was obviously not a man-servant, nor a secretary, but Stratton could not decide what sort of employee he was. The carriage carried them out of London into the countryside, until they reached Darrington Hall, one of the residences owned by the Fieldhurst lineage.

Once inside the home, Davies led Stratton through the foyer and then ushered him into an elegantly appointed study; he closed the doors without entering himself.

Seated at the desk within the study was a barrel-chested man wearing a silk coat and cravat; his broad, deeply creased cheeks were framed by woolly gray muttonchops. Stratton recognized him at once.

"Lord Fieldhurst, it is an honor."

"A pleasure to meet you, Mr. Stratton. You've been doing some excellent work recently."

"You are most kind. I did not realize that my work had become known."

"I make an effort to keep track of such things. Please, tell me what motivated you to develop such automata?"

Stratton explained his plans for manufacturing affordable engines. Fieldhurst listened with interest, occasionally offering cogent suggestions.

"It is an admirable goal," he said, nodding his approval. "I'm pleased to find that you have such philanthropic motives, because I would ask your assistance in a project I'm directing."

"It would be my privilege to help in any way I could."

"Thank you." Fieldhurst's expression became solemn. "This is a matter of grave import. Before I speak further, I must first have your word that you will retain everything I reveal to you in the utmost confidence."

Stratton met the earl's gaze directly. "Upon my honor as a gentleman, sir, I shall not divulge anything you relate to me."

"Thank you, Mr. Stratton. Please come this way." Fieldhurst opened a door in the rear wall of the study and they walked down a short hallway. At the end of the hallway was a laboratory; a long, scrupulously clean work-table held a number of stations, each consisting of a microscope and an articulated brass framework of some sort, equipped with three mutually perpendicular knurled wheels for performing fine adjustments. An elderly man was peering into the microscope at the furthest station; he looked up from his work as they entered.

"Mr. Stratton, I believe you know Dr. Ashbourne."

Stratton, caught off guard, was momentarily speechless. Nicholas Ashbourne had been a lecturer at Trinity when Stratton was studying there, but had left years ago to pursue studies of, it was said, an unorthodox nature. Stratton remembered him as one of his most enthusiastic instructors. Age had narrowed his face somewhat, making his high forehead seem even higher, but his eyes were as bright and alert as ever. He walked over with the help of a carved ivory walking stick.

"Stratton, good to see you again."

"And you, sir. I was truly not expecting to see you here."

"This will be an evening full of surprises, my boy. Prepare yourself." He turned to Fieldhurst. "Would you care to begin?"

They followed Fieldhurst to the far end of the laboratory, where he opened another door and led them down a flight of stairs. "Only a small number of individuals—either Fellows of the Royal Society or Members of Parliament, or both—are privy to this matter. Five years ago, I was contacted confidentially by the Académie des Sciences in Paris. They wished for English scientists to confirm certain experimental findings of theirs."

"Indeed?"

"You can imagine their reluctance. However, they felt the matter outweighed national rivalries, and once I understood the situation, I agreed."

The three of them descended to a cellar. Gas brackets along the walls provided illumination, revealing the cellar's considerable size; its interior was punctuated by an array of stone pillars that rose to form groined vaults. The long cellar contained row upon row of stout wooden tables, each one supporting a tank roughly the size of a bathtub. The tanks were made of zinc and fitted with plate glass windows on all four sides, revealing their contents as a clear, faintly straw-colored fluid.

Stratton looked at the nearest tank. There was a distortion floating in the center of the tank, as if some of the liquid had congealed into a mass of jelly. It was difficult to distinguish the mass's features from the mottled shadows cast on the bottom of the tank, so he moved to another side of the tank and squatted down low to view the mass directly against a flame of a gas lamp. It was then that the coagulum resolved itself into the ghostly figure of a man, clear as aspic, curled up in foetal position.

"Incredible," Stratton whispered.

"We call it a megafoetus," explained Fieldhurst.

"This was grown from a spermatozoon? This must have required decades."

"It did not, more's the wonder. Several years ago, two Parisian naturalists named Dubuisson and Gille developed a method of inducing hypertrophic growth in a seminal foetus. The rapid infusion of nutrients allows such a foetus to reach this size within a fortnight."

By shifting his head back and forth, he saw slight differences in the way the gas-light was refracted, indicating the boundaries of the megafoetus's internal organs. "Is this creature . . . alive?"

"Only in an insensate manner, like a spermatozoon. No artificial process can replace gestation; it is the vital principle within the ovum which quickens the foetus, and the maternal influence which transforms it into a person. All we've done is effect a maturation in size and scale." Fieldhurst gestured toward the megafoetus. "The maternal influence also provides a foetus with pigmentation and all distinguishing physical characteristics. Our megafoetuses have no features beyond their sex. Every male bears the generic appearance you see here, and all the females are likewise identical. Within each sex, it is impossible to distinguish one from another by physical examination, no matter how dissimilar the original fathers might have been; only rigorous record-keeping allows us to identify each megafoetus."

Stratton stood up again. "So what was the intention of the experiment if not to develop an artificial womb?"

"To test the notion of the fixity of species." Realizing that Stratton was not a zoologist, the earl explained further. "Were lens-grinders able to construct microscopes of unlimited magnifying power, biologists could examine the future generations nested in the spermatozoa of any species and see whether their appearance remains fixed, or changes to give rise to a new species. In the latter case, they could also determine if the transition occurs gradually or abruptly.

"However, chromatic aberration imposes an upper limit on the magnifying power of any optical instrument. Messieurs

Dubuisson and Gille hit upon the idea of artificially increasing the size of the foetuses themselves. Once a foetus reaches its adult size, one can extract a spermatozoon from it and enlarge a foetus from the next generation in the same manner." Fieldhurst stepped over to the next table in the row and indicated the tank it supported. "Repetition of the process lets us examine the unborn generations of any given species."

Stratton looked around the room. The rows of tanks took on a new significance. "So they compressed the intervals between 'births' to gain a preliminary view of our genealogical future."

"Precisely."

"Audacious! And what were the results?"

"They tested many animal species, but never observed any changes in form. However, they obtained a peculiar result when working with the seminal foetuses of humans. After no more than five generations, the male foetuses held no more spermatozoa, and the females held no more ova. The line terminated in a sterile generation."

"I imagine that wasn't entirely unexpected," Stratton said, glancing at the jellied form. "Each repetition must further attenuate some essence in the organisms. It's only logical that at some point the offspring would be so feeble that the process would fail."

"That was Dubuisson and Gille's initial assumption as well," agreed Fieldhurst, "so they sought to improve their technique. However, they could find no difference between megafoetuses of succeeding generations in terms of size or vitality. Nor was there any decline in the number of spermatozoa or ova; the penultimate generation was fully as fertile as the first. The transition to sterility was an abrupt one.

"They found another anomaly as well: While some spermatozoa yielded only four or fewer generations, variation occurred only across samples, never within a single sample. They evaluated samples from father and son donors, and in such instances, the father's spermatozoa produced exactly one more generation than the son's. And from what I understand, some of the donors were aged individuals indeed. While their samples held very few spermatozoa, they nonetheless held one more generation than those from sons in the prime of their lives. The progenitive power of the sperm bore no correlation with the health or vigor of the donor; instead, it correlated with the generation to which the donor belonged."

Fieldhurst paused and looked at Stratton gravely. "It was at this point that the Académie contacted me to see if the Royal Society could duplicate their findings. Together we have obtained the same result using samples collected from peoples as varied as the Lapps and the Hottentots. We are in agreement as to the implication of these findings: that the human species has the potential to exist for only a fixed number of generations, and we are within five generations of the final one."

Stratton turned to Ashbourne, half expecting him to confess that it was all an elaborate hoax, but the elder nomenclator looked entirely solemn. Stratton looked at the megafoetus again and frowned, absorbing what he had heard. "If your interpretation is correct, other species must be subject to a similar limitation. Yet from what I know, the extinction of a species has never been observed."

Fieldhurst nodded. "That is true. However, we do have the evidence of the fossil record, which suggests that species remain unchanged for a period of time, and then are abruptly replaced by new forms. The Catastrophists hold that violent upheavals caused species to become extinct. Based on what we've discovered regarding preformation, it now appears that extinctions are merely the result of a species reaching the end of its lifetime. They are natural rather than accidental deaths, in a manner of speaking." He gestured to the doorway from which they had entered. "Shall we return upstairs?"

Following the two other men, Stratton asked, "And what of the origination of new species? If they're not born from existing species, do they arise spontaneously?"

"That is as yet uncertain. Normally only the simplest animals arise by spontaneous generation: maggots and other vermiform creatures, typically under the influence of heat.

The events postulated by Catastrophists—floods, volcanic eruptions, cometary impacts—would entail the release of great energies. Perhaps such energies affect matter so profoundly as to cause the spontaneous generation of an entire race of organisms, nested within a few progenitors. If so, cataclysms are not responsible for mass extinctions, but rather generate new species in their wake."

Back in the laboratory, the two elder men seated themselves in the chairs present. Too agitated to follow suit, Stratton remained standing. "If any animal species were created by the same cataclysm as the human species, they should likewise be nearing the end of their life spans. Have you found another species that evinces a final generation?"

Fieldhurst shook his head. "Not as yet. We believe that other species have different dates of extinction, correlated with the biological complexity of the animal; humans are presumably the most complex organism, and perhaps fewer generations of such complex organisms can be nested inside a spermatozoon."

"By the same token," countered Stratton, "perhaps the complexity of the human organism makes it unsuitable for the process of artificially accelerated growth. Perhaps it is the process whose limits have been discovered, not the species."

"An astute observation, Mr. Stratton. Experiments are continuing with species that more closely resemble humans, such as chimpanzees and ourang-outangs. However, the unequivocal answer to this question may require years, and if our current interpretation is correct, we can ill afford the time spent waiting for confirmation. We must ready a course of action immediately."

"But five generations could be over a century—" He caught himself, embarrassed at having overlooked the obvious: not all persons became parents at the same age.

Fieldhurst read his expression. "You realize why not all the sperm samples from donors of the same age produced the same number of generations: Some lineages are approaching their end faster than others. For a lineage in which the men consistently father children late in life, five generations might mean over two centuries of fertility, but there are undoubtedly lineages that have reached their end already."

Stratton imagined the consequences. "The loss of fertility will become increasingly apparent to the general populace as time passes. Panic may arise well before the end is reached."

"Precisely, and rioting could extinguish our species as effectively as the exhaustion of generations. That is why time is of the essence."

"What is the solution you propose?"

"I shall defer to Dr. Ashbourne to explain further," said the earl.

Ashbourne rose and instinctively adopted the stance of a lecturing professor. "Do you recall why it was that all attempts to make automata out of wood were abandoned?"

Stratton was caught off guard by the question. "It was believed that the natural grain of wood implies a form in conflict with whatever we try to carve upon it. Currently there are efforts to use rubber as a casting material, but none have met with success."

"Indeed. But if the native form of wood were the only obstacle, shouldn't it be possible to animate an animal's corpse with a name? There the form of the body should be ideal."

"It's a macabre notion; I couldn't guess at such an experiment's likelihood of success. Has it ever been attempted?"

"In fact it has: also unsuccessfully. So these two entirely different avenues of research proved fruitless. Does that mean there is no way to animate organic matter using names? This was the question I left Trinity in order to pursue."

"And what did you discover?"

Ashbourne deflected the question with a wave of his hand. "First let us discuss thermodynamics. Have you kept up with recent developments? Then you know the dissipation of heat reflects an increase in disorder at the thermal level. Conversely, when an automaton condenses heat from its environment to perform work, it increases order. This confirms a long-held belief of mine that lexical order induces thermodynamic order. The lexical order of an amulet reinforces the order a body already possesses, thus providing protection against damage. The lexical order of an animating name increases the order of a body, thus providing motive power for an automaton.

"The next question was, how would an increase in order be reflected in organic matter? Since names don't animate dead tissue, obviously organic matter doesn't respond at the thermal level; but perhaps it can be ordered at another level. Consider: a steer can be reduced to a vat of gelatinous broth. The broth comprises the same material as the steer, but which embodies a higher amount of order?"

"The steer, obviously," said Stratton, bewildered.

"Obviously. An organism, by virtue of its physical structure, embodies order; the more complex the organism, the greater the amount of order. It was my hypothesis that increasing the order in organic matter would be evidenced by imparting form to it. However, most living matter has already assumed its ideal form. The question is, what has life but not form?"

The elder nomenclator did not wait for a response. "The answer is, an unfertilized ovum. The ovum contains the vital principle that animates the creature it ultimately gives rise to, but it has no form itself. Ordinarily, the ovum incorporates the form of the foetus compressed within the spermatozoon that fertilizes it. The next step was obvious." Here Ashbourne waited, looking at Stratton expectantly.

Stratton was at a loss. Ashbourne seemed disappointed, and continued. "The next step was to artificially induce the growth of an embryo from an ovum, by application of a name."

"But if the ovum is unfertilized," objected Stratton, "there is no preexisting structure to enlarge."

"Precisely."

"You mean structure would arise out of a homogeneous medium? Impossible."

"Nonetheless, it was my goal for several years to confirm this hypothesis. My first experiments consisted of applying a name to unfertilized frog eggs."

"How did you embed the name into a frog's egg?"

"The name is not actually embedded, but rather impressed by means of a specially manufactured needle." Ashbourne opened a cabinet that sat on the work-table between two of the microscope stations. Inside was a wooden rack filled with small instruments arranged in pairs. Each was tipped with a long glass needle; in some pairs they were nearly as thick as those used for knitting, in others as slender as a hypodermic. He withdrew one from the largest pair and handed it to Stratton to examine. The glass needle was not clear, but instead seemed to contain some sort of dappled core.

Ashbourne explained. "While that may appear to be some sort of medical implement, it is in fact a vehicle for a name, just as the more conventional slip of parchment is. Alas, it requires far more effort to make than taking pen to parchment. To create such a needle, one must first arrange fine strands of black glass within a bundle of clear glass strands so that the name is legible when they are viewed end-on. The strands are then fused into a solid rod, and the rod is drawn out into an ever thinner strand. A skilled glass-maker can retain every detail of the name no matter how thin the strand becomes. Eventually one obtains a needle containing the name in its cross section."

"How did you generate the name that you used?"

"We can discuss that at length later. For the purposes of our current discussion, the only relevant information is that I incorporated the sexual epithet. Are you familiar with it?"

"I know of it." It was one of the few epithets that was dimorphic, having male and female variants.

"I needed two versions of the name, obviously, to induce the generation of both males and females." He indicated the paired arrangement of needles in the cabinet.

Stratton saw that the needle could be clamped into the brass framework with its tip approaching the slide beneath the microscope; the knurled wheels presumably were used to bring the needle into contact with an ovum. He returned the instrument. "You said the name is not embedded, but impressed. Do you mean to tell me that touching the frog's egg with this needle is all that's needed? Removing the name doesn't end its influence?"

"Precisely. The name activates a process in the egg that cannot be reversed. Prolonged contact of the name had no different effect."

"And the egg hatched a tadpole?"

"Not with the names initially tried; the only result was that symmetrical involutions appeared in the surface of the egg. But by incorporating different epithets, I was able to induce the egg to adopt different forms, some of which had every appearance of embryonic frogs. Eventually I found a name that caused the egg not only to assume the form of a tadpole, but also to mature and hatch. The tadpole thus hatched grew into a frog indistinguishable from any other member of the species."

"You had found a euonym for that species of frog," said Stratton.

Ashbourne smiled. "As this method of reproduction does not involve sexual congress, I have termed it 'parthenogenesis.'"

Stratton looked at both him and Fieldhurst. "It's clear what your proposed solution is. The logical conclusion of this research is to discover a euonym for the human species. You wish for mankind to perpetuate itself through nomenclature."

"You find the prospect troubling," said Fieldhurst. "That is to be expected: Dr. Ashbourne and myself initially felt the same way, as has everyone who has considered this. No one relishes the prospect of humans being conceived artificially. But can you offer an alternative?" Stratton was silent, and Fieldhurst went on. "All who are aware of both Dr. Ashbourne's and Dubuisson and Gille's work agree: There is no other solution."

Stratton reminded himself to maintain the dispassionate attitude of a scientist. "Precisely how do you envision this name being used?" he asked.

Ashbourne answered. "When a husband is unable to impregnate his wife, they will seek the services of a physician. The physician will collect the woman's menses, separate out the ovum, impress the name upon it, and then reintroduce it into her womb."

"A child born of this method would have no biological father."

"True, but the father's biological contribution is of minimal importance here. The mother will think of her husband as the child's father, so her imagination will impart a combination of her own and her husband's appearance and character to the foetus. That will not change. And I hardly need mention that name impression would not be made available to unmarried women."

"Are you confident this will result in well-formed children?" asked Stratton. "I'm sure you know to what I refer." They all knew of the disastrous attempt in the previous century to create improved children by mesmerizing women during their pregnancies.

Ashbourne nodded. "We are fortunate in that the ovum is very specific in what it will accept. The set of euonyms for any species of organism is very small; if the lexical order of the impressed name does not closely match the structural order of that species, the resulting foetus does not quicken. This does not remove the need for the mother to maintain a tranquil mind during her pregnancy; name impression cannot guard against maternal agitation. But the ovum's selectivity provides us assurance that any foetus induced will be well-formed in every aspect, except the one anticipated."

Stratton was alarmed. "What aspect is that?"

"Can you not guess? The only incapacity of frogs created by name impression was in the males; they were sterile, for their spermatozoa bore no preformed foetuses inside. By comparison, the female frogs created were fertile: Their eggs could be fertilized in either the conventional manner, or by repeating the impression with the name."

Stratton's relief was considerable. "So the male variant of the name was imperfect. Presumably there needs to be further differences between the male and female variants than simply the sexual epithet."

"Only if one considers the male variant imperfect," said

Ashbourne, "which I do not. Consider: While a fertile male and a fertile female might seem equivalent, they differ radically in the degree of complexity exemplified. A female with viable ova remains a single organism, while a male with viable spermatozoa is actually many organisms: a father and all his potential children. In this light, the two variants of the name are well-matched in their actions: Each induces a single organism, but only in the female sex can a single organism be fertile."

"I see what you mean." Stratton realized he would need practice in thinking about nomenclature in the organic domain. "Have you developed euonyms for other species?"

"Just over a score, of various types; our progress has been rapid. We have only just begun work on a name for the human species, and it has proved far more difficult than our previous names."

"How many nomenclators are engaged in this endeavor?"

"Only a handful," Fieldhurst replied. "We have asked a few Royal Society members, and the Académie has some of France's leading designateurs working on it. You will understand if I do not mention any names at this point, but be assured that we have some of the most distinguished nomenclators in England assisting us."

"Forgive me for asking, but why are you approaching me? I am hardly in that category."

"You have not yet had a long career," said Ashbourne, "but the genus of names you have developed is unique. Automata have always been specialized in form and function, rather like animals: Some are good at climbing, others at digging, but none at both. Yet yours can control human hands, which are uniquely versatile instruments: What else can manipulate everything from a wrench to a piano? The hand's dexterity is the physical manifestation of the mind's ingenuity, and these traits are essential to the name we seek."

"We have been discreetly surveying current nomenclatoral research for any names that demonstrate marked dexterity," said Fieldhurst. "When we learned of what you had accomplished, we sought you out immediately."

"In fact," Ashbourne continued, "the very reason your

names are worrisome to sculptors is the reason we are interested in them: They endow automata with a more human-like manner than any before. So now we ask, will you join us?"

Stratton considered it. This was perhaps the most important task a nomenclator could undertake, and under ordinary circumstances he would have leapt at the opportunity to participate. But before he could embark upon this enterprise in good conscience, there was another matter he had to resolve.

"You honor me with your invitation, but what of my work with dexterous automata? I still firmly believe that inexpensive engines can improve the lives of the labouring class."

"It is a worthy goal," said Fieldhurst, "and I would not ask you to give it up. Indeed, the first thing we wish you to do is to perfect the epithets for dexterity. But your efforts at social reform would be for naught unless we first ensure the survival of our species."

"Obviously, but I do not want the potential for reform that is offered by dexterous names to be neglected. There may never be a better opportunity for restoring dignity to common workers. What kind of victory would we achieve if the continuation of life meant ignoring this opportunity?"

"Well said," acknowledged the earl. "Let me make a proposal. So that you can best make use of your time, the Royal Society will provide support for your development of dexterous automata as needed: securing investors and so forth. I trust you will divide your time between the two projects wisely. Your work on biological nomenclature must remain confidential, obviously. Is that satisfactory?"

"It is. Very well then, gentlemen: I accept." They shook hands.

Some weeks had passed since Stratton last spoke with Willoughby, beyond a chilly exchange of greetings in passing. In fact, he had little interaction with any of the union sculptors, instead spending his time working on letter permutations in his office, trying to refine his epithets for dexterity.

He entered the manufactory through the front gallery, where customers normally perused the catalogue. Today it was crowded with domestic automata, all the same model char-engine. Stratton saw the clerk ensuring they were properly tagged.

"Good morning, Pierce," he said. "What are all these doing here?"

"An improved name is just out for the 'Regent,'" said the clerk. "Everyone's eager to get the latest."

"You're going to be busy this afternoon." The keys for unlocking the automata's name-slots were themselves stored in a safe that required two of Coade's managers to open. The managers were reluctant to keep the safe open for more than a brief period each afternoon.

"I'm certain I can finish these in time."

"You couldn't bear to tell a pretty house-maid that her char-engine wouldn't be ready by tomorrow."

The clerk smiled. "Can you blame me, sir?"

"No, I cannot," said Stratton, chuckling. He turned toward the business offices behind the gallery, when he found himself confronted by Willoughby.

"Perhaps you ought to prop open the safe," said the sculptor, "so that house-maids might not be inconvenienced. Seeing how destroying our institutions seems to be your intent."

"Good morning, Master Willoughby," said Stratton, stiffly. He tried to walk past, but the other man stood in his way.

"I've been informed that Coade will be allowing non-union sculptors on to the premises to assist you."

"Yes, but I assure you, only the most reputable independent sculptors are involved."

"As if such persons exist," said Willoughby scornfully. "You should know that I recommended that our trade-union launch a strike against Coade in protest."

"Surely you're not serious." It had been decades since the last strike launched by the sculptors, and that one had ended in rioting.

"I am. Were the matter put to a vote of the membership, I'm certain it would pass: other sculptors with whom I've discussed your work agree with me about the threat it poses. However, the union leadership will not put it to a vote."

"Ah, so they disagreed with your assessment."

Here Willoughby frowned. "Apparently the Royal Society intervened on your behalf and persuaded the Brotherhood to refrain for the time being. You've found yourself some powerful supporters, Mr. Stratton."

Uncomfortably, Stratton replied, "The Royal Society considers my research worthwhile."

"Perhaps, but do not believe that this matter is ended."

"Your animosity is unwarranted, I tell you," Stratton insisted. "Once you have seen how sculptors can use these automata, you will realize that there is no threat to your profession."

Willoughby merely glowered in response and left.

The next time he saw Lord Fieldhurst, Stratton asked him about the Royal Society's involvement. They were in Fieldhurst's study, and the earl was pouring himself a whiskey.

"Ah yes," he said. "While the Brotherhood of Sculptors as a whole is quite formidable, it is composed of individuals who individually are more amenable to persuasion."

"What manner of persuasion?"

"The Royal Society is aware that members of the trade-union's leadership were party to an as-yet unresolved case of name piracy to the continent. To avoid any scandal, they've agreed to postpone any decision about strikes until after you've given a demonstration of your system of manufacturing."

"I'm grateful for your assistance, Lord Fieldhurst," said Stratton, astonished. "I must admit, I had no idea that the Royal Society employed such tactics."

"Obviously, these are not proper topics for discussion at the general sessions." Lord Fieldhurst smiled in an avuncular manner. "The advancement of science is not always a straightforward affair, Mr. Stratton, and the Royal Society is sometimes required to use both official and unofficial channels."

"I'm beginning to appreciate that."

"Similarly, although the Brotherhood of Sculptors won't initiate a formal strike, they might employ more indirect tactics; for example, the anonymous distribution of pamphlets that arouse public opposition to your automata." He sipped at his whiskey. "Hmm. Perhaps I should have someone keep a watchful eye on Master Willoughby."

Stratton was given accommodations in the guest wing of Darrington Hall, as were the other nomenclators working under Lord Fieldhurst's direction. They were indeed some of the leading members of the profession, including Holcombe, Milburn, and Parker; Stratton felt honored to be working with them, although he could contribute little while he was still learning Ashbourne's techniques for biological nomenclature.

Names for the organic domain employed many of the same epithets as names for automata, but Ashbourne had developed an entirely different system of integration and factorization, which entailed many novel methods of permutation. For Stratton it was almost like returning to university and learning nomenclature all over again. However, it was apparent how these techniques allowed names for species to be developed rapidly; by exploiting similarities suggested by the Linnaean system of classification, one could work from one species to another.

Stratton also learned more about the sexual epithet, traditionally used to confer either male or female qualities to an automaton. He knew of only one such epithet, and was surprised to learn it was the simplest of many extant versions. The topic went undiscussed by nomenclatoral societies, but this epithet was one of the most fully researched in existence; in fact its earliest use was claimed to have occurred in biblical times, when Joseph's brothers created a female *golem* they could share sexually without violating the prohibition against such behavior with a woman. Development of the epithet had continued for centuries in secrecy, primarily in Constantinople, and now the current versions of automatous courtesans were offered by specialized brothels right here in London. Carved from soapstone and polished to a high gloss, heated to blood temperature and sprinkled with scented oils, the automata commanded prices exceeded only by those for incubi and succubi.

It was from such ignoble soil that their research grew. The names animating the courtesans incorporated powerful epithets for human sexuality in its male and female forms. By factoring out the carnality common to both versions, the nomenclators had isolated epithets for generic human masculinity and femininity, ones far more refined than those used when generating animals. Such epithets were the nuclei around which they formed, by accretion, the names they sought.

Gradually Stratton absorbed sufficient information to begin participating in the tests of prospective human names. He worked in collaboration with the other nomenclators in the group, and between them they divided up the vast tree of nominal possibilities, assigning branches for investigation, pruning away those that proved unfruitful, cultivating those that seemed most productive.

The nomenclators paid women—typically young housemaids in good health—for their menses as a source of human ova, which they then impressed with their experimental names and scrutinized under microscopes, looking for forms that resembled human foetuses. Stratton inquired about the possibility of harvesting ova from female megafoetuses, but Ashbourne reminded him that ova were viable only when taken from a living woman. It was a basic dictum of biology: Females were the source of the vital principle that gave the offspring life, while males provided the basic form. Because of this division, neither sex could reproduce by itself.

Of course, that restriction had been lifted by Ashbourne's discovery: the male's participation was no longer necessary since form could be induced lexically. Once a name was found that could generate human foetuses, women could reproduce purely by themselves. Stratton realized that such a discovery might be welcomed by women exhibiting sexual inversion, feeling love for persons of the same rather than the opposite sex. If the name were to become available to such women, they might establish a commune of some sort that reproduced via parthenogenesis. Would such a society flourish by magnifying the finer sensibilities of the gentle sex, or would it collapse under the unrestrained pathology of its membership? It was impossible to guess.

Before Stratton's enlistment, the nomenclators had developed names capable of generating vaguely homuncular forms in an ovum. Using Dubuisson and Gille's methods, they enlarged the forms to a size that allowed detailed examination; the forms resembled automata more than humans, their limbs ending in paddles of fused digits. By incorporating his epithets for dexterity, Stratton was able to separate the digits and refine the overall appearance of the forms. All the while, Ashbourne emphasized the need for an unconventional approach.

"Consider the thermodynamics of what most automata do," said Ashbourne during one of their frequent discussions. "The mining engines dig ore, the reaping engines harvest wheat, the wood-cutting engines fell timber; yet none of these tasks, no matter how useful we find them to be, can be said to create order. While all their names create order at the thermal level, by converting heat into motion, in the vast majority the resulting work is applied at the visible level to create disorder."

"This is an interesting perspective," said Stratton thoughtfully. "Many long-standing deficits in the capabilities of automata become intelligible in this light: the fact that automata are unable to stack crates more neatly than they find them; their inability to sort pieces of crushed ore based on their composition. You believe that the known classes of industrial names are not powerful enough in thermodynamic terms."

"Precisely!" Ashbourne displayed the excitement of a tutor finding an unexpectedly apt pupil. "This is another feature that distinguishes your class of dexterous names. By enabling an automation to perform skilled labour, your names not only create order at the thermal level, they use it to create order at the visible level as well."

"I see a commonality with Milburn's discoveries," said Stratton. Milburn had developed the household automata able to return objects to their proper places. "His work likewise involves the creation of order at the visible level."

"Indeed it does, and this commonality suggests a hypothesis." Ashbourne leaned forward. "Suppose we were able to factor out an epithet common to the names developed by you and Milburn: an epithet expressing the creation of two levels of order. Further suppose that we discover a euonym for the human species, and were able to incorporate this epithet into the name. What do you imagine would be generated by impressing the name? And if you say 'twins' I shall clout you on the head."

Stratton laughed. "I dare say I understand you better than that. You are suggesting that if an epithet is capable of inducing two levels of thermodynamic order in the inorganic domain, it might create two generations in the organic domain. Such a name might create males whose spermatozoa would contain preformed foetuses. Those males would be fertile, although any sons they produced would again be sterile."

His instructor clapped his hands together. "Precisely: order that begets order! An interesting speculation, wouldn't you agree? It would halve the number of medical interventions required for our race to sustain itself."

"And what about inducing the formation of more than two generations of foetuses? What kind of capabilities would an automaton have to possess, for its name to contain such an epithet?"

"The science of thermodynamics has not progressed enough to answer that question, I'm afraid. What would constitute a still higher level of order in the inorganic domain? Automata working cooperatively, perhaps? We do not yet know, but perhaps in time we will."

Stratton gave voice to a question that had posed itself to him some time ago. "Dr. Ashbourne, when I was initiated into our group, Lord Fieldhurst spoke of the possibility that species are born in the wake of catastrophic events. Is it possible that entire species were created by use of nomenclature?"

"Ah, now we tread in the realm of theology. A new species requires progenitors containing vast numbers of descendants nested within their reproductive organs; such forms embody the highest degree of order imaginable. Can a purely physical process create such vast amounts of order? No naturalist has suggested a mechanism by which this could occur. On the other hand, while we do know that a lexical process can create order, the creation of an entire new species would require a name of incalculable power. Such mastery of nomenclature could very well require the capabilities of God; perhaps it is even part of the definition.

"This is a question, Stratton, to which we may never know the answer, but we cannot allow that to affect our current actions. Whether or not a name was responsible for the creation of our species, I believe a name is the best chance for its continuation."

"Agreed," said Stratton. After a pause, he added, "I must confess, much of the time when I am working, I occupy myself solely with the details of permutation and combination, and lose sight of the sheer magnitude of our endeavor. It is sobering to think of what we will have achieved if we are successful."

"I can think of little else," replied Ashbourne.

Seated at his desk in the manufactory, Stratton squinted to read the pamphlet he'd been given on the street. The text was crudely printed, the letters blurred.

"Shall Men be the Masters of NAMES, or shall Names be the masters of MEN? For too long the Capitalists have hoarded Names within their coffers, guarded by Patent and Lock and Key, amassing fortunes by mere possession of LETTERS, while the Common Man must labour for every shilling. They will wring the ALPHABET until they have extracted every last penny from it, and only then discard it for us to use. How long will We allow this to continue?"

Stratton scanned the entire pamphlet, but found nothing new in it. For the past two months he'd been reading them, and encountered only the usual anarchist rants; there was as yet no evidence for Lord Fieldhurst's theory that the sculptors would use them to target Stratton's work. His public demonstration of the dexterous automata was scheduled for next week, and by now Willoughby had largely missed his opportunity to generate public opposition. In fact, it occurred to Stratton that he might distribute pamphlets himself to generate public support. He could explain his goal of bringing the advantages of automata to everyone, and his intention to keep close control over his names' patents, granting licenses only to manufacturers who would use them conscientiously. He could even have a slogan: "Autonomy through Automata," perhaps?

There was a knock at his office door. Stratton tossed the pamphlet into his wastebasket. "Yes?"

A man entered, somberly dressed, and with a long beard. "Mr. Stratton?" he asked. "Please allow me to introduce myself: My name is Benjamin Roth. I am a kabbalist."

Stratton was momentarily speechless. Typically such mystics were offended by the modern view of nomenclature as a science, considering it a secularization of a sacred ritual. He never expected one to visit the manufactory. "A pleasure to meet you. How may I be of assistance?"

"I've heard that you have achieved a great advance in the permutation of letters."

"Why, thank you. I didn't realize it would be of interest to a person like yourself."

Roth smiled awkwardly. "My interest is not in its practical applications. The goal of kabbalists is to better know God. The best means by which to do that is to study the art by which He creates. We meditate upon different names to enter an ecstatic state of consciousness; the more powerful the name, the more closely we approach the Divine."

"I see." Stratton wondered what the kabbalist's reaction would be if he learned about the creation being attempted in the biological nomenclature project. "Please continue."

"Your epithets for dexterity enable a *golem* to sculpt another, thereby reproducing itself. A name capable of creating a being that is, in turn, capable of creation would bring us closer to God than we have ever been before."

"I'm afraid you're mistaken about my work, although you aren't the first to fall under this misapprehension. The ability to manipulate molds does not render an automaton able to reproduce itself. There would be many other skills required."

The Kabbalist nodded. "I am well aware of that. I myself, in the course of my studies, have developed an epithet designating certain other skills necessary."

Stratton leaned forward with sudden interest. After casting a body, the next step would be to animate the body with a name. "Your epithet endows an automaton with the ability to write?" His own automaton could grasp a pencil easily enough, but it couldn't inscribe even the simplest mark. "How is it that your automata possess the dexterity required for scrivening, but not that for manipulating molds?"

Roth shook his head modestly. "My epithet does not endow writing ability, or general manual dexterity. It simply enables a *golem* to write out the name that animates it, and nothing else."

"Ah, I see." So it didn't provide an aptitude for learning a category of skills; it granted a single innate skill. Stratton tried to imagine the nomenclatoral contortions needed to make an automaton instinctively write out a particular sequence of letters. "Very interesting, but I imagine it doesn't have broad application, does it?"

Roth gave a pained smile; Stratton realized he had committed a *faux pas*, and the man was trying to meet it with good humor. "That is one way to view it," admitted Roth, "but we have a different perspective. To us the value of this epithet, like any other, lies not in the usefulness it imparts to a *golem*, but in the ecstatic state it allows us to achieve."

"Of course, of course. And your interest in my epithets for dexterity is the same?"

"Yes. I am hoping that you will share your epithets with us."

Stratton had never heard of a kabbalist making such a request before, and clearly Roth did not relish being the first. He paused to consider. "Must a kabbalist reach a certain rank in order to meditate upon the most powerful ones?"

"Yes, very definitely."

"So you restrict the availability of the names."

"Oh no; my apologies for misunderstanding you. The ecstatic state offered by a name is achievable only after one has mastered the necessary meditative techniques, and it's these techniques that are closely guarded. Without the proper training, attempts to use these techniques could result in madness. But the names themselves, even the most powerful ones, have no ecstatic value to a novice; they can animate clay, nothing more."

"Nothing more," agreed Stratton, thinking how truly different their perspectives were. "In that case, I'm afraid I cannot grant you use of my names."

Roth nodded glumly, as if he'd been expecting that answer. "You desire payment of royalties."

Now it was Stratton who had to overlook the other man's faux pas. "Money is not my objective. However, I have specific intentions for my dexterous automata which require that I retain control over the patent. I cannot jeopardize those plans by releasing the names indiscriminately." Granted, he had shared them with the nomenclators working under Lord Fieldhurst, but they were all gentlemen sworn to an even greater secrecy. He was less confident about mystics.

"I can assure you that we would not use your name for anything other than ecstatic practices."

"I apologize; I believe you are sincere, but the risk is too great. The most I can do is remind you that the patent has a limited duration; once it has expired, you'll be free to use the name however you like."

"But that will take years!"

"Surely you appreciate that there are others whose interests must be taken into account."

"What I see is that commercial considerations are posing an obstacle to spiritual awakening. The error was mine in expecting anything different."

"You are hardly being fair," protested Stratton.

"Fair?" Roth made a visible effort to restrain his anger. "You 'nomenclators' steal techniques meant to honor God and use them to aggrandize yourselves. Your entire industry prostitutes the techniques of yezirah. You are in no position to speak of fairness."

"Now see here—"

"Thank you for speaking with me." With that, Roth took his leave.

Stratton sighed.

Peering through the eyepiece of the microscope, Stratton turned the manipulator's adjustment wheel until the needle pressed against the side of the ovum. There was a sudden enfolding, like the retraction of a mollusc's foot when prodded, transforming the sphere into a tiny foetus. Stratton withdrew the needle from the slide, unclamped it from the framework, and inserted a new one. Next he transferred the slide into the warmth of the incubator and placed another slide, bearing an untouched human ovum, beneath the microscope. Once again he leaned toward the microscope to repeat the process of impression.

Recently, the nomenclators had developed a name capable of inducing a form indistinguishable from a human foetus. The forms did not quicken, however: they remained immobile and unresponsive to stimuli. The consensus was that the name did not accurately describe the non-physical traits of a human being. Accordingly, Stratton and his colleagues had been diligently compiling descriptions of human uniqueness, trying to distill a set of epithets both expressive enough to denote these qualities, and succinct enough to be integrated with the physical epithets into a seventy-two-lettered name.

Stratton transferred the final slide to the incubator and made the appropriate notations in the logbook. At the moment he had no more names drawn in needle form, and it would be a day before the new foetuses were mature enough to test for quickening. He decided to pass the rest of the evening in the drawing room upstairs.

Upon entering the walnut paneled room, he found Fieldhurst and Ashbourne seated in its leather chairs, smoking cigars and sipping brandy. "Ah, Stratton," said Ashbourne. "Do join us."

"I believe I will," said Stratton, heading for the liquor cabinet. He poured himself some brandy from a crystal decanter and seated himself with the others.

"Just up from the laboratory, Stratton?" inquired Fieldhurst.

Stratton nodded. "A few minutes ago I made impressions with my most recent set of names. I feel that my latest permutations are leading in the right direction."

"You are not alone in feeling optimistic; Dr. Ashbourne and I were just discussing how much the outlook has improved since this endeavor began. It now appears that we will have a euonym comfortably in advance of the final generation." Fieldhurst puffed on his cigar and leaned back in his chair until his head rested against the antimacassar. "This disaster may ultimately turn out to be a boon."

"A boon? How so?"

"Why, once we have human reproduction under our control, we will have a means of preventing the poor from having such large families as so many of them persist in having right now."

Stratton was startled, but tried not to show it. "I had not considered that," he said carefully.

Ashbourne also seemed mildly surprised. "I wasn't aware that you intended such a policy."

"I considered it premature to mention it earlier," said Fieldhurst. "Counting one's chickens before they're hatched, as they say."

"Of course."

"You must agree that the potential is enormous. By exercising some judgment when choosing who may bear children or not, our government could preserve the nation's racial stock."

"Is our racial stock under some threat?" asked Stratton.

"Perhaps you have not noticed that the lower classes are reproducing at a rate exceeding that of the nobility and gentry. While commoners are not without virtues, they are lacking in refinement and intellect. These forms of mental impoverishment beget the same: A woman born into low circumstances cannot help but gestate a child destined for the same. Consequent to the great fecundity of the lower classes, our nation would eventually drown in coarse dullards."

"So name impressing will be withheld from the lower classes?"

"Not entirely, and certainly not initially: when the truth about declining fertility is known, it would be an invitation to riot if the lower classes were denied access to name impressing. And of course, the lower classes do have their role to play in our society, as long as their numbers are kept in check. I envision that the policy will go in effect only after some years have passed, by which time people will have grown accustomed to name impression as the method of fertilization. At that point, perhaps in conjunction with the census process, we can impose limits on the number of children a given couple would be permitted to have. The government would regulate the growth and composition of the population thereafter."

"Is this the most appropriate use of such a name?" asked Ashbourne. "Our goal was the survival of the species, not the implementation of partisan politics."

"On the contrary, this is purely scientific. Just as it's our duty to ensure the species survives, it's also our duty to guarantee its health by keeping a proper balance in its population. Politics doesn't enter into it; were the situation reversed and there existed a paucity of labourers, the opposite policy would be called for."

Stratton ventured a suggestion. "I wonder if improvement in conditions for the poor might eventually cause them to gestate more refined children?"

"You are thinking about changes brought about by your cheap engines, aren't you?" asked Fieldhurst with a smile, and Stratton nodded. "Your intended reforms and mine may reinforce each other. Moderating the numbers of the lower classes should make it easier for them to raise their living conditions. However, do not expect that a mere increase in economic comfort will improve the mentality of the lower classes."

"But why not?"

"You forget the self-perpetuating nature of culture," said Fieldhurst. "We have seen that all megafoetuses are identical, yet no one can deny the differences between the populaces of nations, in both physical appearance and temperament. This can only be the result of the maternal influence: The mother's womb is a vessel in which the social environment is incarnated. For example, a woman who has lived her life among Prussians naturally gives birth to a child with Prussian traits; in this manner the national character of that populace has sustained itself for centuries, despite many changes in fortune. It would be unrealistic to think the poor are any different."

"As a zoologist, you are undoubtedly wiser in these matters than we," said Ashbourne, silencing Stratton with a glance. "We will defer to your judgment."

For the remainder of the evening the conversation turned to other topics, and Stratton did his best to conceal his discomfort and maintain a facade of bonhomie. Finally, after Fieldhurst had retired for the evening, Stratton and Ashbourne descended to the laboratory to confer.

"What manner of man have we agreed to help?" exclaimed Stratton as soon as the door was closed. "One who would breed people like livestock?"

"Perhaps we should not be so shocked," said Ashbourne with a sigh. He seated himself upon one of the laboratory stools. "Our group's goal has been to duplicate for humans a procedure that was intended only for animals."

"But not at the expense of individual liberty! I cannot be a party to this."

"Do not be hasty. What would be accomplished by your resigning from the group? To the extent that your efforts contribute to our group's endeavor, your resignation would serve only to endanger the future of the human species. Conversely, if the group attains its goal without your assistance, Lord Fieldhurst's policies will be implemented anyway."

Stratton tried to regain his composure. Ashbourne was right; he could see that. After a moment, he said, "So what course of action should we take? Are there others whom we could contact, Members of Parliament who would oppose the policy that Lord Fieldhurst proposes?"

"I expect that most of the nobility and gentry would share Lord Fieldhurst's opinion on this matter." Ashbourne rested his forehead on the fingertips of one hand, suddenly looking very old. "I should have anticipated this. My error was in viewing humanity purely as a single species. Having seen England and France working toward a common goal, I forgot that nations are not the only factions that oppose one another."

"What if we surreptitiously distributed the name to the labouring classes? They could draw their own needles and impress the name themselves, in secret."

"They could, but the name impression is a delicate procedure best performed in a laboratory. I'm dubious that the operation could be carried out on the scale necessary without attracting governmental attention, and then falling under its control."

"Is there an alternative?"

There was silence for a long moment while they considered. Then Ashbourne said, "Do you recall our speculation about a name that would induce two generations of foetuses?"

"Certainly."

"Suppose we develop such a name but do not reveal this property when we present it to Lord Fieldhurst."

"That's a wily suggestion," said Stratton, surprised. "All the children born of such a name would be fertile, so they would be able to reproduce without governmental restriction."

Ashbourne nodded. "In the period before population control measures go into effect, such a name might be very widely distributed."

"But what of the following generation? Sterility would recur, and the labouring classes would again be dependent upon the government to reproduce."

"True," said Ashbourne, "it would be a short-lived victory. Perhaps the only permanent solution would be a more liberal Parliament, but it is beyond my expertise to suggest how we might bring that about."

Again Stratton thought about the changes that cheap engines might bring; if the situation of the working classes was improved in the manner he hoped, that might demonstrate to the nobility that poverty was not innate. But even if the most favorable sequence of events was obtained, it would require years to sway Parliament. "What if we could induce multiple generations with the initial name impression? A longer period before sterility recurs would increase the chances that more liberal social policies would take hold."

"You're indulging a fancy," replied Ashbourne. "The technical difficulty of inducing multiple generations is such that I'd sooner wager on our successfully sprouting wings and taking flight. Inducing two generations would be ambitious enough."

The two men discussed strategies late into the night. If they were to conceal the true name of any name they presented to Lord Fieldhurst, they would have to forge a lengthy trail of research results. Even without the additional burden of secrecy, they would be engaged in an unequal race, pursuing a highly sophisticated name while the other nomenclators sought a comparatively straightforward euonym. To make the odds less unfavorable, Ashbourne and Stratton would need to recruit others to their cause; with such assistance, it might even be possible to subtly impede the research of others.

"Who in the group do you think shares our political views?" asked Ashbourne.

"I feel confident that Milburn does. I'm not so certain about any of the others."

"Take no chances. We must employ even more caution when approaching prospective members than Lord Fieldhurst did when establishing this group originally."

"Agreed," said Stratton. Then he shook his head in disbelief. "Here we are forming a secret organization nested within a secret organization. If only foetuses were so easily induced."

It was the evening of the following, the sun was setting, and Stratton was strolling across Westminster Bridge as the last remaining costermongers were wheeling their barrows of fruit away. He had just had supper at a club he favored, and was walking back to Coade Manufactory. The previous evening at Darrington Hall had disquieted him, and he had returned to London earlier today to minimize his interaction with Lord Fieldhurst until he was certain his face would not betray his true feelings.

He thought back to the conversation where he and Ashbourne had first entertained the conjecture of factoring out an epithet for creating two levels of order. At the time he had made some efforts to find such an epithet, but they were casual attempts given the superfluous nature of the goal, and they hadn't borne fruit. Now their gauge of achievement had been revised upward: Their previous goal was inadequate, two generations seemed the minimum acceptable, and any additional ones would be invaluable.

He again pondered the thermodynamic behavior induced by his dexterous names: Order at the thermal level animated the automata, allowing them to create order at the visible level. Order begetting order. Ashbourne had suggested that the next level of order might be automata working together in a coordinated fashion. Was that possible? They would have to communicate in order to work together effectively, but automata were intrinsically mute. What other means were there by which automata could exchange in complex behavior?

He suddenly realized he had reached Coade Manufactory. By now it was dark, but he knew the way to his office well enough. Stratton unlocked the building's front door and proceeded through the gallery and past the business offices.

As he reached the hallway fronting the nomenclators' offices, he saw light emanating from the frosted glass window of his office door. Surely he hadn't left the gas on? He unlocked his door to enter, and was shocked by what he saw.

A man lay face down on the floor in front of the desk, hands tied behind his back. Stratton immediately approached to check on the man. It was Benjamin Roth, the kabbalist, and he was dead. Stratton realized several of the man's fingers were broken; he'd been tortured before he was killed.

Pale and trembling, Stratton rose to his feet, and saw that his office was in utter disarray. The shelves of his bookcases were bare; his books lay strewn face-down across the oak floor. His desk had been swept clear; next to it was a stack of its brass-handled drawers, emptied and overturned. A trail of stray papers led to the open door to his studio; in a daze, Stratton stepped forward to see what had been done there.

His dexterous automaton had been destroyed; the lower half of it lay on the floor, the rest of it scattered as plaster fragments and dust. On the work-table, the clay models of the hands were pounded flat, and his sketches of their design torn from the walls. The tubs for mixing plaster were overflowing with the papers from his office. Stratton took a closer look, and saw that they had been doused with lamp oil.

He heard a sound behind him and turned back to face the office. The front door to the office swung closed and a broad-shouldered man stepped out from behind it; he'd been standing there ever since Stratton had entered. "Good of you to come," the man said. He scrutinized Stratton with the predatory gaze of a raptor, an assassin.

Stratton bolted out of the back door of the studio and down the rear hallway. He could hear the man give chase.

He fled through the darkened building, crossing workrooms filled with coke and iron bars, crucibles and molds, all illuminated by the moonlight entering through skylights overhead; he had entered the metalworks portion of the factory. In the next room he paused for breath, and realized how loudly his footsteps had been echoing; skulking would offer a better chance at escape than running. He distantly heard his pursuer's footsteps stop; the assassin had likewise opted for stealth.

Stratton looked around for a promising hiding place. All around him were cast iron automata in various stages of near-completion; he was in the finishing room, where the runners left over from casting were sawed off and the surfaces chased. There was no place to hide, and he was about to move on when he noticed what looked like a bundle of rifles mounted on legs. He looked more closely, and recognized it as a military engine.

These automata were built for the War Office: gun carriages that aimed their own cannon, and rapid-fire rifles, like this one, that cranked their own barrel-clusters. Nasty things, but they'd proven invaluable in the Crimea; their inventor had been granted a peerage. Stratton didn't know any names to animate the weapon—they were military secrets— but only the body on which the rifle was mounted was automatous; the rifle's firing mechanism was strictly mechanical. If he could point the body in the right direction, he might be able to fire the rifle manually.

He cursed himself for his stupidity. There was no ammunition here. He stole into the next room.

It was the packing room, filled with pine crates and loose straw. Staying low between crates, he moved to the far wall. Through the windows he saw the courtyard behind the factory, where finished automata were carted away. He couldn't get out that way; the courtyard gates were locked at night. His only exit was through the factory's front door, but he risked encountering the assassin if he headed back the way he'd come. He needed to cross over to the ceramicworks and double back through that side of the factory.

From the front of the packing room came the sound of footsteps. Stratton ducked behind a row of crates, and then saw a side door only a few feet away. As stealthily as he could, he opened the door, entered, and closed the door behind him. Had his pursuer heard him? He peered through a small grille set in the door; he couldn't see the man, but felt he'd gone unnoticed. The assassin was probably searching the packing room.

Stratton turned around, and immediately realized his mistake. The door to the ceramicworks was in the opposite wall. He had entered a storeroom, filled with ranks of finished automata, but with no other exits. There was no way to lock the door. He had cornered himself.

Was there anything in the room he could use as a weapon? The menagerie of automata included some squat mining engines, whose forelimbs terminated in enormous pickaxes, but the ax-heads were bolted to their limbs. There was no way he could remove one.

Stratton could hear the assassin opening side doors and

searching other storerooms. Then he noticed an automaton standing off to the side: a porter used for moving the inventory about. It was anthropomorphic in form, the only automaton in the room of that type. An idea came to him.

Stratton checked the back of the porter's head. Porters' names had entered the public domain long ago, so there were no locks protecting its name slot; a tab of parchment protruded from the horizontal slot in the iron. He reached into his coat pocket for the notebook and pencil he always carried and tore out a small portion of a blank leaf. In the darkness he quickly wrote seventy-two letters in a familiar combination, and then folded the paper into a tight square.

To the porter, he whispered, "Go stand as close to the door as you can." The cast iron figure stepped forward and headed for the door. Its gait was very smooth, but not rapid, and the assassin would reach this storeroom any moment now. "Faster," hissed Stratton, and the porter obeyed.

Just as it reached the door, Stratton saw through the grille that his pursuer had arrived on the other side. "Get out of the way," barked the man.

Ever obedient, the automaton shifted to take a step back when Stratton yanked out its name. The assassin began pushing against the door, but Stratton was able to insert the new name, cramming the square of paper into the slot as deeply as he could.

The porter resumed walking forward, this time with a fast, stiff gait: his childhood doll, now life-size. It immediately ran into the door and, unperturbed, kept it shut with the force of its marching, its iron hands leaving fresh dents in the door's oaken surface with every swing of its arms, its rubber-shod feet chafing heavily against the brick floor. Stratton retreated to the back of the storeroom.

"Stop," the assassin ordered. "Stop walking, you! Stop!"

The automaton continued marching, oblivious to all commands. The man pushed on the door, but to no avail. He then tried slamming into it with his shoulder, each impact causing the automaton to slide back slightly, but its rapid strides brought it forward again before the man could squeeze inside. There was a brief pause, and then something poked

through the grille in the door; the man was prying it off with
a crowbar. The grille abruptly popped free, leaving an open
window. The man stretched his arm through and reached
around to the back of the automaton's head, his fingers
searching for the name each time its head bobbed forward,
but there was nothing for them to grasp; the paper was
wedged too deeply in the slot.

The arm withdrew. The assassin's face appeared in the
window. "Fancy yourself clever, don't you?" he called out.
Then he disappeared.

Stratton relaxed slightly. Had the man given up? A minute
passed, and Stratton began to think about his next move. He
could wait here until the factory opened; there would be too
many people about for the assassin to remain.

Suddenly the man's arm came through the window again,
this time carrying a jar of fluid. He poured it over the automaton's head, the liquid splattering and dripping down its
back. The man's arm withdrew, and then Stratton heard the
sound of a match being struck and then flaring alight. The
man's arm reappeared bearing the match, and touched it to
the automaton.

The room was flooded with light as the automaton's head
and upper back burst into flames. The man had doused it
with lamp oil. Stratton squinted at the spectacle: Light and
shadow danced across the floor and walls, transforming the
storeroom into the site of some druidic ceremony. The heat
caused the automaton to hasten its vague assault on the door,
like a salamandrine priest dancing with increasing frenzy,
until it abruptly froze: Its name had caught fire, and the letters were being consumed.

The flames gradually died out, and to Stratton's newly
light-adapted eyes the room seemed almost completely
black. More by sound than by sight, he realized the man was
pushing at the door again, this time forcing the automaton
back enough for him to gain entrance.

"Enough of that, then."

Stratton tried to run past him, but the assassin easily
grabbed him and knocked him down with a clout to the
head.

His senses returned almost immediately, but by then the assassin had him face down on the floor, one knee pressed into his back. The man tore the health amulet from Stratton's wrist and then tied his hands together behind his back, drawing the rope tightly enough that the hemp fibers scraped the skin of his wrists.

"What kind of man are you, to do things like this?" Stratton gasped, his cheek flattened against the brick floor.

The assassin chuckled. "Men are no different from your automata; slip a bloke a piece of paper with the proper figures on it, and he'll do your bidding." The room grew light as the man lit an oil lamp.

"What if I paid you more to leave me alone?"

"Can't do it. Have to think about my reputation, haven't I? Now let's get to business." He grasped the smallest finger of Stratton's left hand and abruptly broke it.

The pain was shocking, so intense that for a moment Stratton was insensible to all else. He was distantly aware that he had cried out. Then he heard the man speaking again. "Answer my questions straight now. Do you keep copies of your work at home?"

"Yes." He could only get a few words out at a time. "At my desk. In the study."

"No other copies hidden anywhere? Under the floor, perhaps?"

"No."

"Your friend upstairs didn't have copies. But perhaps someone else does?"

He couldn't direct the man to Darrington Hall. "No one."

The man pulled the notebook out of Stratton's coat pocket. Stratton could hear him leisurely flipping through the pages. "Didn't post any letters? Corresponding with colleagues, that sort of thing?"

"Nothing that anyone could use to reconstruct my work."

"You're lying to me." The man grasped Stratton's ring finger.

"No! It's the truth!" He couldn't keep the hysteria from his voice.

Then Stratton heard a sharp thud, and the pressure in his

back eased. Cautiously, he raised his head and looked around. His assailant lay unconscious on the floor next to him. Standing next to him was Davies, holding a leather blackjack.

Davies pocketed his weapon and crouched to unknot the rope that bound Stratton. "Are you badly hurt, sir?"

"He's broken one of my fingers. Davies, how did you—?"

"Lord Fieldhurst sent me the moment he learned whom Willoughby had contacted."

"Thank God you arrived when you did." Stratton saw the irony of the situation—his rescue ordered by the very man he was plotting against—but he was too grateful to care.

Davies helped Stratton to his feet and handed him his notebook. Then he used the rope to tie up the assassin. "I went to your office first. Who's the fellow there?"

"His name is—was Benjamin Roth." Stratton managed to recount his previous meeting with the kabbalist. "I don't know what he was doing there."

"Many religious types have a bit of the fanatic in them," said Davies, checking the assassin's bonds. "As you wouldn't give him your work, he likely felt justified in taking it himself. He came to your office to look for it, and had the bad luck to be there when this fellow arrived."

Stratton felt a flood of remorse. "I should have given Roth what he asked."

"You couldn't have known."

"It's an outrageous injustice that he was the one to die. He'd nothing to do with this affair."

"It's always that way, sir. Come on, let's tend to that hand of yours."

Davies bandaged Stratton's finger to a splint, assuring him that the Royal Society would discreetly handle any consequences of the night's events. They gathered the oil-stained papers from Stratton's office into a trunk so that Stratton could sift through them at his leisure, away from the manufactory. By the time they were finished, a carriage had arrived to take Stratton back to Darrington Hall; it had set out at the same time as Davies, who had ridden into London on a racing-engine. Stratton boarded the carriage with the trunk of papers, while Davies stayed behind to deal with the assassin and make arrangements for the kabbalist's body.

Stratton spent the carriage ride sipping from a flask of brandy, trying to steady his nerves. He felt a sense of relief when he arrived back at Darrington Hall; although it held its own variety of threats, Stratton knew he'd be safe from assassination there. By the time he reached his room, his panic had largely been converted into exhaustion, and he slept deeply.

He felt much more composed the next morning, and ready to begin sorting through his trunkful of papers. As he was arranging them into stacks approximating their original organization, Stratton found a notebook he didn't recognize. Its pages contained Hebrew letters arranged in the familiar patterns of nominal integration and factorization, but all the notes were in Hebrew as well. With a renewed pang of guilt, he realized it must have belonged to Roth; the assassin must have found it on his person and tossed it in with Stratton's papers to be burned.

He was about to set it aside, but his curiosity bested him: He'd never seen a kabbalist's notebook before. Much of the terminology was archaic, but he could understand it well enough; among the incantations and sephirotic diagrams, he found the epithet enabling an automaton to write its own name. As he read, Stratton realized that Roth's achievement was more elegant that he'd previously thought.

The epithet didn't describe a specific set of physical actions, but instead the general notion of reflexivity. A name incorporating the epithet became an autonym: a self-designating name. The notes indicated that such a name would express its lexical nature through whatever means the body allowed. The animated body wouldn't even need hands to write out its name; if the epithet were incorporated properly, a porcelain horse could likely accomplish the task by dragging a hoof in the dirt.

Combined with one of Stratton's epithets for dexterity, Roth's epithet would indeed let an automaton do most of what was needed to reproduce. An automaton could cast a body identical to its own, write out its own name, and insert it to animate the body. It couldn't train the new one in sculpture, though, since automata couldn't speak. An automaton that could truly reproduce itself without human assistance remained out of reach, but coming this close would undoubtedly have delighted the kabbalists.

It seemed unfair that automata were so much easier to reproduce than humans. It was as if the problem of reproducing automata need be solved only once, while that of reproducing humans was a Sisyphean task, with every additional generation increasing the complexity of the name required.

And abruptly Stratton realized that he didn't need a name that redoubled physical complexity, but one than enabled lexical duplication.

The solution was to impress the ovum with an autonym, and thus induce a foetus that bore its own name.

The name would have two versions, as originally proposed: one used to induce male foetuses, another for female foetuses. The women conceived this way would be fertile as always. The men conceived this way would also be fertile, but not in the typical manner: Their spermatozoa would not contain preformed foetuses, but would instead bear either of two names on their surfaces, the self-expression of the names originally born by the glass needles. And when such a spermatozoon reached an ovum, the name would induce the creation of a new foetus. The species would be able to reproduce itself without medical intervention, because it would carry the name within itself.

He and Dr. Ashbourne had assumed that creating animals capable of reproducing meant giving them preformed foetuses, because that was the method employed by nature. As a result they had overlooked another possibility: that if a creature could be expressed in a name, reproducing that creature was equivalent to transcribing the name. An organism could contain, instead of a tiny analogue of its body, a lexical representation instead.

Humanity would become a vehicle for the name as well as a product of it. Each generation would be both content and vessel, an echo in a self-sustaining reverberation.

Stratton envisioned a day when the human species could survive as long as its own behavior allowed, when it could stand or fall based purely on its own actions, and not simply vanish once some predetermined life span had elapsed. Other species might bloom and wither like flowers over seasons of geologic time, but humans would endure for as long as they determined.

Nor would any group of people control the fecundity of another; in the procreative domain, at least, liberty would be restored to the individual. This was not the application Roth had intended for his epithet, but Stratton hoped the kabbalist would consider it worthwhile. By the time the autonym's true power became apparent, an entire generation consisting of millions of people worldwide would have been born of the name, and there would be no way any government could control their reproduction. Lord Fieldhurst—or his successors—would be outraged, and there would eventually be a price to be paid, but Stratton found he could accept that.

He hastened to his desk, where he opened his own notebook and Roth's side by side. On a blank page, he began writing down ideas on how Roth's epithet might be incorporated into a human euonym. Already in his mind Stratton was transposing the letters, searching for a permutation that denoted both the human body and itself, an ontogenic encoding for the species.

Story Copyrights